Soldier
Soldier

Adrian Gere

Published in 2010 by New Generation Publishing

Chapter 1

It was very cold and wet on that Tuesday morning in November nineteen fifty three as Alan Gray stood on the railway station in Aldershot; he had been driven from Borden Army Camp in Hampshire to the railway station having been demobbed from the army after serving just over three years in the Royal Army Service Corps. He had to admit, he found it bloody daunting to say the least, as he stood on the platform in the drizzle awaiting the train to London. A civilian once again, but with no job, a few quid in his pocket and a few more in the bank, which he had managed to save during his time in the forces. At that point in time he had no idea what he was going to do for a living, probably something to do with transport, possibly a lorry driver, or maybe taxi driver, who knew?

He wasn't even sure right then whether he had made the right decision. After all if he had signed for a further term, he had been offered a brilliant posting to France as a Staff Sergeant at CRASC, the command unit for the RASC in Europe, stationed in Paris and controlling all military transport in Europe. He would even have been working once again with his old Boss Capt, or rather Major Mason. But he had chosen Civvy Street, why he wasn't quite sure.

He looked up at the notice board and saw that his train would be arriving in five minutes but had to switch platforms, he walked over the footbridge just as the train was approaching. Once aboard he placed his luggage, which consisted of a large metal suitcase and a sports holdall in the overhead luggage rack and then settled down in a corner seat for the journey to London and them on to his Mums home in Essex. Sitting there waiting for the train to pull out of the Station he closed his eyes and looked back to how it had all started. Wanting to leave home and be a soldier, doing a bit of fibbing along the way about his Dad giving consent, but somehow getting away with it and all the adventures that he had experienced over the past three years.

His driving ambition to join the army was born out of hearing the stories his Dad used to tell him and his brothers about when he was a soldier during the First World War in France. He was a Corporal in The Middlesex Regiment, they were an infantry outfit and Dad was serving in the in the front line, or so he said. He had been wounded in late nineteen seventeen, a bullet had passed through his left hip and out the other side and he had been sent home to the UK, he was even proud enough to show the scar.

He had received a wonderful commendation letter from the Brigadier who was in charge of the troops where he was stationed, so some of what he said must have been true Alan thought had thought at the time. He used to tell about his experiences in the trenches, being fired at by the Germans, surviving on just one meal each day, the horrendous weather conditions during the winter months and lots more, whether they were all true or not didn't really matter, it was fascinating for Alan and Alan just loved to listen to the stories.

Then of course there were Alan's three elder brothers, all with army experience, which only added to his keenness to join, the stories they used to relate when they were home on leave, Alan thought were also brilliant. Bill the eldest had just been demobbed after serving his National Service with the Royal Signals, spending eighteen months of his two year stint in Egypt. Then there was Charlie who was in Germany with the Royal Artillery, at the time of Alan joining he still had two months of his two years left to serve. And his brother Eddie was serving in Egypt in the RASC. Ed was only just over a year older than Alan and he had been told after joining, that if he wished too he could have joined him in Egypt, but Alan decided he wanted to be his own man and serve his time wherever he was sent.

Alan was one of seven children, he had been born in north London, just a stones throw from the home of Tottenham Hotspurs Football Club, but towards the end of the war in nineteen forty five the family had moved to Essex. His Dad had been medically retired from his work as an underground train driver, because he suffered from Asthma and was forced to stop working. The house they moved to in Essex stood in about three acres of land, with a small wood at the furthest most point. It had in fact been built by Alan's grandfather on his Mums side of the family and she had somehow inherited it when his granddad had died, he never really knew the full details. All Alan remembered, was that one January morning with snow falling heavily, all, seven of them, together with their Mum had left the home they had known in Tottenham and went by train to Brentwood in Essex.

After getting off the train they then had to walk over three miles to the house, because there was only one bus each day and would you guess, they had missed it. His Dad was following in the removal van that was supposedly arriving later in the day. God what a difference he thought, after arriving and looking around their new home. From having all normal mod cons like gas, electric, running water, a proper toilet and a bath, they were to be living in an old dilapidated house with absolutely none of these.

They were going to have to get used to paraffin lamps for lighting, an old fashioned stove that burnt wood or coal for his Mum to cook on, a metal bath that had to be filled from a bucket and water that had to be pumped from a well in the garden. But worst of all Alan thought, was the toilet; it consisted of a bucket with a wooden seat over it, situated in a small hut a twenty yard walk from the back door. He then found out that it had to be emptied each day and the contents would have to be dug into the garden. Alan was twelve at the time and after surveying all that was around him in his new abode, vowed there and then that he would leave home at the first opportunity.

That opportunity presented itself by way of a bet in the late summer of nineteen fifty. Alan had been at football practice with the junior section of Brentwood Football Club, he had been told that he had an exciting future as an inside right, being a natural goal scorer, the previous season having netted thirty five goals in helping his team to win their league and promotion to a higher Division.

The new season was going to be tough, that was why they had started training in July which was much earlier than normal. It was customary after training to go to the local Pub, The Kings Head, for a couple of pints of beer. Although most of the lads were under age, the landlord turned a blind eye, mainly because the team manager was a regular at the Pub and he knew that Alan and the lads were with him, plus the fact that most of them looked old enough, well just about anyway.

After a couple of pints of bitter, two of Alan's mates in the team Ken Long and Brian Harvey started talking about their brothers experiences in the army and Alan soon chipped in, especially having three brothers with army experience. Ken said that he had always wanted to join the Navy and Brian made a claim that he was more interested in the Royal Airforce. Another pint of bitter and the bragging started with a pact being made, this being that the three of them would go to the local recruitment centre in the middle of town and sign on. Alan was of course forgetting at the time that he was technically too young. Ken and Brian were both almost six months older than he was, so they would have no problem and in fact they had been served notice that their call up papers for National Service would be with them during the next three months. But by the time they left the pub they had shaken hands on the fact that by the same time the following week they would all be signed up in their chosen services.

Chapter 2

Alan hadn't told his mates that his Dad probably wouldn't let him join up, but went along to the recruitment office on the Wednesday during his lunch break anyway. He worked at the local Sainsbury's grocery store, which was only a hundred yards or so away from the recruitment office, so it was no problem. They gave Alan a form that he would have to get filled out and then signed by one of his parents, due to the fact that he was under eighteen; he was in fact seventeen and four months. When he got home that evening he went to his bedroom and filled out the form and took a huge gamble by forging his Dad's signature, he knew that his Dad would never sign it for him and his Mum would only say, 'Speak to your Father.' They also required his birth certificate, but Alan decided that he would just have to blag this one; knowing his Mum would never give it to him anyway and he just hoped that he would get away with it just with his Fathers signature, well his forged signature anyway.

The following lunchtime Alan returned the form to the recruitment sergeant who checked the details, he made a comment that they would still require his birth certificate, but he would start the process anyway. On Friday evening when Alan returned home from work there was a large brown envelope for him from the army recruitment office, Alan opened it in the privacy of his bedroom and there was a letter saying that he was invited for an interview and a series of aptitude tests the following Monday. This meant that on the Saturday he would have to ask for a day off work, this of course had to be taken as holiday, which he knew wasn't a problem, because he had still got over a week of his annual entitlement to take.

He daren't say anything to his parents; he just knew that they would have blown a fuse, especially his Dad. With two of his brothers away in the army and his eldest brother not living at home anymore, Alan's wages were important to the household budget. He had to give up half of his earnings each week, which then were three pound seven and sixpence after tax, so after paying his parents he was left with just one pound twelve shillings or there about for his own spending. This was one of the reasons that his Dad would blow his top, because that would disappear if Alan left home.

Alan's Mum did ask what the envelope from the Army was about, but he fobbed her off by saying it was just some standard information relating to when he would receive his National Service papers, luckily she bought his excuse and said no more. He was all of a dither come Monday, he left for work at his normal time but didn't take his normal route, he cycled to the railway station instead and parked his bike. He had to travel to Chelmsford for his interview, which was about twelve miles away and he caught a train at eight thirty. Even though he didn't have to be there until ten o'clock, Alan wanted to find the recruitment office to be sure to get there on time, once he had located it, he then walked to a small café and got himself a cup of tea to pass the time.

At ten minutes to ten Alan entered the very drab looking grey building that he had sussed out earlier and walked hesitatingly to the information desk where a very large army sergeant was standing. "Can I help you son?" He said in a broad cockney accent.

"I'm here for an interview for joining the army,' Alan replied with a little stammer in his voice.

"Bit on the young side aren't you?" he answered back, "lets have a look at your form and I'll see if I can get you sorted." With that he took the letter that Alan had been sent and walked to a back office. After some five minutes he was back behind his desk, "take a seat over there young man," he said pointing to some folding wooden chairs that were against the back wall in the reception area, "someone will be with you in five minutes."

Alan walked to where he had pointed and sat down, but he didn't have to wait long. Another sergeant walked through the door and called his name, 'Alan Gray." Alan stood and walked the short distance to where he was. "Come with me son and we will get things started."

The sergeant took Alan along a short corridor to a small room where there were four wooden desks and chairs and told him to take a seat. The Sergeant then went to a larger desk, which was obviously his and picked up a brown folder from which he extracted some sheets of paper; he walked back and placed these before Alan on the desk top where he was sitting.

"OK lad," he started, "here are some simple tests for you to do, just read the instructions at the top of each sheet and then complete as many of the answers as you can. You've got an hour and a half to do them, so take your time. If you have a problem, call me I will be sitting just over there," he said pointing to his desk.

Alan glanced through the five sheets that he had been given, they were a mixture of different tests, the first was a straightforward maths test, addition, multiplication, division and subtraction, which he completed fairly quickly, he'd always been pretty good at maths, so no problem there. The second was an array of different shapes in lines and the idea was to work out what the next shape should be at the end of each line, a little more difficult, but he got there in the end. Then there was one that had rows of numbers and Alan had to work out which number was at the end of the row and in some cases one had been left out and he had to work out which it was, again more difficult than the previous two, but he gave it his best shot. There was another on a similar vein but using words and finally one that consisted of circles and squares of various colours and sizes and these had to be identified and placed in a specific order, probably something to do with colour blindness he guessed.

It took Alan the full ninety minutes to complete the test papers; he kept going back over what he had done several times just to make sure he had got them right, or as near right as possible. The sergeant stood from his chair and as he approached said, "Have you finished son, because your times up?"

"I've done the best I can," replied Alan, and the Sergeant took the papers from him.

"I'll arrange for a cup of tea and we'll get these checked. Do you take sugar?"

"Yes please, just one spoonful will be fine," Alan answered as the sergeant left the room.

A soldier with two stripes on his arm came into the room with the tea, Alan learned later that he was a corporal, he placed it on the desk and left. Alan sat and waited and sipped the tea, it was luke warm, but comforting all the same.

In all Alan had to wait for about twenty five minutes before the sergeant came back, he had a smile on his face and said, "bright young thing aren't you, did all right with the tests, the Captain will see you in five minutes, I'll call you when he's ready," and with that he left the room once more.

Alan sat thinking and he began wondering, was he doing the right thing, should he have lied about his Dad giving him permission and forging his signature and would they catch him out, if so what then? 'Just have to cross that bridge as and when I come to it,' he thought.

The sergeant came back and took Alan through to a much bigger, much smarter office where the Captain was waiting for him, he had three small crowns on each shoulder of his uniform and that is what apparently showed others what his rank was. It went through Alan mind that he would probably have to learn all about those things if he got through the next phase of his interview and actually joined.

"Thank you Sergeant Jones," the Captain said, "I'll call you when I'm done."

"Yes sir," he replied and left the room.

"Right young man, take a seat," he said. After Alan was seated in a chair opposite him he continued. "So what makes you want to be a soldier at your young age?"

Alan felt nervous right then and started stammering a bit as he spoke saying, "well, well I've got two brothers already in the army and one that's just come out and from what they have told me it sounds like good fun."

The Captain smiled at Alan's answer. "Good fun hey," he said and then he stopped smiling and continued in a very stern voice. "Good fun they tell you, well I will tell you this young man, it's not meant to be fun. A soldiers life is a tough one, if you join you are there to serve your King and Country, so don't start out on the wrong foot by thinking it's going to be fun."

Alan sat bolt upright, a little taken aback by the tone in his voice and the steely look the Captain was giving him.

"So let's start again shall we, why do you want to be a soldier?"

Again with a slight stammer Alan said, "I am very proud of my Brothers being in the army and I want to be like them and serve my Country."

"Now that's what I want to hear," said the Captain the smile returning to his face, "so what do your Brothers do and what sections of the forces are they in?" he asked.

Alan told the Captain about his Brothers service and where they were stationed, which he made some notes before asking. "So have you thought about what you would like to do, given the chance of course?"

"I think I would like to join the Royal Army Service Corps and be a driver like my one of my Brother's is," Alan replied.

"Well there are plenty of career opportunities apart from that in the RASC and if you do make the grade we do have a facility that would allow you to join him where he is stationed, should you choose to do so. That is of course if you complete your basic training satisfactorily. The next stage is to have a medical, so if you want to continue I will arrange for you to see the Medical Officer."

"Does that mean I am being accepted?" Alan asked excitedly.

"Well you seem to be pretty bright and very keen, so if you pass the MO's check over then yes, but not until you are seventeen and a half, which is the youngest age you can join," he said looking at Alan's application form and noting his date of birth, "so that won't be until September. But let's wait and see what the MO has to say."

With that he pressed a buzzer on his desk and the sergeant returned back into the room. "Sergeant Jones, take young

Gray along to the MO's office and get him checked over. When the MO's done, bring him back to me with his report and the necessary papers and we will get things under way."

"Very well sir," replied the sergeant, Alan was then taken to another room for his medical.

The medical took about half an hour, when it was completed Alan had to sit in a waiting area for a further fifteen minutes while the results were being processed, the sergeant then returned and took Alan along to the Captains office once again.

"Well Gray," the Captain started, "it looks like you have checked out OK and if you would like to sign these papers, then we can talk about getting you on a basic training course."

It had all happened so quickly, Alan was somewhat in a daze when he left the recruitment centre. 'I have actually signed on to join the army; God knows what my Dad is going to say, he is going to go ballistic,' he thought, he knew that all too well, but it was too late by then. Alan had been given a date of Monday the fourth of September, nineteen fifty, when he would have to report to the training camp at Farnborough in Hampshire, just four weeks away.

He had still to hand in his notice at Sainsbury's and he also knew his football manager was going to be as sick as a parrot at him leaving, he had been banking on Alan's goal scoring skills for the new season ahead. 'But it's my life,' Alan said to himself as he waited for the train to take him back to Brentwood and the short cycle ride home.

Chapter 3

Alan decided that that he wasn't going to tell his parents until two weeks before he was due to go to Farnborough, this way he hoped that he would reduce the time of suffering that he knew he would be in for from his Dad, he just knew that he was going to go ape shit. On the Tuesday evening he went to football practice and as normal when they had finished went to the Pub for a drink. Alan was sitting with Ken and Brian and asked them how they had got on with what they had been chatting about the previous week, about joining the forces.

They both went a little red and it was Ken that spoke first, "Well actually I haven't done anything, how about you Brian?" he asked.

"No," replied Brian, "when I had sobered up a bit the next day I decided I would wait for National Service to come around, after all I haven't got that long to wait anyway. How about you Alan, what you have you done?"

Alan smiled, "I've actually been and bloody well done it, I've signed on, I start my training in four weeks. I'm joining the Royal Army Service Corps like my brother Eddie."

They both looked Alan with complete surprise, they were both gob smacked and then went on to ask him loads of questions about what he had had to do, where he would be going too and they generally chatted right round until nine thirty, at which time they said their goodbyes and Alan cycled back home. He still had this nagging feeling inside him regarding the forging of his Dads signature and also what his Parents were going to say when he eventually told them.

He had written a letter to his boss at Sainsbury's, which he was handing in the next morning. Although he only had to give one weeks notice, he was in fact giving the Company three and would be having the last week off of work before leaving for Farnborough and his new life of adventure in the army. Well that was the way he was looking at it at that point in time.

On the following Saturday Alan played football with the team in a pre-season friendly, he scored three goals and assisted in making two more for Brian Harvey to score; the Manager was absolutely over the moon. He went over to Alan at the end of the match and said, "keep this up young Alan and we will be topping the new league before too many games are played, well done."

Alan decided there and then to tell him that he would be leaving and he didn't take the news too well. "I don't understand you Son," he said, "you know that both Southend United and Chelmsford City are interested in you, why throw it all away. And what about your dream of playing for Spurs, has that gone out the window as well?"

"I'm sorry Boss," Alan said, "but it's too late now, it's done and dusted. I'm sure I'll get to play a bit in the army from what I have been told by my Brothers, if you're any where near good at any sport, then there's lots of opportunities. I'm just going to have to take my chance."

"And what does your Dad think about this?" he asked.

'Shit', Alan thought, he hadn't given a thought to the fact that the manager knew his Dad, so he just took a flyer saying. "Yeah he's OK about it, thinks I'm doing the right thing. I'm gonna have to do National Service pretty soon anyway, so why wait."

He just grunted and walked away, leaving Alan to get his things together before making his way home. He just had to hope that the manager didn't bump into his Dad before he had gotten around to telling him, otherwise he new he would be in deep, deep trouble. His Dad worked in the foundry at the Ford Motor works near Dagenham, it was no good for his asthma or his health generally, but he had been unable to find any other work, partly due to his age and the fact that all he had ever known was driving underground trains.

His Dad had tried for a few years after the family first moved to Essex, to become a small holding farmer, but the regulations surrounding him getting animal feed for the poultry and pigs had become a nightmare and he had had to give it up. It was through his work at the Ford motor works that Alan's Dad had got to know Jack Hardy the football coach and recommended Alan and he became his team manager. Alan knew he just needed to keep his fingers crossed and hope that their paths wouldn't cross before he actually got around to telling his Dad the news himself.

It was the following Sunday that the shit hit the fan so to speak. Alan's Dad had been to the Kings Head Pub at lunchtime and had returned much earlier than he normally did and Alan could see he had a face like thunder. After removing his jacket and hanging it over the back of his chair he went into the front room and called for Alan to follow, that is when Alan knew he was in real trouble. It wasn't often they ever went into to the front room, that was normally only used for special occasions or when they had visitors, otherwise they spent most of their time in the kitchen or the back room, which was also the dining room.

"Is there something that you're not telling me young man?" he asked Alan in a very stern tone, looking directly at him with what looked like daggers in his eyes.

"I'm sorry Dad I 'm not sure what you mean," replied Alan.

"Let me give your mind a little jog then shall we," he said in an almost sarcastic way. "I have just been talking to Jack Hardy your football manager and he tells me you are leaving the team. Why?" he finished and waited for an answer.

Alan knew there was no use trying to lie his way out of this; he just had to tell the truth and hope for the best, he knew that his Dad knew, so the game was well and truly up. What Alan hadn't expected though was his Dad's reaction when he answered.

"I have been meaning to tell you; and Mum of course. I'm joining the army" Alan said.

"Your joining the army are you, and just when do you join?" he asked.

"On the fourth of September." Alan said quietly.

"So you are leaving home in a couple of week's time and you hadn't got the gumption to tell me or your Mother that you were leaving. What do you think this is going to do to her, what with your other Brothers being away, you're all she's got left right now and what about your contribution to the household, how do we replace that?"

"I'm sorry Dad, I just didn't think this through, but it's too late now, it's done." Alan said in as bold a voice as he could muster.

"Your bloody right it's done," he shouted, "you're done too as far as I'm concerned. Go to your room, pack your bags and get out of my house. I do not want to see you here ever again do you understand me. Going behind my back, making me look a complete fool in front of my work mates by telling them and not telling me, have you any idea of the humiliation you have caused and how that makes me feel? Just pack your things and go!"

Alan was stunned by what his Dad had said, he certainly hadn't expected this reaction, he had guessed that he would be well miffed, but this, bloody hell. Where on earth was he going to go, after all he thought, it was early afternoon on a Sunday where on earth would he sleep, where would he live, he'd still got to get through the next two weeks. 'God if only I had done things differently,' he thought, but it was too late for that now.

He went to his bedroom and took down from the top of the wardrobe an old battered brown suitcase; he had brought it from a second hand shop a year previously when he had gone on his only holiday, three days at Southend on Sea. He had coupled this with a football trial that had been arranged by Jack Hardy. He didn't possess many clothes, but what he did have he packed neatly into the suitcase, along with a wash bag that contained his toothbrush, soap and razor, Alan had only been shaving for a month or so, and this he only did once each week.

In all it took Alan just half an hour, and when he was finished he went downstairs and in to the back room where his Dad was sitting at the table eating his meal, his Mum was crying and had obviously been trying to get his Dad to change his mind, but Alan new all to well that once his Dad had made a decision, there was never any turning back. Alan said goodbye, but his Dad ignored him, his Mum made a start towards him, but his Father told her to stay where she was, Alan turned and left the room. Little did he know right then, that that would be the last time that he would ever see his Father?

Chapter 4

Alan went to the garage and collected his bike, although with the suitcase and his small holdall which had his sports kit in, it was impossible to ride, so he walked with the bags balanced on the seat and the crossbar of the bike. The only place that he could think of going was to his Uncle Les and Aunt Jean; they lived some three miles away in a village called Warley, there was also a large Army Barracks there where the Essex Regiment was stationed. Uncle Les had been in the RAF and there had been some bad blood between him and Alan's Father. Alan never did find out what it was all about, all he knew was that for many years, almost as long as he could remember, the two families never met socially, although Alan's Mum did visit them occasionally, what with Auntie Jean being her sister, but obviously she never let on to his Dad that she did, or she would have been in trouble that's for sure.

It took Alan over an hour to walk to their home; the time was about three thirty when he knocked on the font door. His Uncle Les answered the door and after a short greeting asked him to go inside, which he did after propping his bike against the side fence and placing his bags on the front step.

"So what brings you here young Alan?" he asked. He always called Alan, young Alan, never Alan, something that Alan could never figure out.

Alan stuttered a little as he started to speak, "I need a big favour Uncle Les. I have signed on to join the army and Dad's furious because I didn't tell him before I did it, and he's made

22

me leave home. I have to report for my training in two weeks time and wondered whether you would be able to put me up for a couple of weeks until I leave. I will pay for my keep of course." He finished.

"Blimey lad, you have got a problem, he said, "let's go and have a word with your Auntie Jean. Don't want to cause any more bad feelings with your Parents, there's been enough already," he finished.

He had a slight limp which was due to a shrapnel wound he received while he was flying a Hurricane Bomber during the war, he received a bravery award for his heroics, or so the story went, although Alan had never seen it. Alan followed him into their back room where his Aunt Jean was sitting in her armchair knitting.

"Hello young Alan, it's nice to see you, it's been a while since we last had this pleasure, nothing wrong it there?" She said.

After saying hello to his Aunt it was his Uncle Les that spoke. "Young Alan here's got a slight problem and wondered whether we could help, seems he's had a fall out with his Father and needs a bed for a couple of weeks."

"Oh, I am sorry to hear that," she said, "what has happened, I know he can be a bit hot headed at times, but this must be serious."

Alan explained to them both exactly what had happened, although he didn't mention that he had forged his Dads signature and not provided a birth certificate. They both pondered for a while and asked Alan to pop into the kitchen while they had a chat; they said he would find his cousin Jenny there and that they would call him in a little while. Jenny was nice, Alan was just sorry that she was his cousin because he could easily have fallen for her; she had all the boys chasing her. She was sixteen and a real good looker with long blonde hair and a very sexy figure and also a terrible flirt and tease. Both Alan's mates Brian and Ken had dated Jen from time to time and the last Alan knew was that she had been dating a chap called Brian Jones. In a way it used to make him feel a little bit jealous, silly really, 'after all she is my cousin,' Alan thought.

It must have been fifteen minutes or so before his Uncle Les came into the kitchen where he was sitting with Jenny. "Well young Alan," he started, "we've had a chat and although we know we shouldn't do it, we have decided to let you stay. There is one condition though, and that is that you are never to tell your Father that we put you up, is that understood?"

"Yes of course Uncle Les, this is really good of you, I can't thank you enough," replied Alan.

"You've got your Auntie Jean to thank, she persuaded me, always had a soft spot for you young man. Go and bring your bags in and we will show you which room you can use. Oh, and park your bike around the back by the coal shed." And with that he left the room.

"You're going to be staying here," Jenny said to Alan with a big smile on her face. "What have you been up too, or aren't I allowed to know?" she finished still smiling.

"Let me get my things in and I'll tell you," said Alan, "but you heard what your Dad said, you're not to tell a soul."

Alan wheeled his bike into their back garden and propped it up where his Uncle Les had said and took his two bags into the hall where he was waiting to show Alan to his room. Alan followed him up the narrow stairs, when they reached the top his Uncle stopped and opened a door that was directly in front, it turned out to be a small box room that overlooked the back garden, and they entered.

"Here you are lad, you can use this room, make yourself at home."

Their home was a three bedroom semi-detached house in a small cul-de-sac of about twenty houses, Jenny being the only child had the larger second bedroom and the third bedroom or box room as it was sometimes called was where they were going to let Alan sleep. The big advantage for him was that they had all mod cons, so at least there were some plus points in this for Alan, he would be able to have a proper bath and use a proper toilet.

Alan set about unpacking his few belongings and hanging them in the small wardrobe his Uncle had said he could use, he then went back downstairs and into the back room to see his Uncle Les and Aunt Jean; they were both sitting when he entered. Aunt Jean was still doing her knitting and Uncle Les reading the newspaper. "I would like to talk about how much I can give you each week that I am staying here, to help towards my keep, I don't want to be a burden," Alan said. "At home I used to give my Parents half of my wages which is one pound twelve shillings and sixpence; if that is not enough I can always give you a little more." He stopped and waited for their response.

Aunt Jean answered, "You don't have to be obliged young Alan, after all you are family, but if you would like to contribute, well that will be fine by us. Do you agree Les?" she said turning to Alan's Uncle.

"That would be very considerate of you young Alan, I always had you down to be a fair lad, so that's agreed then." And he went back to reading his newspaper and smoking his pipe.

Aunt Jean said, "If you would like to go to the kitchen and ask Jenny, she will show you the ropes, show you where everything is and she can tell you about our normal rota so that you can fit in around that. Is that's alright with you?"

"That's fine Auntie Jean and thank you both very much," Alan said and made his way to the kitchen.

Jenny was still sitting at the kitchen table reading a magazine when Alan entered and she turned and smiled, "welcome to our humble home, so how long are you staying and more to the point, why?" she asked with an impish look in her eye.

Alan explained to Jenny that he had signed up to join the army and would be leaving in two weeks, he told her about the row with his Dad and that he had told him leave home and hence here he was now seeking the help of her Parents. He told her how grateful he was to her Mum and Dad and so glad that they were able to help. He said he would try to get back home during the daytime when his Dad was at work to see his Mum before he left for Farnborough, but he would do that just a couple of days before he was due to leave.

"So have you finished work at Sainsbury's now?" Jenny asked.

"No, I have given them my notice, but I still have another week to work. I am taking the last week off, I'm not sure why now, because I won't know what to do with myself now that I'm not at home. Still too late for that now," he finished.

"Well I won't be working that week either," said Jenny with a twinkle in her eye, "I am sure we will think of something."

Alan smiled inwardly, he wasn't sure what Jenny was eluding too, but he also knew that she had always fancied him, even though they were cousins. 'Just have to be careful here he thought, especially as her Parents are being so good to me,'

Jenny and Alan were moved from the kitchen at just after five o'clock by her Mother saying, "I'd better get some dinner cooking or we'll all starve." So Alan, together with Jen went into the back room where Uncle Les was still reading his newspaper.

He looked up when they entered and said, "Tell me young Alan, what section of the army are you joining and where are you going to be stationed?"

Alan gave his Uncle the background information from what he knew, but as it was very little at that point in time, there wasn't much to say. They just chatted generally for a further ten minutes and his Uncle returned to reading his newspaper. Jenny suggested that they could perhaps go upstairs and listen to some of her records, she had a record player in her room and she had several new records she wanted to play. They sat on her bed and listened and chatted, she was interested in why Alan wanted to join the army and was there anywhere in the world that he would like to go. She asked endless questions and they chatted until just after six thirty, when her Mum called out that dinner was ready. 'This is quite cosy, just the two of us, I could easily get used to this' Alan thought, as they left her bedroom.

Chapter 5

On the Monday Alan took his turn in the bathroom after both his Uncle Les and Aunt Jean had finished. Because he had to leave for work before Jenny, Alan was allowed to use the bathroom third and once he was finished he got himself dressed in his work clothes. Then after eating some toast that his Aunt had prepared, he set off on his bike for the ride to Brentwood and his last week at his job at Sainsbury's.

Although he had quit the football team, Alan decided that he would still go to the training session on that Tuesday evening anyway; and just about everyone was interested in why he was joining the army before he had too. Alan didn't have any real answers, because it had been done on a whim, but nevertheless it made for some good banter as the evening wore on and after training they all trouped to the Pub. They had also arranged that as the following Tuesday would be Alan's last night before leaving, they would have a small celebration. Something that Alan was looking forward too.

The week passed very quickly and on Saturday at four o'clock Alan said a final farewell to all his workmates at Sainsbury's. They had clubbed together and bought him a wrist watch, which was something that he had never owned before and he was really chuffed. There was a mixture of joy and sadness as he finally left, with Alan saying that he would keep in touch and let them know what exotic parts of the world he was serving in. They all laughed and waved goodbye as Alan got on his bike to ride back home, or rather back to his Uncle Les's home, for the last time from the shop where he had worked for the past three years.

Every month there was a dance at the local Town Hall in Brentwood and Alan felt that this would be a good way of saying cheerio to his mates, because he knew that most of them would all be there as normal, it was the highlight of each month. Jenny had already arranged to go, so it was decided they would go together, although once there Alan knew she would split and join her group of girlfriends like she normally did. Things panned out exactly as he had thought, they got a bus from the end of her road to the town centre and walked the hundred yards or so to the hall, and it was packed as usual. This was the place where most dates were made, the boys out to get a girl and vice versa, Alan left Jenny and joined his normal group of friends who were seated at the far end of the hall, near to the band.

Jitterbug and jive were all the rage, having been brought over to England towards the end of the war by the Americans, the band was a Glen Miller style group, but without as many instruments, but they still did a good job. It wasn't long before Alan spotted Jenny dancing with one of her girl friends and there was a group of Essex Regiment soldiers standing and admiring them. Again Alan felt a pang of jealousy course through him, although he knew he shouldn't, knowing she was his cousin, but he just couldn't help it. Perhaps it was just being protective towards her, he thought, he didn't really know.

As the evening drifted by Alan had a few dances with several of the girls that he knew, each one saying they were going to miss him madly, not that he really believed them, but it made for a bit of a laugh anyway. It was just after ten o'clock when Jenny sidled up to Alan and asked, "Aren't you going to ask me to dance then?"

"Jenny Hi, if you would like too, I would love it," said Alan, and with that took her in his arms as they made a pretty good attempt at a quickstep, although their feet did get a little tangled on a couple of occasions. Alan was actually a very good dancer; he just had a natural sense of rhythm and felt that the errors were mainly caused because he was finding it very hard to concentrate on his dancing, with Jenny in his arms pressing her soft body firmly against his.

After a few circuits of the hall she said to Alan, "Let's jive, I know you're good at that," and with that they broke apart and jived to the next two numbers. Although they hadn't jived together before, they seemed to hit it off straight away and it wasn't long before they were the centre of attention, as the music got faster and faster so did they, building into a crescendo at the end, with everyone clapping and cheering, Alan couldn't help think what a real buzz it had been.

"Pity we didn't realise how good we were together before now, we've wasted a lot of time," Jenny said as the dance finished. "I am reserving the last dance with you Alan Gray and no arguments," and with that she turned and rejoined her girlfriends. Alan noticed that as Jen and her friends were talking together they kept looking in his direction; he never did know what they were talking about, but obviously something to do with him he guessed.

At just before eleven thirty, the band struck up a waltz and Jenny made a beeline across the hall towards Alan, a smile lighting up her face. "Well," she said, "are you just going to stand there, or are we dancing?"

With that she slipped into Alan's arms, pushing herself as close as she could against his body as they started to waltz. Although Alan new most dance steps, including the waltz, he decided to just ease his way around the dance floor in what was no more than a soft shoe shuffle, slowly guiding Jenny around the hall, the experience of holding her so close was almost intoxicating and one that Alan was thoroughly enjoying.

The band played three numbers in all and the longer the dance went on the closer she seemed to push herself towards him, moving her body in a sensual manner as she did. When the band stopped, Alan didn't want it to end and just stood there holding her in his arms, she looked up in his face smiling, "the music's finished, I think we'd better go. I'll just go and say goodbye to the girls and get my coat."

She slipped away from Alan and it took him some seconds before he gathered himself together. He walked towards his mates, although most of them had paired up with girls and were leaving and they said their goodbyes to him, wishing him all the best. Then he made his way to the exit door and waited for Jenny. It was several minutes before she appeared, looking rather flushed, again with that lovely smile she always seemed to be wearing. They left the hall and walked towards the bus stop, there was a late night bus to Warley which left at eleven fifty and they were just in time to catch it. On the bus they sat next to each other and she slid her hand into Alan's, turning her head smiling, they didn't say anything during the journey, which anyway only took ten minutes.

The bus stopped and they got off at the stop just past the end of Jenny's road. They crossed the road to the entrance to the cu-de-sac where she lived, where there was a clump of trees at the corner of the road. When they reached them Jenny stopped and turned towards Alan, raising her face towards his and their lips met. Alan's heart was racing, he knew they shouldn't be doing this, but he couldn't stop himself, there had been all those years of him fancying Jenny like hell and now here she was in his arms offering herself to him. The kiss was endless; he had never kissed another girl in the way that they were kissing and it seemed so right, even though he knew it wasn't.

It must have been at least ten minutes before their lips eventually parted, Alan looked deep into Jenny's easy saying, "Jen, we shouldn't be doing this, after all you are my cousin."

"Well that's not really true Alan," she said, "I am my Dad's daughter, but my Mum isn't my real Mum. When I was sixteen my Mum explained to me that my real Mum had died in childbirth and she had married Dad six months later and has brought me up as her own. So although everyone thinks we are cousins, in fact we aren't, so it's OK. I've always fancied you Alan, but couldn't do anything about it until I knew just a few weeks ago and the thought of you going away and never knowing, I couldn't let that happen, the feelings I have for you are so powerful."

Alan wasn't quite sure how to react, but before he had a chance to say anything else, she had placed her lips against his once again. He then felt her take his hand and push it inside her small jacket placing it firmly on her breast; he couldn't help but respond and gently fondled her, their kissing becoming more passionate by the minute. She had obviously felt the bulge in Alan's trousers pushing against her body and gently rotated her hips against him.

This continued for quite some time, before Alan broke off the kiss, saying, "Shouldn't we be getting home, your Parents will wonder where you are, or we are even."

"You're right I suppose, although they feel happy that I am with you knowing that you will be looking after me," Jenny replied, "but I've got big plans for next week. Let's go." And with that they walked hand in hand towards Jennie's home, only separating when they were in sight of her front door.

It took Alan ages to get to sleep, his mind was racing and he couldn't get the images out of his head of him and Jenny, he felt it was wrong even after Jennies explanation, but it was so enjoyable and what did she mean when she said she had plans for next week?

Chapter 6

Eventually Alan slipped into a deep sleep and it was only hearing the sound of water running in the bathroom that awoke him, his room was next to the bathroom and he could hear almost every noise, even the loo flushing. He looked at the bedside clock, the time was seven thirty, he new that it was probably his Uncle Les in the bathroom and by the time Aunt Jean and then Jenny had used the facilities, it would be his turn. So he turned over and dozed off to sleep again, thinking that it would probably be another hour or so before he got a look in. He was right, because it was eight thirty when there was a knock on the door, Jenny called out that the bathroom was free. Alan got out of bed and after pulling his old dressing gown around him; he made his way next door to the bathroom to freshen up.

When he had finished and dressed he made his way downstairs, Aunt Jean was preparing breakfast, "Did you have a good time last night young Alan? Jenny tells me that you had several dances together, that was nice. Thank you for looking after her."

Alan was sure that he blushed, but responded by saying, "Yes it was very nice and we managed to get the last bus home, so we weren't too late."

"You're a good boy young Alan, thank you," she replied.

Alan wondered whether she would be saying that if she knew what had really happened, but hopefully she would understand, he just had to keep a cap on things and make sure that he doesn't do anything that would upset them, after all they were being very good to him, he thought.

Alan was playing football for the team for the last time at two thirty and would have to leave their home about midday. Jenny had said over breakfast that she would like to go and watch Alan play and although he said she would be bored, she insisted and her Parents also said that she could go along with him. So at just before twelve o'clock they set off on their bikes for the football club at Brentwood.

"I really enjoyed myself last night," Jenny said as they cycled towards the town.

"I did as well Jen," Alan replied, "I've never felt anything as good before, but we do have to be careful, what if your Mum and Dad ever found out, I certainly wouldn't be flavour of the month that's for sure, even though as you explained we aren't really related."

"Don't worry, no ones going to find out anything, I just can't help the way I feel about you Alan. It's a silly law anyway, but it doesn't apply to us, if two people like each other whether they are semi-related or not, it should be up to them and no one else," she said in an almost defiant voice.

Alan didn't respond as they continued their short journey to the football club. The team Alan was playing against were in the league that Brentwood would be playing in during the forthcoming season; they had finished fourth in the table and were supposed to be pretty good, so Alan new it would be a tough test. Not that there would be anything that he could do about things in the future, because he wouldn't be around for the new season. The Boss had made Alan Captain for the day as it was his last match and he was really chuffed. The whole team played really well and they beat the opponent's four goals to two, with Alan scoring two of the goals. He was elated as were all the others, although there was an element of sorrow based on the fact that Alan wasn't going to around the next season to help them with his goal scoring.

Jenny was beaming when the match was finished, "I never realised you were so good," she said as he made his way to the changing rooms, "I'll wait for you out here, don't be long."

After he had showered and changed, Alan made his way outside after saying his final farewells to all his team mates, they all wished him well and the Boss gave him an extra special hug, something he had never done before. "Were going to miss you Son, you just take care of yourself. And I'm sorry if I got you into some trouble with your Dad, I just didn't realise you hadn't told him. But you take care."

Alan met Jenny outside and they got on their bikes and headed for her home. When they got there she couldn't stop talking to her Parents about how good he was, it was a bit embarrassing really Alan felt, although somewhat flattering as well. Aunt Jean had prepared a typical Sunday Roast and Alan sat with them around the table and really enjoyed the meal, thanking her afterwards for such a lovely dinner.

Jenny had said during dinner that there was a very good film on at the cinema and was it all right if she went, 'perhaps

Alan would like to come as well,' she had added. Her Parents were all in favour, her Dad saying, "If young Alan is there to look after you, then that's Ok with us."

They caught the bus at six thirty; the film started at seven fifteen and would end at around ten o'clock, just in time to catch the last bus back to her home. Alan paid for the tickets, although Jenny had tried to insist that she paid for her own, but he wouldn't let her on account of how kind her Parents had been. He bought the most expensive tickets, which gave them seats in the very back row, they looked around as they entered the cinema and luckily didn't see anyone else that they knew. Alan had also bought a bag of popcorn that they could share. They chose two seats at the farthest end of the row where it would be difficult to be seen, just in case anyone who knew them did come in later.

It wasn't long before the lights dimmed and the film started, it was a love story starring Audrey Hepburn and Noel Coward, not that they saw much of the film. No sooner had the lights gone down, when Jenny pulled Alan towards her planting her lips on his and they kissed long and hard for several minutes. She then took his hand and placed it inside her blouse at the same time sliding her other hand between his legs and stroking him, Alan was in a state of pure bliss. They stayed like that for absolutely ages, touching and caressing and kissing, Alan totally forget any feelings of this being wrong; he was enjoying the whole sensation too much. Half way through the film the lights came back on and there was a short interlude, they both sat up and straightened themselves trying to look as normal as they could and Alan opened the popcorn, not that either of them had much of an appetite for it, too hungry for other things.

After fifteen minutes the lights dimmed once again and they were soon back in the positions they had been before, only this time Alan didn't need any encouragement from Jenny. He had slipped her Bra off of her breasts and was enjoying feeling the full softness of them, at the same time she had slipped her hand inside his trousers and he was having the most difficult job of keeping control of himself. The time flew by and before they knew it the lights were being put on once again at the end of the film, it was then a case of making themselves look as decent as possible before leaving the cinema. They got the bus back to Jen's and again stood under the trees and kissed before they eventually went back to Jenny's home.

Her Parents were in bed when Jen let them in the front door and they went to the kitchen as quietly as possible and she poured a soft drink for them both. After drinking down the lemonade Jen slipped into Alan's arms and kissed him, saying that this had been the most wonderful evening of her life. They didn't dare to stay in that position too long, just in case one her Parents came downstairs to see what was going on, so they said goodnight and both made their way to their separate rooms for the night. Again it took Alan ages to get off to sleep, he had had a few girl friends over the past couple of years, but none that had been as forward or as sexy as Jenny was, he just couldn't get the evenings events out of his head, he just kept reliving each moment again and again.

Chapter 7

Alan didn't have to get up for work on the Monday and as Jen was also having a week's holiday neither did she. Jenny was a trainee hairdresser at a small salon in Brentwood and she had booked the week's holiday some months previously, so it had nothing to do with the fact that Alan was not at work. Uncle Les was an Assistant Bank Manager at the Barclays Bank in Brentwood High Street and Aunt Jean was a seamstress at Burtons Men's Outfitters, she did all the tailoring on the made to measure suits. They left for their respective places of work together each morning at a quarter past eight. Uncle Les drove an Austin Seven car, it was his pride and joy and after dropping Aunt Jean off at Burton's he would park it in his designated parking spot at the Bank, but Aunt Jean only worked until two in the afternoon, so she caught the bus home on her own.

Uncle Les kept his car in a wooden garage at the side of the house and Alan heard him getting ready to leave, both he and Aunt Jean had said goodbye to Jenny and then he heard the sound of the tyres on the gravel drive as it drove off. It was only a couple of minutes later that the door to his bedroom opened and Jenny walked in wearing just her shortie nightie, which was semi see through, Alan gulped just looking at her. She smiled and moved to the side of his bed sitting on the edge and leant down and kissed him, after a little while she stretched out and laid on the top of the bed covers next to Alan, wrapping her arms around his neck and pulling him closer.

Jenny then pulled away and stood up saying, "come into my bedroom, the beds much bigger than this one," and with that she was gone.

Alan slowly got out of the bed and followed, when he entered her room she had her back towards him and was pulling the nightie over her head, she then turned towards him naked with a big smile on her lips. Seeing her naked only went to heighten his desire, she then leaned towards him and pulled the cord that held up his pyjama bottoms and they slid to the floor. Her eyes widened and she let out a little gasp when she saw the size of Alan, he was exceptionally well endowed and had been since a very early age. When he was in the showers after football he always got ribbed, the lads used to say things like, 'you obviously had no toys when you were a kid,' in a way they were almost right, he thought.

It probably all stemmed back to that day during the school holidays when he was twelve, in the first summer that they had moved to Brentwood; he had gone home after playing football at the local rec with some mates and on entering the house heard noises coming from upstairs. Not knowing who was home he had crept up to find out what was happening. The door of the bedroom he shared with his brother Eddie was slightly open and that was where the noises were coming from, Alan had crept to the door and looked in. He couldn't believe what he saw, a friend of theirs called Ellen, who lived a hundred yards down the lane from them, was sitting on the bed with her blouse undone and her breasts were uncovered, and his brother Eddie was sitting next to her stroking them and she had her hand inside his trousers.

Alan tried to creep away without them knowing, but as he moved a loose floor board creaked and Eddie called out, "is anyone there?"

Alan ducked away, but not before Eddie was out on the landing, with Ellen standing next to him still bare breasted and he said in an angry voice, "You bloody little snitch, coming in and spying like that."

Ellen was fifteen at the time and fully matured, but although Eddie was only just over a year older than Alan, he was exceptionally well matured for his age; which Alan had noticed when they undressed for bed at night, because they shared a bedroom together and slept in the same bed. As for Alan, he was only just starting to get arousal type feelings, he could feel his body was changing but he wanted it to happen much quicker than it appeared to be. Alan realised there and then why Eddie had matured the way he had.

Alan wasn't sure what made him say what he did, but he knew that he never regretted it for one moment, he just blurted out, "if you don't let me join in, I'm going to tell Dad and Ellen's Mum and then you'll both be in dead trouble."

Eddie stood there on the landing and Alan could see the large swelling in his trousers and he had to admit he was envious. Eddie looked at Ellen and said, "It doesn't look as though we've got much choice."

And then he said to Alan, "whatever goes on between the three of us has to be top secret, is that understood, otherwise you'll get the biggest hiding you've ever had."

Alan was blushing and stammering all at the same time, "Yes, yes of course, but only if I can join in now." And that was the start of it.

They used to have regular trysts, at least once each week and sometimes more; Alan used to get to touch and feel Ellen as she would him. They sometimes met at their house when no one was home and sometimes at Ellen's; they also met in an old barn type building that was tucked away in the woods at the end of their land, where they had managed to get an old sofa. Alan even had Ellen to himself on many occasions when Eddie wasn't around which he had really enjoyed, he used to get her full attention and they would fondle each other for ages getting him fully aroused.

Alan had found it very exciting and as the months wore on his body had grown beyond all recognition to those first days, even Ellen was amazed at how large Alan had grown in such a short time, and by the time Alan was thirteen even his brother Eddie was jealous of him, because he had grown even larger than he was, thanks to all the encouragement given by Ellen.

Unfortunately it all came to an end when Alan was thirteen and a half; Ellen had got herself pregnant by a local Farmers son. She was sent away to a convent to have the baby and no one ever saw either the baby or Ellen again.

Jenny pulled back the bedcovers and slipped underneath saying, "come and join me."

Alan didn't need a second invitation and climbed in the bed beside her, she was right, her bed was at least twelve inches wider than the one he was sleeping in and there was ample room for the both of them. As he slipped under the covers Jenny turned towards Alan and they were in each others arms in an instant, completely naked. Their bodies rotated and pushed against each other as they started exploring each other with their hands.

Jenny slid her hand down Alan's body took hold of his large erection in her hand and said, "Gosh you are so big and lovely I can't wait to have you inside me, although I must admit it's a bit scary."

Alan had never had full sex before, although he had come very close several times with a couple of previous girl friends and also with Ellen, but always just managing to stop before going too far, but there was to be no stopping today. Jenny had told him that she had never done it before and only knew from what her Mum had told her and from books she had read, so it was going to be a first for both of them, which made Alan a little scared. He didn't want to disappoint and didn't really know what was expected, so he just let things develop and happen as naturally as possible. Jenny had also told him she had a good supply of French letters for protection, they sold them in the hairdressers where she worked, so they were easily available without embarrassment.

The more Jenny touched Alan and the more he touched her, the closer he was getting to having a complete explosion and he didn't want that to happen too quickly. Jenny then called out, "Oh Alan let's do it, please let's do it, I can't wait any longer."

Alan reached across for a protective rubber, which Jenny helped him to put on; she had a look of apprehension in her eyes as she took in just how big he was. Being aware of this, Alan didn't want to do anything that might hurt Jen, especially as this was her first time also and his and having had no previous experience to call upon. So he tried to be as gentle as was possible in his state of heightened excitement, when he started to enter her body. Jen let out several gasps as he gradually eased himself inside her and it was some time before their bodies were joined as if one. At which point she let out a huge sigh saying, "My god that is amazing."

They started to move their bodies slowly together, but the sexiness of the whole thing had gotten to Alan and he was now so excited that he just couldn't control himself and within less than a couple of minutes he had totally lost control and had the most tumultuous climax. He knew it was too early but just couldn't stop it. Jenny cried out at the same time, but Alan wasn't sure whether that was with her climax or not. He collapsed on top of her, his body going limp and they just lay there in each others arms. Their bodies still joined together.

It must have been half an hour later, while they were kissing and fondling that Alan felt himself start to grow inside her body, Jenny could also feel it as well and said how nice it felt. A further ten minutes and he was fully erect inside her ready for a second go, but this time it seemed to last for ever, there was no quick explosion. Alan was able to control himself and after more than fifteen minutes of pure joy, Jenny let out a whimper saying, "oh god Alan I'm cumming, I'm cumming, don't stop, oh god that's so lovely" and with that her body felt like it was exploding beneath him, they were both pushing harder and harder with every thrust until they came together in an almighty climax and collapsed into the bed locked in each others arms.

That was the start of the most amazing week of Alan's life, each day they made love, each day it got better than the previous day and the better it got the more they wanted to do it, sometimes doing it as many as three times before lunchtime, which was their deadline because of her Mum coming home from work. But on the Friday, as her Mum was doing the weekly shop, they stayed in bed until three o'clock in the afternoon and Alan lost count of the number of times they actually made love, it had been superb, but that would be it for some considerable time, because on Monday Alan was off to become a soldier.

He knew they shouldn't have been doing what they were, but he had no hang up's after what Jen had told him about their true relationship, it had been wonderful and even though everyone thought Jenny was Alan's cousin, he truly felt that he loved her and he knew she felt the same way about him.

Chapter 8

On the Thursday afternoon, after his lovemaking session with Jenny, Alan had cycled home to say goodbye to his Mum. She was very tearful and said that his Father had made it quite clear that he never wanted to see Alan again and that she was to have nothing to do with him either. She had found out he was staying with Uncle Les and Aunt Jean and had promised not to say anything to Alan's Dad, but was pleased about the fact that he had found somewhere to stay, short term anyway. Little did she know what had been going on there with Jenny and Alan, and he just hoped that neither she nor anyone else ever did. In all Alan stayed just over half an hour and after a short hug he kissed his Mum on the cheek and after saying a final goodbye, he cycled back to Warley to his Uncles home.

Friday evening was spent at Jenny's Parents home. After eating the meal that his Aunt Jean had prepared, which was fish and chips with green peas, Jen and Alan went to her room, supposedly to listen to her record player. Although they wanted too, they knew they daren't make love again in case her Parents heard, but they spent most of the time kissing and canoodling until eventually Alan went back to his room at just after ten o'clock.

The major bonus for Alan, was that after wakening on the Saturday morning, Jen's Parents announced that they were going to Romford, a nearby town where there was a large market to do some shopping, leaving Jen and Alan with a couple of hours to engage as they wished. Over breakfast Jen kept looking at Alan and smiling, he just hoped that her Parents didn't notice the way she was looking.

Her parents had barely left the house when Jen grabbed Alan by the hand and almost dragged him up the stairs, once in her room she threw her clothes off, as did Alan and they were soon in her bed making love once again, Alan also knew that this would definitely be the last time before he left on Monday, so made the most of it. They also had to be careful that they were re-dressed and looking fairly normal before her Parents got home. Alan felt it was a wonderful bonus and had loved every minute of it, promising that he would write regularly when he was away. He just hoped that he could keep that promise; bearing in mind he didn't really know what was ahead of him; plus the fact that writing had never been one of his strong points.

Jenny and Alan went into town on the Saturday evening, they had eaten at her home before they left and called in to two or three of the Pubs where Alan knew he would get served and just spent a relaxing evening, even managing to get a gin and orange for Jen at the Kings Head, where he was well known from his football. They caught a bus back to her home at just after ten o'clock and after stopping under the trees at the end of her road for what would be a final kiss and cuddle, they walked the short distance to her door, Jen made them each a cup of cocoa and they sat in the kitchen chatting until just after eleven, before making their way upstairs to bed.

The Sunday passed very quickly, Alan packed his suitcase and sports bag ready for Monday morning; he was catching a train from Brentwood to Liverpool Street Station and then transferring across London to Waterloo Station to catch the train to take him to Farnborough. He had said goodbye to Jennies Parents and thanked them for having him during the past two weeks, prior to them leaving for work. Jenny didn't have to leave until half an hour after her parents, she normally travelled in to town by bus, so they were able to spend quite some time saying their goodbyes, Jenny was in floods of tears. Alan had decided that he would travel with her and then wait around for his train; even though it didn't leave Brentwood until ten fifteen.

Chapter 9

It was the fourth of September 1950 when Alan reported to Farnborough Barracks in Hampshire, the time was one thirty. After he got off the train he wandered outside the station, it had just started to rain, as he looked around he spotted an army lorry parked in the car park and after making enquiries found out that it was waiting to pick him up, together with half a dozen other new recruits. It was a further half an hour before they were all assembled and they then piled into the back of the truck, after throwing their suitcases with their personal belongings in first and the lorry bumped its way to the Army Barracks.

They started introducing themselves as the lorry trundled along; everyone was of a similar age. The chap standing next to Alan was called Les Fraser, he was from Leeds, there was also another Yorkshire chap named Bill Blowers, then a Londoner named Larry Hall, who preferred to be called Cocker, another chap from Colchester in Essex called Charley Harris, a Scot who introduced himself as Jock Ferny and the last one was a Welsh chap called Geoff Stevens, so quite a mix, Alan thought.

The lorry drove through the Barrack gates and stopped at a building marked 'Stores' where they were told to get out. After a couple of minutes a corporal with two stripes on his arm arrived and told them to get in a straight line, which they did, he then read their names off of a list he had on a clipboard and re-arranged the line in alphabetical order. He seemed friendly enough Alan thought, as he told everyone about the procedure for the afternoon, but little did he or any of the others know that that was the last time he would be in any way friendly.

As their individual name was called they walked forward into the stores and were fitted out with their uniforms and general army kit, what Alan had never realised was just how much of it there would be. Two khaki suits which were called battledress, two pairs of boiler suite type overalls which were called fatigues, in fact two pairs of everything almost, boots, shirts, underwear, pyjamas, sports shirts and shorts, ties, berets, the exception being, that they had four pairs of socks and one overcoat, called a greatcoat. Then there was an array of odd items, a square metal tray with a handle called a mess tin, which was for eating food out of, a metal mug, a knife, fork and spoon, various holdall type bags made of some sort of webbing material and to top it all a large canvas bag which was about four feet long and twenty inches round called a kitbag, this was for stowing all the kit in for when they were on the move.

Alan was then told by the storeman to fold everything up and pack it in the kitbag, which he did, or rather he tried too. There was so much kit that it just seemed too much to fit in, but eventually he managed after a lot of pushing and shoving, while all the others were doing the same after receiving their kit. In all it took something over an hour for this process to be completed and the corporal, whose name they had learnt was Smith had re-appeared.

This was when Alan and the others saw the change. He shouted so loud that it made everyone jump. "Right then you horrible lot, get outside and line up as you were before."

Once lined up he continued, "Put your kitbags on your shoulders," he shouted, "turn to your right and start marching, follow me." They did as ordered and followed him some hundred yards or so to a brick building where he shouted for them to halt.

"This will be your home for the next four months," he continued in a loud voice, this was obviously done to show who was in charge. "Get inside and find yourself a bed, there are still a few spare ones, then get yourself out of your civvies and in to a pair of fatigues with your boots on. You will then be shown how you need to fold your kit and also how to make your beds each day. Come on now, move!" And they did.

They all trooped into to the barrack room, Alan was looking around for an empty bed as he walked down the centre aisle. There were in fact two empty beds next to each other about half way along the barrack room, so he threw his kitbag on the bed to bag it and as he did, Les Fraser did the same on the one next to it. Alan and the others started to sort out what they had been told were the fatigues to change in to. He took off his civvy clothing and pulled on a khaki shirt and the fatigues, which were in fact in two parts, a jacket and trousers suit, then a pair of thick socks and finally the boots that he had been issued with. In all it took about ten minutes to change and with the rest he stood by the side of his bed waiting for what they had to do next.

Corporal Smith was then joined by another soldier with one stripe on his arm, who was a lance corporal; he was in fact Lance Corporal Jones and he would be the one who did most of the showing of what had to be done. He started with the bed making and everyone gathered around his bed for a demonstration. The bed had to made in a special way, first the two sheets had to be placed on the mattress, then one blanket had to be stretched tight over the bed and then tucked in at the corners in what they called envelope fashion. The top sheet then had to be folded over the blanket about eighteen inches. The remaining blankets had to then be folded so that they were the same width as the bed and these then had to be stacked one on top of the other at the head of the bed, with the pillows on top of those.

By the side of each bed was a metal locker, which was in fact a wardrobe for their clothes and Lance Corporal Jones showed how each piece of their kit had to be folded and stacked on the various shelves in the locker? Alan's Brothers had never really told him about this side of things and it was coming as a bit of a shock, not just to him, but to the others as well, Alan could tell by the expressions on their faces. This whole process took well over an hour and after the demonstration, each of them had to go to their own bed and have a stab at making it correctly and then at putting their things away in the manner they had been shown. Lance Corporal Jones's bed was at the end of the Barrack Room and was there to use as a guide if they had forgotten just how it should be done.

Each Barrack Room had twenty eight beds in, occupied by twenty seven of the new recruits, and one lance corporal or corporal; in Alan's barrack room it was Lance Corporal Jones. At the end of the Barrack room was the washroom where there was a row of toilet cubicles, a row of hand basins

53

and also a long open shower area with a dozen shower heads, and then beyond that was another Barrack Room the same as the one Alan was in. So in all there were fifty four private soldiers and two corporals, known as NCOs, or non commissioned officers, which made up the Platoon, and they were designated as B Platoon.

The time was approaching five o'clock when Corporal Smith arrived back to the Barrack Room "Right oh you lot, get outside!" he shouted, "It's time to visit the barber for a shampoo and set."

And with that they all trooped outside and stood in a line, where again he shouted for them to turn to the right and march behind him to the Barbers, were everyone was in for a severe shock. Shampoo and set, Cpl Smith was obviously joking, Alan thought, as he watched what was happening, more like a bloody sheep shearing shed. Alan never had particularly long hair, it was just above his collar, with a parting down the left hand side, mainly due to the requirements at Sainsbury's because of working with food, but by the time the barber had finished, there was barely anything left. The Barber used an electric hand trimmer and started at the back of the neck and went straight over the top to the forehead, shearing off everything in its wake. When they were all done they again went outside and were escorted back to their Barrack Room, all of them in a daze, Les Fraser especially, as he had had very long black wavy hair at the outset, but not any more.

Back in the Barrack Room Corporal Smith did an inspection of the first efforts at laying out the kit and making the beds, Alan's in fact wasn't too bad, but he noticed that some of them hadn't got a clue. Smithy ranted and raved, pulling everything out of Bill Blowers locker and throwing it on the floor, telling him he was a useless idle little bugger and if he didn't do better next time he would be on Jankers the next day. Jankers, it turned out was a form of punishment, where you were given some extra work to do in your own time, like cleaning the toilets or scrubbing the steps of the Barrack Room, cleaning the heating stove in the middle of the room, all of which were some form of menial task and normally something that was visual to everyone else, obviously used as a deterrent.

Alan looked across at Bill when Smithy was gone, "do you want a hand?" he asked.

Bill looked up, "could you, I just can't get the bloody hang of these blanket corners, or the shirts and things in the locker, they just keep collapsing."

Alan walked across to his bed to help and he set about trying to get Bills things in better order, it only took about ten minutes, Les Fraser had also lent a hand as well, so that helped, Les did the bed while Alan concentrated on the locker.

Fifteen minutes later Corporal Smith was back for a look. "That's better Blowers, now you just make sure it always looks like that, do you understand, you horrible little man?"

"Yes Corporal," he said in reply.

Corporal Smith stood back from Bill and shouted, "stand to attention when you talk to me soldier and address me as Corporal Smith, not just Corporal," and leaning right up to Bill's ear he shouted, "do you understand me laddie?"

Bill stood upright and said, "Yes Corporal Smith." And with that Smithy turned and left the Barrack Room.

Dinner was served at six o'clock in the canteen, or rather the cookhouse, because that is what it was known as and Lance Corporal Jones had arrived in the Barrack Room at five minutes too and he marched the platoon the hundred yards or so across the parade square. By then Alan was absolutely starving; he had only had a mug of tea and a bun at the railway station since his breakfast at his Uncle Les's and had had nothing since. The cookhouse was jam packed with squaddies, squaddies being a slang name used for soldiers, together with Les and Bill, Alan joined the end of the queue after picking up a plastic tray. They chatted as the queue moved slowly towards the serving hatch and each in turn held out their plates to be served. Dinner consisted of a meat stew, boiled potatoes, cabbage and parsnips and a plate of fruit pie with thick stodgy custard for pudding, not very appetising, but being as hungry as he was, just about anything would have done right then, Alan thought.

The three of them wandered to a half empty table, the table's seated about twenty four people; with twelve each side and they managed to get on the end together. Although the food was pretty lousy, Alan had to admit he enjoyed it, mainly he thought because he was so damned hungry. They chatted as they ate; Les had a steady girlfriend back home in

Leeds who was pretty cut up about him joining the army, Bill had no one special, but looking at the size of him Alan wasn't too surprised. It wasn't that he was overweight; it was just that he was an awkward shape, large head, barrel chest, fairly modest waist but a huge backside. But all in all he seemed a nice enough guy Alan felt, even if he was a bit slow on the uptake. They were joined after five minutes by Cocker Hall, Alan found out that he had a steady girl friend back home in London, but he never let on too much about himself, only saying that yes he had had several girlfriends and yes there was someone at present, but not sure how long it would last now that he had joined up.

The dinner was washed down with a large mug of very strong tea and when they were finished they had to report back to the Barrack Room, the time was about ten minutes to seven. Corporal Smith and Lance Corporal Jones were there waiting for everyone and spent the next hour outlining the training programme over the next month. This would consist of two weeks of nothing but square bashing, that's the name given to marching up and down the parade square doing various drills. They would learn how to march properly, how turn left and right, how to halt, how to salute Officers. Then after the first week they would be introduced to marching with a rifle on their shoulder, as well as all the additional drills that had to be learned with the rifle and they were to find out later these had nothing to do with shooting.

Lance Corporal Jones then spent some time showing them how to shine their boots; the toecaps had to shine like a mirror, a pretty tough task Alan thought as he looked at the rough black leather on the toe caps of his boots. Jonesy showed them the trick of what he called, spit and polish, where you spread black boot polish on the leather and then literally spit on it and rub it in with a duster using small circular motions. They were to spend the rest of the evening getting their boots looking something like the ones Jonesy had left on his locker for all to see.

Alan sat on the side of his bed with one boot between his knees and started what at first seemed to be a hopeless task, but was surprised at how soon an inkling of a shine started to appear. He varied the amount of spit and polish combinations and after an hour, with one aching wrist he was quite proud of his efforts and started on the second boot. Bill Blowers wandered over looking a bit gloomy with one of his boots, he had hardly made any impression at all, so Alan gave him a few tips, which he thanked him for and wandered back to his bed to carry on. Lance Corporal Jones arrived back into the Barrack Room at nine thirty and after a general look to see how they were getting on, told them all to start getting ready for bed as lights out was at ten thirty and Reveille, which was the morning wake up call, would be at six o'clock.

After putting his boots in the bottom of his locker Alan headed for the toilet block, he went to the loo first and then had a quick wash before getting in to bed, he wasn't just tired, he was absolutely knackered, and this was only the end of his first day. He then pulled on his new blue and white stripped army supply pyjamas, which were made out of a winceyette type material, which in all fairness were fairly cosy for the time of year he thought. He was asleep almost before his head had even touched the pillow; he certainly didn't need any rocking that was for sure.

Chapter 10

When Alan had arrived with his six chums on the Monday, most of the other beds in the Barrack Room were already occupied, most of them having arrived during the latter part of the previous week, it seemed that they liked to stagger the intake over a period of several days prior to the serious training getting underway, which was to start on the Tuesday morning. Alan was awakened by a loud trumpet sound playing a tune that he was to learn later was Reveille and was the normal wake up call used throughout the armed forces, just as at night they played the Last Post when it was time for lights out. This was obviously a tradition that had been carried down the years, Alan also found out that it wasn't a trumpet; it was in fact a bugle.

Lance Corporal Jones was up immediately and shouting out, "Come on you lazy lot, let's be having you, wakey, wakey." And he was off to the wash room.

Alan slowly raised himself up and stretched, then after a couple of minutes eased himself out of his bed, grabbed a towel from his locker together with his washing and shaving kit and made his way to the washroom. They had been told the night before that they would have half an hour to get ready before breakfast, which was at six thirty and then had to be on parade at seven thirty. Although Alan shaved, he only had what could be described as bum fluff on his chin, so it only took a few minutes and he was back in the Barrack Room and dressed in his fatigues by ten minutes to seven. Les and Bill were also ready and Cocker called out to them to wait for him, which they did.

Together the four of them made their way to the cookhouse for breakfast. It was real greasy spoon stuff, eggs, bacon, baked beans, and fried potatoes, the potatoes were probably left over's from dinner the night before, and all cooked in gallons of fat, with a couple of slices of bread and margarine and large mug of strong tea. Alan asked the others if they thought the tea tasted funny, but they didn't make any real comment, he certainly thought it did and was to find out later in the day why.

When they got back from breakfast, Corporal Smith had also turned up and was already starting his shouting, yelling at everyone and anyone in his sight to get dressed properly and get outside on parade and ready for inspection. Everyone had to wear fatigues over a khaki shirt and tie, but also had to wear a pair of webbing gaiters around the ankles. The gaiters rested on the upper part of the boots, the idea was to fold and tuck the bottom of the trousers into the gaiters to keep them from flapping about. They also had a webbing belt with brass buckles on around their waists and on their heads they wore a navy blue beret, which had to be pulled down to the right hand side, the beret sported a brass badge, the badge of the RASC.

Once outside Lance Corporal Jones started getting the whole platoon of fifty four recruits in some form of order, they were in three lines, or ranks as they were known, facing the front. He was doing his best to size everyone, tallest on the left as he faced them and shortest on the right and so on, he'd obviously done this many times before and it didn't take him too long to get it somewhere about right.

It was then that they were about to meet their Platoon Officer, Second Lieutenant Harding; he had one crown, or pip as they were known, on his shoulder denoting his rank. He was only about twenty one years of age, very tall and thin, with ginger hair and a moustache; obviously the moustache was there to make him look older than his years Alan thought, plus he had an awfully posh voice. "Thank you Corporal Smith," he started, "Good morning B Platoon and welcome to Farnborough, where I know you will be very well looked after by Corporal's Smith and Jones. Sergeant Harrison your platoon Sgt will be back with us next week, but until then I want you to do exactly as you are instructed, so that when Sergeant Harrison returns he will be proud of you. Is that understood?"

All in chorus they shouted, "Yes Sir!"

Cpl Smith then shouted, "Front rank, take one pace forward," to which those in the front line did as instructed. This was followed by, "The rear rank, take one step backwards," again they responded. This was later to be changed to 'open order march,' where both ranks would do this on the one order, the idea being to allow the officers and NCOs to walk between the ranks for inspection purposes.

Lt Harding followed by Cpl's Smith and Jones then started walking along each line of the platoon, looking at each soldier in turn.

As they walked Lt Harding would say something to Cpl Smith, who would then address the soldier they had stopped in front of, the first of these, was Jock Ferny. "Did you shave this morning soldier?" he shouted at Jock.

"Yes Cpl Smith," replied Jock.

"Well laddie, tomorrow morning make sure you stand one pace closer to your bloody razor and you might make a better job of it. Do you understand me laddie?"

"Yes Cpl Smith," came back Jock's reply.

They moved on. The next soldier they stopped at was Bill Blowers. "What is your name soldier?" shouted Cpl Smith.

"Private Blowers, Cpl Smith," Bill answered.

"Well private Blowers, you look like a bag of spuds tied up in the middle, you are a disgrace to the uniform you are wearing. I will be keeping a close eye on you soldier, you need to smarten yourself up and quickly, otherwise you will find yourself on Jankers for the foreseeable future. Is that understood?"

"Yes Cpl Smith," Bill said, and they moved on.

There were several more stops for the small group as they made there way between the ranks, and several more rantings by Smithy, ones that Alan felt sure he practiced time and time again, but after twenty minutes they were finished.

When they reached the end of the final line in the Platoon, Lt Harding stood back saying, "Ok Corporal Smith, get then on the square and see what they can do."

With that he saluted, turned and marched away, leaving the platoon with the two Corporals.

It was Corporal Smith who took charge from thereon in. Using Jonesy as a model the platoon were shown how to stand to attention. This started from what was called the standing easy position, where you stood with feet apart and hands behind the back and fairly relaxed. The next move was to stand at ease; all this consisted of was literally a bracing of the body which was done by pushing the hands down the back, finishing in a more upright stance. Then finally coming to attention was achieved by lifting the left knee to waist high and then banging the foot onto to the ground next to the right foot, at the same time bringing the arms to the side of the body with the thumbs in line with the pockets of your trousers and pointing towards the ground.

After several run throughs, and when everyone had got the hang of things, it was on to turning right, turning left and turning about from a stationary position. Each of these moves was made in a similar way, from standing to attention it was a case of turning the way instructed, then lifting the knee to waist height and then banging the foot back onto the ground, so you were in fact still standing at attention, just facing in a different direction.

All the turns were done to a count of three; you would count one on the initial turn, then two and three as a pause between the move and then one again for the final move. So in your head you were counting, one two three, one, this was to try to make sure that everyone finished with the stamping of the foot at the same time.

Then it was on to learning how to march properly, always starting off the with the left foot forward first, while swinging the right arm forward, the arms had to swing back and forth to shoulder height making sure that the hand was clenched with the thumb pointing straight down the line of the hand. From the marching it was then a case of learning to stop, or halt, which was the term they used, but trying to make this happen as a unit all in unison with each other.

They were then shown how to left turn while still marching, first to the left, then to the right and then an about turn, facing in the opposite direction. This done, they were then shown how to salute with the right hand, bending the arm until the fingers of the hand were touching the forehead. Next they were shown how to do an eyes right and eyes left while marching, these two functions being a way that respect was shown to Officers by a platoon while marching. The NCO that was in charge of the platoon would himself salute the officer, while all those in the platoon turned their head as instructed, left or right. In all it took just over an hour for the two corporals to show the whole routine and then it was the turn of the new recruits.

What an absolute bugger up it was too. Alan was positioned about six from the right hand end of the Platoon in the front rank; he had Jock Ferny to his right and Les to his left. When they were doing the stationary bits things weren't too bad, the stand easy to the attention position was OK, the turning right and left was fairly OK, but when they started the marching it was horrendous. When they turned right Jock would be marching in front of Alan, on the face of it, it shouldn't have been a problem, but the silly sod didn't seem to know his right from his left.

When Corporal Smith shouted, "Right Turn," there was Jock looking straight into Alan's eyes. Corporal Smith was there like a shot, "which is your right side soldier?" he shouted at Jock.

Jock stammered saying as he pointed, "this side Corporal Smith."

"Then why the bloody hell did you turn the other way you dozy sod. Tell me laddie is there something going on between you two that we don't know about? Do you like gazing into his eyes, do you soldier?"

"No Corporal Smith," Jock replied.

"Then turn the other bloody way then," he shouted right into his ear.

Jock turned to face the correct way and they waited for the next command.

Corporal Smith shouted out, "Platoon, quick march."

As Alan went to put his left foot forward it rammed straight into the back of Jock's left leg, because he had started off with his right foot and right arm swinging together as he marched forward. Alan stumbled as he tried to march and regain his balance this also caused Les Fraser who was behind Alan to stumble, while at the same time putting all those behind them in a right mess.

Corporal Smith was back to where Les and Alan were trying to regain their balance, with Jock Ferny striding away kicking hell out of the chap in front of him.

"Halt!" Smithy screamed at the top of his voice and everyone came to a stop. He stared at Alan, his face no more than an inch away from his and then he shouted, "So who is to blame for this little shambles soldier. Do you know you're left from your right?"

"Yes Corporal Smith," said Alan.

"So what happened then?" he finished.

"I think we all got a bit mixed up Corporal Smith," Alan continued.

"You're not blaming that great big Scottish lummox who's in front of you then?"

"No Corporal Smith."

"Why not, because you should be he's a bloody clown not a soldier." Cpl Smith then walked along to Jock Ferny and standing with his mouth close to Jock's ear he shouted, "What's your name soldier?"

"Ferny, Cpl Smith," Jock replied.

"Well Private Ferny, the next time you do that I will put my dick in your ear and I will fuck some sense in to you. Do you understand me soldier?"

"Yes Cpl. Smith," Jock said in answer.

"Right, let's all get fell in again and see if we can get it right this time," he shouted.

Alan couldn't help but grin at Smithy's little jibe at Jock and it was one that was going to be heard time and time again during the next few weeks, he would find out.

They all got back into their positions and while they were doing this Alan whispered to Jock, "For god's sake Jock start with your left foot this time."

"Sorry, got a bit muddled," was all he said in his broad Scottish accent.

Thankfully the second time around he got it right, Jock started off with his left foot and they were away. They marched up and down the parade square it must have been twenty times, doing left turns, right turns and about turns. The about turns were the worst, Jock kept getting out of step when they did this and Alan had to kick his legs and make him skip to get his proper leg moving correctly. Luckily neither of the Corporals noticed this and they somehow got away with it. It was ten o'clock before they had a break and like most of the others Alan's legs ached like hell. They were called to a halt, told to stand at ease and then stand easy and finally dismissed. They had half an hour to go to the loo if needed and get a cup of tea; Alan needed both in that order. Then it was back to the square bashing right up until lunchtime at twelve thirty.

When break time came Alan just needed to cool his feet down, what with all the marching and the banging down of the feet when coming to attention and turning. He went back to the Barrack Room and took off his boots, walked to the washroom and let some water fall into the shower tray and stood in it, 'blimey this is great,' he thought, the best feeling for a long time. After ten minutes of foot bathing, he re-joined the others and they made their way to the cookhouse for lunch. Lunch was much the same as dinner, some meat and veg with thick gravy and a piece of cake, together with the obligatory cup of tea, definitely something odd about the taste, Alan thought again, he just didn't know why the others hadn't noticed it.

They were back on parade at one thirty. The first session of the afternoon was just more of what they had done in the morning, marching up and down the parade square turning left, then right, then turning about, backwards and forwards. Then at four o'clock after they had had their afternoon break they were being taken to the medical centre for what they called an FFI, a free from infection examination by the camp Medical Officer, or MO as he was better known. These were to become a regular occurrence throughout Alan's army life he would soon learn. The Army were big on things like cleanliness and personal hygiene, so it was easy to understand; it only took one bad apple, so to speak. Alan had to admit that the FFI was one of the funniest hours that he had spent in a long time. The Platoon was marched to the Medical Centre and after being dismissed they were told to form an orderly line in a long corridor.

Lance Corporal Jones was with the Platoon and told them to start getting their kit off, right down to their underpants. Everyone gradually stripped off and when the MO said he was ready to start, Jonesy called out, "Right you lot, get your pants off, now!"

Slowly each of one of the Platoon slipped their underpants off and threw them on their respective pile of clothes on the floor where they were standing. It was the next order that made Alan laugh like a drain, Jonesy shouted, "Mark time."

Well, marking time is the same as running on the spot, but a little slower and the sight of fifty odd chaps in the nude bouncing up and down; well Alan just saw the funny side of it. Some were holding themselves, some were laughing, as he was, and some were totally embarrassed. After some five minutes of this Jonesy called halt and they all stood and waited, it was time for the FFI to get started.

A medical NCO came into the corridor and started to get those at the front to move in single file into the room where the MO was waiting, sitting behind a desk with one junior Officer each side of him. The FFI consisted of stopping in front of the MO, stating your name and the last four digits of you army number, then standing with your feet apart holding your arms upwards and outstretched so they could see under your armpits, then turning around and bending over so they could see your rear end.

When it was Alan's turn the MO looked at him, he was gazing at his size down below, being as well endowed as he was, "What's your name soldier?" he asked.

"Private Gray, Sir." Alan replied

He then turned to the younger officer on his left he said, "Make sure this man has double bromide, looks like he could need it. Liase with Lance Corporal Jones as soon as we are finished here."

Quite what they meant Alan didn't know right then, but was to find out a little later. He was also to find out what the funny taste in the tea was, because it turned out that they put a substance called bromide in the tea, it helps to reduce the male tendency to get horny and aroused, bearing in mind they are all boys together. Jonesy saw Alan after the FFI examinations were finished and it was arranged that he had to report to him every morning and he would make sure that he had a bromide tablet over and above what they were dosing him with already in the tea. Luckily he wasn't going to be seeing Jennie for a while, 'because that could be very disappointing,' he thought.

The funny thing was, that Smithy's saying of 'I'll put my dick in your ear,' was changed, he would follow it up sometimes by saying 'and if that doesn't work then I will get Private Gray to put his dick in your ear and see if that has the desired effect,' which caused a great laugh with all the lads.

Chapter 11

The first week at Farnborough flew by and everyone was gradually getting better at the marching and the turning, but they were now going to have to learn to do it with a rifle on their shoulder. On the Monday morning the Platoon was marched to the armoury where each Soldier was issued with a 303 Rifle, which had to be signed for. Each rifle had a serial number and once assigned, it was your responsibility and had to be returned to the armoury each evening. They were then marched back to the parade square where again using Jonesy as the model, Corporal Smith went through all the movements that had to be learned with a rifle.

When standing easy or at ease, the butt end of the rifle was on the ground, while the top of the barrel was held in the right hand protruding in front of the body, then when moving to the attention position, the rifle had to be pulled in tightly to the side of the body. The next position was called slope arms, this meant a sharp movement where the rifle was thrown up the right hand side of the body, being caught with both hands, the left arm reaching across the body to catch hold of the upper part of the rifle and the right hand catching the rifle around the area of the trigger guard, about midway along the length of the rifle. It then had to be moved with both hands across the body and laid it on the left shoulder with the left hand moving down to support the rifle at the butt end, finally moving the right hand back to the side of the body, all of this done using the one two three timing. This caused some fun as you can imagine, especially with Bill Blowers and Jock and also a few of the others, they just couldn't get the hang of it, they seemed to have no coordination; rifles were falling on the ground all over the place, with Corporal Smith getting more and more enraged by the minute. There were more dicks in ears that morning than ever before.

From the slope arms with the rifle on the left shoulder, the next move was to get it back down to the where it started from; this was called order arms, which in fact was a reversal of the slope arms. The rifle had to drop down the left side of the body with the butt still being held in the left hand, at the same time the right arm was brought across the body to take hold of the rifle about half way up its length. From there it was a matter of carrying it across the body with the right hand and placing the butt of the rifle on the ground, with the left arm returning to the side, still standing at attention, again using the one two three timing.

After practising the slope arms and the order arms for about half an hour, until Smithy was satisfied that the Platoon had all got it somewhere near right, they then moved on to the present arms. The present arms was used as a salute to officers using a rifle. From the slope arms position, the rifle had to be moved to the centre of the body and held in front with both hands and at the same time the right foot had to be lifted and placed at an angle behind the left foot. All very confusing, but after a couple of attempts Alan felt he had got it pretty well OK.

After that it was a case of going through the whole routine from stand at ease, getting to attention, sloping arms, then turning right and marching, keeping rifle balanced on the left shoulder while swinging the right arm. Up and down, up and down, all morning they were at it, until Corporal Smith was satisfied that they had all got it about right, and then thank god it was time for some lunch, thought Alan.

Sergeant Harrison had retuned to Barracks on the Tuesday morning and he was introduced by the Platoon Officer at the morning parade. He was well over six feet tall, with a large frame and was probably about forty years of age, he like Corporal Smith had a very loud voice and liked to use it. He took control of the morning session, with the Platoon marching up and down both with and without the rifle; he seemed quite impressed with what he saw bearing in mind this was only the second week of training, but he wasn't going to say so that's for sure, thought Alan.

And so the week continued, sometimes with Sergeant Harrison sometimes Corporal Smith, it was a case of marching and more marching, Alan lost count of the number of times that they went from one end of the parade ground to the other, all he did know was that at the end of each day he was knackered and each night he slept like a log.

During the evenings of the second week they were shown by Jonesy how to Blanco the items of webbing they had been issued with. Blanco was a brownish block of what could only be described as a cross between soap and polish, which with the aid of some water had to be brushed onto the webbing to form a waterproof protection as well as enhancing the look of it. The webbing items consisted of the belt, the gaiters and the various back packs and pouches that had been supplied when they had been kitted out. The packs and pouches were not so bad, they just had to have a matt finish to them, so a couple of coats was sufficient, but the belt and gaiters had to have a polished finish to them, so again the spit and polish routine was used to get this sheen on them. The gaiters had black straps that held them in place and these had to be treated in the same way as the boots, again using the spit and polish technique. Plus the fact that the brass buckle on the belt, together with the hat badge and the buttons on the greatcoats had to be highly polished. All this was done during the evenings between dinner and lights out using Brasso.

By the end of the second week most of the Platoon were starting to look and act something like soldiers. Their marching and use of the rifle was pretty good, their turnout was one hundred percent better than at the end of the first week and all in all Sergeant H, Smithy and Jonesy were pretty pleased with the overall progress. On the Friday morning parade, even Lieutenant Harding complimented them on the Platoon turnout, didn't compliment the squaddies themselves who had done all the hard work, obviously felt it was the NCOs hard work that had got them thus far, nothing to do with their own effort, but that's the way it seemed to be, so just something that had to be accepted, thought Alan.

Saturday's were a half day, so they didn't do any square bashing; instead they had to do chores. Between them they had to clean the Barrack Room from top to bottom, they scrubbed the washroom, swept the outside area around the Barrack Room and generally spent the whole morning cleaning. They also had to mark all of their kit with their surname and the last four digits of their personal army number.

When Alan and the others had collected their kit on the first day, they had also been provided with what was called a pay book or pass book, this was a small brown book about four inches by six inches. Inside was a number, which was to be Alan's army number throughout his service , this being 21970430, it also had the address of the Farnborough Barracks as his Home Station and several blank pages for future postings to be written in. There was a space for next of kin, where Alan had written his Mothers name and her address in case this was ever needed. Then there were pages which would be used in the event of promotions and details of any courses attended and examinations passed, giving a comprehensive record of a soldier's time in the service. It also had to be used on pay day; there were pages inside for this to be stamped by the Pay Corps Officer, showing the amount paid and date.

In fact they had had to use them on the previous Thursday, because that was their first pay day. Pay Parade had been just after lunch and they all had to line up outside the Pay Masters Office and went in one by one, they had to stand to attention and state their name, rank and number. The Paymaster would take the pay book and make the entry and pass over a small brown envelope, containing their wages. Once outside, Alan eagerly ripped open his envelope, which contained four pounds one shilling. His weekly wage was two pound seven shilling and sixpence, but as there were an extra few days from the previous week, this had been lumped together. He felt like a millionaire. Trouble was he couldn't go out anywhere to spend it.

On Sunday Alan wrote a letter to Jenny, he gave her some background information of what he were doing, but as it was so much repetition of the previous week, there wasn't too much knew to tell. He kept it to just one page and signed it Alan, and added just one small kiss under his name, had to be very careful in case her parents ever read them.

Chapter 12

Things started to get much more interesting during the weeks that followed. The whole Platoon had started going to the gym regularly each morning for an hour after the morning inspection parade. In the middle of October they also went to a firing range to shoot their rifles, but before doing any shooting they had to learn how to strip and clean them. They were each given a special cleaning kit, which consisted of a soft cloth, a small can of oil and what was called a 'pull through', the pull though was basically a tapered piece of rope about three feet long; and at the thin end there was a weight. The idea was, that the weighted end was dropped into the breach end of the barrel and once it protruded out the other end, it had to be pulled through the length of the barrel, the thicker end of the rope therefore cleaning any carbon deposits that may be left after shooting and oiling the barrel at the same time. This was something they had to do both before and after firing.

Alan really enjoyed his time at the firing range, it turned out that he apparently was a pretty good shot, seemed to have a natural talent for it and this in fact got him his first entry into his pass book, stating that he was 'a first class shot', marksman being the top award, which no one got. By the end of the week he had also learned how to use a Sten gun, which was a small automatic gun and a Bren gun, which was like a large rifle that had a tripod at the front end, this was fired while laying down on the ground balancing the front end of the barrel on the tripod, the Bren Gun was also automatic, and firing this Alan felt was a really brilliant experience.

The other thing that they now had to do was guard duty, this happened about once every three weeks. Alan's first experience came during the last week in September, together with Cocker and Bill he had reported to the guard house along with thirteen others from B Platoon at five thirty in the evening. The Guard Commander on that first occasion was Sgt Harrison. He got the Platoon fell in, in two ranks and awaited the duty Officer, who was Lt Harding, to carry out the inspection. This was really pretty straightforward, he just walked along the ranks making a few comments as he did and they were then dismissed.

Guard duty meant just what it sounded like; it was each soldier's job to take it in turns to guard the perimeter of the camp, this was done in two hour stints. Alan was on the first shift of six o'clock to eight o'clock with seven of the others, they were marched to their posts and then had to patrol an area which had been detailed to them earlier by the Guard Commander. Alan's walk was about one hundred and fifty yards long from one end to the other and he had to keep marching up and down for the whole two hours. If he encountered anyone in his area of patrol, he had to point his rifle and shout, "Halt who goes there." A bit of a giggle really, he thought.

They had all practised this during one of the training sessions the previous week, Alan just hoped that he wouldn't encounter anyone, especially on his first stint, but if he did he would then have to act on whatever the response was. The response should come back either friend or foe. If they were supposedly friend then the guard had to say, "step forward and be recognised." It was a case of that person doing as instructed and then being allowed on there way, providing of course they were a friend, a friend being another soldier who would have to produce his ID, or identity. If the response was foe and they couldn't identify themselves, then they had to be marched to the Guard Room.

Alan was just pleased when his first stint was over because he was then allowed to have his supper. The first stint had been OK, but when he had to go back out at ten o'clock for his next session it was much more eerie, the trees swayed in the wind throwing shadows everywhere and there were times when Alan wasn't sure whether there was anyone there or not. The worst stint of all though Alan thought was the two o'clock until four o'clock one, he was just glad when it was over. He felt it was just so bloody creepy out there and that's no shit, although he would never say that to any of the others guys, but he also knew that they were feeling the same.

As the months were to go by, Alan did find that the guard duties weren't really that bad, it was something that one just got used too over time and took in your stride, in fact just another learning curve he felt.

Towards the end of October they started doing five mile marches and the five mile runs, together with tackling the assault course. The assault course was one of Alan's favourites. The first time it was done wearing just sports kit, but by the end of the week it had to be done while fully kitted out with back packs on and carrying a rifle, which Alan found, as did the others, was a different proposition. The assault course was about a mile long in total and consisted of crawling under netting, swinging across water on ropes, walking on a log that was suspended over a river, climbing a large netting wall and also getting over a six foot tall brick wall, plus of course all the running through the woods, clambering up slippery river banks, wading through a river and lots more.

But Alan loved every minute of it. The only real drawback was that at the end of the day the kit they had been wearing was absolutely filthy and it all had to be cleaned and Re-Blanco'd. Luckily they only wore their second pair of boots and fatigues for these jaunts, so scuffing the toecaps didn't matter quite as much, although they were still expected to be clean with a hint of a shine.

At the end of eight weeks continual training, Alan felt that he was really becoming a soldier and all the hard work was paying off. They had been told by Cpl Smith, that providing the Platoon passed a full inspection, which included a full marching exercise in front of the Camp Commander and an inspection of the Barrack Room by Lieutenant Harding and his boss Captain Jameson the Adjutant, everyone would receive a forty eight hour weekend pass. Everyone was on tenterhooks. Alan, together with Les Fraser and Cocker Hall had gone around all those blokes who they knew had had some problems with kit layout, like Jock and Bill, plus a couple of others, and gave then a last minute helping hand to make sure there would be no mess ups. It was great, the marching was good and the room inspection was A OK and they all got to go home for the weekend.

Alan had written to Jenny about every two weeks and in his last letter had told her that he may be able to come home for this particular weekend and would her Parents mind if he stayed. The answer came back a big yes, so Alan was quite excited. The weekend pass lasted from Friday evening at five thirty, until five thirty on Sunday evening.

Alan travelled to London with Les, Bill and Cocker. Les and Bill would get the underground to Kings Cross Station and then a train together to Leeds, and then Bill would get another train from Leeds to take him to his home in Bradford. Cocker in the meantime would just need to get the underground to Islington. The train to London was at just after six o'clock and they all boarded and had a good chat on the journey about what had happened during the past weeks and also a few laughs as well.

Once at Waterloo Alan said his goodbyes to the three of them and made his way to the underground, he had to get the Northern Line and then change at Embankment to the Circle Line that took him to Liverpool Street, where he would get his train back to Brentwood. By the time he arrived at Brentwood it was almost half past eight, he walked to the bus stop and got the bus to Warley and ten minutes later was walking into the cul-de-sac where Jenny lived. He rang the doorbell and she answered the door; on seeing Alan she gave the biggest smile he'd ever seen and just threw herself at him with a big hug and kiss.

Right at that point her Mum called out, "who is it Jenny?"

Jenny pulled away from Alan and called back, "it's only Alan, he's just got here."

"Bring him in dear, don't keep him stranding out in the cold," her Mum called again. And with that Jenny took Alan's hand and led him into the front living room releasing his hand as they entered, where both her Mum and Dad were sitting.

Alan was dressed in his full uniform and Uncle Les said, "My, my, what a smart lad you are. Looks like you've been a soldier a lot longer than a couple of months; they've done a jolly good job with you young Alan."

Jen stood there looking at Alan, there was a look in her eyes that said, 'I am so proud of you,' he just hoped that her Parents hadn't been looking too closely to see. Aunt Jean got up from the table and said, "I'll go and put the kettle on, would you like something to eat young Alan?"

He hesitated, but then said, "A sandwich will be fine, if that's not too much trouble?"

"I'll make you a nice corn beef sandwich, just opened a tin this evening, wont be a minute." And she left the room.

Uncle Les was keen to hear what Alan had been up too and he spent the next half an hour telling him loads of the things that he'd been doing, especially the rifle shooting, Uncle Les was really interested and Jenny just sat there with her mouth open, hanging on every word Alan said. He did think that he had glamorised it a bit, but felt sure, what with Uncle Les being an ex-serviceman himself, he would probably read between the lines, but all the same he had to admit he enjoyed the story telling. It wasn't long before his Aunt Jean was back with the sandwich and a cup of real tea;

Alan was getting fed up with the bromide stuff that they were forcing down him each day and the real tea tasted just great.

The time had crept round to nine thirty and Jen's Mum said she was going to get ready for bed and Uncle Les followed fifteen minutes later, leaving Jen and Alan on their own to chat, "Don't you be too late to bed young lady, don't go keeping young Alan up, he's probably tired from his long day," he said as he left the living room.

"OK Dad," replied Jenny, giving Alan a smile and a wink at the same time.

As soon as her Dad had left the room, she walked around the table and sat on Alan's lap putting her arms around his neck and kissing him in that wonderful way that she did.

"We had better be careful," Alan said, "what happens if they come back down and catch us?"

"They wont don't worry. Once they've gone to bed they're gone." And she continued to kiss and hug him, like there was no tomorrow.

After ten minutes she finally broke away and said in an excited voice, "I've got some really good news. Mum and Dad are going to Romford Market tomorrow morning, so we will have a couple of hours on our own together, that's if you want too of course?" She said this with that devilish smile of hers.

"I'd love that Jen, but there may be a problem," Alan said.

She looked quite serious and said, "Problem, what sort of problem, there's nothing wrong is there?" She was quite concerned.

Alan explained the bromide situation to her and she screeched with laughter, he told her to be quiet or her Parents would hear and come down wondering what was wrong, so she tried to control herself a little.

She slipped her hand down his trousers and he actually felt himself respond a little, and she said, "that will be no problem, it might take a little longer, but I don't mind, could be fun," she said, again that devilish smile.

It was just after ten thirty when they both went to bed, Alan had to admit it was nice to be in a soft bed once again, he hadn't realised just how hard the ones at the camp were. The day had been exhausting, what with the parade and then the travelling home, or rather to his Uncles home and Alan went out like a light. He slept soundly until he heard a knock on his door, Jen poked her head round and told him the bathroom was free and her Mum was cooking breakfast. He looked at the bedside clock, it was almost eight o'clock, he staggered out of the bed and after pulling his dressing gown around him went to the bathroom. After ten minutes and a good freshen up he felt a different person.

Alan's Uncle and Aunt were sitting at the breakfast table with Jenny when he entered the dining room and after saying good morning, his Aunt stood to get his plate, together with Jenny's, which she had placed in the oven to keep warm.

They had started their breakfast, Uncle Les saying that they needed to be away as early as possible, because as it was getting close to Christmas car parking would be difficult. Alan said he understood and of course it was alright with him, but as Jen had waited until he arrived, they ate together, while her Mum cleared some of the things away, asking Jenny if she would be good enough to wash the remaining plates and dishes and put them away, which of course she agreed.

The time was nine o'clock when her Parents said goodbye to them both and left for their trip to the market, Uncle Les had already got the car out of the garage and had it waiting on the drive for Aunt Jean to get in, they then drove away. Jen reached across the table and took Alan's hand, squeezing it gently, she smiled then stood and walked round the table to sit on his lap, they kissed and it wasn't long before she was dragging him up the stairs to her bedroom. Their clothes were off in a trice and they slipped under the bedclothes and in to each others arms. The bromide was certainly doing its job, but Jen was determined to get the better of it and she did. It took over half an hour of her stroking and generally playing with Alan, coupled with their kissing and Alan exploring her body, but then it was all systems go. It was wonderful and Alan was beginning to wonder if joining the army had been such a wise choice after all, thinking of what he was missing and would be missing while he's away, but too late now, was all he could think right then.

Knowing that her Parents would be home at about one o'clock, they had to make sure that they were properly dressed and the dishes all done before that, but it had been a perfect three hours of sheer bliss for Alan. Towards the end,

Jen was saying how much she wished he wasn't going to be away so much, but promised that she would wait for him coming home on leave and to make sure he got home as much as he could, which Alan had decided there and then that he would, thinking that this was just too good to miss.

The weekend passed all too quickly, but before Alan left he thanked her parents for having him and he gave his Aunt Jean a large box of chocolates and his Uncle a pack of tobacco for his pipe, both of which he had purchased on the Saturday while Jen and himself were in Brentwood. "You shouldn't have done that young Alan," they both had said, "after all you are family and you're always welcome." But Alan felt better for it, hopefully showing that he wasn't taking them and matters generally for granted.

Alan had to leave Brentwood on the two o'clock train to be sure of getting back to Barracks before five thirty. Jen went to the station with him; catching the bus from Warley at a quarter past one. They had half an hour to wait on the station and they went into the waiting room and had a final kiss and cuddle before the train pulled into the Station, Jen was in floods of tears as the train pulled out and Alan waved to her out of the window until the platform disappeared from view.

Chapter 13

Luckily, the trains were pretty much on time and after crossing London to Waterloo Station, Alan caught his connection and was back in Farnborough at a quarter to five in the afternoon. He reported to the guard room and booked himself back from his weekend leave and made his way to the Barrack Room. Les and Bill were already there when Alan arrived and they chatted generally about their respective weekends and after about half an hour Cocker arrived and all four of them went to the cookhouse for their evening meal.

The Barrack Room notice board showed that on Monday everyone in the Platoon would be having their vocational interviews; these would decide what trade each of them would undertake once the initial training was completed. Alan had already decided that he wanted to be a Driver, as had Les, Bill and Cocker, but Jock was erring more towards a storeman's job, felt it would keep him out of the cold and the whole group had laughed at his reasoning.

After the normal early morning parade on the Monday, the Platoon was marched to the main camp offices where the interviews would take place. In all there were six interviewers, ranging from Lt Harding, Sgt Harrison, Sgt Major Brown and three other officers who Alan hadn't seen before. His name was called by Sgt Harrison and Alan marched to his desk and waited to be told to sit down. Once seated the Sergeant went over Alan's progress since joining, saying that he was a promising soldier and to make sure that his selection of trade would be one that would test him throughout his army career. Quite what he was getting at Alan wasn't sure, but his mind was already made up, a driver he wanted to be and he was sticking to that no matter what.

After the preliminaries were over and Sgt Harrison had covered all the various trades that Alan could be considered for, he said "So Gray, what are your thoughts, how do you want to spend the rest of your time in the RASC?"

Alan's response was immediate, "I want to be a Driver, Sgt Harrison," he said.

"And why a Driver, Gray? There are many other trades as I have explained that I feel would suit your aptitude better."

Alan answered by saying, "I have a Brother in the RASC in Egypt who is a Driver and I have set my heart on following him, which was one of my main reasons for joining."

"Are you hoping to join him where he is stationed? because that can be arranged." He asked, "providing of course you pass your test OK."

"No Sgt Harrison, I want to make my own way, but I have decided that I want to be a Driver, as I said earlier that is what I joined up for," Alan finished.

"Determined young man I can see. Well I will put you forward, but you have to remember that you only get two shots at your driving test. The course lasts one week and at the end of the week you will take your driving test, if you pass, then OK, but if you don't, you get to take it early the following week. If you fail, then it'll probably be the stores or an admin job, do you understand?"

"Yes Sgt Harrison, I'm prepared to take that Chance," Alan replied.

"Right; the driving course proper starts a week today, but there will be an introduction during Thursday and Friday of this week, the details will be on the Bulletin Board in your Barrack Room." He made the necessary notes on his pad and Alan was dismissed.

After the interview Alan walked away feeling really chuffed.

At Lunchtime on the Monday following their vocational interviews, Alan met up with Les, Bill and Cocker and they went to the cookhouse; they all sat at one of the long dining tables after getting their regulation meat, potatoes and veg from the serving hatch. They had also been put forward for the driving course and they chatted about any experience that they had had already, which in Alan case was zilch. Bill said he had driven a tractor on a farm where he had worked and Les had driven his dad's car on a couple of occasions, but only around a factory estate. So all in all, Alan felt they all had an exciting week coming up.

And it was exciting Alan had to admit, even if the first couple of days were hilarious rather than serious, but he felt that without those couple of days he may well have struggled. The first day was a bit more serious though, teaching the group the Highway Code and the general form filling involved when a vehicle is assigned to an individual driver. They would have to complete a written test on the Highway Code prior to taking their driving tests as well as being asked questions by the examiner, but Alan felt that with a bit of swatting, this shouldn't be too much of a problem.

For Alan and the rest of the group the second day was a real hoot; in the training room there were eight mock ups of a drivers cab, there was a seat, a steering wheel, a gear lever, a hand brake, three foot pedals and a lever to operate two directional indicators. The idea was that you sat on the seat and then pretended to be driving; steering, changing gear and using the indicators. One of the main things that they had to practice and get used to, was that with a lorry the driver has to double de-clutch, which meant pressing the clutch in with your foot twice, once when taking it out of gear and again when it is put into the next gear. For someone like Alan and a lot of the others in fact who were uninitiated this had been a real boon, because Alan really got the feeling that he was driving, even though he wasn't moving. They were watched over by several army driving instructors, called DI's for short, each of them was a Lance Corporal; the one assigned to Alan specifically was Lance Cpl Adams, he was about nineteen and a National Serviceman.

Alan's first actual experience at driving came on the Monday morning. After morning parade those on the course had to go to the driving centre where the Lorries were parked and waiting, each sporting a very large red L plate for Learner, back and front. Lance Cpl Adams was waiting and after climbing aboard he drove the lorry out of the camp and headed towards some quiet roads between Farnborough and Guildford, obviously ones he had used time and time again.

As he drove he explained to Alan what he was doing and what he was looking for on the road, emphasising the importance of getting used to mainly using the wing mirrors, because when the lorry was loaded the interior mirror was pretty useless. He spent a lot of time demonstrating how to double de-clutch, changing gear again and again, which Alan found useful. After about half an hour he stopped and jumped out saying, "OK matey, it's now your turn."

Alan had to admit, he was scared shitless, really scared, no secret about that. He sat there shaking; sitting at the steering wheel of a bloody great three ton lorry for the first time in his life, who wouldn't have been scared? He thought.

"We can't bloody sit here all day," said Lance Cpl Adams, "start it up, get it in first gear and let's go, come on, do you want to be a driver or don't you?"

After making sure that the gears were in neutral, Alan turned the ignition key and the engine started, he then put his foot on the clutch and pushed it to the floor and engaged first gear. Then gripping the steering wheel like crazy he let the hand brake off and let out the clutch and the lorry was moving forward with him in control, well not fully, but trying dammed hard to be. The lorry lurched forward and the engine stalled, Alan jammed on the foot brake and then the hand brake.

Lance Cpl Adams looked across at Alan with a grin and said, "Got a bloody kangaroo in the tank have we. Come on, get it started again. Don't waste time, we haven't got all day."

Alan re-started the engine and tried again to pull away, this time with a little more success, the lorry inched forward, but just as it did a car was overtaking him and he blasted on his hooter, but Alan kept the vehicle moving forward.

"You're supposed to look in your bloody wing mirror and make sure it's clear before pulling away you silly bugger, it does help," said the DI.

But the lorry continued with Alan steering. He tried to change into the second gear and there was an almighty crunching noise as he tried to get the gear engaged.

"Keep your bloody foot on the clutch when you're trying to get in it gear, then it might go in without all this noise," the DI shouted across at him.

Eventually it engaged and their speed increased, Alan then changed into third gear with a bit more success, just a little rumble from the gearbox and by then they were doing about twenty five miles an hour, Christ he thought 'I hope I can stop the ruddy thing when I have too.' And then finally he got it into fourth gear, without too much grinding of the gears.

"That's better," said Lance Cpl Adams, "just keep going as you are."

Luckily the road was fairly straight, so steering wasn't a big issue for Alan at that point in time. They had driven along for about a mile with just fairly slight bends in the road, which he was able to manoeuvre around quite successfully. Lance Cpl Adams then told Alan to stop, he pressed his foot on the footbrake and the DI shot forward almost banging his head on the windscreen.

"You bloody fool, do it gently? You don't have to jam down the bloody pedal as hard as that. Right, let's pull away again and have another go through the gears, but look in your mirror before you do."

After checking in the wing mirror that the road was clear Alan pulled away again, changing gears much better now, well with much less crunching anyway. This time they drove a little further than before and Alan saw that they were approaching a stop sign and a main road ahead of them. Bloody hell he thought, what do we do here?

Lance Cpl Adams said, "Just start pushing your foot on the brake, but gently this time, I don't want to go banging my head against the windscreen. Right, now change down to third gear at the same time that you're braking. Just before the white lines push the footbrake full on, but don't ram it, do it gently but firmly as you did just now, then depress the clutch at the same time and put the gears in neutral and then pull on the handbrake."

Christ, all that to remember and do at the same time and in such a short time, Alan thought, bloody hell, but he did manage to do as he was told and the lorry stopped.

"OK, that wasn't bad for a first time," the DI said, "we're turning left here, so indicate, make sure there's no traffic coming from your right, put it in first gear, then as you pull away start to steer around the corner, pull your left hand down and push your right hand up and it'll make it a lot easier."

Alan did as he was told, after letting the clutch out the lorry moved forward and he began turning the wheel hard at the same time, but suddenly he felt a bump at the rear as the back wheels bounced over the kerb, but he kept going and then straightened the lorry up along the new road ahead.

"Not too bad, but you do have to give a much wider turn to get the rear of the truck around the corner, you have to remember how long it is" Lance Cpl Adams said. "Now just drive along this road, change gears and keep looking in your wing mirrors from time to time. This road runs about a mile and a half and then we're going to turn right. Do just the same as you did before as we approach the tee junction, but turn the other way at the junction, just make sure you take a wide enough sweep as you turn."

As they approached the Tee junction Alan slowed the lorry to a halt, indicated and when the road was clear he pulled forward and turned the wheel to the right. There were hedges along the side of the road and the wing mirror on Lance Cpl Adams side brushed through a large clump as the lorry got a bit too close to his side of the road, Alan then did his best to get the lorry back straight as soon as he could trying to judge the width, while at the same time trying to change gears as he did so.

"Well, not bad for your first attempt," he said. "We'll try that again at the next junction in about five hundred yards."

It was just as well that there wasn't too much traffic on the roads he had chosen, Alan thought as they trundled along, but that was probably the reason the DI used these particular roads. Alan indicated quite a way before the turning and changed down the gears coming to a complete stop. He went to pull forward, but the engine stalled, and he realised that he had put it in third gear and not first. After pulling on the handbrake and re-starting the engine he had a second go, this time with more success, not brushing the wing mirror into the hedge as he had before.

They carried on driving for two hours, Alan realised that they had in fact gone over the same route several times, but each time he got to a junction he became more confident and by the end of the session was quite chuffed with what he had achieved, especially as he had never driven in his life before, let alone a bloody great three ton truck.

On Cpl Adams instructions Alan had stopped in a small lay-by along the main A3 road south of Guildford where there was a small wooden café, there were three other lorry's already parked, obviously a natural watering hole Alan guessed, that they used on a regular basis. They got out of the lorry and Alan locked the doors before entering the café, Les Fraser was there with his DI and two of the other chaps from camp. Alan got a cup of tea and sat with Les to chat about the experience. It sounded as though he had done about as well as Alan had, with a few shaky moments along the way.

Tuesday, Wednesday and Thursday were all much of the same, except each day they drove a little faster and also on much bigger roads where there was far more traffic, they also drove through several villages and a couple of towns, including Guildford and Farnham, but Alan felt he had coped pretty well. On the Thursday morning as they were driving along the main A3 road from the south, which was a very long slow hill, they were about half way up when Cpl Adams told Alan to stop, which he did after making sure that he had indicated and there was nothing too close behind him.

The DI then said to Alan, "Do you smoke Gray?"

To which he answered. "No." Alan had had the odd fag in the past, just to try it out, but had never taken it up seriously.

"Well I do," continued the DI and took out a packet of ten Woodbines. "Get out and place these under the rear wheels, then get back in. We're going to do a hill start and if you go backwards and crush my fags, it will cost you double," and he smiled.

Alan did as he was told and after getting back into the cab proceeded to pull away on the hill. He was ecstatic; he in fact did it on three occasions, each time without rolling backwards. Alan then handed the DI back his unharmed Woodbines. The DI just grinned.

Alan's driving test was on the Friday at twelve forty five in Slough. He had spent the morning driving, firstly on the roads that he had gotten to know very well and then at eleven o'clock Cpl Adams headed him in the lorry towards Slough. They drove around the route that the DI expected the tester to take Alan, so that he would at least be fairly familiar with what to expect, what Alan hadn't bargained for though was the amount of traffic at lunch time. At twelve thirty he drove to the test centre and with Cpl Adams went into the building where they filled out the necessary forms, at exactly a quarter to one the examiner walked through a door at the rear and introduced himself to Alan and walked out to his lorry with him.

The first fifteen minutes were taken up with questions on the Highway Code, which Alan had read and re-read over the past week and felt that he had answered all the questions fairly OK. The examiner then told him to start the engine and drive forward. Alan felt that the next forty five minutes were the most important that he had had to face so far since he'd joined the army, and right then he was bloody nervous, but tried his hardest not to show this to the examiner.

The examiner gave Alan continual instructions as they drove, turn left at the next junction, turn right at the tee junction, straight ahead at the next roundabout and so on. In all they passed through at least ten sets of traffic lights and had to negotiate three roundabouts on their route. On the main A4 road Alan was able to increase his speed, but kept within the forty mile limit allowed, then all of a sudden the examiner shouted, "Emergency stop." Although Alan was expecting this at some point, it still came as a bit of a surprise to him, he pressed the brakes on hard, but without actually jamming them on, putting his foot on the clutch at the same time and came to a stop, making sure that he had indicated and had checked the rear view mirrors at the same time.

The examiner made a few notes on the pad on his clip board and told Alan to engage first gear and pull away once again, He did as instructed, making sure he checked his mirrors and indicated. Again following the Examiners instructions, Alan drove to a housing estate where there was not too much traffic, he then instructed Alan to stop at the corner of the junction that was in front of them and explained that Alan was now required to reverse the lorry around the corner. This is something that Alan had practised and practised with Cpl Adams, the one thing he had impressed upon him was not to hit the kerb and to make sure that when he stopped, he was lined up parallel with the kerb about nine to twelve inches away. It went great, smooth as you like first time and again after making some more notes the Instructor told Alan to pull away again and with him guiding Alan as before, left here, right there, they drove back to the testing centre. Alan parked the lorry and waited.

"Well done Driver Gray, you've passed, you can take your L plates off now." the Instructor said and with that he was gone.

Cpl Adams came out of the office ten minutes later with a big smile on his face and some documents for Alan, which were tantamount to his knew driving licence, telling him that the official licence would take a week or so to be processed through the system. And with that they drove back to the Barracks at Farnborough, minus L plates.

Although Alan had got his licence so to speak, the driver training wasn't quite over, because the following week they had to do a night drive from Farnborough to Portsmouth and back and this had to be completed before they were officially deemed to be full blown Drivers. It was good fun though Alan thought; they set off at six thirty on the Tuesday evening in convoy, twelve Lorries in all and it was hammering down with rain. The only vehicle to have head lights on was the lead vehicle driven by Lance Cpl Adams; Alan was the second vehicle in the convoy and like all the others just had side lights on, but at the rear of each Lorry was a special light that shone on to the white painted rear gear axle housing. So all Alan could see ahead of him was two small red rear lights and the white light on the rear axle of the lorry in front. Once they got out of the town and onto the main A3 highway they then had to switch off the sidelights and just rely on the white axle light, it was quite eerie really Alan thought, even more so to any one looking at the convoy driving along.

The drive took just over an hour to get to Portsmouth and after a short break of thirty minutes they made the return journey, with Alan this time halfway along the convoy; Les Fraser was in the vehicle in front and Cocker in the one behind, with Bill being the very last lorry, having all passed their tests on the previous Friday. The time was just after nine thirty when they eventually had the Lorries all safely parked and the four of them went to the NAAFI for a well deserved beer before turning in for the night. The NAAFI, for those that don't know, is like a cross between a shop and a club where as normal soldiers you could buy sweets, magazines, cigarettes, toiletries, plus tea and coffee and soft drinks and they also had a licensed bar.

Chapter 14

It was the middle of November and the Platoon were over half way through their basic training, the square bashing was all but over, except for practising for the final passing out parade, Alan had become a Driver, so at least his trade was sorted out and during the next four weeks running up until Christmas they were having a series of what were called manoeuvres. These were designed to make the rookies into real soldiers as they put it, trying to put them in positions that they could and would find themselves in, in the year's ahead, dependant on where they each got posted too.

The first of these was to be a night manoeuvre. The Platoon was kitted out in full gear, back packs, rifle the lot, but no ammunition. They were then going to be taken in groups of eight to an unknown location by lorry; they would be dropped off at midnight and had until six o'clock the following morning to rendezvous at a given location marked on the map they had been given. They would have to use the map reading skills, which they had been learning in the previous weeks. There were six other groups being dropped off in a similar location about half a mile apart, the main missions were to rendezvous at the correct place and time and not to be seen by any of the other groups. If your group was seen, they were deemed to be captured, so the art of camouflage was of the essence, again something that they had also been learning during the previous week.

In the same group with Alan were Les, Cocker, Bill Blowers, Jock Ferny and three others, John Hardy, Harry Crook and Bob Barnet, all good blokes. They couldn't see out of the sides or rear of the lorry as it trundled to their destination, because the tarpaulin covers had been tied firmly in place. Alan had his watch on and it took forty-five minutes to reach the drop off point, during this time they had discussed the issue of who would be the leader and after not too much discussion it fell on Alan's shoulders and he in turn nominated Les to be his number two. The group then set about smearing their faces with the camouflage paste that they had been supplied, it was a brownie green paste and they smeared it on, also helping each other to make sure their faces were well covered.

The lorry stopped and the canvas back was opened and L/Cpl Jones, who had been driving, told the group to get out, as soon as they were all out he said his goodbyes and drove off. It was pitch black and drizzling with rain, the only lights they had were very small pen torches, but they also knew that they would have to use these carefully so as not to be seen by any of the other groups. Alan saw a clump of bushes about twenty yards away and the group, on Alan's command, headed towards them for cover, once there they then set about getting their bearings. Alan got the compass out and found north, then sent Les out of the clump of bushes to see if he could see any landmarks, he returned after ten minutes quite chipper.

"Towards the south of us, about four hundred yards or so, there's a church steeple, and to the left of that is a windmill," he said.

"OK," Alan said, "we will go south and find out the name of the church, that will tell us exactly where we are and we can then get a bearing on our rendezvous point and start to plot our route. Let's go. Single file and let's do it low and slow. Keep your eyes peeled for any signs that may help and keep listening, any noise and we stop and drop to the ground. Understood?"

They all gave a thumb's up and the group moved out very stealthily.

It took ten minutes to get to the church; they hadn't seen or heard anything. They sank low against the walls of the churchyard and Alan told Cocker to go in slowly and take down whatever details he could off of the board at the church entrance. He came back after a few minutes and handed Alan his notes which he read. The church was St. Peters in the village of West Liss; Alan found it on the map which he had clipped to a flat board and marked a line in pencil between where they were and the rendezvous point, the distance was about fifteen miles. With the help of Les, Alan then plotted a route that would take them through Liss Forest, there they would cross the main A3 road and then follow a line north, keeping to the western side of a smallish main road which should take them to Bucks Horn Oak, very near to their destination. This decided the group set off, knowing that time was of the essence.

The trek through the forest slowed them down, but at least it gave good cover. It took three quarters of an hour to get to the main A3 road, on checking, Alan worked out that they were just north of a village called Greatham, he signalled for the group to stop and sent Les to do a recy to make sure it was all clear. After a couple of minutes he was back and reported that apart from some slow moving traffic, mainly lorries, it was an ideal spot to cross.

Alan decided that it would be better to go in pairs and split the group accordingly; Les went first with Bob Barnet. They slid down the bank towards the road feet first, then weaving between small clumps of bushes they crossed the wide grass verge and after checking for traffic and making sure the road was clear, they ran across the road and dived into the bushes opposite. Once across Les signalled with his pen torch that they were OK and for the next two to go. As soon as Alan had received the signal from Les he tapped Bill on the shoulder saying, "right mate your turn, go!"

Bill Blowers and John Harding went next, again feet first sliding down the bank, across the verge and then across the road diving into the bushes to safety, again the signal from Les and it was time for Cocker and Harry Crook to go, with them safely across also it just left Alan and Jock. Just as they were about to go, Alan spotted movement about two hundred yards south and nearer to the village, he could see three people reflected in a small street lamp. He used his pen torch to signal to Les, who flashed back in acknowledgement, knowing that something was wrong. Alan and Jock lay still for about ten minutes until Alan was sure that whoever it was had moved away and he felt it was safe to make their crossing.

Alan went first sliding easily down the bank and once on the grass verge looked to make sure Jock was OK, he looked up and saw Jock dangling head first with his foot caught in some roots of the bushes they had been sheltering behind.

"What the hell are you doing Jock, why didn't you come out feet first?" Alan called quietly.

"I'm sorry Alan, thought I'd come down head first, hoped it would be easier and look at the mess I'm in," he said in his broad Scots accent.

Alan climbed up the bank and released Jock's foot and he fell head over heels down the bank, landing in a heap on the verge. "Come on you big lummox," Alan said, "Let's move it."

Once across, Alan re-grouped with the others and after checking that they were all in good shape, they set off north walking in single file in the fields at the edge of the road. What Alan hadn't bargained for, was that they would stumble across an Army Barracks some three miles further up the road in a village called Borden, one that Alan would in fact visit on several occasion in the future, although he didn't know that at that moment in the time. He decided that they would need to give this a wide berth and after a consultation with Les chose to cross the small main road they had been following, using the same ploy as previously, then to go some hundred yards into the fields before striking north once again. The time was just after three o'clock and by Alan's estimation they were just about on schedule. They then came to a small village called Lindford and skirted this on the west side, not wanting to go through the centre, then half a mile further north they re-crossed the road.

The rain had got worse and they were all cold and wet through, so Alan decided that they would stop and take on some refreshment. They all carried drinks and hard tack biscuits which were designed to give a burst of energy, which was something that Alan felt they all needed right then. By his reckoning they still had some six miles to go to the rendezvous point and luckily had so far seen none of the other groups, or rather they hadn't seen Alan's group, or at least he hoped they hadn't. A quick check of his watch showed that they had two hours to go and he signalled for the group to move off once again.

It was tough going through the fields, the grass was long and the bushes hampered their progress, but they were still on schedule he felt. At one point they in fact walked across a golf course, which made the going a bit easier for about a mile, although Jock did manage to fall into one of the sand bunkers, just to hamper things a little. The actual destination for the rendezvous was about a mile north of Bucks Horn Oak at a place called Holt Pound, where a small camp was supposedly set up for the arrival of all the groups, with breakfast laid on.

Alan stopped the group in a small clump of woods to get their final bearings, he sent Les off to see if he could see a church steeple, which was the landmark that Alan had marked just to be sure that they were on the right track. If Les could see one, then Alan knew that the rendezvous was only about half a mile from that point and they would use that line for their approach, rather than entering directly from the south, hoping that they could arrive without being seen. It meant re-crossing the small road once again, which they did as before and made for the church; St. James's just on the edge of a village called Rowledge. Once there and in the cover of the churchyard, he worked out their final approach to Holt Pound, which meant crossing two fields, a distance of about half a mile.

The time was just after five thirty, so Alan knew they were in good time. The group kept in single file and made their approach from the north of the camp, it was quiet, although there were lights on within the tarpaulin tenting that had been erected. As they got closer they could see shapes of people inside and hear muffled voices talking. They halted and made the final plans for entering the camp.

Just as Alan's group were about to break cover and get on to the road, Cocker grabbed his arm and pointed to a point about two hundred and fifty yards south, there was another group approaching, but not making any attempt to cover up the fact that they were there. Cocker smiled and said, "Shall we capture the buggers Skip, be a bit of a coup at the last minute don't you think?"

Alan grinned back and consulted the group; they were all up for it. They quickly changed their tactics circling south and west and getting themselves in a position behind a hedge where the other group would have to pass and they would be able to make their attack. The other group were strolling along the main road towards Holt Pound totally unaware of what was in store for them, thinking that they had made it back safely. Les had found a small gap in the hedge and as the opposition group drew level, all eight of them burst through the hedge, quickly surrounding the other group and shouting, "You're captured."

They just stood there gob smacked, absolutely gutted and Alan and his party marched them into the camp, much to the surprise of the NCOs that were there waiting, they had heard the noise from just a hundred yards or so away but never dreamt of the final outcome.

Once in the camp everyone had a good laugh, even the captured group saw the funny side of it and they were all ready to tuck into the breakfast that the cooks had prepared, eggs, bacon, sausage, fried potato's and baked beans, with a couple of slices of bread and marge, all washed down with a mug of the obligatory bromide flavoured tea. Alan's group were on a real high, thanks mainly to Cocker's observations, the final ten minutes of the exercise had been a real hoot.

Back at Barracks Alan and the rest of the Platoon had the task of getting their kit cleaned up before they were allowed to get into their beds until lunchtime, then it was a de-brief of the exercise and forward planning about the next manoeuvre. This would take place the following week, but this time would include the Lorries and would last for four days. It was to be in the New Forest which was south west of Southampton. It would include a night drive to the sight, then the camouflaging of the vehicles and setting up camp for the night. The following day there would be attacks from the air and land. After the exercise that Alan had just finished, he was really up for this new one, couldn't wait.

Chapter 15

Now that the basic training stuff was almost out of the way, everyone was getting more time for other activities including football and it wasn't long before the Physical Training Instructor, PTI for short, spotted Alan's potential and singled him out for a place in the Company Team. After several training sessions a team was picked to play in the annual Garrison championships during early December. In the competition they would play teams from the likes of the Royal Artillery, the Medical Corps, the Royal Engineers plus several others and Alan had been selected to play centre forward. During the week long tournament there were also other sports that were being contested and for some reason one of the other PTI's had also picked Alan for the boxing team.

Although Alan had never really boxed at a club, his Dad had taught him, together with the help of his brothers. It had all started when Alan was eight; he had taken a fairly good hiding from the school bully, a boy called Charley Wager. Alan had stuck up for a little skinny kid called Henry Brown, who was forever the butt of Charley, he was always bullying him, knowing that he wouldn't or couldn't fight back. Alan had tried to help Henry out on one occasion and although he had put up a pretty good fight, Charley was older and much bigger than Alan was and he got himself a good beating; he skulked home with a beauty of a black eye and a cut on his cheek.

When Alan's Dad saw the state he was in he went ape, and said that he was going to teach him to take care of himself properly. The first thing his Dad did was to go out and buy some boxing gloves, then over the next few weeks Alan boxed against his brothers, with his Dad giving advice, he apparently used to box when he was in the Army. Alan got a few more bruises along the way, but it wasn't too long before he had become pretty nifty. When his Dad was happy that he could handle himself, he told him that he had to go to school and give Charley Wager a good hiding, to repay him for the bruises he had received a few weeks earlier. The trouble was it almost got Alan expelled from the school.

It wasn't as though Alan could just go and pick a fight with Charley; he had to wait for the right opportunity. The opportunity came one lunch break a couple of weeks later; Charley Wager was once again giving his favourite punch bag Henry a real going over when Alan stepped in.

At first Charley just laughed, saying, "Plucky little Gray again is it, you want some more of what I gave you last time do you, well here goes?" and he swung a punch which Alan dodged.

Well the next five minutes was a real humdinger and it only stopped when the sports teacher pulled Alan off. Charley was a right mess and Alan was then hauled before the Head Master Mr White. After Alan gave him a full explanation of how Charley Wager was for ever bullying the other kids, he understood, but said that he would have to wait to see if there were any reprisals from the parents of Charley Wager, if so he could be in serious trouble. Luckily for Alan there were none and the matter was forgotten, but Charley Wager never bullied any one at school ever again.

During one PT session at Farnborough, sometime during the fourth week of training, everyone in the Platoon had had a couple of rounds in the boxing ring and it must have been then that the PTI had noticed Alan's natural ability. Over the few weeks that had followed he had again singled Alan out for further sessions during normal PT stints and he had also had to attend some evening training sessions. Alan didn't mind actually, because he enjoyed the workouts, but when the PTI said he would be fighting for the Company as well as playing football, he was a bit taken aback. Alan's natural weight meant that he should have been fighting as a middle weight, but was then told, that as they had another very good middle weight, they wanted Alan to step up to light heavy, even though he protested it made no difference, all Alan was told was, "that an order is an order". 'Some compensation that is,' thought Alan.

It was on the Monday evening of the last week in November that the Platoon set off for the New Forest for the four day manoeuvre. In all there were ten trucks involved, of which Alan was driving one and on board were five others from the Platoon, Les, Cocker and Bill were also driving their own vehicles. The Officers and NCOs travelled in Jeeps and other smaller vehicles. There had been a briefing during the afternoon telling everyone what was expected. As they left Farnborough it was once again raining and they drove in convoy, Alan's was the third lorry. The drive took just over three hours; the convoy trundled along between thirty five and forty miles per hour, they joined the main A31 road near Farnham which took them directly the New Forest, bypassing Winchester and Southampton en route.

It was eleven o'clock when the convoy turned off of the main road and headed into the forest the rain still hammering on the roof of Alan's lorry, he had Jock Ferny sitting alongside him, although Jock had dozed off until the bumping on the uneven surface woke him up. They were called to a halt by Sgt Harrison and each lorry was pointed into various directions forming a wide circle, they were told to pull into the trees where they were thickest and to start to camouflage the vehicles. The five guys in the back, who included Taffy Jones, Harry Crook and Bob Barnet, all got out, bringing with them the green netting. Luckily most of the trees were some form of fir tree, so being evergreen's it helped tremendously.

Between the five of them they pulled the netting over the top of the lorry, making sure that it was interwoven with the firs, just as they had been shown back at Farnborough. It took about forty five minutes, but when done Alan was really chuffed with the result. Sgt Harrison came by and checked on their progress and remarked on the good job that they had done. It was time then to bed down for the night, bed being inside a sleeping bag which was laid on a rubber groundsheet under the lorry.

Alan was awakened by a roar from overhead of aircraft flying very low. He wriggled out of his sleeping bag and crept to the edge of the lorry and peered upwards. It was just breaking light; a quick look at his watch told him it was just before seven o'clock. They had been warned of something like this, but didn't expect it so soon. By now all the others were awake and had joined Alan at the side of the lorry, he could see someone approaching, dodging between the trees

111

using them as cover, and as he drew closer Alan could see it was L/Cpl Jones.

"Better be ready for the full on attack anytime now," he said. "The main thing is to stay well covered, they will be dropping bags of flour and if you get hit, then you are considered done for. This raid will last about ten minutes and then its breakfast, so be alert." And with that he was off, crouching low as he left to move along to the next vehicle.

It must have been half an hour before Alan heard the drone of the planes in the distance, they had waited for full light to appear, but luckily it was still raining and very cloudy and misty overhead so their visibility was not that good. The first approach came quick and they just dropped bags and bags of flour which were bursting all over the area, it was like some sort of scatter tactic, just hoping to hit a target more by luck than judgement, this told Alan that they were not really seeing their target too well, so he felt that they must have done a pretty good job with the camouflage. The planes disappeared in the distance only to return almost immediately with another scattering to try to hit a target, but from where Alan was he couldn't see whether they had hit any of the other trucks, all he knew was they had not spotted theirs. Everyone waited until they were given the all clear by Jonesy and were then told to get fell in for morning parade.

Lt. Harding was well pleased with everyone's efforts and confirmed that there had been no hits. He went on to explain that the planes would be back later in the day, probably sometime after midday, when the weather was supposed to clear a little, in the meantime everyone was told to do more work on the camouflage to make sure that the trucks weren't going to be seen from the air. They were also told that later in the day the whole Platoon would be moving to another location, so it would be a case of more of the same all over again. The afternoon raid came at about one thirty, but again they made no direct hits, mainly Alan thought due to the heavy mist that had persisted. There were a few near misses and Sgt Harrison was quick to make the point to the two vehicles that had had the near misses. The order for moving out came at five o'clock, just as it was getting dark, so Alan and the rest had to start the balls aching job of stripping the camouflage off of the lorry, then loading it in the back and getting ready for the move.

After a twenty minute drive deeper into the forest the Platoon was ordered to stop and once again had to repeat the process of re-camouflaging, everyone was knackered at the end of it, but the cookhouse had been set up and by seven thirty they were eating. It wasn't too appetising, but it was hot and filling, which as far as Alan and the rest of the lads were concerned was the main thing. They then spent the rest of the evening generally chatting, until it was time for lights out and bed.

The first raid came during the night, the planes roared over the forest where they were encamped at about four thirty, they had lights blazing trying to pick out a target, probably looking for some sort of reflection off the windscreens or mirrors. During the first pass they didn't drop any flour bags, but they were back within a couple of minutes for their second run and bags were pouring from the sky. Alan's truck had a near miss, but the lorry next to his had a direct hit, the driver was John

Harding and later on he got a right rollicking, he hadn't covered his windscreen properly and they must have got a glint from it to home on to, probably why there had been a bag dropped near to his truck, Alan had thought. The rest of the night was quiet and the whole team kipped under the lorry until they were woken by Jonesy at six thirty. Once they had paraded and had breakfast, they then had to start packing up ready for the drive back to Farnborough.

Once back at the Barracks they had the lorry's to clean and also their kit, which was pretty much caked in mud from the exercise, but Alan felt it had been a real hoot. When they had finished the clean up and had there evening meal, Alan and Les, together with Cocker and Bill went to the NAAFI for a beer and a chat about the last few days, wondering just how near that was to the real thing and would they in fact ever actually do it for real one day. Something that none of them knew right then.

Chapter 16

The week of the Garrison competitions had arrived and Alan was spending quite a lot of time in training, both for the football and the boxing. Cocker went with him to the gym on several occasions and they sparred a few rounds together, Cocker was a lightweight, weighing ten stone and was a pretty nifty little boxer, he used to belong to the Bethnal Green Boxing Club, which had produced a few good boxers over the years. Luckily for him he was fighting at his correct weight, but as Alan was fighting above his own weight, he decided that he would spar with the heavyweight on the team to get a feel for what it was like with the bigger chaps, his name was Geordie Harper. Christ didn't he pack a wallop, Alan thought, because he caught Alan a few times, he was just glad he had his protective head gear on. Alan was scheduled to play football on Tuesday, Thursday and Saturday and was boxing on Wednesday, Friday and Saturday, and realised that he was going to be fairly knackered at the end of the week, so had put in plenty of training over the weekend and also got as much kip as he could.

The Tuesday football match was against the Royal Ordinance Corps, who in fact had won the tournament the previous year, and they were good. It was a very close fought affair, with the RASC taking the lead after fifteen minutes;

Alan had scored after being put through with a great pass from the right half. But at half time the Ordinance team were leading by two goals to one and looking very strong. After the break the PTI decided to push Alan out on the right wing knowing that he was a two footed player and their left back was a bit suspect; and it worked. After ten minutes Alan floated a cross into the six yard box which was headed in by the team centre half, who had made a great run from the middle of the field and they were now level two goals apiece. It wasn't until ten minutes from time that the opportunity came for Alan to score the winner. A neat bit of inter passing between Alan and the inside left gave him the chance of hammering in a real scorcher from about fifteen yards out and the team ran out winners by three goals to two. The PTI was dead chuffed.

On Wednesday evening Alan's boxing match started at half past eight and he had put in a few rounds of sparring with Geordie Harper once again and when it was his turn to enter the ring he just couldn't believe what was standing the other side, it was bloody man mountain. Alan thought he must have been a full heavyweight, but tough shit, he was stuck with him. The PTI in Alan's corner said, "Just get on yer bike as much as possible and keep out of his reach, try to tire him down and wait for an opening," it was alright for him to say, but trying to do it was a different bloody matter for Alan though.

When the bell went for the first round the big guy lumbered across the ring swinging punches from all angles and Alan back pedalled away from him holding his guard high around his head. Alan was prodding out his left fist and trying to jab him in he face, but the big guy just kept moving forward right through his punches and caught Alan with a couple of real heavy stinging blows to the head, and he only just about managed to stay upright on more than one occasion. Alan was just glad that the rounds were only two minutes long and, at the end of the first round he slumped on his stool in the corner, with the PTI splattering water all over him. "Just keep away from him," he said, "I can see he's really puffing, he's totally unfit and you see, you'll get your chance."

'It's all right for you to say that you're not the one getting the bloody thumping,' Alan thought, so he just nodded and got up as the bell went for the second round. Man Mountain stormed across the ring towards him with his arms flailing once again, Alan had backed up to the ropes at the edge of the ring and quickly side stepped out of his way, but there was no stopping Man Mountain. He was charging so fast across the ring he couldn't stop and as Alan side stepped and he just kept on going, he went straight through the ropes and landed in a heap on the floor. Alan hadn't even touched him. As he lay there on the floor the PTI who was in his corner ran around to assist him, but by the look of him he was in no fit state to continue, Alan couldn't help but do a grin. After some five minutes of attention, it was decided that he couldn't go on so the referee declared Alan the winner, it was a bloody miracle and the RASC lads in the audience were going barmy, he'd hardly landed a punch on him, but still won.

For his endeavours Alan was allowed an extra hour in bed the following morning, which he was pleased for. The football match was at two thirty and they were playing against the Royal Artillery; Alan had been told beforehand that they were a bunch of thugs and that proved to be the case. They were quick to notice Alan's skills on the ball, so every time he received the ball there were three of them barging and kicking hell out of him. Two other players in Alan's team had in fact been stretchered off in the first half an hour; luckily they were not too badly injured and after treatment were able to continue. After ten minutes of the first half the Artillery lads scored while one of Alan's team was off for treatment, even though he appeared to be yards offside. The match continued at a hell of a pace, it was real end to end stuff, and it was just before half time when Alan received a good pass from the centre half, he dribbled the ball some fifteen yards and slotted a pass through to Taffy, playing at inside left and he skipped around their full back and knocked the ball in at the near post, so they turned around one goal a piece.

The second half was as rough as the first, with tackles flying in every which way, and with only five minutes left to play there had been no more goals. With time running out the RASC team made one last gasp attack, there were several passes between Alan and Taffy on the right wing, Alan finally slipped the ball between two of their defenders to Taffy and just as he was about to shoot he was brought down with a scything tackle in the penalty box just as he was about to score in an open goal. The referee at last saw some sense and awarded a penalty to Alan's team. With the score still at one goal each no one offered to take the spot kick, so the Captain, a chap called Harry Brown walked towards Alan and handed him the ball saying, "I think you've got the best chance Alan, give it a go mate."

'Bloody hell, not the pressure that I liked, but here goes,' thought Alan. Luckily Alan had noticed that their keeper wasn't particularly good and guessed that he would dive either to his left or his right, which seemed to be the normal thing keepers did, so he decided that he would hit the ball dead centre. Alan ran up to take the kick and just pumped the ball straight into the middle of an empty goal, the keeper doing just what Alan had thought he would diving to his right. In an instant all the players in the team were crowding around him and slapping him on the back saying things like, 'well done mate,' and 'great goal,' as they made their way back to restart the game. The whistle went for full time almost immediately after the opponents had kicked off.

When Alan turned up for his boxing match on the Friday evening, the PTI told him that his opponent had withdrawn due to illness, he then went on and joked saying, "He probably heard about your giant killing act on Wednesday and chickened out." and they both laughed.

But Alan was really pleased and relieved, he thought, football that's my thing, but although he knew he could handle himself pretty well, boxing was not his favourite pass time. So that left him with a free evening to watch the others, he even got a look at the chap he would be fighting on the Saturday which was useful; he was in the Catering Corps. Alan could see that he was much bigger than he was, even bigger than his previous opponent, but he was flabby with a very large gut, obviously came as part of his job, working with food all the time Alan thought. Alan did feel for the guy though, because he got a real good hiding from his opponent who was in the Royal Engineers, Alan was just glad he hadn't had to face him, because he was bloody good.

After another lie in on Saturday morning Alan got taken to the football match which had a three o'clock kick off, this game would decide who had won the football tournament. Alan's teams' opponents were the Royal Signals who apparently had been runners up the previous year, so were probably out for a win to avenge the previous year he thought. The PTI had told the team that the Signals were very good and he was right. It was a battle royal, a real cup final and the Signals lads took the lead just before half time.

After a pep talk from the PTI, Alan switched positions to the left wing, again his thinking was that their right back was probably their weak link and with Alan's speed and skill on the ball, if he could hopefully get in behind him they then stood a good chance of opening them up. It worked like a dream, within fifteen minutes they had scored twice and were a goal in front, the goals came from crosses that Alan was able to get in from the wing by easily getting around their right back just as the PTI had said.

Their PTI football coach was furious and was shouting from the touchline for one of their defenders to take Alan out of the game and bloody hell didn't they just. Their centre half raced across towards Alan just as he was about to cross the ball from the wing, he clattered into Alan and laid him out for the count. The Ref blew the whistle and their centre half was sent off, but sadly that was the end of the game for Alan. Taffy took the free kick from where Alan had been fouled and it was nodded into their goal by the centre half running in unchallenged and the RASC team ran out three one winners, so Alan felt it had been worth it in the end, even though he was feeling pretty bruised and groggy.

The big problem for the boxing PTI though, was getting Alan in shape for the evening match, his leg was badly bruised, but he arranged for some massage and bandaged it up, but only after putting witch hazel on to bring out the bruising which stung like hell. The PTI said he would look again fifteen minutes before Alan was due to fight, to see if he was up for it. As it happened, after a bite of food and couple of mugs of tea Alan was feeling fairly OK, 'must have been the magic bromide,' he thought with a grin to himself. Alan's fight wasn't due to start until nine o'clock and by then he was feeling pretty good and after a quick spar with Geordie, who gave him a few tips on how to handle the bigger guy, Alan made his way to the ring.

When Alan was in the ring his opponent looked much bigger than he had on the Thursday evening, although he was podgy around the middle. It made Alan remember something that his Dad had told him all those years ago, 'work the body and the head will fall.' So Alan did just that. The big guy was fairly hesitant in his approach, but kept his guard very high, this meant that Alan had loads of room when they got to close quarters to work on his gut, at every opportunity he pummelled him as hard as he could, keeping himself too close for his opponent to get off any of his big shots to Alan's head.

At the end of the first round the boxing PTI said they were about all square and to just do more of the same. But Alan got careless in the second round and as he was pulling away from the big guy after giving him a good roughing up inside, he caught Alan with a real haymaker, he just didn't see it coming and bam, he was flat on his back. All Alan could hear was the slow count of the referee, four, five, six, and at the same time he heard the PTI shouting, "get up, bloody well get up, come on get up." Alan rolled over and managed to push himself upright just before the count got to ten. The referee gave Alan a good looking at and asked was he OK to continue, he just nodded.

The last half minute of the round was a blur, Alan just kept going backwards as the big guy was hunting him down looking for the kill, punching Alan continually, but he would not go down, he just kept his hands to the side of his head to take most of the force out of the punches. When Alan got back to the corner the PTI poured water over him to get his senses working once again and said, "go to work inside again, that burst of his took more out of him than it did out of you. Work the body and if you get a chance to put in a good uppercut while you're in close, really let one go.'

It was then that Alan remembered a move that his brother Eddie had taught him during one of their sessions. When you're in close working on the body, the idea was to use your left arm to lift the opponents guard making the room to get an uppercut away that would travel close to his chest and you could score a good hit right under the jaw. As the final round started and the big guy went across the ring towards Alan, Alan could see that he was still breathing heavy from the last round, so the PTI had been right. Alan took his time, just pushing out a few jabs in the big guy's direction waiting for the opportunity to get inside his long arms. It must have been during the second minute of the round when the opportunity came, there hadn't been too many exchanges, Alan felt that the big guy was holding back hoping that he had done enough by the knock down in the previous round to win the contest.

Alan worked his way inside the his guard and executed the move just as Eddie had taught him, with his left arm he pushed upwards against his arms creating the gap that he needed, and then with all of his strength he launched an uppercut that caught him flush under his jaw. He stopped dead in his tracks and dropped in a heap on the canvas floor of the ring, Alan just stood there not believing that he had done it, while the referee counted to ten and raised his arm. The lads again gave Alan a mighty roar as he left the ring. Even though he had won, the team actually lost the boxing tournament, but it had been a hoot Alan felt anyway and he was dead chuffed they had won the football, so as far as Alan was concerned it had been a great week.

Chapter 17

The weeks leading up to Christmas were hectic, the platoon went on more manoeuvres, both night and day, they did several five mile runs in full kit, further rifle shooting and assault course exercises, all things to build up stamina for whatever may be thrown at them in the months and years ahead. Alan thoroughly enjoyed it, even though it left him knackered at the end of each day, it was certainly a good sleeping pill that was for sure, and Alan slept like a log every night.

Everyone was granted a week's leave at Christmas, Alan had been writing to Jen regularly over the past weeks and she was thrilled to think that he would be home for a whole week. Christmas day was on a Monday and Alan left camp on the Saturday morning and had to be back on the following Saturday which was the day before New Years Eve. Jen had set it up so that he could stay with her Parents once again and Alan decided that he would make a point of buying them a small gift, as well as giving them some money towards his stay, in the same way he had previously. Even though they always made a big thing about it by saying he shouldn't bother and that they were just happy to have him and after all he was family, but there was never any real hesitation about taking the money when it was offered, not that Alan minded, he was just very grateful to them.

Alan travelled to London with Les, Cocker and Bill after saying goodbye to the rest of the lads before they left barracks on the Saturday morning; they caught the train to Waterloo which was where they parted company for their separate journeys. Alan caught the underground and after changing trains once, arrived at Liverpool Street for the journey to Brentwood. He had told Jenny which train he would be on and she was at the station to meet him, it was great and Alan felt really chuffed. As they kissed, passers by smiled and some whistled, Alan thought that they may probably have been thinking that he was back from the war or something like that, but he had to admit it felt really good, even better that he had Jen in his arms once again.

Eventually they made there way to their favourite café in centre of town and had a coffee before catching the bus home to her Parents; she said that she wanted Alan to herself for a little while before going home, which was nice he thought. They eventually caught a bus at four o'clock back to her home and Uncle Les and Aunt Jean where there to greet them. Aunt Jean also told Alan that she had arranged for his Mum to visit on the Sunday, so he was very happy at the prospect of seeing his Mum once again; he felt it had been ages since he'd last seen her, it had in fact been almost four months.

When Alan did see his Mum, she was very emotional and tearful, asking would he try to make it up with his Dad, but he told her it was down to him really, he had chucked Alan out; and he felt that he couldn't just go walking back in. He knew what his Dad was like and being that it was Christmas; Alan didn't want to spoil it for his Mum and the others. She understood and said that she would try to work on him and make him come round, but Alan didn't hold his breath, he knew that once his Dad had made a decision there was never normally any turning back.

Aunt Jean had arranged a fairly traditional Christmas, well as traditional as it can be with the shortage of so many items since the end of the war, even though rationing had ended in nineteen forty six, there were still so many food items in short supply. But for all that it was very pleasant, everyone exchanged presents on Christmas morning, Alan had bought Jen a silver plated necklace and for her Mum & Dad he had bought a small radio for their kitchen, he had noticed from when he had stayed previously that they hadn't got one, so thought it may prove useful. They were delighted, or they appeared to be he thought, as was Jen with her present. Jen had bought Alan a picture frame; she said that he could put a family picture in to keep while he was away to remind him of those back home. What she didn't tell her Parents was that the picture she wanted Alan to put in the frame was one of her, which she gave him later in the day, and it was one of her in a very sexy pose.

Jen's Parents had to return to work on the day after Boxing Day, which was a Wednesday, but Jen didn't have to go back until the Thursday and no sooner had her parents left the house, she was in Alan's bedroom and lying next to him. They kissed and cuddled just lying there for some time before she got up, and pulling Alan with her dragged him into her own bedroom, they were laughing as they undressed each other and got under the bedclothes exploring each others bodies as they did. In spite of the bromide effect, Jen seemed to be able to work wonders with Alan and it wasn't long before they were making love, but in their hast Alan had forgotten to put on a French letter, Jen said not to worry as she should be at her safe time of the month. The bromide was actually doing Alan a favour, because it meant it took much longer for him to climax, making their sessions more enjoyable.

This had probably been the best time ever Alan thought, well for him anyway, it went through his mind that it may have been because he wasn't using any protection, but it was wonderful and they just lay there in each others arms enjoying the moment. It was then that their cosy little world came crashing down around them. In the throes of their passion they had not heard the front door open, the next thing they heard was Jen's Dad outside her bedroom door on the landing calling both her and Alan. Then the door opened slowly and he was there in the doorway, trying to take in the scene that was before him.

"Just what is going on Jennifer? I can't believe what I am seeing!" he shouted. "So this is what the pair of you get up to when we are out of the house, we trusted you Alan and now you have betrayed that trust completely. Don't you realise that you are cousins and even though you may be old enough, this just isn't allowed in law and especially under my roof."

Alan just lay there with the sheets pulled around him; Jen was the first to respond. "Dad we are not cousins, you know that, we may be to everyone in the family but we are not related in any way at all so it's alright."

"It is not alright as far as I'm concerned young lady!" he shouted back at her, "this is a disgrace and you could bring disgrace on our family. How could you do this after the way we have treated you Alan, we took you in when your own

Father threw you out and you repay us like this. I want you to leave right now, I will give you ten minutes to pack your things and I want you gone and you are never, and I mean never, to contact Jennifer ever again." With that he shut the bedroom door and made his way down the stairs.

Turning to Jen Alan said, "Christ that's done it, I'm so sorry Jen, but I never heard him come back. Will you be alright?"

"I'll be fine," she said, "But what about you, where will you go?" she asked."

"I've got no choice really; I'll just have to return to camp. Not much of a prospect though, because there won't be many chaps there, just a few that are on duty, but I'll just have to make the most of it," said Alan shaking his head.

"We have got to meet up somewhere before you go Alan. I don't know what brought Dad home, but he will have to go back to work at some time and I will sneak out then. Wait for me in the café in town; if I'm not there by midday then you'll have to take it that I couldn't make it. But I'm sure I will." She lent across and kissed Alan gently on the lips.

Alan got off of the bed and retreated to his bedroom; he got dressed and packed his things in his small weekend bag. When he had finished, he went downstairs and into the back living room where he knew his Uncle Les would be sitting. "Uncle Les all I can say is I'm sorry, we can't help the way we feel about each and it only happened after Jen told me that we weren't really related, I don't know what else to say."

"Then say nothing more lad, just leave. I will make some excuse to your Aunt as to why you had to leave. I will not be telling her what I saw, because it would break her heart. I don't want you contacting Jennifer ever again, is that understood, this is where it ends," he finished and looked down at the newspaper he had been reading.

Alan remembered mumbling something, trying to apologise even more, but Uncle Les wasn't looking or listening so he stopped and left.

The time was just after ten thirty when Alan left Jens house and wandered to the bus stop, he had noticed that Uncle Les's car wasn't in the drive and wondered how he had got home and why at that time of the day, but what the heck, it was all too late now. He waited twenty minutes for a bus to come along, got off in the centre of town and walked almost aimlessly to the café where Jen said she would meet him. Once inside he ordered a large cup of tea and sat slowly drinking to while the time away, a couple of times the young waitress asked him if he was OK and did he want something else, but Alan just told her he was meeting someone and that they must be late, and she left him alone with his thoughts.

In fact it was fifteen minutes past twelve when Alan saw the top of Jen's head pass the window of the café and she entered the door and gave a huge sigh of relief when she saw him still sitting there. She hurried to the table where he was sitting and gave him a kiss. "Oh Alan I'm so sorry, I thought you would be gone by now, I'm so glad you waited. What a mess, I don't know how we're going to get out of this?" she said in a resigned voice.

"Nor me," Alan replied. "Did your Dad explain what had brought him home, because I noticed that his car wasn't in the drive when I left?"

"If it wasn't for his stupid car, we wouldn't have got caught like that'" she started. "The bloody silly thing broke down on his way to work and after he managed to get there with a lift by a friend, he had come back home to get some details that he needed to get it repaired and that's why he was there and how he caught us." And she started to cry.

"Perhaps it was meant to happen," Alan said. "After all we have been lucky up until now, I suppose it couldn't go on without something like this happening. But where does that leave us now Jen. He has told me that I have got to stay away from you, I mustn't write, or contact you in any way, so what next?"

"I don't quite know what to say," she said, with tears rolling down her cheeks. "I do love you Alan, I can't bear the thought of not seeing you or being with you, but how I just don't know. Bloody silly Parents, why won't they understand?"

Alan reached out and held her hands across the table, "I'm not sure either Jen, but if it's meant to be then I'm sure we will."

She gave a little smile, "I do hope so Alan, I really do. I've got to go now because my Mum will be home soon, but I will write, I will find a way. Perhaps I can get one of my friends to receive your letters and pass them on to me, I'll let you know."

They both stood and left the café; together they made the short walk to the bus stop where Jen would catch her bus home to Warley. Alan took her in his arms for one last time and they kissed, the bus came and she got on, again with tears streaming down her face, they both waved until the bus was out of site, then Alan slowly made his way to the Railway Station to get a train back to Farnborough.

The rest of Christmas and New Year were fairly miserable for Alan. He arrived back at the Barracks and signed in at the guard room, the Corporal on duty was surprised to see him, but made no comment, other than to say "you're going to be bloody lonely mate." And he was right.

Chapter 18

The final passing out parade for the platoon was on Wednesday January the seventeenth, it was to be the culmination of everything that they had worked for during the past four months. The day would start with a normal morning parade, except they would all be wearing their best battledress. This would be followed immediately by a barrack room inspection, which would be carried out by the Commanding Officer, with the whole entourage of Platoon officers and NCOs.

Everyone in the barrack room had worked hard over the previous two days making sure that everything was top class, their kit was laid out properly, their boots shone like glass, the barrack room floor shone, windows were cleaned, no stone had been left unturned for this day. Cpl Smith had been on top form, shouting his orders and getting everybody up for the day. Alan had to admit that even Jock looked good, and that was saying something, he normally resembled a bag of spuds tied up in the middle.

Luckily the sun was shining even though it was bloody cold; the temperature couldn't have been much above freezing point. The Officers were pleased with the barrack room and all that was left was the parade which would take place at midday. Firstly the platoon was to be inspected by the Commanding Officer; this would be followed by an exhibition of marching which would last for half an hour.

The platoon had rehearsed and then rehearsed again to make sure it would be alright on the day, and it was, even Sgt Harrison and Cpl Smith were proud of everyone, even Jock, saying that this had been one of the best intakes for many a year. When it was finished, they were then fallen out and it was time for lunch, Alan was famished as were all the lads. The next highlight would be the individual postings, which were due on the bulletin board immediately after lunch at two o'clock.

Alan, together with Les, Cocker and Bill went to lunch, chatting generally about the day and also looking forward to where they would each be posted too, none of them had any preconceived ideas, just take what comes seemed to be the general consensus. Although at the time Alan thought that it would be nice to have at least one of his muckers with him, wherever it was he was going to be sent.

The barrack room was a hive of activity and noise when they returned from the cookhouse, then at just before two o'clock Jonesy entered with a list which he fixed to the notice board with a couple of drawing pins. There was an immediate rush towards the board and a few whoops accompanied by a few groans; some pleased some not so pleased. Alan waited until it had died down a bit before he walked over and had a look. By the side of his name was 20 Company RASC and he quickly looked down to see that Les had been given the same posting, together with Bill Blowers, Bob Barnet and Harry Crook, but Cocker was going to York, as was Jock.

Each soldier in the Platoon was then given a folder that contained some information about their future posting, the dates that they were expected to report and the location. 20 Company was in fact situated at Regents Park Barracks in London and was predominantly a staff car company, chauffeuring Officers around. There was also a large Platoon of specially equipped lorry's, used for transporting soldiers around London, mainly Guardsmen from the Chelsea Barracks and Westminster Barracks to their places of duty, such as Buckingham Palace, Horse Guards Parade and many more. Alan was really chuffed and excited at the opportunity of seeing all these famous places, places that he had only heard and read about. Cocker was probably the least chuffed of the lot, because a posting to London would have been almost home from home for him, but going to York seemed to him to be a long, long way from home.

It was then a matter of everyone getting themselves packed ready for their respective journeys, first home on leave and then to their new postings. They wouldn't in fact be leaving until the following morning, so at least they had one last night when they could all celebrate together and the four of them decided to have a night out in Aldershot. And celebrate they did, all finishing up with rather thick heads the next morning.

Alan knew he was going to miss Cocker a lot, because next to Les he was his best buddy. He also remembered that he had the little problem of no where to stay in between leaving Farnborough and going to his new posting in London, all the other lads were talking about what they would be getting up too on their four day break, because they were all on leave until the following Sunday evening, but for Alan he had no where. He had a word with Sgt Harrison, without going into too much detail, and it was arranged that it would be OK for him to stay on in camp, he cleared it that he could move in to one of the barrack rooms used by the on site squaddies and he would leave from there to report to 20 Company on the Sunday afternoon.

Jenny had written Alan just one letter since the awful Christmas affair and he had written back care of one of her best friends, a girl called Lucy, but had not received a reply. As he had loads of time on his hands he wrote once again, telling her where he was to be posted too and a little about what went on their, although of course he didn't know just what function he would perform. It also gave him the opportunity of giving her the new address. The next few days dragged by, but Alan managed to fill them with some extra spit and polish on his kit in general, ready for the new adventure that lay ahead.

On the Sunday morning after Alan had eaten breakfast he dressed ready for his journey. He wore his best battledress and carried his overcoat, everything else had been packed into his kitbag and back pack, what a tussle it had been to get it all in, it was like getting a quart into a pint pot and being the first time he'd done it, it was trial and error, a case of pack and re-pack until he finally got it all in. This was in fact the first time that he had had to carry all his kit and he hadn't realised just how bloody heavy it was, the kitbag alone must have weighed at least forty pound and the only way to carry it was on his shoulder. Alan managed to get a lift to Farnborough station in one of the trucks and after being dropped off walked to the platform where his train would depart from, he had a free rail pass, so didn't have to pay.

Once on the train he hoisted the kitbag and back pack onto the luggage rack and sat in a vacant seat for the fifty minute journey. Alan had to use the underground trains to get across London, the nearest station was Great Portland Street and he had to cross the Euston Road and walk up a road called Albany Street towards Regents Park, what a bloody long walk that turned out to be, especially carrying his kitbag. By the time he got to the Barracks, after stopping several times for a break, he was well and truly knackered, didn't want to do that too many times that's for sure, was his main thought right then.

Alan dropped his kitbag on the floor of the Guardroom and reported in; the Corporal on duty got one of the other ranks to take him to his billet which was on the far side the parade ground opposite the main entrance where he had entered the camp. He was a nice sort of bloke Alan thought, probably about twenty or so, he had been at 20 Company for nine months, 'really cushy posting,' he said as they chatted. He showed Alan to the bed that had been allocated to him in his new billet and left to go back to his guard duty. The time was just after four o'clock as Alan unpacked his kit, placing things in his locker in the way he had been taught at Farnborough, although he wasn't sure what the format would be at his knew unit. He knew that Les and Bill should be arriving about six, and as they would still be serving the evening meal in the cookhouse, Alan decided to await their arrival before eating, even though he was starving, having had nothing since breakfast.

It was in fact just before five thirty when Les and Bill arrived, they had travelled down from the north together and Alan was pleased to find that they were all to be billeted in the same barrack room. The barrack room had twenty beds and a separate room at the end which was apparently where the NCO in charge of the barrack room slept, his name was Cpl Lawrie and he was from Scotland. The barrack room was much better than at Farnborough, less Spartan with a much more homely feel about it, there were even curtains at the windows and large heating radiators on the walls, but what did he know about homely feelings right then, he thought.

The washroom was situated at the end of the barrack room and was very similar to Farnborough with a line of washbasins, toilet cubicles and a long communal shower, which was shared with the next billet to the one Alan was in. He gave Les and Bill a hand with their unpacking and then they all made their way together to the cookhouse for something to eat. They were both full of their weekend at home, but Alan didn't say anything about his; they never knew that he had stayed at Farnborough and he wasn't going to say, well not then anyway.

Chapter 19

Reveille was at six thirty and everyone aroused themselves and made their way to the washroom, they then started dressing for the day ahead, Alan was gradually getting to know the chaps around him, introducing himself before trouping off to breakfast with Les and Bill, they all seemed a fairly decent bunch of chaps, only time would tell, he thought. The three of them fell in with the others at eight o'clock for morning parade and got their first introduction to the Platoon Officer Lt Graham and Also the Platoon sergeant, Sgt Broad, they had met Cpl Lawrie the previous evening, he had arrived back at camp just after Alan and the others had returned from the cookhouse.

After the parade was over, the three of them, together with Bob Barnet and Harry Crook, who were in fact sleeping in the adjoining barrack room, were marched to the Adjutants office, a Capt Hardy, who went through what their individual duties would be. Les was to be a staff car driver, while Alan and Bill were going to be driving the troop carrying trucks and Bob and Harry were to be on normal transport duties. They were then taken to their respective places of duty, which was where they would report each day after morning parade was over.

The staff car garage and the truck garage were adjacent to each other, but had separate operating offices, so while Les went one way Alan was taken along with Bill to the larger truck garage. The sergeant in charge of truck transport was Sgt Haig-Humphries, they found out later that he was referred to as Sgt HH, a real bull of a man, but fairly nice with it Alan felt. He explained the procedures that they would have to go through when taking charge of a vehicle and that they would initially be assigned to be with another driver. The idea behind this was firstly to help them learn the various routes and also as they were both fairly new to driving anyway, to get used to driving in London, because this was a bit different from driving in the country, which was what they had been used too up until that point in time.

The driver that Alan was assigned to was a chap called George Grant; he was from Gloucester and had been at 20 Company for just over six months, the only difference being, that he was a National Serviceman in for just two years, but turned out to be a real nice bloke. The truck that Alan was in with George was due out at twelve o'clock to pick up Coldstream Guards from Chelsea Barracks and take them to Horseguards Parade in Whitehall, not far from Trafalgar Square. Alan was quite exited about the whole thing, seeing the sights of London as they drove, passing Marble Arch and Hyde Park Corner on the way to Chelsea Barracks and then The Houses of Parliament and Trafalgar Square on the return journey.

George drove the truck into the barracks and parked and that's when Alan saw all the Guardsmen in their full dress uniforms, red jackets, black Busby's on their heads, the polished breastplates in fact the whole caboodle, he was gob smacked at just being so close to the action, so to speak. The Guards then clambered into the back of the truck, which had a row of seating all the way along each side and a row down the middle. Once they were all aboard, George drove off to drop them at the designated point, just off of Whitehall. This was Alan's first proper sighting of Big Ben and the Houses of Parliament; it was like a free sightseeing tour and getting paid at the same time.

The days that followed were just as exciting for Alan; they went to Buckingham Palace, The Tower of London, Windsor Castle and numerous places around the capital where the Guards were on sentry duty one way or another. And after two weeks Alan was doing it all by himself, driving through the Palace gates was the best buzz for him he thought. It didn't take Alan long to have a wonderful knowledge of London, he could get from A to B with his eyes shut after the first two months and was really enjoying himself.

It was the beginning of March that Sgt HH called Alan into his office and suggested that perhaps he should consider sitting the exams for becoming an NCO.

"I really think you've got what it takes Gray," he said during their conversation. "We had a good report from Farnborough on your leadership skills and this place could do with a few chaps like you. Give it some serious thought; we'll have another chat in a few days." And they did, chat that is, and a week later Alan started to study to become an NCO, while at the same time still ferrying the Guards all over London.

As it happened, Les had also been approached about becoming an NCO, at first he had said he wasn't interested, but once he knew that Alan was up for it he had said yes also. The course was a mixture of self study, which they did during the evenings and classroom lessons, given by Capt Hardy and Sgt Broad. Then there was the parade ground bit, where they actually had to learn to command a platoon of soldiers on parade, this was taken by Regimental Sergeant Major Bull. Bull by name and bull by nature was a truism if ever there was one Alan thought. He shouted louder than Cpl Smith had during training at Farnborough, and frightened the bloody life out of Alan the first time he had them on the parade square.

The course lasted one month in all and at the end of it they had to take a written exam, followed by the session on the parade ground with a small squad of fifteen other soldiers. The small squad was made up of mostly their daily mates, other squaddies that they worked with and of course RSM Bull was there to see that they did it right. Luckily the lads in the squad knew the drill and what it was all about and did both Alan and Les proud, responding to all their commands, in fact making them look better than they probably were. That was the thing that Alan was fast learning since joining the army, the camaraderie, your mates were real mates, standing by you and pulling out all the stops.

It was the ninth of April that Alan was promoted to L/Cpl, as was Les and they went out and celebrated in some style at the weekend.

Another bonus for Alan being stationed at Regents Park Barracks was that when he wasn't on duty on a Saturday, he was able to go and watch his favourite football team Tottenham, Hotspur. They had won the Division One championship the previous year and were on track to repeat the performance and Alan managed to make three visits to home matches during March. He saw them beat Chelsea two goals to one, West Bromwich Albion five goals to one and Everton three goals to one. Les went with Alan on two occasions when he wasn't working during the day on the Saturday. The major difference between their driving roles, was that Les found that he had lots of evening trips with the Officers and very often these would be at weekends as well.

Alan hadn't heard from Jen in all the time he had been at 20 Company, even though he had written on three occasions and felt that the time had come where he would have to move on. She had obviously had to heed what her Dad had said, so it was probably now well and truly over.

There was a very nice girl that worked in the NAAFI called Nancy and Alan had this feeling that she fancied him, so he decided to try to date her. She was over the moon. "I've been wondering when you were going to get around to asking me," she had said.

Even though Les had still got his girlfriend back in Leeds, it didn't stop him from chatting and dating the girls down in London and with Alan now going out with Nancy, they would often make up a foursome. Alan found it was good fun, the four of them exploring London, the good thing for the lads was that the girls knew it better than they did, well as far as the best places to go in the evenings and weekends was concerned. They used to go to Leicester Square, China Town, Soho, Covent Garden and sometimes went to Hammersmith

Palaise dancing. They also went to Streatham Ice Rink several times and had a whale of a time when they did.

Alan had never done ice skating before his first visit, but he had been pretty good on roller skates. Before joining the army he often used to go to the roller rink near Romford and was quite a star turn, he could do most of the tricks and jumps and even a bit of dancing. But the ice skates were a slightly different proposition and it took him quite a while to get the knack. He had the natural balance, but found balancing on the thin blade played havoc with his ankles, compared with being on four wheels which he was used too. Nancy was good though, she had had lessons as a schoolgirl and whizzed around the ice like a real pro.

Spurs were playing their last game of the season on the fifth of May and Les couldn't go with Alan because he was working, so Alan asked Nancy if she would like to go with him, she jumped at the idea, because she had never been to a football match before. They were playing against Liverpool and it turned out to be a great football match with Spurs winning three goals to one which meant that they also celebrated winning the Division One Championship once again, which made it a tremendous day out. Being in his uniform Alan was getting star treatment from the other supporters around him, who were obviously in a great mood and they went into a couple of the pubs near the ground after the match and had a whale of a time, without it costing Alan hardly anything.

Although Nancy was from Newcastle, she had lived and worked in London for just over three years, she was two years older than Alan, not that that made any difference. She had worked at the NAAFI for a year and lived in a rented flat just five hundred yards away from the Barracks, which made it easy for Alan after their dates, just a short walk home so to speak. Alan had been dating Nancy for just over five weeks, it was in fact the week after they had gone to the football match, and together with Les and the girl he was dating called Jane, they had been out dancing at the Hammersmith Palaise. They had said goodnight to the other two and Alan walked Nancy to her door and he was in for a nice surprise.

As they reached Nancy's flat they stopped and stood in the doorway as they usually did, Alan held her in his arms as they kissed, then after a short while she broke away and said, "Would you like to come in for a nightcap?" Alan didn't need a second invitation and she unlocked the door and they went inside.

The nightcap turned out to be a little more than just a nightcap. Once inside Nancy's flat they kissed some more then after a short while Nancy said, "if you'd like to go in the living room and pour a couple of drinks, I'm just gonna get into something a bit more casual. You'll find the drinks in the cabinet over there," she said pointing, before turning and walking away, "I'll have a gin and orange."

Alan wandered into the small living room and went to the cabinet. After opening the cabinet door he took out two glasses and rooted around for the gin, he poured a large measure into one glass; he then found a bottle of Schweppes orange which he also poured in. After a further rummage he found a bottle of whiskey and poured himself a small shot, then added some Schweppes ginger ale from a part used bottle.

As he took the drinks to a small coffee table, he heard the door behind him open and looked up. Nancy's idea of something more casual turned out to be a baby doll nightie which was completely transparent, leaving nothing to the imagination. Alan just gulped.

"I take it you like what you see?" she said with a smile.

"Like it, I just love it," replied Alan walking towards her as he did.

"I do think you are a teeny bit overdressed young man," she said teasingly, "come on let's do something about that shall we?"

With Nancy's willing help Alan undressed, taking off his jacket, shirt and trousers and socks, leaving just his underpants, complete with very large bulge.

"My, my," said Nancy, her eyes widening as she stared at Alan, "what have we got here, something pretty special by the looks of it."

They came together in a clinch, their bodies pressing against each other and Alan growing larger by the minute. "I think we'll forget the drinks for a while," said Nancy holding Alan's hand and walking him towards what turned out to be her bedroom.

Once inside and on the bed they started to explore each others bodies and it wasn't long before the nightie and the underpants were off. When Nancy saw Alan in all his glory she almost fainted, not believing what she was seeing and couldn't resist taking him in her hand and stroking him. It had been five months since Alan had last made love and he was raring to go, which probably also went to enhance his size, but he had a very willing Nancy, who was starting to breathe very heavily and was soon begging him to make love to her. After slipping on a French letter, Alan happily obliged.

And that was the start of a very nice relationship, albeit short lived as Alan was to find out later in the year.

Because Alan wasn't allowed to stay out of Barracks weekdays overnight, he wasn't able to stay the night with Nancy, but he was allowed weekend passes. So what he used to do was to arrange to have a weekend pass for a Friday and Saturday night, and this meant that he would be allowed to stay out. Alan would use these passes to stay the five hundred yards from Barracks at Nancy's, well he didn't really have anywhere else to go for a weekend, so it made sense, well to Alan anyway and Nancy didn't complain. She was very good in bed, being that much older than Alan she had had some previous experience of boyfriends and it was good, in fact very good and it did help to pass the weeks and months that was for sure.

Chapter 20

Les's promotion didn't really make too much difference to him; he continued to drive his staff car, but was now driving higher ranking officers than before, but for Alan it was a complete turnaround. He was put in charge of a small Platoon which was called the Kings Baggage Platoon. This Platoon was made up of four vehicles, all Ford Thames Trader trucks which were normal three ton lorries, the difference being that they were all highly polished and the ropes holding the tarpaulin cover over the back were brilliant white nylon ropes, with highly polished chrome fittings. The tyres were treated with a special black polish, while the wheels themselves were painted white. All in all a real bullshit job and it was part of Alan's job to make sure that they were maintained at this high level at all times.

The function of the Platoon was transporting the Kings Baggage between the various homes that he occupied, from Buckingham Palace to places like Windsor Castle, Sandringham in Norfolk and also Balmoral Castle in Scotland. Although when the family went to Scotland they travelled by train, as did the baggage, the platoon's role then was taking the baggage to Euston Railway Station for the onwards journey. Alan was soon to learn that whenever the Royal Family moved home for a break, they would take almost half the contents of the Palace with them, right down to kitchen utensils, cutlery, as well as crates and crates of clothing. Then of course there were the royal grandchildren's toys, which took up a couple of crates on their own, but Alan enjoyed his new role and felt it was a really great job.

Alan also got to see the inside of the various Palaces from a very different viewpoint, a bit like upstairs, downstairs. He could even boast of having had breakfast, lunch and dinner at Buckingham Palace and Windsor Castle, albeit in the servant's quarters, but still something to treasure and remember and to tell the grandchildren about in the future, if he ever have any of course.

Every time that the platoon did a run, all the drivers and Alan as the NCO in charge, would receive what was known as the Kings Crown, a five bob bit. Alan thought afterwards, 'if only I had kept one as a souvenir,' but to him and the other lads at the time it was just money. In all he carried out this role for five months, and during the second week of July he had been made up to a full corporal with two stripes, but only after completing the necessary training and passing the required exams. The brilliant thing for him was that each promotion gave him more wages each week, so he was up for it big time and he didn't mind the extra responsibility that came with the job.

The promotion meant that Alan became Guard Commander instead of just doing guard duty; this was something that occurred about once a month. He also got to take the morning Parade occasionally, which again was something that Alan enjoyed; all in all he was having a ball. The only sadness was that he still hadn't heard from Jennie, although as he was enjoying his new romance with Nancy, he felt that it took the edge off of it somewhat.

Alan had leave entitlement of one week every four months, but due to his circumstances had not taken advantage of this during his time at 20 Company, He had just been having the forty eight hour passes to stay with Nancy. But then out of the blue in July Les suggested that perhaps he would like to go home with him and spend a few days up in Leeds. Alan jumped at the idea and because he had never been there before he was really looking forward to it.

They left London together on the afternoon of Friday 20th and caught the train from Kings Cross Station to Leeds. Les in fact lived in a suburb called Horseforth which was just outside the City centre and they arrived at his home after a short bus ride, at seven in the evening. His Mum was nice, a very homely lady and his Dad was just what Alan had expected from what he had heard about Yorkshire men and also the way Les had described him. He worked at a local colliery, although he didn't actually go down the pit, he operated the lift that took the miners to and from the coal face. He was sitting at the kitchen table when Alan arrived with Les, with a pair of corduroy trousers on, tied at the knee with tape, with a pair of red braces over his shirt and his shirt sleeves rolled up to his elbows. Alan could see immediately where Les got his rugged looks from.

When they entered and Alan had been introduced, the very next thing Les's Dad said was, "I bet you lads could do with a pint after your journey, I'll go get me jacket. We'll be back in an hour mother," he called to Les's Mum and with that they walked straight back out of the door.

The Pub was only about a two hundred yard walk, it was called The Old Halfway House and when the two of them entered wearing uniforms, all heads turned towards them. Les's Dad, whose name was Harry, pushed his way to the bar and ordered each of them a pint of bitter and himself a pint of mild and bitter. Les spotted a couple of his old pals and they gathered round for a chat, but before long his Dad was back by their sides and full of questions as to what they were getting up to and the like.

Alan found it was great fun actually, because him and Les were able to stretch the truth a little and make things sound much more exciting than they really were and his pals just hung on every word that they said, them not having been called up for National Service for one reason or another. Although back in London Les's Yorkshire accent was obviously noticeable, amongst his mates and with his Dad he seemed to have drifted back into a much broader accent, almost trying to let them know that he was still one of them so to speak.

After an hour and another two pints of bitter, Les's dad said, "better be going lads, Mother will be fretting with the dinner, cooking something special so she said. Can always come back later, they don't close till eleven on a Friday." And with that they left the Pub, Les saying several farewells as they did.

Back at Les's home, his Mother had prepared a steak and kidney pudding with all the vegetable trimmings, Alan thought it looked just great, a real treat after some of the army food that they had endured during the past year, this was real home cooking. She had placed their plates in front of them after they sat down, and Alan was sitting politely waiting for Les's Mum to be seated before he started eating, when Les's Dad said, "don't just sit there lad, get stuck in," and he did just that, it was delicious.

Alan and Les were due back at barracks in London on the following Friday by six o'clock in the evening, but the week they had in Leeds was great. On the Saturday afternoon they went to watch Leeds United football team playing against Birmingham City in a pre-season friendly in Division two and they played out a one all draw. Unfortunately their star defender John Charles wasn't playing, because he had been called up for his National Service, but it was an alright sort of game, 'not a patch on Spurs though,' Alan had thought.

On the Saturday evening Les had arranged to meet up with his girlfriend Jean and she in turn had said that she would take along a friend to keep Alan company. They met at the Old Halfway House Pub at just after seven o'clock, the idea being that they would have a drink there and then get fish and chips at the local chippy. They were half way through their first pint when the girls arrived, and Alan's eyes almost popped out of his head, he had seen a photo of Jean, so he recognised her, but the friend, well Alan was speechless. She had the largest pair of knockers Alan had ever seen and as she walked in she was getting whistles from a bunch of lads at the bar, who all looked envious when she teamed up with Alan and Les. After he popped his eyes back in, Alan said 'hello,' her name was Molly and Alan offered to buy them both a drink.

"I'll have a gin and orange," said Molly in a broad Yorkshire accent and Jean, just as broad, said she'd have a snowball, which was a babycham with advocaat.

After the drinks arrived and Alan had paid for them, they found a table at the end of the bar away from the door, so they wouldn't have people walking by them all the time, being as the Pub was so busy. Jean sat holding Les's hand and looking at him with big moony eyes, not saying too much and Molly made sure her chair was very close to Alan and their legs were touching. Also, every time she took a drink from her glass she replaced it back on the table, leaning across Alan so her boobs brushed against his arm.

They just chatted generally, Jean wanted to know how Les was getting on and was he missing her and Molly was asking lots of questions of Alan, like, 'where he lived,' 'had he got a girlfriend,' 'why did he join the army,' and all manner of things. Alan was OK with that and just went along with the flow, after all he thought, 'this is a one off,' and he was enjoying the feeling of her boobs rubbing against him. What also crossed his mind right then was, 'would he actually get any closer to them.'

Les got another round of drinks in and after they had downed them, they decided to stroll to the chippy. Les had always gone on about how good the fish and chips were in Leeds compared with down south, so now was judgement time, Alan thought. They all ordered cod, chips and mushy peas, they didn't sell alcohol so they had to be satisfied with a Coca-Cola to wash it down, Alan had never had mushy peas before, so for him if was a first. But Alan had to admit to himself afterwards that Les had been right about the fish and chips, they were bloody great. They sat at a round table in the chippy and devoured them. Molly was still doing all she could to rub her boobs, or whatever part of her body she could against Alan and once again he decided he wasn't going to stop her.

Once they were finished they strolled the short distance back to the Pub and as they did Molly pushed her arm through Alan's, again pressing those ample boobs against his side as she did. Alan re-ordered some drinks when they got back to the Pub, but as they couldn't find a table to sit down, they just stood near to the bar, which was when Molly went full on. She was about six inches shorter than Alan and she had positioned herself directly in front of him, now pushing her boobs right into his chest. He then felt her hand start to fondle him in the crutch, he remembered Les telling him when they were doing their training just how forward the girls back home in Leeds were, compared with southerners and this was proving to be the case right then for Alan. To show he was interested, he slipped his arm around Molly's waist and this only went to encourage her to push herself even closer against him and she was also trying to get her hands inside his trousers, 'bloody hell,' he thought.

Another couple of drinks and an hour later, the time was almost half past ten, Molly pulled Alan's head down towards her mouth and said, in her broad Yorkshire accent, "Do you fancy a bunk up, you feel pretty tasty in their?" she said giving him a squeeze as she did.

Although Alan was a bit taken aback, he replied, "sounds a good idea to me, any ideas where?"

"Me Mam and Dad are out tonight, won't be back till gone midnight, so we can go back to my place if you like. Les'l probably be taking Jean home and I bet they'll be at it, so it'll save you missing out," she finished, again giving him another squeeze.

"I need to nip to the loo before we go, I'll be back in a sec," Alan said and made his way to the men's toilets, just hoping that there was a French letter machine on the wall in there. The problem was he hadn't come prepared for this and just hoped he would be in luck, because he hadn't really looked when he was in the loo earlier. 'Yippee,' he said to himself as he saw the machine on the wall at the far end of the loo's and put the necessary coins in to get a packet of three, which he slipped into his battledress top pocket. He had to laugh at the motto that had been scrawled across the face of the machine, it read, 'Buy me and stop one.'

Once back at the Bar, Les said that he was going to take Jean home and that he would see Alan outside the Pub at about midnight. Then out of earshot of the girls he said to Alan, "looks like your lucks in mate, go and enjoy yourself, there's enough of her to enjoy that's for sure." He ginned as he said the last words.

Outside the Pub, Molly grabbed Alan by the hand and started walking briskly, saying as she almost dragged him along, "better get a move on, I want to make the most of what you've got in those pants, and we aint got that long."

It only took five minutes to get to Molly's house; she lived in the middle of a terrace block of about eight houses. She let go of Alan's hand as she fished in her handbag for the keys and after opening the front door, she pushed him inside. They had barely got a foot over the doorstep when she was on to Alan like a tigress, thrusting herself towards him, her lips almost smashing against his. He could feel the real fullness of her boobs against his body as she did, which only helped to arouse him further.

After five minutes she broke away and grabbing Alan again by the hand said, "follow me," and with that she was off up the stairs, with Alan in pursuit.

Alan almost stumbled as they got near the top; she was in such a hurry. Molly pushed open a bedroom door and pulled him on to the bed, almost jumping on top of him. Again they kissed.

Molly grabbed Alan between the legs saying as she did, "come on big boy; let's see what you southerners are made of."

Alan needed no more encouragement, he turned Molly onto her back and started to remove her blouse and then her bra, he gazed at the sight below him and just said to himself, "bloody hell," at the same time stroking and kissing her enormous nipples, which were like organ stops, he thought.

At the same time, Molly was trying to pull Alan's trousers down and he had to stand to get them fully removed, pulling off his underpants at the same time. As he stood in front of her naked, Molly's eyes widened when she saw the size of him, because he had now grown to his full length. She gasped before saying, "bloody hell as like, what a beauty, god I hope I can get it all inside me. Come on lets give it a bloody go."

With that, she laid legs akimbo on the bed waiting for Alan to move towards her, but he had to put on a protective rubber first. She let out a small scream when he first started pushing inside her, but gradually after several half pushes, he was fully inside and then there was no stopping her. They worked their bodies against each other with ever increasing passion and after almost ten minutes Molly screamed out, "oh my god I'm cumming, faster, oh Christ faster,"

And Alan obliged until he was also ready for his climax and they exploded in unison together and collapsed on to the bed, with Alan lying on top and snuggling his face into Molly's boobs as he did.

After some ten minutes, Molly said, "that was bloody earth shattering; I take back everything I thought about southerners being a bit wimpish, if they're all like you that is?"

Alan smiled to himself saying as he did, "they're not all like me, but they're also not all wimps, I can speak from what I've seen since being in the army. Us southerners can hold out against the best from anywhere around the country."

"OK then," said Molly in her broad accent, "prove you're no bloody wimp and give me another fuck."

Alan didn't need a second invitation and within a further ten minutes he was fully aroused and they were going hammer and tong once again.

During the course of the week, Alan met up with Molly twice more and each time it was as mind blowing as the first time, just wham, bam, thank you mam. On the last occasion, she had even taken time off of work so she could see Alan and they could make love, or have sex was probably the best way to describe it, it was just pure full on lust and she said that she just couldn't get enough of him.

The rest of the week they were in Leeds Alan and Les mainly spent their time in the Pub's, ones that Les had used in the past. Like Alan, he had always been able to fool the Landlord with the age thing prior to reaching his eighteenth birthday, but now of course that wasn't a problem. It was also amazing how generous the Yorkies were towards servicemen, they both had so many free pints they lost count, 'saved us a bob or two though,' Alan thought at the time.

The week came to an end all too quickly, they had said goodbye to Les's Dad the previous evening after a good session at the Old Halfway House, because he was up and at work by six in the morning. When Les said goodbye to his Mum, she got very upset, telling him to take care and make sure that he wrote at least once each month, which he promised he would.

Alan thanked Les's Mum for having him, he had bought her a large box of chocolates which she was really overcome about, "No one ever bought me anything like this before young Alan, thank you, you're a good friend to Les, he's told me so many times in his letters. You take care also won't you?" And with that they left and got the bus to the railway station to start our journey back to barracks.

Chapter 21

Life at 20 Company continued much the same during the last week of July and in to August; Alan was still dating Nancy and enjoying the occasional weekend with her as and when the opportunity arose. Very different to his few days in Yorkshire with Molly, not the northern slam bam thank you mam approach, much more romantic, which Alan really preferred, although he felt that the Leeds experience had been amazing and certainly one he wouldn't have missed for the world.

But it was on the eight of August that both Alan and Les both got the shock of their lives. It was a Monday and they had been on a training course together learning about controlling a Platoon in an active service theatre, which is one where armed fighting is taking place. When they returned to the barrack room they looked at the bulletin board to see what was in store for them the following day, and posted on the board was information stating that they were both being posted to Korea at the end of the month?

They just stood there in shock almost, although they both knew that these things were always possibilities, to actually see your name printed on a bulletin saying, 'Posting to Korea,' Alan felt it was quite scary. They just looked at each other with their mouths open, not quite knowing what to say.

It was in fact Bill Blowers who broke the silence, he had seen them looking at the bulletin board from his bed and said, "lucky sods, I wish I were coming. I'm gonna be stuck here on my own now."

"No your not," Alan said, "you've made loads of mates here and you'll forget us as soon as we're gone."

"No I won't." he said in a doleful tone, "you two have been the best buddies anyone could ever want, all those scrapes you got me out of during training and since we've been here. I know I aint got what it takes to be an NCO or anything like that, but you two still treat me the same in spite of that."

"Come on don't get all maudlin on us Bill, you'll be fine and I promise we'll keep in touch, isn't that a deal Les?" Alan finished.

"Sure is with me, we've had some fun together and we will never forget that, or you Bill for that matter, just keep your head down, you'll be fine mate," answered Les.

It took several days for Alan to actually take in the enormity of what was to happen. Together with Les they had been called before the Adjutant the following morning, who explained to them the procedures over the next few weeks. On the nineteenth of the month, which was a Sunday, they would be transported to Borden Camp in Hampshire, which was the transit camp. Alan grinned inside, remembering it from the night manoeuvre all those months before; it was the camp that they had had to skirt around to reach their rendezvous point. There they would be kitted out with new equipment and also have a whole series of inoculations against things like yellow fever, typhoid, cholera, malaria, TB and many other tropical type diseases. That in itself was scary Alan felt, the thought that he might catch something like that, blimey.

Alan and Les were both given a week's leave before they had to report to Borden and Les was going home to Leeds. As for Alan, he was staying at Camp knowing that he couldn't go home, although he had arranged for a four day pass which allowed him to stay out of Camp and had planned to stay with Nancy. He enjoyed four fabulous days and nights with her, during the days they went out and about in London and then at nights they enjoyed some of the best sex that Alan had ever had, well he certainly thought so at the time. Nancy was really upset at Alan going away and on their last day together they in fact stayed at home and spent most of the time in bed, Alan was bloody knackered when it was time for him to report back to Camp, but he had to admit, it had been bloody wonderful.

He had been writing regularly to his Mum once a month, he would post the letter at the weekend and she would receive it during the week when his Dad was at work, this way the old man never knew that Alan had been keeping in touch. When Alan wrote about going to Korea, his Mum wrote back, again begging him to try to make it up with his Dad, but Alan had repeatedly told her that he wouldn't want to know and his Mums letter to him in August confirmed his thinking. She said that she had told him where Alan was going and the possible risks, but apparently he refused to discuss the matter. Alan did however go home on the Friday before he was due to go to Borden while his Dad was still at work and his Mum was very upset, but Alan told her he would be OK, not to worry and all that, but he knew she would.

161

The small one ton lorry was parked at the main Barrack gates waiting for Alan and Les at ten o'clock on the Sunday morning, they had said most of their goodbyes to the lads the night before, in fact they all got pretty pissed in the NAAFI and Alan had one hell of a hangover, not the best start to the day he felt. Bill Blowers was there to see them off from 20 Company and the big bugger was almost in tears as they left.

It only took an hour and a half to get to the Camp, and they were met by a Sergeant, Sgt Harris, who took them to a reception centre to join up with another thirty or so chaps, there were a couple of other NCOs but the bulk of them were mainly non rankers, drivers, storemen and the like. An Officer, a Second Lieutenant called Brady, arrived soon afterwards and introduced himself as their Officer in Charge, they were given a Platoon Number which was TDO3, god knows what it meant Alan thought, but felt sure it did mean something to someone. The next step was to be kitted out, all very similar to Alan's very first day as a soldier back at Farnborough the previous year.

The whole group of thirty or so trouped in line through the stores collecting their new kit and had to hand back some of their existing kit as it would not be needed in their new location, although they had been told that the main winter kit for Korea would be supplied when they got to Kure in Japan. They were all supplied with lightweight jackets and trousers, called 'Olive Greens,' these would be used during their journey on the troop ship, mainly due to the increase in temperatures once they had reached the Mediterranean Sea. 'Christ knows how all this was going to fit in to the kitbag,'

Alan thought, but when he reached the end of the line they were each given another kitbag, 'thank God for that, but how the hell they were expected to carry two,' Alan wasn't quite sure right then. The whole process took well over an hour and when completed they were taken to the barrack room, or rather split up in to two groups and taken to two separate barrack rooms.

Les stayed together with Alan and they entered the barrack room where they were to be billeted for the next week; there were already a number of other squaddies in the barrack room when they arrived. Alan heard a commotion as they entered and saw two of the squaddies squaring up to each other, Alan dumped his bags down and made his way to where the rumpus was going on to break them apart. He couldn't believe his eyes, one of the two guys was Cocker Hall. When he saw Alan he stopped what he was about to do, but unfortunately for him the other chappie didn't and he caught Cocker with a sharp right hander to the side of his head, bringing a smear of blood and a bloody great swelling under his left eye. It was all Alan could do, with Les's help, to restrain him, but thankfully they did. Alan made the other chap stand to attention and said that he would be on a charge; he gave Alan a mouthful of abuse but did as Alan had said. It was at that point that Sgt Harris entered the barrack room and Alan handed matters over to him to sort out.

As it turned out, Cocker and the other chap, Geordie Brown, were both sent before the Commanding Officer and had three nights of Jankers, he had apparently said to them to save their fighting skills for when they got to Korea, because they would need them there. Good advice Alan thought. But

Alan was chuffed to see Cocker again and as soon as his Jankers were over the three of them went to the NAAFI and celebrated with a few beers.

The week flew by; the worst bit for Alan was the jabs, he thought they were bloody awful. His arm, as did most of the other lads, swelled up like a balloon and ached like bloody hell, 'just as well we didn't have to do much work,' Alan thought, apart from learning to get their kit in the kitbags ready for travelling. They were sailing on a ship called the Empire Orwell, which was sailing from Southampton on Thursday the thirtieth of the month, they would be taken by lorry early in the morning and embark ready for departing at about five in the afternoon. Alan had never been on a ship before, neither had Les or Cocker, so they were all feeling a bit queasy about the whole thing. The ship would take just over four weeks to get to Japan and after a short stay there, they would then be shipped across to Korea.

Chapter 22

At ten minutes past five on a bright August afternoon in nineteen fifty one the Empire Orwell steamed out of Southampton harbour. Once their kit had been stowed in the hold, Alan and all the rest of the troops had formed lines all along the ships railings the whole length of the deck. Alan thought it was really quite something; the quayside was packed with hundreds of people all waving the troops off, it made them all feel like heroes going off to war, a really funny feeling, but in a way there was an element of truth. Alan stayed with the rest, lining the rails of the ship until the harbour was out of sight and then, together with Les and Cocker they made their way back down to their troop decks, which were five floors down from the main deck.

Alan had been put in charge of one half of the deck, which was C Deck, while Les as a L/Cpl had been made second in command of D Deck under a Sgt Jones who was in the Signals, D Deck neighboured on to C Deck, which was quite convenient for both of them. The bunks were three high in long lines down the length of the Deck and they folded away during the day. Being the NCO in charge, Alan had fortunately been assigned to the top bunk at the very end of the deck nearest to the staircase; each person was also allocated a locker to store their kit in. The lockers were also in long lines down the centre of the ship, in all there were four rows of bunks with the lockers between each row. They had had to be selective with the choice of clothing for the journey, because one kit bag with clothing and other items that would not be wanted on the voyage was placed in the hold and wouldn't be seen again until their arrival in Japan.

It was Alan's job to make sure that the deck was clean and tidy at all times and that everyone carried out proper daily hygiene, also he had to get them on morning parade for inspection by Lt. Brady. The rest of each day up until around three o'clock, would be spent doing a mixture of physical training, education and generally learning about what it would be like when they eventually arrived in Korea. After three o'clock the remainder of the day was free, where they could choose some form of entertainment such as, deck quoits, volleyball, table tennis, rifle shooting and there was also a small swimming pool, although this did get very over-crowded.

The Empire Orwell was a fairly old ship and had been used for troop carrying and also as a hospital ship towards the end of the Second World War; it was originally designed as a passenger liner to carry just over four hundred passengers. The ship had been converted to carry one thousand five hundred troops and had a crew of about one hundred and fifty. On board was the 1st Battalion Royal Norfolk Regiment, which made up the largest single group and this was mixed in with the RASC, the REME, which is the outfit that carry out the repairs to the army vehicles, then there were Royal Signals, Medical Corps, Royal Engineers, in fact a fair smattering of most of the support units.

The route for the journey was across the English Chanel, around the coast of northern France and then through the Bay of Biscay. From there it would follow the coast of Spain and Portugal to the Rock of Gibraltar, then through the Mediterranean Sea until the ship reached Port Said in Egypt, which would be the first port of call. Then the ship would continue through the Suez Canal and down the Red Sea, stopping at a place called Aden, before setting forth across the Indian Ocean towards Colombo in Ceylon.

After Colombo the ship was due to stop at Singapore where it would be dropping off several troops, then it would continue on to Hong Kong where further troops would disembark, before the last stage of the journey which took them to Kure in Japan. After a short stay in Kure, they were due to board a much smaller boat to take them the final stage to Inchon in Korea. To Alan this was the greatest adventure of his life; London had been exciting when he first went there, but this wow. Seeing all these places that he had only read and learned about during geography lessons at school, this to him was a dream come true. He felt at the time that the same went for most of the lads, well certainly for Les and Cocker that was for sure, from what they had said.

The first encounter of bad weather came when the ship was crossing the Bay of Biscay, Alan had heard that it could be rough, and rough it was. Luckily for him he seemed to handle it pretty OK, but several of the lads on the deck were sea sick, puking everywhere. This caused a right scene, with Alan and some of the deck-hands moping up after them as they lay on their bunks as white as sheets. Alan, together with his helpers had buckets and squeegees and were mopping it up as best they could and tipping it down the toilets, then pouring gallons of disinfectant everywhere, as much as anything to try to cover the smell of the sick. Alan learned later that Les had had the same problem on his troop deck.

The good thing though, was that when it was time for dinner the mess deck was half empty, which was great for Alan and those not affected, because there was plenty of grub to go around and they all ate heartily.

Once around the corner of Gibraltar the ship steamed along the Med and the temperature started to rise and by the time it passed Malta and headed towards Suez it was really hotting up, with temperatures of about seventy five to eighty degrees and they were told that it would get even hotter when they got through the canal. It was in fact the heat that caused the first problem relating to personal hygiene.

During a morning inspection by Lt Brady, he remarked on a bad smell that was coming from somewhere at the end of the troop deck. On closer inspection Alan pulled out a dirty sock from between the mattress on the bed of a Private Duffy, he was in the Pioneer Corps, he always appeared to be on the scruffy side and had already been warned about his turnout, but this was something different, the sock stank to high heaven.

Lt Brady took Alan to one side saying, "check that mans locker Cpl Gray and report back to me what you find. I want this sorted right away, do you understand?"

"Yes Sir," Alan replied, "I'll see to it immediately." Alan then dismissed the remainder of the troop deck, but only after telling them that he wanted them all back in one hour's time for a full locker inspection, after he had dealt with the Duffy situation.

When Duffy opened his locker it took Alan's breath away, how he hadn't noticed it before lord knows, it was disgusting. He made him pack everything in to his kit bag and carry it up to the top deck, where Alan had an area cordoned off; he then made Duffy lay out all his kit on the deck. After that was done he then took him to the maintenance area where they borrowed two large buckets a scrubbing brush and soap powder, one of the crew also rigged up a hose pipe and tap to supply water for Duffy's task and also to wash the deck down after he was finished. The task being, that he had to scrub every item of his kit and lay it out on the deck to dry, luckily the sun was up and Alan knew they where in for a long hot day, so it should be dry by the end of the day. Alan then got L/Cpl Hutchins, who was his second in command on C deck, to watch over Duffy while he reported back to Lt. Brady.

What a bloody fiasco, Alan thought, dirty little bastard, that wasn't going happen again that's for sure. Although Duffy wasn't little, he was in fact a great big slob of a man. He didn't really want to be on the ship, or in the Army for that matter, he was a National Serviceman doing his time against his wishes, and not the only one that was for sure. Although luckily, Alan felt that most of the other National Service lads on board were knuckling down and accepting their lot.

After leaving Hutchins to watch over Duffy Alan returned to the troop deck to carry out the locker inspection. Everyone was present and together with Lt. Brady, Alan checked every locker for any similar occurrence of the Duffy situation, luckily most of the lads were a pretty good bunch, even most of the NS boys where OK. Always the odd bad apple; and Alan realised that living in such close proximity, even more so than at Barracks, he was going to have to keep a much closer watch on everyone of them from now on. Lt. Brady was happy with the inspection and told Alan to escort Duffy to his Cabin after he had finished his task. He in fact was placed on fatigues for a week, helping out the deck hands scrubbing and sweeping the decks, cleaning windows and portholes and generally carrying out menial task all around the ship. Served him right, the dirty sod; was all Alan could think right then.

Chapter 23

They had been at sea for ten days when the ship docked at Port Said in Egypt. It had in fact docked overnight and Alan awoke to a babble of noise coming from the side of the ship, when he went to the top deck with Les and Cocker, they were amazed at the sight that they saw. The ship was almost surrounded by little boats, which they found out later were nicknamed 'bum boats,' and the locals on board these boats were trying to sell their wares, watches, cigarette lighters, cameras, in fact a whole array of things. Everyone had been told previously to expect this, but Alan just never realised the extent of the greeting they were receiving, if it could be called that. They had also been told not to try to trade over the side of the ship, because once you had passed them any money, they would probably move away and you would never receive the purchases that you had hoped to make.

After Alan and the others had eaten breakfast they were to be allowed ashore for four hours, with the ship setting off again at four in the afternoon, after taking on board fuel and rations. It was a tremendous experience. The three of them made their way down the gangplank and wandered into the town, it was a fifteen minute trip, the sun was very hot and the streets were filthy with dust and dirt, obviously blown in from the desert that surrounded the area. The shops, or bazaars as they were called, were stacked high with carpets, pots and pans, furniture and of course there were the ones that sold the tourist type things like the bum boats had been trying to sell to them earlier.

They were stopped at almost every shop they passed, with the Arab owners trying to coax them inside to buy their goods. It took ages just to walk a few yards, but after half an hour of this constant badgering they learnt how to avoid them, by just keeping on going past them and not showing any interest in the goods they had on offer. They had to admit though, that it was much easier said than done.

Alan had never owned a camera and wanted to try to record some of the places they would be visiting, so he succumbed to the offers being made at one of the gift type shops. He didn't know too much about cameras or photography for that matter, but finished up buying a Japanese Ricoh 35mm job and loads of spools of film to use in it. Les in the meantime bought a cigarette lighter and Cocker bought a watch. They appeared to be excellent value, but in all fairness they were names that none of them had ever heard of before and lord knows just how long they would last. But then Alan thought, at the prices they had paid it didn't really matter.

Once he had got used to the badgering, Alan found it really good fun, what with the bartering with the locals to get the best deal. This was something that Cocker was brilliant at, being a cockney and having worked as a barrow boy at the weekends with his Dad on the markets in East London, he managed to get some real good deals for everyone.

At three o'clock they were back on board and ready for the next stage of the journey. If the rest was going to be like this, Alan thought, 'then it's just fine by me,' he was having a ball, in spite of the Duffy thing. Again all the troops lined the ships railings as the Empire Orwell steamed out of Port Said harbour, the locals lining the quayside shouting and waving, Alan had that lovely feeling of being someone special again and looked forward to the next time they entered and left a port on their journey, but this time he was able to take some photo's to help remember the occasion, which he felt was great and he was really chuffed.

When Alan woke up the following morning he couldn't believe what he saw out of the porthole that was just to one side of his bunk, it looked like huge walls of sand. He quickly went to the washroom and washed and shaved, then after dressing he gave Les a shout and together with Cocker they made their way up to the top deck. The ship was steaming through the Suez Canal.

Alan had learned about the canal in geography at school and here he was steaming through it, he just felt it was so hard to take in. On the top deck they could see above the sides of the Canal and the desert stretched endlessly in front of them for miles, there were small groups of camels shading under palm trees in the distance and Alan went about taking more photo's with his new camera, he just hoped it worked, mainly because of the silly price he had paid for it. He was in awe of the whole scene and had to pinch himself just to make sure this was for real.

Alan made a point later to learn more about the Canal. It was about one hundred miles long and for large stretches could only take a single ship, there were three large lakes at intervals along its course, the largest being the most southerly called The Bitter Lake, this in itself was some twenty miles long. It was in these lakes that the ships would have to anchor and await clearance before starting along the next section, on one occasion they in fact had had to wait six hours before they could make their way through the next stage. The ship was still in the Canal when evening came and it wouldn't be until they awoke the next morning that they would have completed the journey and would then be steaming through the Red Sea.

The next port of call was Aden, which was at the southern end of the Red Sea; the Red Sea was in fact about one thousand miles long, so they were in for several days at sea before reaching the next destination, this was when Alan got involved in rifle shooting. Lt. Brady had asked for volunteers with a good shooting record to make up a team to compete against the other regiments on board and as Alan had been classed as a first class shot during training at Farnborough, he was really up for it.

They met for a practise session on the second day after they had left the Suez Canal behind; the targets were balloons which were set free at the rear of the ship. The rifles were the standard 303 issue, so Alan was well used to them. There were ten RASC lads initially; competing for four places on the team and after an hour of competitive shooting the team was picked. It was made up of Alan, Cocker, a L/Cpl Paul Harris who was from Norwich and had been stationed at York with Cocker and a Driver named John Brown from Guildford in Surrey, Les was a substitute if needed.

There were in all ten teams competing and the competition was to be staged over two days, the first later in the day being the heats, with the semi final and final the second day. The RASC team managed to get through to the final, but were well beaten by the team from the Norfolk Regiment, probably because they were infantrymen and shooting was one of their main skills. But all in all Alan and his team were well chuffed to get that far, he felt it had been a great event and one that he hoped that they may repeat before they finished their voyage.

The ship arrived at Aden the day after the shooting final and everyone was looking forward to going ashore once again. Alan found that Aden was a real shit hole; it smelt, it was dirty, the people were pushy, trying to get you to buy their goods, but the bargains that were to be had were amazing. Alan felt that if they had going home it would be a a different story, a real haven for gifts, but there was nothing really that he wanted to buy to take with him to Korea. He could have bought his camera for less than he had paid in Port Said, but as far as he was concerned he had a bargain, so it didn't matter too much. Alan was almost glad to get back on board the ship, but hoped that they would stop here en-route to blighty when they eventually got to go home, 'buy the place up,' he thought.

Once back on board, it wasn't long before the crew were untying the ropes at the dockside and the ship was steaming out to sea. The next leg of the journey was to take them across the Indian Ocean towards Ceylon, where it would be stopping at Colombo the capital, the journey time was supposed to be somewhere in the region of five days, but the sea had other ideas. They were just one day out from Aden when the first swells hit the ship and everyone was warned that they were heading into a monsoon. The Captain was taking the ship off of the normal route and steering due north to try to get some shelter from the storm, but without too much luck. For Alan and probably a lot of the others, it turned into one of the most frightening experiences of his life, although luckily for him he wasn't seasick.

The ship was tossed about in the ocean like a toy boat, it heaved up and down for three days and four nights before coming through the end of the storm. Alan had been told by one of the crew that the best way to get adjusted was to go as far forward on the top deck as one dared in those conditions and hold on to the rails and just go up and down with the ship. The idea being that when you got back down below the wallowing of the ship would seem less apparent, up to a point he was right Alan thought, but still bloody scary to say the least. There were times when Alan felt that the ship just couldn't take any more of the pounding from the weather and would certainly sink, but luckily it didn't.

Alan, together with Les and Cocker and a few other brave souls, spent almost forty eight hours clearing up sick from the troop decks with the help of a couple of members of the crew, it was the Bay of Biscay all over again, only multiplied by four, but at least Alan felt it kept him occupied. It was a further two days after the storm had subsided before the smell of sick had finally disappeared from the troop deck and Alan for one was pleased about that.

Due to the storm, the ship was a full day behind schedule when it finally arrived in Colombo and shore leave was cut to just three hours, Alan found that the weirdest sensation was walking on dry land again; he felt it was almost like being drunk. On shore in Colombo was a different experience yet again for Alan, they had now moved from Africans to Asians, not that it made a lot of difference, because Alan couldn't understand either language anyway.

The one thing that stood out in his mind though and what he found most amazing, was that no matter what country they had visited, the locals all spoke some form of English, certainly enough to make him and the others understand. The saddest thing for Alan though was the young kids begging at the roadside. They had been told before going ashore not to give them anything, otherwise they would go and tell their friends and you would be surrounded by dozens of them. Alan kept his money firmly inside his pockets, he wasn't taking any chances, and certainly wasn't ready for an instant adopted family.

Alan was really looking forward to their next stop which would be in another four days, it was Singapore, where several of the troops would be disembarking when the ship docked, and would be serving in Malaya. The good thing as far as Alan was concerned was that this meant the ship would be staying for almost two days. Alan had been told about a famous Hotel in Singapore called Raffles where they had an unusual Bar, so together with Les and Cocker they decided to find it and give it a try as part of their day out.

After disembarking from the ship they got a taxi ride into town and had a browse around the shops, they popped into a couple of bars for a beer or two, or three as the case was, before eventually ending up at Raffles. This place was just amazing   Alan thought, it was awfully, awfully posh, but it had this one bar upstairs where the floor was covered in sawdust and everyone appeared to eat monkey nuts and then throw the shells on the floor for good measure. This really seemed so out of character with the rest of the place it was almost surreal, it was just very different and yet another boast, Alan thought, to be able to say, 'I've been to Raffles.'

They didn't arrive back on board the ship until almost nine o'clock in the evening, they were all pretty pickled, but in a nice giggly way, all in all they had had a real ball, just another thing to remember for the rest of their lives.

Their second day in Singapore was somewhat different. They were woken up by the sound of thunder and Alan could see the bolts of lightening almost zinging down all around the ship. Alan had never seen rain or lightening like it, it was awry and a bit scary at the same time. They in fact had to wait almost until midday before it stopped and they dared to venture ashore, but only for a couple of hours or so, because the ship left at six in the evening. They just visited a few bars and had a few drinks before returning to the ship ready for the off.

Sleep came easy for Alan the night after Singapore, what with the drinks and the buzz of it all and when he awoke the next morning they were full steam ahead bound for Hong Kong, The journey time was only just over three days and again they would be dropping off several troops, so Alan was pleased that another all day stay was on the agenda.

As soon as they docked, Alan felt that Hong Kong was something different; it was in fact really an island stuck on the end of the mainland, the main town being Kowloon. The place was full shops and bars and Alan noticed something that hadn't been too prevalent at the previous stops, and that was girls offering their services. They had been warned at one of the talks on board ship about the diseases that could easily be picked up by going with them, so although it was very tempting, Alan had decided, along with the others just to enjoy themselves with a few beers and a laugh. The ship was sailing at nine o'clock and they had to be back on board by seven and just for a laugh they had each got a rickshaw to take them back to the quayside, more photograph opportunities Alan felt and he had to admit it was a real hoot.

Alan knew that they were now getting ever closer to Korea, just the one stop in Japan before they would make that final leg of the journey. Like most of the guys he was getting a little bit tense and apprehensive, especially with all the talks that they had had to prepare them for what was ahead. Not that Alan thought any talk could ever prepare you for the unknown, which it what they were about to enter.

From Hong Kong the sea journey was around five days; they would disembark with all their kit and be taken to the Army Base just outside the town of Kure. Here they would attend several instruction courses, mainly about climate and the right clothing to wear in the winter, which was apparently fast approaching. They also learned that the temperatures can go down to minus forty degrees and that to Alan sounded bloody cold, even though the special clothing that they were going to be supplied with was supposed to combat this, just have to wait and see, he thought.

Chapter 24

It was Monday the first of October when the Empire Orwell finally docked at Kure in Japan; the weather was fairly miserable, not unlike any October day back in the UK really Alan thought. After the ship was all tied up at the dockside, the kitbags started being unloaded from the hold and it was one hell of a problem for all the troops in sorting them out, the thing was that all the kitbags looked the same, the only difference was that each soldiers name and army number were stamped upon them in white and spotting them was difficult. The crew were busy sorting through them and calling out names and after some two hours most of the chaps had got their own kit and were ready to go.

Alan got the lads from his troop deck in line and they marched towards and then down the gangplank to the quayside. Lorry's were lined up along the dock and Alan, together with the rest of the troops half walked half marched towards them, each carrying two bloody great heavy kit bags. The driver of the lorry that was to transport Alan and the RASC boy's, was holding up a large placard with 78 Coy. marked in bold letters. The three of them, together with the rest of the group that were going to 78 Coy made there way towards the truck and got on board.

The time was three thirty in the afternoon when they eventually arrived at the Base and were taken to a barrack room where they would stay for three days before the short trip to Korea. The first day was spent getting kitted out for

Korea, changing a lot of the standard equipment for special stuff that was specifically designed for the weather that they were going to experience.

For the winter in Korea each soldier was supplied with special extra thick jackets and trousers that had an insulating type of material in the lining, these were called combat suits. Then there were special boots with extra thick soles almost like a car tyre and a there was a mesh liner to fit inside, the idea being to form an air pocket between your foot and the base of the boot. Then there was something called a Parka, which was a coat that was similar to an anorak, except that it was lined with lamb's wool, and had a large hood that was wired around the front to fold in and protect the face from the cold.

Then there were the smaller items, like several pairs of extra thick woollen socks, long john underwear and long sleeved vests and a whole array of other paraphernalia, including something called a poncho. A poncho was apparently a rain protector or rain coat for want of a better way to describe it. It was really no more that a circular rubber sheet with a hole in the centre so that it went over the head and just hung to somewhere between the waist and the knees, dependant mainly on how tall a person was, 'take a rain check on that one,' Alan thought, grinning at his own pun.

Alan also grinned to himself at the thought of wearing long johns, 'not too sure about that,' he thought at the time, little did he know just how glad he would be that he had them when he was in Korea and also how glad he would be of the poncho. Another thing that struck Alan as strange was that they were also keeping their Olive Greens for the summer, this was obviously due to the huge swings in temperature that were experienced in Korea.

They were also issued with a month's supply of Primaquine tablets, these had to be taken on a daily basis and further supplies would be given once they were in Korea. These tablets it was explained; were to help to keep them immune from malaria, should they get bitten by a mosquito bearing the disease. At the same time they were given a packet of salt tablets, again these had to be taken daily and again further supplies would be available from the stores when they arrived at their new location.

The following two days were spent giving everyone the background to the war that was currently happening and what each soldiers role would be once they were there. Alan would be in B Platoon as would Lt. Brady; he would be taking over as Platoon Commander and Alan would be his senior NCO. Alan felt that it had been good to get to know him on the trip out, so there was going to be no unexpected shocks when he got there and he was pleased that they had got on pretty well together during the past four weeks. The role of B Platoon it appeared was the transportation of food, ammunition and general supplies to the front line, 'bloody hell,' Alan thought, this sounds a bit scary.

Les was to be staff car driver to a Brigadier, who in fact was the Commanding Officer and Cocker was to be in C Platoon which was attached to field ambulance rescue, driving an ambulance, all very different, so at that point in time they didn't quite know just how much they would see of each other once in situ, only time would tell.

They didn't have too much leisure time while they were in Kure, just time enough to visit a few bars during their couple of evenings in town and to suss out the best spots to visit for the future, if an when they returned. As in Hong Kong, Alan noticed that during the evenings there were plenty of girls hanging around the street corners trying to pick up the soldiers, obviously prostitutes, but again he kept away, just admiring them at a distance and some of them were bloody gorgeous he had to admit.

On Thursday the fourth of the month Alan had got the group on parade ready for their final journey, Lt. Brady did a brief inspection and afterwards they climbed aboard the lorry to take them to the dock at ten o'clock. Once there they boarded the Wo Sang, which was a small steam ship that carried just over two hundred troops and a crew of about twenty. The first thing they each had to do once on board was to remove their boots and to put on flat soled shoes with a thong that went between the big toe and the second toe, they were called flip-flops and made of a soft plastic type material. Alan had seen these worn by the people in both Singapore and Hong Kong, and thought at the time how uncomfortable they looked, and he was now about to find out for himself. And just as he had thought, they were uncomfortable, bloody uncomfortable in fact.

The biggest problem for all of them was the jokers who kept treading on the back of the things as you went to take a step forward, jarring the thong between your toes, and from Alan's own experience, it hurt like hell. In the end he had to put a stop to it with a firm warning, otherwise someone was going to get injured, no fun especially bearing in mind what they were about to enter in to, didn't want damaged feet right then that's for sure.

The sleeping arrangements were a mixture of mattresses laid on the deck and hammocks strung between the pillars down the centre of the boat, it had been quite a laugh seeing some of the lads trying to get into the hammocks and god knows how they would sleep in the bloody things all night. Alan had opted for a mattress on the deck and was glad of his choice; at least he managed to get a pretty good sleep each night. The journey was to take two days and the boat being small and the sea being very choppy, they were in for another fun filled experience. Luckily no one was seasick, so no clearing up to do which was a blessing and something that Alan felt he could certainly do without.

It was planned that the boat would arrive at Inchon in Korea at daybreak on Sunday morning and Landing Craft, which were flat bottomed sea going troop carriers would be waiting to take them ashore, the weather was dry, although it was cold. They were all dressed in fatigues when the ship anchored about half a mile from the shore, the kit was sorted and they were all ready to leave, with Lt. Brady in charge. There was a rope ladder hanging down the side of the Wo Sang dangling into the

Landing Craft and after tossing his kit bags into the Craft, Alan was the first to board, he made his way down the ladder and dragged his kitbags with him to the front of the Landing Craft, next down was the Lt. and then the others followed one by one.

Each Landing Craft held about fifty troops and once the first one was loaded it pulled away from the side of the ship and made its way the half mile or so to the shore. Alan could see as they approached, several lorries parked on the quayside probably awaiting their arrival, there was also about a hundred or so troops lined up standing on the edge of the quay, who he learned later were leaving, their tour of duty done. The Landing Craft came to a halt and lowered the front ramp ready for them to disembark, the trouble was the driver, an American, hadn't got in close enough to the shore and they had to wade through about a foot of water, bloody great Alan thought; and welcome to Korea.

Alan just about managed to keep his kitbags dry and walked up the slope towards the waiting trucks, the squaddies standing along the quayside all started shouting 'good luck lads,' as the new boys passed and one very deep Scottish voice from somewhere within their ranks shouted, 'you'll bloody well need it.' Alan couldn't help but grin as he continued his walk to the waiting trucks.

They were greeted by a Sergeant; who Alan would find out later was Sgt. Brown, he was in charge of the transport section at 78 Coy; his job was the deployment of all vehicles in the operational area and Alan would in fact have a very close working relationship with him in the months ahead, although he didn't know that at the time. The trip to the Base only took just over twenty minutes, Inchon town was just a ramshackle of buildings, the whole place looked desolate. The roads were full of deep pot holes and as the truck drove along it lurched from side to side, thrown about by the shear size of them, just another something to get used to Alan thought.

There were in fact twelve altogether in the lorry, eight RASC, Alan and Les being the only NCOs, the remainder were a mix of Drivers, which included Cocker and the others were Storemen. There were also four REME squaddies, the REME it appeared had their workshop on the same Base as 78 Coy, Alan felt it made sense really when you thought about it, no different to back in the UK, at 20 Company they had a REME unit attached to them.

The lorry stopped in front of the Guardroom and they disembarked, one of the storemen a chap called George Green stayed on the truck and passed the kit bags down which were then laid on the ground. As the senior NCO Alan got the group in line and awaited Lt. Brady's instruction, he had gone inside the Guardroom and after speaking to a Corporal that was on duty, the small group marched to the main Admin building some fifty yards away.

A Major came from within the building and greeted Lt. Brady; he then introduced himself as Major Upson and welcomed everyone to 78 Coy. He said that they would be escorted to their respective barrack rooms to offload their kit and then after some breakfast there would be a meeting in the main assembly hall, which was adjacent to the Admin building. A L/Cpl called Hudson then came out of the building, and after a brief chat with the Major he guided the group to what was to be their new homes.

As Cocker was in a different Platoon's to Alan and Les, they would be sleeping in different barrack rooms, although the six barrack rooms were all situated next to each other. Les was also in B Platoon along with Alan; although their roles would be very different, as were two of the other drivers that had arrived with them. Beds had been put aside for each of the new arrivals, and it just happened that Alan's and Les's beds were in fact opposite each other, both being at the end closest to the door.

The barrack rooms were really something quite different, the outside was corrugated iron sheeting and the inside was lined with a thin sheet boarding, some sort of plywood type material. In the centre was a large black stove that burned a mixture of wood and coal and that was the full sum of the heating, Alan thought that at least it could be called central heating being in the middle of the room, ha, bloody ha, he thought. They had been told that they would have to report to the stores after they had eaten to collect their bedding, but from what Alan could see, this consisted of not much more than a sleeping bag and a couple of extra blankets.

Alan turned to Les and said, "what do you think mate?"

He just grinned, replying, "Bloody home from home aint it?" and they both cracked up with laugher.

After breakfast they all made their way to the Assembly Room and after seating themselves waited for Major Upson to arrive. He did so some fifteen minutes later, along with Lt. Brady and a Captain Jones, who was the Adjutant.

It was Major Upson who spoke first. "Again I would like to welcome you to 78 Coy and look forward to working with you in the year ahead. I'll be honest, it is not the best time to arrive, because within a month the place will be freezing, the temperatures will gradually fall to zero and by Christmas it will probably be twenty degrees or even more below that, with probably eight to ten inches of snow to help matters. The clothes that you have been kitted out with should suffice, but make sure that you put plenty of layers on, otherwise you'll freeze."

After ten minutes he excused himself and handed proceeding over to Capt Jones. Capt. Jones was Welsh as the name would suggest, but appeared to be an OK sort of chap. He was somewhere in his early forties and had seen service towards the end of World War two, so was no ones fool. He briefed everyone on their respective roles and who each person would be reporting too, in Alan's case it would be Sgt. Brown, although of course Lt Brady was Alan's Platoon Officer. Les also would report directly to Sgt Brown, as he and another NCO called Cpl Bligh, were the duty staff car drivers. They would receive their daily instructions directly from Sgt Brown at eight am each day, if not the previous evening.

It turned out that Alan was in fact the senior NCO in B Platoon, while both A and C Platoons had Sergeants in charge. There was another NCO by the name of L/Cpl Brian May, who would be Alan's second in command, he had been in Korea it turned out for three months, so Alan thought he should be a great help, well he hoped so anyway.

When they were finally dismissed, Alan, together with Les and Cocker made their way back to the barrack rooms to sort out their kit and collect their bedding from the stores. Lunch was from midday onwards and as they were all starving they in fact decided on an early one. The lads from the Catering Corps did them proud and after a warm welcome, served them up with huge portions of bangers and mash and some apple pie to follow, all washed down with a large mug of hot tea, Alan felt it was pretty good, even if the bangers had come out of a tin and the mash was made from powder and water.

"So how are you looking forward to your new chauffeuring job," Alan asked Les.

"Don't know really, it will certainly be different from 20 Company that's for sure. It just depends on who the old man is I guess and whether I get just one, or several of the old goats to drive around. I'll let you know in a week or so and if I don't like it I'll ask for a new posting, probably to Hong Kong, at least the girls there were pretty terrific," they all laughed.

Cocker was quite chipper about his new job. "Never driven an ambulance before, be great with the blue lights flashing and a nice cute little nurse on board," he said, again laughter all round, but they all knew it was nervous laughter, none of them really knowing what lay ahead over the next weeks, months or the whole year come to that.

Chapter 25

After eating, the three of them made their way back to their Barrack Rooms, Alan said that he needed the loo and would see them a bit later. He made his way to the hut that they had been told was the toilet block and what a shock he got, he just couldn't believe his eyes. Again, like all the other buildings, the wash room was a corrugated iron structure and inside along one wall was a long wooden bench with about fifteen enamel bowls laid out, some more chipped than others. There were about ten taps interspersed along the bench for filling the bowls.

On the opposite side of the room was a slab of concrete with slatted boarding laid down, with a drain at one end and overhead was a piece of steel tubing that went the length of the building, with about six metal shower heads hanging down, they looked a bit like the roses that you get on a watering can Alan thought. He turned on a tap and got some dirty brown coloured luke warm water dribbling out over one of the bowls. Bloody hell he thought, this really is home from home.

What Alan didn't realise, was that he was in for an even bigger shock when he walked across to the toilet building next door. He could smell it before he even opened the door. The toilet block was made up on one side of a long plank of wood with about ten holes cut out, where you were expected to sit, then below was a row of metal buckets, either full or half full of piss and

192

shit, then on the other side of the building was a long trough to pee in, which sloped down towards a large barrel at the end of the building to catch the pee.

Christ, Alan thought you need breathing apparatus just to go to the loo. He found out later that the buckets were emptied once every couple of days by a local operator, the general term used for his lorry was the 'Honey Cart.' Bloody Norah, Alan said to himself, a whole year of this, what the hell am I going to look and smell like at the end of it, or even during it as well, he thought. Then he decided it was time to go and tell the lads, let them know what a treat they're in for.

Les and Cocker, just like Alan had been, were absolutely gob smacked at what they saw. They didn't believe him when he first told them. "Come and have a bloody look for yourselves then," he had said. And they did.

Alan had always been very fussy over his cleanliness and hygiene, even with the limited facilities that he had been used to at home with his Parents, so just how he was going to manage he wasn't quite sure. But felt sure that he would devise a way somehow, only time would tell.

The time was two o'clock in the afternoon and although Alan had been told that they had the rest of the day off to familiarise themselves with their new surroundings, he decided that he would go to the transport office and make himself known properly to Sgt

Brown. He was a nice guy and Alan was pleased that they seemed tom hit it off and get on well from the start. Sgt Brown spent time going over the normal daily procedures, better coming from him Alan had thought, than from Lt Brady, who was as green as he was over these matters and Brady would expect Alan to get clued up anyway. The vehicles in Alan's Platoon were like most others on the base, clapped out three ton Bedford QL trucks, real bone shakers, as they had already experienced on their drive from the Port of Inchon to the barracks when they had arrived.

"There are sixteen trucks in your Platoon and twenty Drivers. The spare drivers are in case of fatigue or sickness, so that all the trucks can be operable on a daily basis. Normally a daily convoy of trucks goes to the front line which is just outside a place called Tokchon, about a five hour drive. They are loaded with just about everything but the kitchen sink on board, usually leaving at around seven in the morning. The remainder of the trucks then make local deliveries to Kimpo, which is the Air Base, and also to the main Battalion HQ, which as you know is now the Norfolk Regiment, they are stationed about two miles away. Then late in the afternoon the trucks are loaded ready for the Tokchon run the next day. So as you can see it's like a production line, with the Drivers rotating to give them a change of scenery and a break from the longer Tokchon run, which at times can be a real killer, I don't mean that literally." He finished with a wry smile.

194

"How many trucks make the supply runs," Alan asked.

"Normally between seven and eight, depending on what is required by the troops on the front line and of course one Water Bowser and probably once a week a petrol tanker. We get the orders in the office daily from Battalion HQ and then have to send trucks to the various pick up points, which all vary for things like food, ammo and of course there is the water. There is also a field bakery that makes the bread. So you can see it is fairly complex," he said.

"So what will my role be, apart from general NCO duties?" Alan again asked.

"It's normal that either you or L/Cpl May would accompany the convoy. I also sometimes go, as does Capt Mason, mainly to keep ourselves in touch with what the conditions are like and the problems likely to be encountered. We know it can be bloody rough going, but you get used to it, after time that is," he said, again with that wry half smile.

"What are the main problems that I should look out for?" Alan asked Sgt Brown.

"The biggest problems are fatigue and boredom. Driving these bloody awful trucks in the conditions they do is extremely tiring, so they need maximum rest. But when they aren't driving there's bugger all to do apart from general duties, it's a waste of time cleaning the trucks, in any case they are better camouflaged with all the crap that they pick up than if they tried to do the job themselves. The major factor that then comes into play is the Beer Hall, next to the NAAFI. The hours are limited, but sometimes the blighters go over the top and that's not good when they've got to drive the next day. This is something you will need to watch closely. Whatever you do you must check every one of them very carefully each morning before they leave; anyone that smells even a hint of drink doesn't go and is on a charge. So be warned and watch out very closely for it, because it happens quite often," he finished.

This had been a useful half an hour and Alan thanked him, but not before asking, "So when is my first run?"

"Tomorrow morning, your number two is doing it today and you normally do alternate days. Best that you get stuck in straight away and get some experience before the bad weather really hits us. The convoy will be leaving in the morning at seven a.m., see L/Cpl May when he gets back tonight, he'll give you the low down. Cpl James from C Platoon has been filling in today; he has been arranging the pickups today from stores, so everything will be ready for all systems go. Cpl May could do with a rest, the poor sod's been doing double shifts the last three days waiting for you to arrive. Oh, and by the way, good luck," he said and turned back to the other matters he needed to attend too.

After leaving the Transport Office Alan wandered over to the NAAFI, just to check out what he could buy

196

there, and the hours of opening and the like. He hadn't bargained for the surprise that he was going to get when he went in. The building was about forty feet by thirty, so not particularly large, but behind the counter stood two WVS ladies, the WVS being the Women's Voluntary Service. Now although this was quite normal to see back in the UK, Alan was amazed to see that there were two very attractive WVS girls there in Korea. He walked to the counter and introduced himself, although they had realised straight away that he was a new arrival.

The elder one reached her hand over the counter taking Alan's and saying, "Hi, I'm Susan and this is Charlotte, Charlie to her friends."

"And what do I have to do to be considered a friend, or as a new boy am I excused the preliminaries and accepted as a friend," Alan said with a grin, directing his gaze towards Charlotte.

She had stunning eyes, they were almost emerald green and they looked out from a perfectly shaped face, topped with a head of honey blonde hair, which was cut at shoulder length, 'very American,' Alan thought.

"Time will tell, but right now I will say yes," she replied with the most gorgeous smile. "What can we get you?"

"A cup of coffee would be good for starters," Alan said.

"And for seconds," Charlie said with a wicked little grin.

"Ah, now that depends what's on offer." he replied, looking straight into those magnificent green eyes.

"Again, time will tell," she said, again with that smile.

"Enough of this teasing," said Sue. "Here's your coffee Alan, she's got a ten minute break coming up, so you go and sit yourself down over there," she said pointing to a table in the corner, "and she can join you for a chat when she gets off, fill you in on all the local gossip, so to speak."

With that Alan paid for the coffee, thanked Sue and walked to the table she had suggested. To say he paid her wasn't exactly true, because in Korea the forces didn't have real money, they were issued with what were called BAFFs, these were special army vouchers with a face value the same as pounds, which were used as currency, no good to man or beast other than a soldier in Korea, still never mind, Alan thought, as long as they do the job while I'm here that was all that mattered.

The NAAFI was quite nicely decorated, well in comparison with the rest of the camp that Alan had seen thus far and they had a good stock of sweets, magazines, cigarettes, not that Alan smoked, as well as items like boot polish, metal polish and all the general toiletry items that one needed to supply for oneself. It was ten minutes later when Charlie joined him at the table with a cup of coffee in her hand.

"So what do you think of it so far?" she asked with a knowing smile, almost pre-empting what his answer was going to be.

"Pretty grim is all I can say at present from what I've seen and probably even grimmer when I get down to my duties," he replied. "But what brings two such lovely ladies to a hell hole like this?"

"Well thank you for the compliment," she said smiling, "it's a long story. But briefly, Sue and I have been working together for about four years, she was married, but her husband died on active service in Malaya two years ago. He was also in the RASC, so we have a soft spot for you guys. As for me, my Dad is a General in the Royal Artillery and stationed in Whitehall, Mummy lives in Wiltshire and I was bored after completing college, so Mummy suggested I join the WVS. I've spent a lot of time in the UK, that's where I first met Sue, then this opportunity came along and we took it, really as an adventure."

"And has it been; an adventure that is?" Alan asked.

"Yes it has; a real eye opener in fact. At least I have been able to pick the men from the boys and the gentlemen from the scum bags." She scowled as she said the last few words.

"I bet," he answered, "but how do you manage with these awful facilities?" Alan enquired.

"We are pretty OK really. We live in the building next door. It's made up of two bedrooms, a small living room come kitchen and a bathroom. The bathroom facilities are a lot better than you have, not the Ritz, but adequate enough for us, otherwise we wouldn't be here I can assure you."

"Don't you have trouble being the only two females on the base though?" he asked.

"We could do, but we make it quite clear and the guys mainly know their place, they treat us with respect in the main. There's always the odd arsehole, but we get by."

"And what category do you place me in after this brief introduction?" Alan asked, again with a smile as he did so.

"I don't normally make snap judgements," she said, "but in your case I will. I think you're pretty dishy, and a gentleman with it." Again she gave that lovely smile.

"I'm very flattered," Alan said, "I hope we see much more of each other over the coming weeks. But right now I've got to go and sort my detail out for tomorrow, my first run to the front line, I'm the NCO in charge of B Platoon, so I better get my skates on. See you soon and thanks for the coffee and chat." And with that Alan got up and left.

Charlie said as he departed, "you're very welcome, but don't make it too long." Again she smiled.

Alan was on cloud nine, she was bloody lovely and 'why me,' he thought as he strolled to his next port of call, which was the Platoon Office to see Lt Brady. He then immediately had a re-think, trying to be rational and logical about what had just happened, 'she's probably like this with all the guys, just teasing me, egging me along, maybe a little game she plays with all the new boys. But on the other hand, he thought again, if she's not, then wow.' But right then he knew it had to be one hundred percent full concentration and back to the task in hand.

The Platoon Office was situated alongside the Transport Office, when Alan entered Lt Brady was already there seated at a desk. After saluting, Alan told the Lt that he had been checking things over with Sgt Brown regarding the next day's operations, at which he seemed surprised but pleased. He pointed to where Alan would make his base while in camp, which was at a desk in the opposite corner of the office to the Lt., not very large, but adequate, Alan thought at the time.

"L/Cpl May is due back in Camp at around seven, I think you should wait around to see him to discuss arrangements for tomorrow." The Lt said to Alan

"I have already decided on doing that Sir, especially after my chat with Sgt Brown, he thinks its imperative." replied Alan, "I'm just off to the compound to check up with Cpl James, who's been standing in on the local runs, just to make sure that all the vehicles are ready for the off at first light."

Alan then wandered out to the compound where about eight trucks were parked and saw several squaddies around them including a Corporal. He walked over and introduced himself.

The Corporal turned to Alan saying, "I'm bloody glad you've arrived, I'm Bill James,' and they shook hands. "I've been standing in for you for the past three days, just been getting everything ready for the run tomorrow. Brian May should be back in a couple of hours, but I'm gonna get something to eat, if you'd like to join me we can go over a few things you may find useful?"

"Yeah that sounds great; I'm a bit hungry anyway." And together they made their way to the cookhouse; it was just after five o'clock.

They ate and chatted for about an hour before Bill said he was off back to his own Platoon, "Better go and get my own lot sorted for the morning now," he said as he left.

About five minutes later Alan left the cookhouse and wandered back to B Platoon office. He sat at his new desk and made a few notes while he was waiting for Brian May to arrive back. It was dark when Alan heard the rumble of trucks entering the base and he made his way outside as they drove into the compound and parked. The drivers climbed down all looking weary from their day and Alan walked towards them, as he did so he was joined by Lt Brady.

"Let's go and find L/Cpl May," the Lt said as he came to Alan's side.

Brian May was just climbing down from the lead truck as they arrived by the side of it. On seeing Lt Brady he stood to attention and saluted, saying, "L/Cpl May reporting back from Tokchon Sir."

"At ease Cpl," said the Lt. "I'm Lt Brady the new Platoon Officer and this is Cpl Gray, he will be taking over the Platoon from hereon in, but I hear you've done an excellent job, well done."

"Thank you Sir. It's been tough, but we've managed," he finished.

"Perhaps you would go over the duties for tomorrow with Cpl Gray, to get him up to speed so to speak and then report to me back at the Platoon office," Lt. Brady said.

"Yes Sir, I'll do that right away," he said and saluted as Lt. Brady made his way back to the Platoon office.

Brian May and Alan shook hands after the Lt. had gone, he seemed an OK sort of guy and certainly someone that Alan felt he would be happy to work with. Sgt Brown was right though, he did look knackered.

"So what's the SP for tomorrow?" Alan asked him.

"I'd better report in to Sgt Brown at the Transport Office first, come with me if you like and then you'll see what the procedure is," he replied.

"Sounds good to me," Alan said and they walked off together.

After entering the Transport Office he spoke with Sgt Brown, handing over a batch of documents, obviously the weigh bills or whatever they called them. He then collected a new wad of papers and took Alan to a vacant desk and explained too him what the procedure was, some of which Sgt Brown had already covered, but Alan didn't let on and he just let Brian give him the full info first hand, so to speak.

In all they were there for about fifteen minutes before Brian suggested that they go back to the Platoon Office and arrange with Lt Brady the detail of the morning Parade. 'Christ,' Alan thought, 'even got to do parade's out her. Oh well, some thing's never change.'

Lt Brady was in his office, probably wanting to know the procedure for the following day, being the new boy like Alan, he obviously wasn't too clued up on what took place. Brian May explained to Lt. Brady what the normal routine was, and that his predecessor Lt. Hall normally had an early morning parade at six forty five where the men and the vehicles would be inspected. As far as the men were concerned it was a case of checking that there were no signs of alcohol and as far as the trucks were concerned that the loads were firmly secured.

Brian May also said to Alan, "I'll introduce you to as many of the Drivers as possible during the evening and the rest after Parade in the morning before you leave."

That done, they saluted the Lt and took their leave; saying that we would be on Parade sharp the following morning.

As they walked back to the Barrack room, Brian explained the trip Alan was going to be doing the following day. "It's a straightforward run to 29th Brigade at Tokchon, which is north of the Imjim River. You'll need to be on your guard just north of the Gloster Valley, there was quite a bit of small arm's fire today" He said, "I'd suggest you ride with Paddy Gregson; he's the most experienced of the Drivers going on the run, he knows the route and he knows his stuff, so you'll be OK with him. Let's go and see if he's inside, or he may still be at dinner."

Paddy was in the Barrack Room and Brian introduced him to Alan, whose first impression was that he seemed a good guy, he certainly needed him to be that was for sure, what with all this new responsibility and the like, were Alan's main concerns. Brian then left to get his evening meal, having not eaten since just after midday, he said he was starving and Alan could imagine just how he felt.

Chapter 26

Alan couldn't say that he slept well that first night in Korea, what with it being a strange bed and new surroundings, plus the thought of the possibility of coming under small arms fire so soon after arriving, bloody hell he thought. But as most of the other lad's were in bed and tucked up early by Alan's normal standards, probably due to the knackering days they had, at least it was fairly quiet. Well that was until the early morning wake up call at six o'clock, which was carried out by one of the squaddies on guard duty.

The guard duty lads were taken from a mixture of the storemen, the catering corps and the REME but not the Drivers, this was mainly because of the exhausting days that they experienced and something that Alan was quite pleased about. Just another something that he felt he could well do without.

Once awake, Alan went to the washhouse where he washed and shaved, before making his way to breakfast in the cookhouse, the place was buzzing. Once this was done, he was now ready for his first proper day in Korea. He made his way to the Platoon Office, Lt. Brady was already there and as the Drivers arrived Alan got them lined up ready for inspection. He was just thankful that the Lt. kept the Parade short and sweet, just a cursory walk along the front rank, before saying,

"Very well Cpl Gray, dismiss them and get them to their vehicles."

Alan saluted, saying, "Yes Sir."

With that the platoon walked across to the vehicle compound where the Lorries were parked. The compound was surrounded, as was the whole camp, by twelve foot high wire fencing. There were in fact two fences and between them were rolls of barbed wire and the whole fence was topped with three rows of barbed wire. Obviously to dissuade any unwanted visitors. In each corner of the compound was a lookout tower erected about thirty feet off the ground, where a guard was on duty twenty four seven, 'must be bloody cold on a winters night,' Alan thought.

L/Cpl May called the guys together and made a formal introduction and Alan made a point of going to each of them and shaking their hand, not really the normal thing, but under the new circumstances that he found himself in, Alan wanted to be buddies as well as their NCO in charge. He just hoped that it would help generate a good working relationship, especially as he was the new kid on the block, so to speak. Paddy Gregson was there and talked Alan through the normal procedure adopted for daytime convoys. Each Driver carried a Sten Gun which was held in a rack to the side of the Drivers seat and ample ammunition was in an ammo box situated between the two front seats. The first thing to check was that they had been properly cleaned and oiled and a magazine of rounds was in place and the safety catches were on.

Together, they then checked in the rear of each truck to make sure that the loads were properly secured, as Paddy pointed out, the roads were so bloody bad that if things weren't tied down correctly, it could cause havoc on the journey. Once Alan was happy that things were in order, guided by Paddy, they were ready for the off.

It was a wet miserable morning and the wind had got up somewhat, there was also a heavy mist hanging in the air, hopefully the wind would blow it away to make visibility better Alan hoped, Paddy at least seemed to think it would. There were in fact seven trucks in the convoy for the day, plus one Water Bowser, three were carrying rations, three ammunition and the last a general array of spare parts for equipment that needed repairing in the field. Alan travelled in the first truck driven by Paddy and the convoy pulled out of the camp at five minutes past seven.

The journey to Seoul, which was only about twenty five miles due east of Inchon was quite straightforward, even though Alan could see the roads were bloody awful. The potholes made the trucks lurch and with the road not being very wide, made it difficult to pass oncoming vehicles, especially with the paddy fields. Paddy Fields are where they grow the rice and line both side of the road, they're between twelve to twenty four inches below the road surface and are just a sea of mud and water. Although it was only twenty five miles to

Inchon, the journey took almost an hour. When they entered Seoul, which was the Capital City, 'what a mess,' Alan thought, buildings had been bombed and partly destroyed by the enemy and a real feeling of poverty seemed to reek from every angle. The Chinese had occupied the town for some months and it had only been retaken by the commonwealth troops earlier in the year.

It was noticeable to Alan that there were little or no road signs anywhere and it was a case of every man for himself with local knowledge being key. Paddy guided the truck through the City, pointing out various reference points that Alan should bear in mind for future trips, which he made notes of. Once out of the City the trucks headed north towards what had come to be known as the Gloster Valley, due to the heroics of the Gloucester Regiment at the end of the previous year, where many of them were killed and wounded, but had still managed to force the enemy into retreat. Alan could remember learning about that when he was on the Troopship on his way out, during the time that they were being given a background of what to expect.

Once the City was out of sight, the roads got steadily worse and the hills became a little more mountainous and the weather just got bloody worse. It was another three hours to their destination, Paddy said, mainly because of the slow progress due to the terrain. They stopped several times en route to check that the Drivers were coping OK and that the loads were still secure, which thankfully they were. This was a fairly

210

experienced crew on Alan's first day, which he was especially pleased about.

From the air it must have looked like an anthill, what with the various troop vehicles that they passed coming from the opposite direction. Paddy explained that there would already be one or two convoys ahead of them and probably another two or three behind, possibly Yanks, Canadians or even the Aussies. The Canadians in fact shared the compound at 78 Coy in Inchon, but Paddy went on to explain that their quarters were one hundred percent better than those of the RASC, he had had several invites for a beer during the weekends, "Great bunch of guys too," he finished.

The worst bit was going through the Valley. When a convoy was travelling in the opposite direction the trucks were so close to the edge that it was a wonder there weren't accidents everyday, although Paddy did say that there had been several fatalities during his period in Korea. The Bedford QL trucks they had to drive were right hand drive, designed for the UK, but as traffic drove on the right hand side of the road, the driver did at least have the benefit of being able to hug the edge with more control than he would otherwise have had. The downside when passing another convoy was judging the width of the truck, which was that much more difficult and more scratches and gouges were on the left hand side of the trucks because of that reason. The REME must have had their hands full in maintaining them that was for sure, Alan had thought as they drove.

They drove through the Valley without incident, which Alan was pleased about, although he sat with his Sten gun at the ready just in case. Paddy also explained to Alan that as the convoy approached Tokchon there would be quite a barrage of firing by the Artillery from their 25lb guns, just to ward off any of the Chinese that may by lurking in the vicinity. The observation crew would spot the trucks through their field glasses as they approached and then the Artillery would let off their barrage. Alan was just pleased he had been warned; because it was bloody hairy to say the least and if he hadn't known it was friendly fire he thought he may have had a heart attack.

The convoy of trucks eventually arrived at the Base a mile or so outside Tokchon at just before one o'clock Alan was starving, as he was sure all the lads were. Paddy had told him that grub would be supplied when they arrived and they all tucked in to bangers and mash, although the mash was made from powder and the bangers were out of a tin as Alan had experience the previous day, but it wasn't bad he thought, especially being as hungry as he was right then. It also seemed from Alan's experience thus far, that bangers and mash was the staple diet.

A team of Ordinance Corps lads unloaded the ammunition and another team of Norfolk Regiment lads got to grips with the rations and general stores items. The whole time that they were at the Base, guns were constantly being fired from both sides and on one occasion they had had to dive for cover as shells exploded within a hundred yards or so of where they were grouped, the noise was deafening, 'bugger being here all the time,' Alan thought and was bloody glad when they were on the move once again away from the mayhem. In all it took the lads at the front line an hour to get the trucks unloaded and ready for the return run and at two o'clock after saying their goodbyes they left the Base for the journey back to Inchon.

The return journey took almost as long as the outward run had, even though the trucks weren't carrying any loads, this was again mainly due to the state of the roads and the fact that darkness had gradually descended making it an almost impossible task to drive, especially for the following drivers with no headlights. They used exactly the same format for night driving that Alan had learned during his driver training back in Farnborough, which is that only the front truck had headlights on, although the ones on these trucks had been shaded in such a way so as not to give off too much upward light that could be seem from above. The following vehicles had to follow the white light shining on the centre of the rear axle of the truck in front, not easy, especially when the white was a muddy white due to the muck and mud thrown up as the trucks drove, speed was therefore reduced considerably.

Again Alan felt that driving through the Valley was the worst, especially as they had to pass three convoys that were going north, but once they reached Seoul, at least there was a smidgeon of street lighting to help them through. It was ten minutes past seven when Alan and his first convoy arrived back at the camp at Inchon, each of them as knackered as one another from the length of the day and the bumping about that they all received from the QLs.

Once back at camp the lorries were parked in the compound and immediately a team of REME lads got to work, checking out the engines, cleaning the spark plugs, double checking on the condition of the wheels and tyres, checking the springs which take one hell of a hammering on each journey and generally making them ready for their next trip the following day.

Alan's first port of call was the Transport Office to check in and report their return with no mishaps, Sgt Brown was still there and he chatted with Alan about the journey and he briefed him on the convoys for the next day. L/Cpl May had been taken ill with some form of food poisoning and Alan would need to be in charge again the following day, again leaving at seven in the morning. Sgt Brown gave Alan the list of Drivers selected for the trip and then told him about one of them, a chap named Hopkins.

Hopkins apparently was an old soldier with some fifteen years service and despised any one with authority, especially if they were younger and had less service in than him. He also had a booze problem and had in the past been on several charges due to this and on one occasion had been banned from driving for a month due to the problem.

"Just keep an eye on him," Sgt Brown said. "I would suggest that you make him lead Driver and travel with him, it won't be pleasant, but at least you can keep him in your sights. I hope you remembered the key points that I know Paddy would have pointed out to you today, because Hopkins has had a habit of trying to make up his own route. He once took a new NCO way off track and got the whole bloody convoy lost. They needed a motor cycle outrider to rescue them, could have been nasty if they had got in enemy hands." Nice one Alan thought.

When Alan had completed everything at the Transport Office, together with the Platoon members that had been with him on the run earlier, he made his way to the cookhouse for their evening meal. The Catering Corps lads were terrific, even though their resources were pretty limited, they always seemed to rustle up something that was edible and everyone tucked in. As soon as he was finished eating Alan went to the loo, holding his breath all the time as he did so, well as long as was possible anyway and then got himself tucked up in his sleeping bag for the night, after arranging a call for six in the morning. Christ, Alan thought, 'I really do need some kip,' and he was out like a light.

Chapter 27

Alan woke to another wet morning and it was definitely getting colder, after a quick wash and shave and visit to the loo, again with maximum breath holding, he went along to the cookhouse for some breakfast, scrambled egg made from powder, some fried potato, which was again powdered mash rolled into balls and fried and a rasher of bacon that came out of a tin, together with a couple of slices of bread, but at least it filled a hole and he was ready for the day ahead, although a little tense thinking of the Hopkins situation.

Everyone was on Parade at five minutes to seven and after an inspection by Lt. Brady; they all climbed aboard the Trucks ready for the journey to Tokchon. Hopkins wasn't too enamoured at being in the lead truck at the outset, especially with Alan along side him, but after Alan had buttered him up a little by saying things like, 'one of our most experienced Drivers,' etc, etc, he seemed OK about it. Alan was just glad that Sgt Brown had given him that bit of background info about Hopkins that he had, because at least he was on his guard.

On the previous day when Paddy had been the lead Truck, Alan had made copious notes regarding the route as he had pointed them out to him throughout the journey and just hoped that he would remember them now. As Bill Hopkins drove, Alan managed to get him chatting about his past service, the places he had been to and the action he had faced and on the face of it he appeared to be an OK sort of chap, but on no account was Alan going to let him fool him into a false sense of security and allow him to get the upper hand in any way.

There were a couple of times during the outward journey that Hopkins had wanted to go his own route, but each time Alan had made him keep to the way that Paddy had taken him the previous day. On one of the stops Alan caught him drinking from a bottle of beer and confiscated it from him, much to his annoyance, but Alan had decided there was only going to be one boss. Hopkins never spoke for the remainder of the journey, he just occasionally looked across at Alan with a sneer on his face, as much as to say 'I'll get you.' But Alan wasn't too worried as long as he drove the vehicle where he wanted him too.

Fortunately they had got through the Gloster Valley without incident and it was around one o'clock when the convoy arrived at 29 Brigade and again the same procedure took place for the unloading, amidst the banging off of the guns. Then after grabbing a bite to eat and a visit to the loo, they started their return journey back to Inchon.

After about an hour or so from Tokchon, Hopkins was in a foul mood and he started turning the steering wheel violently, first left and then right bumping the truck on and off the road surface, such as it was, causing

Alan to be thrown about in the cab, on one occasion banging his head against the bracket that holds the Sten Gun in place. By this time Alan had had enough.

"Stop the truck Driver Hopkins," Alan shouted across to him, but he ignored Alan and kept driving.

"Driver Hopkins, stop this truck. That's an order!" Alan shouted once again and this time he did, putting the brakes on fiercely almost making Alan bang his head into the windscreen, luckily Alan had his hands firmly on the dashboard and this just about saved him.

Alan jumped down from the truck and signalled to the other trucks to pull in behind them. Then he walked around to the driver's side saying, "get out Hopkins and get into the passenger seat, now!"

Although Hopkins protested at first, saying that he was in charge of the truck and it was his responsibility, Alan made it quite clear that no one would be moving anywhere until he did as Alan had said. The remainder of the lads looked on with some trepidation, they knew his background much better than Alan did, but Alan had decided that he wasn't going be fucked about by a tosser like Hopkins, especially not in front of the other members of his Platoon, even if he had only been there a couple of days.

Alan drove the QL back to Inchon with not a sound coming from Hopkins, he had gone to sleep, or he was doing a very good impersonation of doing so. Driving

218

was much more strenuous than riding shotgun as Alan had the previous day, it's only when you do it, he thought, that you realise the strain it puts on every muscle in the body, just trying to keep the bloody truck on the road, what with all the ruts and bumps. But the convoy still made pretty good time arriving at Camp at seven fifteen. It was now that Alan had a big decision to make, does he charge Hopkins or let it go this time with just a warning. Alan was thinking this over as he drove into the compound and after parking dismounted from the cab, as Alan shut the door with a bang; Hopkins awoke and slowly climbed down.

Hopkins looked at Alan with a sneer saying, "you jumped up little Pratt, only been here five bloody minutes and already throwing your weight about. Well I'll make your life fucking hell from now on," and that was all it took for Alan to make his decision.

Alan looked him square on and said, "Driver Hopkins you are formally on a charge. Stand to attention," he looked at Alan in dismay but did as he had said and Alan then shouted at him, "quick march." Which he did as Alan marched him to the Guard House

"You'll regret this," Hopkins said as they marched.

"Just keep quiet or you'll make it worse for yourself," Alan said still marching by his side.

When they got to the Guard Room and Alan had brought Hopkins to a halt, he asked the Guard

Commander, Sgt Hawkins, to put him in the cell while he discussed the matter with Lt Brady, which he did. Once he was locked up, the Sergeant said, "So what's he been up to now?"

Alan told Sgt Hawkins what had happened on the journey to and from Tokchon, the beer and the driving and he said, "This is not the first time and probably won't be the last, nasty piece of work that one. I'll wait for you to report back on what we do with him."

Alan's next job was checking in at the Transport Office and luckily Sgt Brown was still at his desk. "How did it go, did Hopkins behave?" he asked.

Alan told him what had happened and he agreed with the way that he had handled matters and that he should go straight to Lt Brady to decide the next step. He in fact phoned the Officers Mess to arrange for Alan to see Lt Brady at the Mess and he walked straight over to get the matter resolved.

After Alan had explained to the Lieutenant everything that had taken place, he made the decision that Hopkins should stay in the Guard House overnight and appear in front of the Commanding Officer the following day, the only problem being that Alan was supposed to be taking the convoy to Tokchon once again.

Lt Brady said, "Leave it with me Cpl Gray; I will try to get the hearing arranged for eight o'clock tomorrow evening when you have returned. I will get back to you before the end of the day. Where will I find you?" he finished.

"I will be in the cookhouse for about half an hour and then back in my Barrack Room Sir," Alan replied. After saluting, he left the Officers Mess and made his way to the cookhouse for some food, he felt bloody hungry and he needed food; it had been a long day and somewhat stressful at the same time.

Lt Brady caught up with Alan before he left the cookhouse and said that the hearing had been arranged with the Adjutant at eight fifteen the following evening. Alan was to put a full report together and let him have it in the morning before leaving with the convoy to the front line. Alan then had to go back to the Guard Room to let the Duty Sergeant know the score with Hopkins and collected from him the formal report that he then had to complete.

It took Alan about an hour to complete the report, it was the first one that he had done and wanted to make sure that he got it right; it was a painstaking task to say the least and one that Alan hoped he wouldn't have to repeat too often. By the time he had completed the form and had a crap and a wash the time was almost eleven o'clock before he finally bedded down for the night.

After breakfast the following morning Alan got the lads on Parade ready for inspection by Lt Brady and after handing the report to the Lt; they boarded their respective trucks and pulled out of the camp for another round trip to Tokchon. Alan was pleased to say that everything went according to plan, no mishaps or delays and they were back at Inchon just before seven o'clock. After parking the trucks in the compound and reporting at the Transport Office to check in and collect the next day's schedule, Alan went to the cookhouse for a quick bite to eat before getting ready for the Charge Hearing by the Adjutant.

As it was a fairly formal affair, Alan changed out of his fatigues and into his normal day wear uniform, complete with tie, also putting on clean boots and gaiters. He called in at the Guard House and the Duty Sergeant, Sgt Smith, informed him hat he was ready to march Hopkins to the Adjutants office, which he did at double quick time. Once there the Adjutant, Capt Jones, called them into his office where he read out the formal charges against Hopkins.

'Driving without due care and attention likely to cause damage to Army equipment,' 'drinking alcohol whilst on duty,' and finally 'insubordination to an NCO.'

"What have you to say Hopkins," the Adjutant asked.

"Not guilty on any of the charges, Sir," he said.

The Adjutant looked at the report and read from it, "It states that on the afternoon of the eight of October you continually swerved your lorry for no obvious reason from side to side, which could have made the vehicle topple over the edge and into a Paddy Field. You were ordered by Cpl Gray to cease, but you continued until he again ordered you to stop the lorry. Is that correct?"

"Up to a point Sir, yes," said Hopkins, "But I was testing the steering to make sure that it was OK, I had had some problems earlier and just wanted to make sure that it was responding properly."

"But when ordered to stop by Cpl Gray, because he thought it was dangerous to drive in that manner, you still continued?" the Adjutant continued.

"Yes Sir, but I wanted to make sure."

The Adjutant stopped him saying, "Driver Hopkins just answer the question, did you refuse when told to stop swerving the lorry around by Cpl Gray?"

"Yes Sir," was all Hopkins said in reply.

"Did you on the same day in question drink alcohol whilst on duty?" the Adjutant asked.

"Yes Sir, but it was for medicinal purposes, I have been suffering from a heavy cold and thought that it would help me get through the day," Hopkins said.

"Beer Hopkins is not for medicinal use. Where you drinking from a bottle of beer?" asked the Adjutant.

"Yes Sir," was all Hopkins said.

"Did you also on the same day say to Cpl Gray 'I will make your life hell from now on,' Driver Hopkins."

"I can't remember what I said Sir. I was angry at being told what to do by a young jumped up bloody sprog who's only been a soldier for five minutes," said Hopkins.

"Driver Hopkins, I don't care how long Cpl Gary has been a soldier, what I do know is that he has proved worthy of being promoted to the rank of Corporal and as long as he has two stripes on his arm you will take orders from him like all other ordinary rank soldiers, irrespective of how long you have served. Is that clear?" The Adjutants last words were said in a raised voice to get the message home to Hopkins obviously.

"Yes Sir." Was all Hopkins said once again?

The Adjutant sat in thought for a while before saying, "I have had time to give this quite some thought, having had the report from Cpl Gray earlier in the day and also having the facts corroborated by three other Drivers who were on the convoy on the day in question and have decided the following. I am going to sentence you to seven days in the Guard Room. Take him away Sgt Smith." And with that the Duty Sergeant shouted at Hopkins to quick march and they headed out of the Adjutants office and back to the Guard Room.

"Cpl Gray" began the Adjutant, when Sgt Smith and Hopkins had left his office, "You have only been here a few days, but already I have heard good reports of how you conduct yourself. There are not many NCOs on the base that would have handled Hopkins the way that you have, we know he is a bad lot but we're stuck with him, just watch your back is all I would say right now."

"Thank you Sir, I will," Alan replied and saluted before leaving his office.

Chapter 28

The next sixteen days were the same as the previous three had been for Alan, backwards and forwards to the front line at Tokchon, he was getting used to the gun fire now, almost blasé about it as though it was the norm, he thought, 'well I suppose it is really, after all there is a bloody war going on.'

The long days were taking there toll and Alan was pleased when Lt Brady told him that L/Cpl May would be resuming duties the following day which was a Sunday. Alan met up with him and briefed him late on the Saturday evening after he had returned with the convoy; Brian May also briefed Alan on the format of the Local collections and drops for the following day, also saying that Sgt Brown would fill him in fully the next morning. When Alan returned to the Barrack Room, Les was there, they hadn't laid eyes on each other since they had arrived three weeks earlier and they spent an hour swapping stories of what had happened to each of them thus far.

"Bloody brave thing you did with that Hopkins chap," Les said, "he's a right shit from what I've heard and he's been talking a lot about revenge, so you need to watch yourself."

"Yeah, I know," replied Alan, "but the Adjutants got his marker, so if there is any trouble he'll really be for the high jump. But yeah, thanks for the warning anyway, I'll certainly keep my eyes open. Luckily most of the lads were pleased I did what I did, most of em seem a bit scared of him, a right bully from what I've heard, but I will be careful. So what's your Gaffer like and what's it like driving a great big Buick around?" Alan asked.

"He's great really, doesn't say a lot. I get my orders from Sgt Brown each day; they sometimes get changed, but mostly local stuff. I go to Seoul a lot and of course Kimpo. There's a great PX there, we must go there when we get a bit of free time."

A PX is the American version of the NAAFI, but from what Les said much bigger and much grander, with a brilliant array of goodies on offer.

"I do have a lot of late nights though," Les continued, "the Gaffer does a lot of dining around with the Yanks and the Aussies. But during the day I'm fairly quiet, although there are a couple of other high rankers that I take around to meetings and the like. But all in all, I'm pretty chuffed and a bloody lovely motor to drive."

Neither of them had seen Cocker, but Alan knew from Sgt Brown that he had been on detachment to MASH, the American hospital operation just outside of Inchon, but should be back in camp on the following Monday. They both said that they would keep an eye out for him to find out how he was doing.

"I want to see what he's pretty little nurse is like," Alan said and they both laughed. They chatted until after midnight, but eventually the late nights for both of them had caught up and they went out like lights.

Since Hopkins had finished his seven days in the Guard House he had been on convoys with Alan on three occasions and on each of these he had behaved impeccably. He kept his distance and hadn't spoken a word to Alan, making sure that he just got into his cab and got on with the job in hand, which suited Alan fine. Alan was looking forward to having the next three days doing just the local runs before returning to the front line convoys, which he would hopefully then rotate with Brian May on a daily basis from thereon in.

On the Sunday morning at just after seven thirty Alan went to the Transport Office to sort out the various local routes for the day. Sgt Brown was there as always and gave him a list of what had to be done, he got the remainder of the Platoon on Parade for Lt Brady to inspect and then went to the Platoon Office to allocate the various runs from the sheaf that Sgt Brown had given him. In the meantime he had told the guys to get the Lorries fuelled up and ready to go.

With the help of one of the Drivers a chap called Billy Starr, who had been in Inchon for seven months and knew the routes well, Alan put together the work loads for each Driver, as it happened Hopkins was one of those on Alan's team this particular day. Alan then went to each of them in turn and gave them their worksheet for the day.

When he got to Hopkins, who would be accompanied for the day by another driver, a chap called Glen Williams, Alan handed him his work sheets, he would be going to the main stores and then to Battalion HQ. Hopkins took the sheets from Alan saying in a loud sarcastic way, "Thank you Corporal Sir," and then under his breath said, "I haven't forgot you matey, just watch your fucking back, you're dead meat." And he was gone; he had said it so that none of the others would have heard. Alan just stared at him as he walked away; as he did Hopkins turned and gave Alan a sneering grin as he continued walking.

When all the vehicles were gone except one, Alan boarded this with a Driver called Harry Jackson, a quiet unassuming chap from St. Albans in Hertfordshire, he had been in Korea about five months and was just about getting the hang of things. The days schedule was a trip to the main stores in Inchon, near to the Port, then to the Ordnance Corps base for ammunition and this was then being delivered to the Kimpo Air Base.

While they were at Kimpo, Alan got Harry to point out where the PX was and as he did, he said, "We can stop there if you like Corp, I often do. They have a much better selection of stuff than we do in the NAAFI."

"We're due a break, so why not?" Alan replied.

He was right, as Les had said when Alan and he had chatted the previous day, the array of goodies was amazing, 'the Yanks certainly get spoilt in comparison to us,' he thought. They had a cup of coffee and Alan also bought some chocolate flavoured milk in waxed cartons and some deodorant spray, he hadn't seen anything like that in the NAFFI before. 'What a bloody good idea,' he thought, 'it may help to keep me smelling a bit fresher; and if it works, I'll probably get some more.'

After a twenty minute stop, they made their way back to the main stores to collect rations that were to be delivered the following day to the front line. After checking with Alan that everything was in order, Harry Jackson Headed back to base at 78 Coy.

They arrived back at half past four, but Alan had to wait for the remainder of the trucks to return before he could knock off for the day, the last one arrived at five thirty. Once he had checked them in, Alan took the Log Sheets to Sgt Brown for him to prepare the runs for Monday to Tokchon and at just after six o'clock, and by then starving, Alan went to the cookhouse for some food. As he entered he saw Cocker sitting at a table with a very large chap chatting as they ate, Alan wandered over. When Cocker saw Alan he stood up and they shook hands and then they gave each other a big hug.

"God it's good to see you," Cocker said, "how's life been?"

"Not bad, it's been pretty hectic, working twenty four seven, but probably no more than you. How are you enjoying yourself and more to the point, what is your pretty little nurse like?" Alan asked.

"Let me introduce you," said cocker and turned to the chap sitting at the table, "I'd like you to meet my nurse, John Hardy."

John stood up and shook hands with Alan, "so this is the pretty little nurse you were hoping for," Alan said with a smile, and then told John the joke that they had made when they last spoke, before he was assigned to MASH. The three of them had a good laugh; Alan then made his way to get some food before re-joining them.

Cocker spun a few yarns about what he had been up too, bringing back the wounded from the front line, limbs lying about everywhere and then ferrying the wounded to Kimpo for repatriation flights home and so on. Alan filled him in with some stories of his own, taking the supplies to Tokchon and some of the other bits, including a bit about the problem with Hopkins. They chatted away for over an hour before Cocker said they had to leave, this had been a flying visit to get his Ambulance checked over by the REME and they now had to get back to MASH at Inchon, so they said their goodbyes.

Alan decided that he would go to the Washhouse to see if he could get a shower, that was providing the water was at least luke warm and he struck lucky, it was. He also decided to try out his new purchase of the deodorant spray he had bought at the PX, on the face of it, it smelt pretty good, he just hoped it worked. After going back to the Barrack Room and changing from his soiled clothing into a clean set of fatigues, he wandered over to the NAAFI. He saw Susan at the counter chatting to a couple of the Drivers, Billy Starr, and Harry Jackson who Alan had been with earlier in the day, when she saw Alan she broke away from chatting to them and walked towards him.

"Alan, it's nice to see you, it seems ages though, we thought you had done a runner, well at least Charlie did. She's been pining for you," she smiled as she said the last words.

"Now why on earth would Charlie be pining for me? After all we only chatted for a few minutes," Alan said.

"You made a big impression young man," she said still smiling. "It's her night off, but I'm sure if I told her you were here she'd be out like a shot."

"Go on then, try it, but I bet she won't," he said, not thinking for one minute she would.

"You're on," Susan replied and with that walked to the doorway at the end of the building, which was where Charlie had explained their living quarters were.

Two minutes later Susan reappeared, "She's on her way. I told you so," she said with a triumphal smile on her face, "you owe me," and she walked back to the counter to continue her conversation with the two lads.

It must have been just over five minutes before Charlie appeared at the end of the room wearing that wonderful smile that she wore so well. "Well Alan Gray, it's taken you a long time. The last time we spoke I remember saying to you quite clearly, not to make it too long before you visited me again and it's been three whole weeks. What is going on?"

"Time fly's Charlie, it doesn't seem that long. But since I arrived I just haven't stopped," Alan said, "back and forth to Tokchon for twenty one days without a break."

"And you couldn't find just a few little minutes to call and see me?" she said with a pout on her lips.

"Charlie, what can I say? I know we chatted, but it was for such a short while I just didn't realise that I'd made that sort of impression on you, after all as I said then, you must get chatted up all the time, why me?"

"You just don't get it Alan Gray do you? I also told you that I am very capable of fobbing them off and I do it all the time. But with you, I don't know, it just felt different, I can't put a finger on it, but I've not felt like this in a long time."

"So you have felt like this before then?" Alan asked.

"Yes, once. But that was a couple of years ago. He died in a car crash and I've never had a boyfriend since. Then you come along and Bingo."

She had a sad look on her face, as though she had told Alan something that she had never told anyone else.

"Charlie I'm sorry, I just hadn't got a clue. After all we don't even know each other, just a twenty minute chat, how can you be so sure?"

"Oh, I'm sure," Charlie said, "all I can say is that you melted my heart. I know it sounds corny and very American type film stuff, but that's just how it is."

Alan was somewhat taken aback by what Charlie was saying and said, "So, where do we go from here? After all let's face it, the circumstances we both find ourselves in aren't actually ideal for a serious relationship, or any sort of relationship come to think of it. I'm stuck in Barracks and working almost twenty four seven and you're sharing with Sue. My hours are completely unknown; you work funny shifts and who knows I may even get killed in the situations that I find myself in with guns banging all around me at the front line."

"Alan, don't you think I've thought of all the obstacles, after all I've had three long weeks to do so. I know it's almost impossible, but it's worth a chance isn't it?" she finished and looked at Alan with those green eyes, almost imploring him.

"Christ Charlie, I'm not sure whether I'm dreaming, or whether this is some sort of game. You're bloody gorgeous and could have the pick of the bunch, what man wouldn't give his right arm to be with you? I'm just; well I'm just gob smacked, I'm just so flattered. When I walked out of here three weeks ago, I'll be honest with you; I felt ten feet tall the way you had chatted to me. I then thought that perhaps it was just a game you were playing and maybe something you did with all the new guys. But I never thought for a moment that I would have made this sort of impression on you and that you would end up feeling like this. Blimey."

"Well I do, and it's not a game" Charlie responded. "So what are we going to do about it?"

Alan thought for a moment before answering. "Well the first thing we need to do is to get to know each other a bit more, quite how and when I'm not sure. After all you know absolutely nothing about me, other than my name and I only know a teeny little bit about you and that you're lovely. So I will definitely spend as much time as I possibly can here in the NAAFI to get to know you, when I am not working that is. It would of course be better if there was somewhere where we could meet, without all the prying eyes that is. But my Barrack room isn't the nicest place for a beautiful lady I can assure you." She laughed.

"I've been chatting to Sue over the past week or so," Charlie said, "I've told her how I feel and she suggested that perhaps you could visit me on my days off, providing they coincide with yours that is, in our quarters. After all Sue would be on duty and we would have the place to ourselves, for a few hours anyway. What do you think?"

"Sounds like a great idea to me, but is it allowed and what if we get caught?"

"No it's not allowed, but as only Sue and I work here, no one is likely to find out and if we do get caught, then we would have to cross that bridge as and when we came to it. Worth a try though isn't it?" She finished, looking at Alan with those green eyes, willing him to say yes.

"Charlie, for you I'm prepared to take whatever risks there are, after all I spend all day taking much bigger ones. God I'm a lucky guy, that's all I can say right now."

"I'm the lucky one," she said. "Come, let me show you my quarters, then at least you will know where we will be making our own little love nest." The last words were said with a wicked twinkle in those lovely green eyes of hers.

"I will go first, give me a couple of minutes to tell Sue and I will leave the door open. Just walk around the back of the screen as though you're going to use the loos and I'll be waiting." And with that she stood and walked away.

Alan's heart was going ten to the dozen; he certainly hadn't expected this to be happening on this particular evening and quite what he was expecting he wasn't really sure. Alan sat and waited a few minutes before he made his move, then casually got up from his chair and walked to where the toilets were and then on to where Charlie was waiting outside the door to her quarters. She beckoned for him to go inside, which he did.

Hardly had she shut the door, when she had turned and was in his arms, her lips seeking out his in a long passionate kiss, she pressed her body close to Alan's, he was glad that he had had the forethought to shower and apply his new body spray, 'this would really be a test for it,' he thought as they kissed.

They stayed by the door kissing for several minutes before she broke away, saying, "that was worth the wait, come on let's sit down."

They sat on a smallish settee against one of the walls; the room was fairly comfortably furnished, although not quite out of Vogue. After they were seated she cuddled up to Alan and he placed his arm around her shoulder pulling her towards him, they kissed again, only this time more softly and after what seemed an age they parted once again.

Charlie looked up at Alan saying, "So let's get to know each other, you go first," this she said with a wide smile on that beautiful face.

"Well," he started, "I live in Essex, I've been in the army for just over a year, I've had one serious girlfriend before joining up and as you know I've been in Korea for just three weeks, that's about it. Now it's your turn."

"That's a very short life story," she said, "Surely there's more than that?"

"Not really, other than the fact that I'm a pretty good footballer, or was before joining up, I played for a team called Brentwood and was their top scorer and I did have high hopes of being a professional one day. I have three brothers and three sisters of which I'm the next to youngest. I used to have a very exciting job; I worked in a large grocery store and served the customers with bacon, butter, cheese and all things like that. Now it really is your turn"

She laughed at Alan's last remarks before saying, "Ok, I've already told you that my Dad is in the Army in London, Mummy lives in the country on the family estate looking after the horses. As for me I was a bored little girl looking for adventure and here I am."

"What about your boyfriend, or is that too difficult to talk about," Alan asked.

"No, I'm over it now. It was tough at the time, but time is a good healer, as they say. We went out for two years, he wanted to get married, but I felt I was too young at the time, and then he had his accident. End of really. What about your girlfriend?" she asked.

Alan explained the complications of her supposedly being his cousin and they had skirted around each other for several years and then the revelation that she wasn't and their short relationship just before he had joined the army. He didn't go into the bit about being caught by her Dad and all that, thought that was best left alone. Alan did tell her about his Dad telling him to leave home when he found out he was joining up, she couldn't believe that anyone could be like that, especially a parent. Over the next hour or so more small points came out about each of them, their schooling, their general interests, the music they liked and so on, overall Alan felt it was a really good chat and he felt that he really knew Charlie at the end of it.

Alan glanced at his watch and saw that it was a quarter to eleven, "blimey," he said, "I'd better go. I've got to do the Barrack Room head count before eleven."

"Do you really have too?" she said.

"I really do," Alan replied.

They stood and she pushed herself into his arms once again, giving Alan the full taste of that wonderful body, she turned her face up towards his and they kissed once again, a long lingering kiss.

When they finally broke away she said, "Now Alan Gray, you just make sure you visit me every evening for the next three days before you start your front line runs, is that understood?"

"Loud and clear Ma'm," Alan said in a mocking voice, saluting at the same time. And they both laughed.

"You will though won't you?" she said.

"Of course I will, wild horses couldn't keep me away," and they kissed once again before Alan made a dash for the Barrack Room.

Chapter 29

As Alan walked towards the Barrack Room it was as though he was floating on cloud seven, it had been a very unexpected and a really wonderful evening and more to the point, he thought, something to look forward too in the weeks and months ahead. He slowed his pace on his final approach to the Barrack Room and was just about to enter, when he got the feeling that there was someone in the vicinity, but before Alan could even reach the door to enter he was felled from behind. The blow to his head took him by surprise and was so severe that he fell forward to the ground, smashing his face into the gravel as he did.

Alan didn't remember any more for twenty four hours apparently. He was discovered by one of the Guards on duty doing his rounds at eleven thirty, he then aroused the Duty Sergeant and Alan was taken to the medical centre where he was treated for concussion.

When he eventually woke up, Alan couldn't remember what had happened, he couldn't even remember who he was or where he was, in fact Alan lay in the Medical Centre bed for three days before things started to come back to him. He kept getting pictures in his mind of a beautiful blonde girl and them both kissing, then the guns would start pounding in his head, then there was the awful shaking and rattling of being in a lorry and the noise of the engine, then the beautiful girl again and then the most awful thump on his head, like his head had exploded. Alan's face was a hell of a mess, apparently from falling face down in the gravel and he had the most awful headache, although with all the medication that the Doc seemed to be pumping into him, he felt this was gradually easing as the days had passed.

It wasn't until the fourth day that Alan started putting things in their proper places, with a bit of help from the Medic who was looking after him. He had remembered he was in Korea and the guns he could hear where when he had been driving to the front line at Tokchon and then the final piece of the jigsaw fell in place, Charlie.

'Oh God,' Alan thought, 'Of course, Charlie. I had arranged to see her each evening after our super Sunday together, what must she be thinking? How can I get a message to her, or did she already know?' He just knew he had to get out of that place and see her. He called the Medical Orderly over.

"Look Doc, I've got to get out of here, I have something important to do. I need to get back to camp at 78 Coy."

"I'm not too sure whether you're ready to leave yet, but let me see the boss," he said.

He was gone for about fifteen minutes and on his return he said, "I've had a word with the MO and I need to go through a few things with you. We need the bed, so providing you can get through my final check; I'll get a vehicle to take you back, but only if."

With that he started asking lots of questions, checking to see if Alan had got his faculties back, he took his pulse, his blood pressure and tested his reflexes, this went on for twenty minutes or so and at the end of this he said. "Well it seems that you have come through this pretty well, I'll just get you some pills that you are to keep taking for the next four days and also a medical note saying you are not to return to full duties for another three days. Then I'll arrange a vehicle to take you back."

Alan was so relieved he could have kissed him, but resisted the urge. As soon as the Medic was gone Alan got out of the pyjamas that they had provided and got dressed into his uniform, the same one that he had had on that Sunday evening. It was dirty all down the front where he had laid on the ground for half an hour or so before he was found, but so what, that could soon be put right, he thought, get it straight in the laundry. His face had started to heal and at a distance didn't look to bad; it was only right up close that the scars still showed, large areas of gravel rash and a large gash on his forehead and of course the huge bump that was still on the back of his head. The time was almost five thirty in the afternoon and it was completely dark when the Jeep arrived to take Alan the short journey back to 78 Coy, It took just over ten minutes.

As the driver pulled into to the gates, Alan asked to be dropped off at the NAAFI, which he did and after saying cheerio, drove off leaving Alan standing there.

He walked slowly forwards, still very unsteady on his legs, he hadn't walked any distance at all for four day and his legs felt like jelly. As Alan entered the NAAFI he spotted Charlie talking to Sue at the counter, when she saw him enter she just turned and ran out towards her quarters not looking back at him.

As Alan approached the counter, Sue turned to him and said in a very trite voice, "You are not really welcome here anymore. You get a girls hopes sky high and then drop her like a ton of bricks, what the hell sort of game are you playing?"

Alan just couldn't believe what he was hearing, it was obvious that they didn't know what had happened and must have thought that he was playing Charlie along. He carried on walking towards Sue and again she said, "I don't want to hear your silly excuses, why don't you just leave?"

"Sue you don't understand. I've been in hospital for four days; I got hit over the head on Sunday evening as I was going back to the Barrack Room after I left Charlie, and I've been unconscious for most of that time."

"Oh God Alan, it was you they were talking about. No one said who it was. We just put two and two together and thought that you were messing Charlie around. Oh my God I am so sorry I had better go and tell her, you poor bloke." And with that she left to get Charlie.

She came out and called to Alan, "you had better go and see her, she's in bits."

When Alan entered their quarters, Charlie sat on the settee sobbing. When she saw Alan she jumped up and flung her arms around his neck saying, "Oh Alan, I was so hurt and upset when you didn't turn up, if only you had got a message to me, or if someone had said it was you in that rumpus. I could have even come over to see you. God I am so sorry for thinking the worst. I should have known better, but, oh I don't know, I feel so rotten. How are you, you poor darling. Let me have a look at you. Who did this awful thing to you; I don't know anyone that says a bad word against you, so why?"

"I can only take a guess, I don't know for sure, but I think it was Bill Hopkins, he's had it in for me from day one. Jealous I reckon, but as I say I don't know for sure." Alan said.

They kissed and chatted for a further ten minutes, Charlie had to get back to work and Alan needed to let Lt Brady know that he was back and also Sgt Brown. That done he went to the Cookhouse for something to eat; Alan hadn't eaten very much over the past four days and was starting to get a little weakened by the lack of food. The Catering Corps Corporal in the cookhouse did him proud, he rustled up some sausage meat with mash and greens, it may not sound like a feast, but to Alan right then it was. This, washed down with a couple of mugs of hot tea, it was like eating at the Ritz he felt, the way he was feeling.

After eating Alan wandered back to the Barrack Room, there were several of the lads there, Harry Jackson, Billy Starr and also Paddy Gregson, and at the far end sitting on his bed was Hopkins. Paddy was the first to walk over to Alan, "Bloody hell Corp, you look a mess," he said.

"Yeah, been under the weather that's for sure," Alan answered.

"What the hell happened? I've asked around, but no one seems to know anything other than the fact you were found laying outside the Barrack Room door. Did you trip, or did someone clobber you?" he finished.

Alan answered in a fairly loud voice so that Hopkins would hear as well as the others, "I'm not sure Paddy, but whatever happened and whoever it was hasn't heard the last of this. I'll break his bloody neck when I do find out and risk getting busted, it'll be worth it."

They chatted on for a further five minutes or so and they left, saying they were off to the NAAFI for a nightcap before turning in; they were on the Front Line run the following morning and had to be up at the crack of dawn. At least Alan had a couple of days to rest, make the most of them that's for sure, he thought. After checking his bed was OK, Alan also decided to nip back to the NAAFI for an hour, he hoped he might get a chance to have a further chat with Charlie.

Just as Alan was leaving the Barrack Room Hopkins called out, "Got a nasty bang on the back of the head did you Corporal Sir. Nasty headache as well I bet, I do hope it gets better soon? You should watch your back you know, I did warn you." he said in a taunting voice.

"I've got no proof Hopkins, but I know it was you. You're the one who needs to watch his back," Alan said, "When I get the proof I need, I'll get you fucking Court Marshalled, the army doesn't need scumbags like you." And with that he walked out without looking back. Alan wasn't sure what he was going to do, but he would think of something, he felt sure, and he then put Hopkins out of his mind.

Charlie was serving a couple of chaps when Alan entered the NAAFI, but as soon as she was done she made a beeline for him. "Would you like a drink?" she asked.

"Just a coffee will be fine," Alan replied and she walked away to make the drink for him. He couldn't help but admire her from the back as she went, she had the cutest backside he had ever seen, sent shivers down his spine. 'Aren't I the lucky one,' he thought, 'out of all the guys around here it was me she fancied.' He still couldn't really believe it.

Charlie was back at his table in a couple of minutes with a large mug of steaming coffee. "For my special man," she said with that gorgeous smile. As it was fairly quiet they were able to have a good chat, with her having to wander off to serve from time to time. But at just after ten o'clock Alan said that he had to go, he was just about all in; the events of what had happened were really catching up on him that was for sure.

After saying goodnight to Charlie and to Sue, Alan walked towards the Barrack Room, but this time with his ears and eyes working overtime, listening and looking. Once inside he checked that Hopkins was in his bed, as were most of the guys, Brian May was doing the head check, so Alan hadn't got that to worry about, he was also doing the Front Line run and Sgt Brown was taking care of the local run scheduling for the time being. It was now just a matter of getting as much rest as he could and getting back into action once again. As Alan fell asleep he was wondering how he was going to catch Hopkins out, or would he be foolish enough to be the architect of his own undoing.

Chapter 30

It was the fifth of November, a Monday and fireworks day would you believe when Alan resumed duties and was immediately back on the front line run, he had volunteered to get right back in the fray and try to put the Hopkins incident out of his mind. Except it was difficult, because Hopkins was scheduled to be on the front line runs as well over the next three days? Probably just as well though Alan thought, at least he could keep his eye on him.

It really was a fifth of November affair at the front line when Alan arrived with the convoy, he felt that the bloody Chinese must have read about Guy Fawkes and were letting the lads at the front line have hell when they arrived. Shells were dropping all around the whole camp and all Alan wanted to do was to execute a quick about turn and get to hell out of there and back to quieter climes. Within the hour the convoy was making it's way back to Inchon and luckily out of firing distance, Hopkins had behaved as well as Alan could have hoped, the only thing that was still annoying him was the continual use of the 'Corporal Sir,' bit, but Alan had decided to ignore it as best he could.

The next two days went much according to plan and Hopkins had again behaved, but it was on the following morning that trouble reared its ugly head. Hopkins wasn't scheduled to be on the front line run and should have had an extra lie in, which was normal, but due to one of the other Drivers being sick Alan had to tell him that he would be required to fill in, and he was not amused. After breakfast Alan got the Platoon on Parade for Lt Brady to inspect and this is where the trouble started.

Lt Brady called Alan to one side after he had done the inspection saying, "I'm not too happy with Hopkins, Cpl Gray, he smells to high heaven of beer. What do we do?"

As they were still standing at attention, Alan decided to do a walk past himself and when he was opposite Hopkins said, "Driver Hopkins I think you've been drinking, are you in a fit state to drive?"

He looked at Alan with a sneer appearing on his face, saying, "I'm always fit to drive Corporal Sir?"

"Driver Hopkins," Alan said, "I have reason to agree with Lt Brady that you are still under the influence of alcohol and are therefore not fit to drive today."

"I 'm a bloody site fitter than you, you jumped up Pratt," he shouted.

At that point Lt Brady stepped in, "Driver Hopkins, I am charging you with being on Parade while still under the influence of alcohol and unable to carry out your duties and of insubordination to an NCO. Fall out and I will march you to the Guard Room."

Lt Brady then went to Alan saying, "You'll have to get another Driver for the run Cpl Gray, I will deal with Hopkins."

"Yes Sir," Alan replied and after saluting, went to the Barrack Room to roust one of the other Drivers up to take the place of Hopkins.

Because of all the hassle with Hopkins, the convoy was thirty minutes late setting off that morning, but still made good progress and they were at Tokchon eating a plate of egg and fried potatoes by one o'clock and then back on their way to Camp just after two. When Alan returned, the first thing he did was check in with the Transport Office and Sgt Brown filled him in on the Hopkins saga.

"Lt Brady had him in front of the Adjutant at ten o'clock and he's got four days Jankers," he explained, "would have been more if I'd had my way, but we can't spare the Drivers that's the bloody trouble. He really is a nasty piece of work that one."

Jankers on active service meant that not only would Hopkins spend all his days doing menial tasks around the Camp accompanied by one of the Military Police, or MP's as they were known, but he would sleep in the Guard House at night, being under the supervision of the Guard Commander and the Duty Officer. He was released back to normal duties on the Sunday evening, Alan had made sure that Hopkins was not on the Tokchon run on the Monday, because the schedule allowed him several days on locals, so L/Cpl May would have to cope with him for the time being anyway, although he wasn't too keen, knowing that Hopkins would be fuming after his stay in the Nick.

As Alan was on the early run the following morning, he had made just a brief visit to the NAAFI and had a short chat with Charlie before making his way back to bed, Brian May was on head count duty so Alan was able to get his head down before ten o'clock. He wasn't sure how long he had been in bed, but he was woken by someone shaking his shoulders, Alan turned his head and saw Brian May standing above him.

"Alan," he said in a quiet voice, "you had better be on your guard mate. I've just overheard Hopkins talking to some of his cronies; he said that he's going to get you once and for all tonight."

Alan sat up, rubbing his eyes trying to adjust to the lights "did he say how, or when?" He asked

"No, all he said was what I just told you, but definitely tonight. And he is well and truly tanked up; he's been there since they opened apparently."

"Well the only way to deal with him properly is to let him come and do whatever he has in mind, but thanks to you I will be ready for him this time. I'll unzip my sleeping bag so that I can at least protect myself or retaliate to whatever he does, I'll pretend to be sleeping and just wait. If you could lay up on your bed with the lights out, you can switch them on as and when he starts and we'll have the bastard." Alan finished.

"Should I go and tell the Duty Sergeant?" Brian asked.

"No, lets not pre-empt anything, if he does start, then you can go and get him. Let's just play it by ear. And by the way Brian Thanks." And with that Alan lay back on his bed, his heart pounding, just waiting for whatever Hopkins had in mind to happen.

Alan must have lain there coiled like a spring ready to act for almost half an hour before he heard footsteps approaching, he heard some rustling around the side of the Barrack Room wall before the door was opened, Alan tensed his body and waited. The first blow caught him on the shoulders and he winced, but at the same time he swung his left arm outwards towards where he thought Hopkins would be standing and Alan heard a muffled grunt.

"You bastard, want to make a fight of it do you," came the slurred voice of Hopkins.

The second blow hit struck Alan across the chest. He had turned on his back as he had flung his left arm at Hopkins and this meant he had rotated so that his chest was uppermost and caught the full force of the second blow. Christ that hurt, Alan thought, but tried to push the pain out of his mind.

At that moment the lights were switched on by Brian May and the blaze caught Hopkins by surprise. Alan jumped out of his bed, flinging Hopkins to the floor as he did so and lay on his chest with his arm cocked ready to beat seven bells out of him. It was only Brian that stopped Alan from doing so.

"He's not worth it Alan," he said grabbing Alan's wrist to restrain him, "we've got him now, let the system bang him to rights." And he was right, Alan thought.

Alan lay straddled across Hopkins chest gripping his arms across his throat, while Brian May went to get the Duty Sergeant. By then all the lads in the Barrack Room were awake and standing ready in case Hopkins did try to make a break for it, not that he could, because Alan had him well and truly held down. Within five minutes Hopkins was hauled away to the Guard Room and locked up for the night and the following day he, together with Alan and the rest of the lads would know his fate. Alan also gave Sgt Hawkins, who was the Duty Sergeant, the pick axe handle that Hopkins had used to hit him with.

After returning from Tokchon the following evening Alan reported to Lt Brady and asked about news regarding Hopkins. The Lt explained that he had been sentenced to six months in the Nick, he was being shipped out the following morning and would start to serve his time in Kure awaiting a troop ship to take him back to the UK. Once back in the UK he would complete his sentence at the Colchester Correction

Establishment, and he would then receive a dishonourable discharge from the army. He also explained that the pick axe handle had also been used to hit Alan over the head previously; they had matched up some blood samples. Bloody hell, Alan thought, what a couple of weeks, but that was now behind him and it was back to work big time.

Chapter 31

The weeks leading up to Christmas were as hectic as ever, Alan was taking it in turns with Brian May driving the convoys every other day to the front line at Tokchon. The weather had deteriorated considerably during December and the snow was falling steadily, getting heavier and deeper as the days went by. The snow apparently wasn't as deep as the previous winter had been, from what had been said, but was still quite something to contend with on those awful Korean roads, Alan thought. The driving backwards and forwards to the front line each day was becoming more treacherous and far more tiring.

The REME lads had fitted snow chains on the rear wheels of each truck, which made driving and road holding a little better for everyone, however the chains had other downsides because of the additional jolting that they produced for the drivers. Alan was also now experiencing just how cold it got; the temperature had dropped to twenty degrees below freezing, enough to freeze the balls off a brass monkey was the way Alan was thinking right then and it was set to get even colder, 'that'll be even tougher on the monkeys,' he thought, with a grin. He was also very glad of his long johns, even though he had laughed at them when they had been issued, god wasn't he glad of them right then.

Alan was seeing as much as he could of Charlie, although this was limited due to his workload, but very pleasant as and when they managed too. On the Sunday afternoon during the second week in December, Alan had finished attending to the local runs and had sorted out everything for the following day; he wandered to the shower block and managed to get a luke warm shower. After dressing in a clean set of clothing, he went to the NAAFI to see Charlie, knowing it was her day off and hoping he would be able to spend some time together with her in her room. When he arrived, Sue said for Alan to go straight through and that Charlie was expecting him, he knocked on the door and Charlie called for him to go in, and wow what a surprise he got.

Charlie was lying on the couch in a slinky black and red negligee, which she told Alan later she had bought from the PX at Kimpo, just for him. "Come and join me handsome," she said in a very suggestive voice, with that wicked grin of hers spreading across her face.

Alan didn't need a second invitation and the moment he sat down she pulled him down on top of her and kissed him, it was one of her special long lingering kisses, her tongue exploring Alan's lips and mouth as she did. It was obvious she was highly aroused and it wasn't long before they were taking each others clothes off, not that Charlie had much to take off. This was the first time that they had been naked together and Charlie looked absolutely gorgeous, she had beautiful full breasts with lovely turned up nipples at the end, she took Alan's hand and placed it against one of her bosoms, his fingers gently stroked the nipple and he watched as it became erect, jutting out from the softness of her full breasts.

Alan had grown to his full size and she gasped when she saw him, gently taking hold of him in her hand saying, "Oh Alan you're so huge, it's beautiful."

From what Charlie had told Alan during their chats during the previous months, it had been a long time since her boyfriend and also since she had made love, for Alan it had also been several months, in fact not since Nancy in August. They gently fondled each other for ages, just enjoying the feel of each others bodies, then finally Charlie said in a slightly slurred voice "Alan, I can't wait any longer, love me, please love me." And after slipping on a French letter, he did.

It was quite earth shattering, the most wonderful love making that Alan had ever had, Jen had been good and Nancy even better due to her experience, but with Charlie it had an added maturity about it, he just couldn't put a finger on it, but just wow!

They lay in each others arms for an hour, just holding, kissing, touching, until Charlie said softly, "can we do that again?" And they did.

That was the start of something special for Alan, it had been special just knowing that she fancied him amongst all those that she could have picked from, but after that day, well that was it, Alan was really smitten. Over the weeks ahead they did all they could to meet and as often as possible they made love, Charlie had a good supply of French Letters luckily, she got them

258

supplied, 'just in case,' she had said, so there was no problem there.

Christmas nineteen fifty one came and went in a flash; Alan had managed to buy Charlie some perfume from the PX which she was delighted with and she had bought him some after shave lotion, again she got this from the PX on one of her visits there.

Both Alan and Charlie had had to work on Christmas Day, but they still managed to spend the evening together. Alan had seen Les and Cocker on Christmas Eve; and they had managed a couple of beers together and spent some time catching up with what had been happening. Les was dating an American girl who worked at the PX and, Cocker had finally got his little nurse, although John Hardy was still his Ambulance Nurse, he was dating a nurse at MASH again an American. It was then that Alan decided to tell them about Charlie, they were both pleased, saying 'what a lucky bugger he was,' because they both knew her from the NAFFI and also knew just how gorgeous she was

Even though they were on active service, Christmas Lunch had been made into a bit of a fun affair in the Cookhouse; the Catering Corps lads had done a brilliant job with the rations that they had, serving up chicken with roast spuds, cabbage and even a Yorkshire pudding, and this was followed by something that almost resembled a Christmas pudding, with hot custard poured over it. Everyone also received a bottle of beer, and dinner was served up by the Officers and Sergeants.

Chapter 32

And so it was in to January and a new year, the snow was really thick and the trips to Tokchon were becoming more hazardous by the day. The trucks were all fitted with snow chains on the rear wheels and some had had them fitted on the front as well, but as Alan had recalled earlier, this only went to make the journey even more horrific, with the extra shaking that each driver had to suffer. There wasn't a day went by without an incident of some sort, either a truck slipping off the road into the Paddy Fields, or a bump with another vehicle, not so bad when it was a military one, but as Alan was to find out a real bugger when it was a local's vehicle. Alan and all the drivers had been warned that that type of accident was to be avoided like the plague; the blighters would demand a brand new vehicle to replace their old wreck, even if it had been their fault and it usually was.

January flew by, with the daily convoys back and forth to Tokchon and of course there were the various local journeys that had to be organised getting the supplies ready to take to the front line. All the Platoons were working flat out, almost twenty four seven, or so it seemed Alan thought, which unfortunately meant that there was very little time for Charlie, but when they were together it was quite amazing. In fact during the whole month they only managed to see each other on just two occasions.

During February the weather had worsened somewhat, but from what Alan had been told, with any luck it should start to change during the next few weeks and hopefully by the middle of March the snow should be gone or at least going, again something he was led to believe. The routine continued without much let up, but they had been informed by the Adjutant that extra troops, mainly drivers, were being shipped out to try to relieve the load somewhat. But for the time being everyone had to make the best they could of things. It was so knackering that most of the lads, including Alan were in bed by nine o'clock almost every night throughout the month.

Then, right out of the blue on the last day of the month, Lt Brady called Alan to one side saying, "I'd like to make the trip tomorrow, Cpl Gray, I've arranged for the use of the Transport Captains Ford Willys Jeep, so you can drive me in that. I've also arranged for an extra Driver to take your Lorry. I want to see what the real conditions that you chap's are facing each day in this awful weather."

"Very well Sir," Alan said, "I'll have the Jeep made ready for seven tomorrow." He saluted and left thinking, 'I could bloody well do with this, but he's the boss.'

After the brief Parade the following morning, the convoy moved out of Barracks, with Alan leading in the Jeep and Lt Brady by his side. Although the Lt had been out and about since arriving in Korea, the furthest that he had been was Seoul, so today was going to be a rude awakening for him, especially when they left the better roads behind them and moved towards the front line at Tokchon.

Lt Brady was appalled at the conditions that the drivers had to cope with, even though they had the snow chains on the rear wheels for extra grip. On the Jeep that Alan was driving, they had special lightweight road grippers made of rope rather than chain, so the juddering wasn't so apparent, but it still didn't make the journey much better. At the first stop about half an hour outside of Seoul, the Lt asked if he could ride in one of the lorries so he could experience that aspect of things, exactly what a Driver has to cope with. So Alan suggested he ride with Paddy Gregson, although Paddy wasn't too keen on the idea.

Alan had to give the Lieutenant his due though, when the convoy arrived at Tokchon he mucked in with the rest of the lads to get the trucks unloaded. When they were out of earshot of the others, Paddy told Alan that the Lt had nearly shit himself when he heard the barrage of guns as they had approached the front line base camp; 'he had thought that was it for everyone and that they were all goners, he thought that the guns were being fired at the convoy.' Paddy also said that he hadn't told Lt Brady about the gun fire, he just let him experience it as it happened and Alan and Paddy both laughed like drains.

"All part of the learning curve," Alan had said.

Lt Brady rejoined Alan in the Ford Willy Jeep for the drive back to Inchon; luckily the Jeep had a fitted canopy wrapped around it to keep some of the cold out, but still not much better than the trucks. The main problem with the trucks was their age, the heaters were practically useless and the gaps in the floor where the foot pedals went through let in the cold draughts and froze your feet. Then there was the draughts that came in around the doors and the side windows and the smell of the fumes from the fuel was bloody awful. All in all not a nice drive as the Lieutenant had found out for himself, just as he had wanted too.

When the convoy got just outside of Inchon Lt Brady said, "Would it be alright if I drove through the town Cpl Gray? I'd like the experience."

"Yeah, that's fine by me sir," Alan said. "I'll stop when we reach the outskirts of town where the lighting, such as it is, comes on. I'll guide you through."

Alan stopped the convoy, and they had a short break and stretched their legs before the final push back to Base, but now with the Lieutenant driving the Jeep. He was an OK driver and although Alan had to give him directions they were making good time; that was until the Korean kid ran out in front of the convoy. He bounced off the front of the Jeep and Lt Brady froze, slamming the brakes on and skidding badly on the snow as he tried to bring the jeep to a halt. As the kid lay in the road a crowd started to gather and Alan knew he had to act quickly.

"Jump out Sir and change seats," Alan shouted at him.

"But what about the boy?" he said, getting out of the jeep and starting to walk towards him lying in the road.

"Just get back in the jeep and change seats Sir, and forget the kid," Alan almost shouted, "I'll explain as we get going."

"But," he said again.

"No buts Sir," said Alan.

The Lt got back into the passenger seat, Alan had already slid across to the driver's side and after they were re-seated Alan pulled away, making a path through the on looking crowd that had gathered, with the lorries in tow behind him forcing them aside.

After the convoy had cleared a way through and was moving along OK, Lt Brady said, "What was all that about Cpl Gray, shouldn't we have stopped and seen to the boy?"

"No Sir," Alan replied, "these kids throw themselves in front of us all the time, if we stop they accuse us of hitting them and they could claim thousands of pound in compensation. Their Parents put them up to it. There is an unwritten rule that says when this happens you just drive on, then there's no hassle. You can check with Sgt

Brown and Capt Mason when we get back to base if you don't agree."

Lt Brady made no more comments about what had happened, but as soon as they arrived back at camp he was off to the Transport Office like a rocket. Once the trucks were all parked in the compound Alan walked to the Transport Office to hand in the dockets and collect those for the following morning and sure enough Lt Brady was in the main office speaking with Capt Mason. Alan just hoped that the Captain would back up his actions. After mentioning this to Sgt Brown, he assured Alan that he had done the right thing and that Capt Mason was putting Lt Brady right on the issue as they spoke.

Chapter 33

Each serving soldier in Korea has an entitlement to what is known as R&R, Rest and Recuperation, these being a one week break for every six months served, so at the end of March Alan would be able to take week's leave. Normally these breaks were in Tokyo the capital of Japan, which Alan thought sounded a great idea for a holiday. He broached the subject with Charlie to see if she got a similar entitlement and was dead chuffed to learn that she did and as she hadn't used hers as yet, suggested that perhaps they could book their trips at the same time.

She was ecstatic at the thought, "Oh Alan that would be so wonderful," she had said when he first mentioned it. "Let's see what we can arrange," and it was left there for the time being, anyway.

Alan managed to meet up with Les and Cocker during the third week in March, although it was difficult to see each other on a regular basis due to their different roles at 78 Coy. They were both getting on fine; Cocker was still with his big nurse and his little nurse and Les with his PX girlfriend. Alan mentioned the idea of R&R, which they were both aware about and it was decided that they would try to arrange their leave at the same time as Alan, although he did tell them that he would be hopefully having Charlie with him as well. They were fine with that, so it was just a matter of fixing up the dates.

Later in the day Alan spoke with Lt Brady and agreed a date at the beginning of April for seven days R&R, he then got messages to both Les and Cocker and also got the OK from Charlie that this would be fine with her, so they were all set. Alan, Les and Cocker would be flying out from Kimpo on the seventh of April on a large troop carrying plane, while Charlie would be going on a small twelve seater earlier the same day.

The sleeping arrangements when they were in Tokyo were going to be difficult though, because the men would be sleeping in a dormitory at the YMCA and although they could stay out overnight, they had to report in once at some point during each day. As far as Charlie was concerned, she would be billeted about a mile away in a special WVS house and again would be under similar rules to the guys, a bit of a fag, but they felt they would get over this somehow.

Alan, along with the others was ready for seven days of fun and freedom. They would be wearing their normal Battledress uniforms, certainly make a nice change from fatigues and combat suits Alan thought. They left camp in a small people carrier for the airport at ten thirty; Charlie had already left and would be there several hours before Alan and the others arrived. Alan had a telephone number where he could contact her and they had arranged that as soon as he arrived that he would call her.

Alan had never flown before, neither had the other two, so this was a new experience yet again for all of them. The plane was huge; it was an American Douglas C47 Skytrain, which was used for transporting goods, as well as troops. The plane was boarded by walking up a long gangplank arrangement from the rear, and then as you entered the interior there was a row of webbing harness's hanging from each side of the plane, which you had to strap yourself in to. There were probably about fifty troops in all, a mix of Brits, Americans, Aussies, Kiwis and Canadians, all going on R&R and all in a very happy mood.

The journey was to take about two and a half hours, Alan's heart was racing as the plane roared along the runway for takeoff, he actually closed his eyes for a moment until they were in the air, although he didn't let on to the others. He then turned and looked out of the window to see the ground disappearing as the plane climbed into the sky, 'this is bloody exhilarating,' was all that Alan could think right then.

The plane landed on the runway at Tokyo Military Airport at half past two with a huge bump, the plane seemed to bounce at it hit the ground and gradually came to a halt opposite a large Aircraft Hanger. They disembarked from the plane and walked to the Hanger, then after a few formalities they were ushered towards a group of coaches where they all boarded for the short journeys to their various accommodations. The YMCA was Ok, the beds looked comfortable, not that Alan had much intention of using his, except probably for the last night and after getting a cup of tea and some food, he phoned the number that Charlie had given him.

It took Alan several attempts to get through; he had trouble with their dialling system, but got there in the end and a female voice asked who he would like to speak too. The next voice Alan heard was Charlie.

"Alan you've made it; how was your flight?" she said.

"Yep, I'm here and the flight was alright, never flown before, so quiet exciting really. How was yours?"

"Yes it was fine; luckily for me I've flown several times, so not as exciting, but for me very quick. I've been here since just after midday and I can't wait to see you. What are the plans?" she finished.

"I'll get a taxi over to your place and then we'll look at one of the Hotels, I've managed to get quite a good a list, so loads to choose from. Then we can get ourselves sorted out and take a look at the town."

"Not quiet in that order," she replied and Alan could hear a little giggle in her voice as she said it. "I've got other ideas for what we're going to do before we see the town. See you in a little while." And with that she replaced the receiver.

Alan couldn't help smiling and Les, who was standing next to him said, "What's making you smile mate, on a promise?"

"Something like that," he replied, "but we must keep in touch, we must all go out for a bite to eat together one night, that'd be good, what do you say?"

"Yeah it would, but we don't want to cramp your style mate, you've got to make the most of it, the times gonna fly by, you just wait and see," Les replied.

"Yes, but one evening won't hurt. Let's say Thursday; we'll all meet up at some prominent place, let's look at the map." And with that Alan opened up the small map of the City that they had each been given.

After a short look and a chat, it was agreed they would meet at the entrance to the Ginza Mart, which was apparently a well known and very large shopping market. "That's a done deal then, six o'clock?" Alan said and they shook hands before he left for his trip across town.

Les and Cocker had no set plans; they were just going to take it as it came. Les had said that he may get a girl for a couple of nights, but Cocker was against that, mainly because of his growing relationship with his nurse back at Inchon, plus as he had said, 'I don't want to get the clap.' Anyway, Alan felt sure they'd have a great time whatever they did.

Alan left the YMCA and walked a few yards before hailing a taxi, he gave the driver the address and he drove like a bat out of hell, as they all seemed to do, across town to where Charlie was staying. She was waiting for Alan at the door of the WVS building and as soon as she saw him getting out of the taxi ran across and gave him a huge hug, even before he had had time to pay the taxi driver. She went inside and collected her small suitcase before they wandered off to find a bar for a drink and then to find a Hotel. Alan ordered Charlie a gin and orange and himself a bottle of beer, he took them to the table where she was sitting and they toasted each other to the week ahead.

The map that Alan had been given had a whole host of Hotel adverts in it and they selected one that looked pretty nice and was not too far from the Ginza Mart, which as it happened appeared to be at the centre of most of what went on in Tokyo. It was within easy walking distance of the bar, so after finishing off their drinks they set out to find the Hilton Hotel.

It was rather grand but what the heck, Alan thought, he was hear with the girl of his dreams for a whole week and he wasn't going to stint on anything, after all he had spent hardly any of his wages for the past six months, so he was pretty flush right then. Alan asked at the check in desk if there were any special rates for servicemen and was delighted to be told that they would get a thirty percent discount off the normal prices, so he booked there and then for six nights.

They were shown to their room on the twelfth floor by a young Japanese boy who wheeled their bags to the room on a trolley. Alan gave him a tip of ten Yen, which was about one shilling, he looked a bit disappointed, but after all Alan thought, 'I'm only a soldier and not one of the wealthy businessmen he usually escorts to their rooms.'

Once inside the room Charlie wasted no time, she almost jumped on Alan and within seconds they were lying on the bed in each others arms. They kissed and then slowly started to remove each others clothes, kissing each part of one another's body as they did. She had beautiful breasts which Alan enjoyed stroking, and after a short while he took the nipple of one into his mouth, running his tongue in little circles around it, she let out little screams of pleasure. Her hand reached down and took hold of Alan and she gently stoked her hand up and down his full length, Alan had to ease her hand away after a while, because he didn't want to cum too quickly, he wanted to be inside her when he did.

They must have kept this up for almost half an hour, just enjoying each others bodies, until Charlie said in a husky voice, "Alan I can't wait any longer, please fuck me, really fuck me." And with that Alan turned her over on her back and sliding his knees between her legs he entered her, gently easing himself inside her soft fleshy lips until he was completely home. They lay there not moving at first, just enjoying the feeling of togetherness and then she pulled away slightly and they started a slow rhythm, in and out, in and out, gradually increasing their speed and intensity with every thrust, until they were both at the point of no return.

"Oh God Alan, I'm Cumming," she cried, "don't stop, don't stop, oh God I love you, love me, love me, oh fuck me, fuck me."

Within a few minutes they both came with the most tumultuous climax, she just shuddered beneath Alan's body, convulsing backwards and forwards, pushing against him like she was trying to get even more of Alan inside her, or that was how it felt to Alan. Then she relaxed and laid still, her arms around Alan's neck and she pulled his mouth towards hers and they gently kissed.

"That was the best fuck I have ever had in my life, you are amazing," she said. "I'm sorry I can't help saying that word, fuck that is, you just turn me on so much I just can't help it." And she giggled as she said it.

She had never used the 'F' word before when they had made love, and Alan thought that for some reason it sounded really sexy the way she had used it. They lay in each others arms, just enjoying that lovely feeling of togetherness. Alan was totally relaxed and after a short while they turned on their sides so as to take any weight off of Charlie, although Alan had been using his elbows to take most of it.

They kissed and caressed for what seemed like ages and Alan could feel himself growing hard inside her, she was gently squeezing her thighs together massaging Alan with her movements, which only went to heighten his feelings and it wasn't long before they were making love once again. This time it lasted much longer, it seemed that neither of them wanted to cum as Alan eased himself in and out of her beautiful body, Charlie was gyrating her hips when their two bodies came together trying to increase the pleasure for both of them. But it was inevitable it couldn't last for ever, she started breathing more deeply and panting, again saying those words, "fuck me Alan, fuck me, oh God fuck me, fuck me." All Alan could think right then was 'this is bloody fantastic.'

After lying there for a further half an hour, Alan suggested that perhaps they should go and get a bite to eat; he was famished having only had a small snack at the YMCA since breakfast. Reluctantly she agreed and they slowly started to re-dress, but with loads of interference along the way from Charlie, it seemed that she just couldn't stop herself from touching Alan and he was starting to really grow once again, but said that it would have to wait for later and continued dressing.

"You spoil sport," she said with a smile and they kissed.

"Mustn't be too greedy," Alan said, "we've got loads of time for lots more of that and I really am starving."

They made their way to the reception area, handed in the key at the desk and walked outside, it had grown dark and the neon lights were shining brightly everywhere, 'so different to Korea,' Alan thought. They held hands as they walked, doing some window shopping as they did. It didn't take them long to find what looked like a nice restaurant and after looking at the menu outside, they went in and were shown to a table.

Alan was just amazed how well the English language travelled, because everyone wherever he had been since leaving home all those months ago spoke some English, even the Gooks who worked on the Base back in Korea.

"Have you ever eaten Chinese food before?" Alan asked Charlie.

"Yes, a couple of times, but I must admit I don't really know too much about it, other than the rice that is," and they both laughed.

"Just have to take pot luck," Alan said, "Perhaps the waiter can help us some," and he was pleased to say that he did.

The waiter that was serving them spoke very good English and suggested several dishes that he thought they may like, mainly chicken and pork, but cooked and served with sweet sauces. Then an array of vegetables, again cooked in sweet sauces, with bean shoots and rice. Alan thought it was delicious, he had never tasted food that was so spicy and sweet all at the same time and Charlie loved it as well. It was quite funny really, both sitting there trying to use chop stick to eat with, especially when it came to the rice, they both gave it a good go, but in the end had to ask for a fork and spoon, so as not to waste any of the gorgeous food, as they set about clearing their plates. Alan realised that Charlie must have been starving as well the way she had polished off the food, although she hadn't admitted to that back at the Hotel, the only thing she had said she was hungry for was Alan's body.

After paying the Bill, Alan and Charlie strolled out into the evening air; it was fresh, but very pleasant, almost like an early summers evening back home. They wandered along the streets looking in the shops as they did, Alan was amazed at the wide array of goods that they had for sale, they seemed wanting for nothing. He couldn't help thinking that it hadn't been all that many years ago that they had been almost crushed by the west towards the end of the Second World War and here they were a rejuvenated nation.

The time had drifted around to nine o'clock when Charlie stopped in her tracks and pulled Alan towards her, then lifting her face to his kissed him saying. "Alan Gray, I want some more of your body, lets go back to the Hotel. We can look at this lot tomorrow, but right now I've got a serious itch." And she grinned as she said it.

Once back in their bedroom Charlie started to undress saying, "I'm going to have a bath, come and join me if you want to."

Alan didn't need any further encouragement and was out of his clothes in a flash and followed her into the bathroom. It was the largest bath that Alan had ever seen, not that he had seen many, but when Charlie leant over to turn on the taps, Alan just couldn't stop himself from going up behind her and reaching round to fondle her breasts. By this time he had grown to his full size and his cock just seemed to slide between her legs as she was bending, although this hadn't been intentional. She let out a little moan when she felt him between her legs and after turning off the taps bent a little further over the edge of the bath and then putting her hand between her legs guided Alan inside her, blimey, he thought, this feels good. He started to move slowly back and forth, at the same time fondling her breasts, Charlie was letting little moaning noises escape from her lips as their pace speeded up until she let out a gasp, again shouting those words, "fuck me Alan, fuck me," until her body went limp as she came to the end of her orgasm.

After easing himself out of her body, she turned towards him and they kissed, she said after a little while "where on earth did you learn to love like this, you are so wonderful."

"I really don't know," Alan said, "it just comes so natural with you, it just happens."

"Let's get in this bath," she said, "see what else you can get up too in there."

And with that she turned the taps on full once again and they climbed in the bath together as the water flowed and the bath filled with lovely clean warm water.

They spent an amazing two hours, both in the bath and out of the bath making love. Alan lost count of how many times, but it seemed that Charlie just had this knack of getting him hard again time and time again; she just couldn't get enough of him. Alan just hoped right then that it wouldn't end and that she would always feel this way, he was in absolute heaven.

The week that followed was wonderful and one that Alan knew would live in his memory forever; it was a mixture of the most fabulous love making, coupled with the most incredible sightseeing. Tokyo had so much to offer, shops, temples, monuments and parks. They even went to a Japanese Play, where all the women were dressed in very colourful costumes which are called Kimono's and their faces were painted white, they didn't understand what it was about, but they both felt it was just an amazing experience. Alan felt so lucky and so happy, Charlie was such a delight to be with; and it wasn't only the love making, she was just such a lovely, lovely person and she also had a brilliant sense of humour.

As arranged on the Thursday, Alan and Charlie met up with Les and Cocker and they had a great night together. They found a really nice restaurant to eat where all the staff were very helpful, the food was delicious and the drink just flowed all evening. It was after eleven o'clock before they eventually parted company and went there separate ways and by then they were all much the worse for wear drink wise, but it had been really good fun.

They had remembered each day to visit their respective Tokyo bases, Alan's being the YMCA and Charlie's the WVS House, just to sign the book saying that they were still around. This apparently was mainly for security reasons, their own specifically, or so they had been told. The Friday would be their last night together, because they each had to be back in their proper digs for the Saturday night, so Alan and Charlie had arranged a special day.

Luckily the drinking on the Thursday night hadn't dampened their ardour for each other and they started the day with a wonderful love making session before going to the restaurant for breakfast. Then after breakfast it was back for round two, more love making until lunchtime. They went out for lunch to a nice little bar that they had frequented on several occasions and the owners had taken a real liking to them, plying them both with extra drinks at no extra cost. Then it was back to the Hotel for more wonderful love making before they went to dinner.

Dinner was at the same restaurant that they had eaten at on their first evening together in Tokyo, but this time Alan had asked for the fork and spoon when he ordered, to save them the embarrassment with the chopsticks and also to make sure they didn't waste any of that wonderful food.

As they strolled slowly back to the Hotel, Charlie stopped and slipped into Alan's arms, she kissed him saying, "Alan, I don't want to go back. This has been the most wonderful week of my life and I don't want it to end. I have fallen for you hook line and sinker, I love you Alan Gray, so much that it hurts."

"I feel the same my darling," Alan said, "but what can we do. After tonight it's back to that godforsaken place and sneaking the odd moments as and when we can, so let's go back to the Hotel and make the most of the moment."

And they did. It was just after ten o'clock when they got back to the Hotel and they spent the rest of most of the night making love, again waking the following morning and doing the same until they were both exhausted. Just when Alan thought his body couldn't take any more, Charlie would kiss him and fondle him bringing him back to full hardness once more and they did it again and again and yet again.

Charlie was in tears when they parted, Alan had taken her by taxi to her digs at the WVS house and they kissed long and hard before she eventually went inside. The taxi took Alan to the YMCA and he crept into bed and just wanted to curl up in a ball and die, he felt so empty after the week that he had had. Alan knew that he would be seeing Charlie when they got back to Korea, but he also knew that it wouldn't be quite the same, they had both got their separate jobs to do, with Alan knowing that his would probably get more difficult as the months went by.

He slept soundly, not even hearing Les and Cocker returning much later, so it wasn't until the morning that they would each catch up on the week's events. R&R was meant to stand for Rest and Recuperation; 'bloody hell,' Alan thought 'after what I've just been through, albeit the most wonderful experience of my life, I truly need a proper week of rest and recuperation to get over it.'

Chapter 34

Alan, together with Les and Cocker left the YMCA in a Jeep that had been arranged to collect them at ten o'clock and take them to the airport; the flight was at eleven thirty. Once aboard the Douglas C17 for the return journey to Korea they started swapping stories about their visit. Les and Cocker had spent most of the time together sightseeing and shopping, except for two nights when Les had decided to give himself a treat with one of the local beauties.

"Bloody marvellous," he said. "We did things that I had never dreamt of before."

Cocker had been faithful to his little nurse at MASH and couldn't wait to get back to Camp to meet up with her again. Alan didn't go into too much detail, but said that he had had the most amazing time and that he felt that he was in love with Charlie; they both agreed that she was a great girl and that Alan was one hell of a lucky guy. Alan dozed off during the flight; he was still tired from the exploits of the week. Charlie wasn't due to take off until the evening, so they hadn't planned to meet, mainly because Alan had an early start on the Monday, because he was scheduled to be back on the front line run, relieving Brian May after his week away.

By the time the plane had landed and they had been transported back to Base, the time had ticked around to three thirty. The first thing the three of them did, was to go to the Cookhouse and see if the Catering lads could rustle up something for them to eat; having eaten nothing since breakfast at the YMCA they were all starving. The cookhouse boys were as good as gold, frying up some bacon and scrambled eggs with fried bread and a large mug of hot tea.

They then said their goodbyes, because they knew they had to go their separate ways, not really knowing when they would get together again, but promising to keep in touch whenever possible. Alan went to the Transport Office to get his orders for the following day and had a long chat with Sgt Brown, who filled him in on the happenings of the previous week.

The rainy season had just started; it was what Alan had decided to call poncho time. He remembered laughing somewhat when he had been issued with his poncho in Kure, but he was really glad of it right then. The beauty of it was that it was so easy to put on and take off and being rubber was excellent against the torrents of rain.

Alan waited for Brian May to return from the Tokchon run and after a chat to catch up on things, he agreed to do the head check so Alan could get an early night. He also briefed Alan on a couple of pointers, firstly regarding a change of route due to some subsidence between Gloster Valley and Tokchon, which he knew would be useful on the day and at least he would be prepared for. And also the fact that the Chinks were again giving some problems en route, some ten miles north of the valley. Even with these thoughts in his mind, no sooner had Alan's head touched the pillow he was in the land of nod and dreaming of the events of a truly unforgettable week.

The morning came around all too quickly and after the six forty five Parade and a quick chat with Lt. Brady, the convoy pulled out of 78 Coy for the round trip to the front line at Tokchon.

Alan was driving the lead truck, it had been agreed two months earlier that there was no real need to have a spare pair of hands just sitting; this gave the platoon much more flexibility with the Drivers, especially as they were still one driver down after the departure of Hopkins. The drive was a bitch, it was raining as they drove and had been apparently for three days non stop and the mud splashing up was playing havoc with the windscreens; they had to stop every five miles or so to scrape and wash them clean. Alan was also thankful that he encountered no hassle from the chinks as Brian May had done the previous week

The continual stopping due to the bloody awful weather had slowed their journey time considerably and it was well after half past one before the convoy arrived at base camp, once again accompanied by the barrage of shell fire from the artillery lads as they did. Alan had forgotten just how loud it was, having been away from it for a week. They did however manage a quick offload and were back on the road home within less than an hour, after scoffing down some bangers and mash. Alan grinned, it seemed that that was all they ever provided them for their lunchtime grub, and if that was all the poor buggers at Tokchon ate, they must be pig sick of it, he thought, grinning at his little pun.

Going back to Inchon was no better for the convoy and as dusk started closing in it added to their woes. With the sludge on the windscreen being sprayed up from the road, the lights from oncoming vehicles dazzled the drivers to the point where it made it almost impossible to see and a couple of times Alan found himself driving with his nearside wheels in the Paddy Field. Luckily they were not too deep and he was able to right matters fairly quickly, but all the same, he thought, a bit bloody scary, the last thing he needed right then was his vehicle or any vehicle for that matter, going completely off the road. Thankfully for all the drivers in the convoy, the lights of Seoul came in to view and Alan knew that worst of it was over, well at least for that day, just a few more miles now, he thought.

Once back at Base with the trucks all parked in the compound, Alan reported to the Transport Office to collect the schedules for the following day, and after a brief chat with Sgt Brown he then reported to Lt Brady and briefed him on the day.

After a meal at the Cookhouse Alan went and cleaned himself up, he was off to the NAAFI to see how Charlie's flight had been, although he knew he couldn't stay late due to the heavy schedule the following day, but he still wanted to see her.

Even though the footpaths around the Camp were fairly well maintained the rain was winning and it was a case of paddling rather than walking as Alan made his way over to the NAAFI, complete with poncho. It seemed that as soon as one hazard went away, like the snow, another one arrived to make life difficult, if it wasn't difficult enough already, he thought as he walked.

Once inside the NAAFI Alan looked around for Charlie, who he knew should be working, but she was nowhere to be seen. He spotted Sue who was at the counter with her back to him, so hadn't seen Alan as he entered, so he walked across.

"Hi Sue, how are you, is Charlie around?" Alan asked.

Sue turned towards Alan, her face was ashen and tears welled up in her eyes when she saw him and the tears were soon streaming down her cheeks.

"Sue, whatever is the matter, are you alright?" Alan asked.

"Yes I think so. Have you heard the news?"

"Sorry I'm not with you, what news I've only just got back from the front line. What is it Sue, what's happened?"

"Oh Alan, I don't know how to begin. God it's so sad," and she really broke down then, unable to speak as her body shook with her crying.

"Come and sit down over here," Alan said, guiding her to a chair and sitting next to her, with his arm around her shoulder to try to comfort her. "Now tell me slowly, what has happened?"

After a short while she regained some composure, "It's Charlie. Her plane never returned from Tokyo. They don't seem to know anything. It took off on time yesterday evening and then nothing. They don't know if it was shot down, or if it's crashed, they just don't know anything Alan, it's just so awful."

Alan sat there next to Sue absolutely stunned. He felt the blood draining from his body and thought he was going to faint, then after trying to regain his senses said, "but are you sure, she was fine yesterday, this can't have happened, where did the information come from?" Alan was just babbling, not really knowing what to say.

Sue looked up, "I had a telephone call from the Flight Officer in charge at Kimpo who told me that the plane has been lost without trace. They log each flight on the radar system, but for some reason her flight just disappeared, they don't know whether it had been shot at, or had had to land in the sea, or it crashed on land, they have been trying to find out all day, but up until an hour ago had no further news." Again she broke down in tears, sobbing her heart out.

Christ, this can't be happening, Alan thought, it's got to be a bad dream. He pinched his leg to make sure he was awake and unfortunately found that he was, he just wished he wasn't and that he was having a bad dream.

"Do her Parents k now?" Alan asked in a doleful voice.

"Yes," she replied, "The WVS HQ was informed and they telephoned me late this afternoon. I just can't believe it, she had so much to live for, especially with you in her life, she thought the world of you, you know."

"Yes, I gathered that from our stay in Tokyo. God this is so unfair," said Alan and he felt tears start to trickle down his face as the sheer enormity of what had happened started to strike home.

Alan sat with Sue for about an hour before deciding that he had better try to get some sleep, if that was going to be possible. After walking the short distance back to the Barrack Room, he undressed and slid down into his sleeping bag trying to shut out everything that he had just learnt, but it was impossible. Alan tossed and turned the whole night, not really sure whether he got any sleep or not.

When morning came Alan was woken by the Orderly Corporal on guard duty, he sat up stretching and tried to get some life going in his body, he felt dead inside, with a nagging ache in his stomach and his heart. He didn't bother with breakfast, he couldn't face it and instead went to see Lt Brady to explain the situation, although Alan knew he still had to get through the day, he felt it better that the Lt knew how he was feeling.

It was a miserable drive to Tokchon, the rain was still pouring down and the mood Alan was in didn't help matters. He tried to be amiable with the crew, but he was finding it bloody difficult and when they were being unloaded at the front line he called them to one side and explained what had happened, so at least they knew what his black mood was about. There we no real incidents on the drive back to Inchon apart from the mud lark that they had to endure, and the convoy was back in the compound by just after seven o'clock.

Once Alan had completed everything for the following morning, he made his way to the NAAFI. As soon as he entered Sue walked across towards him, still looking very sad and she had black rings around her eyes where she obviously hadn't slept the previous night either.

"Have you heard anymore?" Alan asked her.

"Nothing Alan, I have been in touch with the Flight Officer at Kimpo again, but he has no news. The WVS HQ has been on again and they are sending a replacement in the next day or so. But apart from that, nothing."

"Surely there must be an explanation," Alan said, "an aeroplane doesn't just vanish into thin air without a trace?"

"I wish I knew," was all Sue said in reply.

They chatted for a further five minutes before Alan made his way to the Cookhouse for some food, before getting himself bedded down; Alan was out on his feet. Luckily for him he was able to sleep a little better, probably due to sheer exhaustion having had little or no sleep the previous night coupled with the strains of the day. And he knew tomorrow would be no better.

Chapter 35

As the following weeks passed, Alan had thrown himself into the job one hundred and ten percent; now that Charlie was gone he had no other distractions. It was during the last week in April that Alan had learned officially that Charlie's aeroplane had crashed into the sea soon after take off with severe engine problems, wreckage had been found, but no bodies. Alan grieved for weeks; he was in fact a pain in the arse to most of the lads in the Platoon, but he felt sure they had understood the reasons for his moodiness; after all they all knew Charlie and what a loss she was to everyone and to Alan in particular.

Alan had met up with both Les and Cocker during the first weeks that had followed Charlie's death, they were as sad for Alan as he was for himself, they had met her and seen them together as a couple in a very different way and knew what she had meant to him. Les had some bad news though; he had got a dose of clap from the Japanese bird he had slept with while on R&R.

"Christ Les, didn't you use a jonnie?" Alan asked when Les told him.

"No, the bitch told me she was clean and it was safe. Safe my arse. She has got me into awful shit with my Boss, I almost lost my stripe. I was lucky I wasn't on a full blown charge; if I had been I would've lost it, but the Boss got me off, said he wouldn't have any other driver and that was it, so no further action was taken by the MO."

"God you were lucky," Alan said to Les, "does it give you any trouble though?"

"Well me poor old John Thomas is so swollen, I think it's even bigger that yours right now Alan," he said, "and when I pee it's like broken glass coming out, it's bloody awful. I did say to the MO is there any chance of getting rid of the pain, but leaving the swelling in place, but he wasn't amused," and the three of them laughed.

Cocker was still seeing his little nurse, although knowing Alan's situation didn't want to highlight the fact too much, but Alan told him not to be daft about it, he was just pleased for him.

"You're gonna have to introduce us soon, or we wont believe she exists," Alan joked.

"You better believe it. I tell you what, when you feel ready, I mean when you've go yourself over Charlie, how about we all try to meet up at the PX," Cocker said.

"Sounds good to me," Alan replied.

"And me," said Les, "you'd better be careful though because I'm on the lookout for a new bird now that mines gone back to the US of A."

And they all laughed at the joke Les had made, knowing that he wouldn't do anything of the sort as far as Cocker and his girl were concerned.

"I could always bring another nurse along for you Les if you like," said Cocker.

"Better wait until I've got rid of the clap first, then it might be a good idea." Les said, and again they laughed mainly at Les's short term demise.

Chapter 36

The weather was changing considerably as the end of May approached, the temperature was rising and hopefully it was also coming to the end of the rainy season, and Christ hadn't it rained, Alan thought. He had been told that the rainy season would last until the end of May, and driving to Tokchon and back through the Gloster Valley in mud, slush and shit like they had too was no fun, in fact in someway they all felt, probably worse than in the snow. The shit that the lorries were throwing up caused the Drivers in the middle and at the rear of the convoy huge problems and the trucks had to stop time and time again during each trip to clear the screens to give the drivers reasonable visibility. But by the beginning of June the rain had gone and the weather was starting to get much warmer and the days much longer giving them more daylight to complete the front line runs.

It was on June the sixth that Alan got the letter from his Mum telling him that his Dad had died on the sixteenth of May and had been buried a week later, she said he had had a brain haemorrhage, but had died peacefully. She also said how sorry she was that it would be so late in letting Alan know, but didn't know how else to do so other than writing. She also said again that she was sorry that Alan and his Dad hadn't been able to make things right between them, 'bit late for that now,' he thought. For his part he was sad, but there wasn't much he could do about it he felt, being on the other side of the world so to speak.

During June the convoys were receiving some attention from the Chinese; they had somehow managed to infiltrate the front line and had a small position deep in the Gloster Valley. As the convoys drove through the Valley, they were constantly under small arms fire and the occasional mortar bomb attacks and there had been a couple of hits on the convoys, nothing too serious but enough to make it bloody scary, with all the lads on tenterhooks the whole time. Alan had reported this on his arrival at Tokchon on the first occasion it happened and on the following day the Commander in charge at the font had put a small Platoon from the Norfolk Regt in place to protect the trucks as they went through the Valley, but even this didn't seem to deter the bloody Chinks.

It had been decided that they would have to revert to an NCO or an additional driver riding shotgun in the first truck, so that when the attacks started they could at least return fire with the Sten gun. Alan knew it wasn't any good at long range, but it was hoped that the noise of it was enough to keep the buggers at least at arms length. Luckily, this together with the lads from the Norfolk's doing their bit seemed to do the trick, it just added another problem to take care of, if there weren't enough already Alan felt. Fortunately, by the end of June a troop of Para's overran the Chinks during a night time sortie and took them prisoner and thankfully for the lads from 78 Company it was once again back to business as usual.

By the beginning of July the temperature was starting to shoot up, everyone had been wearing their summer clobber since May; this consisted of the olive green lightweight jackets and trousers. But now there were new problems, the heat in the Barrack Room was becoming unbearable, what with the sun pounding down all day on the corrugated iron huts and it was making it difficult to sleep at nights.

The other problem that they were experiencing was the mosquito's, especially so at night time, the little buggers would bite the hell out of each and everyone who dared to leave the smallest part of their body uncovered, and this in spite of having mosquito nets over the beds. They were attracted by a combination of the heat, the damp rising from the paddy fields and of course the squaddies body sweat; the little bastards were having a field day. Luckily everyone was taking their malaria tablets and Primaquine each day, so that if the buggers did carry the disease at least there was hopefully some protection.

What Alan found amazing, was that whatever the weather the trips to Tokchon got no easier, they were just different. They were now faced with rock hard roads and bigger potholes, these were left over's from the winter and the rainy season and there were thick layers of dust covering the roads. It was the dust that was now causing severe engine problems and the REME boys worked overtime to keep the trucks on the road. Every day there were engines overheating, there were blown tyres caused by the potholes, there was the dust getting in the fuel system which was causing problems with spark plugs. In fact it had become a normal event to have to clean the plugs at Tokchon, or even sometimes en route, just to get the engine firing again to get back to base.

It was the third week in July on a Tuesday; Sgt Brown had taken charge of a convoy that was transporting a large Platoon of the Norfolk lads from their Base HQ to a new location some twenty miles east of Tokchon, it was new territory that they were entering. He had chosen to go mainly because it was a new route and he had been given a detailed map by Brigade HQ. The convoy had left at daybreak, an hour before Alan was leaving with his Platoon on the supply run to Tokchon; the weather was now scorching hot with temperatures reaching eighty degrees plus.

It was just before two o'clock in the afternoon, Alan's convoy were about to leave Tokchon for the return journey back to base, when a message was relayed to him via Capt Mason at 78 Coy. The message stated that Sgt Browns convoy had been ambushed after they had turned off on to a dirt road north of the Gloster Valley and there were casualties. Alan was required to make a detour to see what he could do to help. Capt Mason's message also said that he had arranged for two ambulances which were being sent from the field Hospital which was situated midway between Seoul and the Gloster Valley, so they should arrive at the site in about ninety minutes from the time of his message.

After getting the route details to the location from the Station Commander, Alan set off to the new location with one other truck, he sent the remainder of the Platoon back to Inchon, after putting Paddy Gregson in charge. It was almost an hour's drive from Tokchon before they found the turnoff to the track and once they had turned off from the main drag, they found that the track was in really bad condition and Alan made very slow progress for several miles. He could hear what sounded like mortar fire, but kept pushing forward until he saw the convoy about half a mile ahead, they were parked in a tight group and the Norfolk Regt lads had formed a protective line and were firing spasmodic bursts of fire into where they thought the enemy were hidden. There was just the odd return of fire, but very little as Alan made his final approach.

As soon as he had parked, Alan jumped down from his truck and walked to where there was a small group of squaddies standing at the rear of one of the lorries and that was when he saw Sgt Brown laid on the floor with blood around the lower part of his right knee. There were also three Norfolk lads with minor wounds, but it appeared none were too serious.

"Bloody hell, are you OK Sarge?" Alan asked when he saw the state he was in.

"Yeah I'm fine, the buggers just nicked me, bloody bullet came straight through the door, luckily it ricocheted as it came through, otherwise it could have been a bloody site worse," he replied.

"How about the other three?" Alan asked.

"They don't seem to be too bad, just a bloody nuisance really."

"Anyway the ambulance is on its way, should be here anytime now," Alan said before wandering to have a word with the other drivers, just to make sure they were OK. They still had to complete the run poor sods, and that's when it struck Alan, now that Sgt Brown is down, 'Christ, I'll probably have to go with them.' And his appraisal of the situation was just that.

The time was just after three thirty when Alan saw the two ambulances approaching and it didn't take them long to get matters sorted, they dressed the wounds of the injured, including Sgt Brown and after placing them on stretchers they put them onboard the ambulances and they were soon on their way to the field hospital.

Alan was then faced with the task of getting these lads to their destination, hopefully without further problems. He had a meet with the Officer in charge of the Norfolk's and his Sgt Major and between them they devised what they were going to do to try to get to the new location without further problems. It had been decided that they would slightly roll up the canvas sides of the trucks so that the riflemen could be seated and have a good view of where the original attack had come from. They could then train their rifles on this area and let off short bursts every now and again, hoping to keep another attack at bay. Luckily it seemed to work and Alan was pleased that they were able to complete the final six or so miles without further problems.

Once at the location the Norfolk lads soon got to work digging themselves in, there was very little natural cover from shrubs or trees and they had to rely on the undulating terrain to provide their cover for them, but Alan could see that they were experienced at that sort of thing. Alan then had to make the decision as to whether he should stay the night, or return with the convoy to Inchon, bearing in mind that as the time was approaching six o'clock darkness would be with them in just over four hours. He got the Norfolk Officer to contact Capt Mason back at 78 Coy for a decision; he would know what the trucks were needed for the following day because that would have a bearing on matters. The answer came back, 'return to base.' All Alan could think right then was, 'shit.'

There were seven trucks to get back to base, Alan's two and five of the troop carriers that had brought the Norfolk's to the new location. The Sgt Major arranged for twenty of the riflemen to travel with Alan's convoy to the point where the ambush had taken place, once they were passed that and safely on their way, the Norfolk lads would trek back to their new base. The poor buggers, Alan thought, that's well over six miles for them to go, but then it went through his mind that they were probably used to it anyway. Once again the Norfolk lads sat in the troop carriers with the canvas sides rolled part way up, but Alan was thankful that they made it with no further problems and they left the convoy to start their trek back.

It was a bloody awful journey back for Alan and his crew of drivers, by the time they hit the Valley it was starting to get dusk and the roads were difficult with the bloody great potholes causing all sorts of problems and they had to keep their speed down to about 20mph for several miles. Once they were clear of the Valley they were then able to speed up and from then on had a fairly good run back to Seoul and then on to Inchon arriving back at base at just before one o'clock in the morning. Alan and the rest of the lads were absolutely knackered, every man jack of them, but Capt Mason had arranged for the Catering Corps lads in the Cookhouse to have some hot food ready for them on arrival, knowing that they hadn't eaten since midday. It was vegetable soup with warm bread and suet pudding and custard, washed down with several hot mugs of tea, just enough to send all of them off to bed feeling somewhat better for the night.

In spite of his late night, Alan was up on the Wednesday morning at six thirty; he was woken on hearing the other lads in the barrack room moving around and getting ready for their day ahead. Although he was still cream cracker'd from the previous day's events, he got himself out of his pit and got washed and shaved. He had to admit that he felt a lot better for it, especially after ducking his head under the shower for five minutes, which was a sure-fire way of washing the cobwebs away that's for certain. Alan reported to the

Transport Office after he had eaten a quick breakfast, just to get up to speed and see if there was any info on Sgt Brown. It appeared that he was OK, he had had his wounds treated and should be back at base medical centre sometime during the afternoon.

Alan's orders for the day were limited due to the previous day's activities; however he still volunteered to take charge of the local schedule. Cpl George Bingham was standing in for Sgt Brown and was pleased for Alan's help, allowing him to get matters sorted for the following day, together with Capt Mason. It was four o'clock by the time Alan had made sure everything was completed for the day and ready for the following morning. He then borrowed a Jeep from the vehicle pool and drove over to the medical centre to see Sgt Brown. He was in good spirits, but the prognosis wasn't too good.

"The darned bullet's gone and chipped the bone, it apparently went in and lodged and although they have got the bullet out it could be three months before I'm walking properly. So it's crutches for the time being," he finished.

"So when are they going to let you back to Camp Sarge?" Alan asked.

"Not for a week at least, or so they say," he answered."

Alan stayed and chatted on for about half an hour or so and he filled him in on the details of the return journey the previous day; just then a nurse arrived and said that it was time for Alan to go, she had to re-dress the Sgts wound. So after a last cheerio he was on his way back to camp.

The following morning, the Thursday, Alan was once again in charge of the run to Tokchon and they left with eight trucks at seven o'clock, luckily it was a fairly straightforward day as it goes, no mishaps to speak of and the convoy was back in camp at Inchon by seven thirty in the evening. After checking all the trucks into the compound and handing over to the REME lads to check them out, Alan reported to Lt Brady's office to give him his report for the day.

"I'm glad I caught you Cpl Gray," he said, "The Adjutant wants to see you in the morning at nine o'clock, I've rearranged a couple of things to allow you the time."

Bloody hell Alan thought 'what have I done,' he couldn't think of anything, just have to wait and see, and Lt Brady hadn't given him any idea as to what it was about. So on the Friday morning when Alan had finished breakfast, he presented himself at the Adjutants office.

"Thank you for coming Cpl Gray," he started. "I'm not sure whether you are aware of the seriousness of Sgt Brown's injuries, but he will not be functioning properly for at least a month and probably even longer than that.

But as his tour of duty comes to an end at the end of August, it has been decided to repatriate him to the UK, earlier than scheduled. That means we require a replacement to take charge of the Transport Office working under Capt Mason. I've watched your attention to detail and have been very impressed with the effort that you have put in since arriving at 78 Coy, this, coupled with your actions of two days ago makes me feel that you are the right man for the job, which I would like you to accept. You will be promoted to Sergeant forthwith and spend the next week with Sgt Brown, who is being allowed out of the sick bay each day to teach you all you need to know."

Alan didn't quite know what to say, or even what he was expected to say, so he just said, "Yes Sir, thank you Sir. May I ask who will take over my role at B Platoon?"

"Yes, Cpl Gray, or should I say Sgt Gray, L/Cpl May is being made up to full corporal as we speak and he will take over as NCO in change of B Platoon relieving you of your duties immediately. What I want you to do is commence your briefing with Sgt Brown later this morning when he arrives from the Medical Centre. In the meantime if you get yourself over to the stores they will have your new jackets complete with stripes ready for you. Have you any further questions Sergeant?"

"No Sir," Alan replied. And with that he saluted and walked out of his office.

'Blimey,' Alan thought, 'who'd have guessed it, me a bloody Sergeant and what a responsibility to take on.'

As soon as he had his new gear, he made his way to the Transport Office and reported to Capt Mason, who congratulated Alan on his promotion saying, "I'm looking forward to working with you Sgt Gray, Sgt Brown will be here shortly. You know Cpl Bingham of course and the rest of the crew, just make yourself at home and if there's anything you need to ask, just do it, everyone is here to help."

"Yes Sir," Alan replied, "thank you, I'm looking forward to the challenge." And a challenge he knew it was going to be.

Alan met up with Brian May when he returned from the Tokchon run and gave him his congratulations on his promotion, as he did to Alan and they arranged for a beer a little later, after they had both eaten. What hadn't sunk in for Alan was that he would have to move to the Sergeants quarters and use the Sergeants Mess from that point on, no more drinking with the other ranks. 'What the hell will Cocker and Les say when they find out,' Alan thought and grinned at the prospect.

News travelled fast on the bush radio and Alan had visits from both Les and Cocker congratulating him. "Biggest problem," Alan said, "is that we can't have a beer together anymore."

Cocker spoke next, "No Prob Sarg," he said the Sarg bit jokingly, "we can always meet at the PX as and when, cause they don't have a problem with it their."

"Good thinking," Alan replied, and they then parted company for their separate duties. Cocker back to MASH and Les was off to pick up his Boss from Seoul.

Alan also realised that because of his promotion and his move to the Transport Office, he would in fact see much more of Les, because as from that point on he would report directly too Alan, as he had to Sgt Brown beforehand.

Chapter 37

Alan had moved into the Sergeants quarters on the Friday afternoon and bloody hell wasn't he impressed, well compared with what he had had to put up with for the past nine months anyway. Not only had he got a decent bed in a room of his own, but also the use of a half decent shower and washing bowl all of his own. The bog wasn't much better though, still a bucket and chuck it, but at least they were single stalls and not one of a row of twelve.

He also got the use of a Maid, well not actually a Maid, but a local Gook girl who took care of the cleaning of his room and his laundry. Previously Alan had had to put his laundry in a sack and it was taken away and washed together with everyone else's, then returned when it was done the following week, but no longer, the girl would be doing it for him.

Up until then Alan had been too busy with his particular job to take too much notice as to how Sergeants were treated, he realised that Officers got their perks, but hadn't expected what he found in his new quarters. Alan didn't meet the Gook girl until the following day, but when he did his eyes lit up, her name was Kim Song Lee and she was a little cracker. She was about eighteen Alan guessed and under the loose fitting white uniform that she wore he could see that she had a very shapely little body.

Kim Song spoke quite a bit English; she had learned it from her father who was the odd job man around the camp. When she ended a sentence she would always finish it by adding San. Like 'Can I get you anything Sgt San,' and 'I have finished your room Sgt San,' it was some kind of politeness thing, but coming from her it sounded really cute. 'Could really get used to having her around,' Alan thought with a smile.

It was quite ironic in fact, because Kim Song's father wasn't just the camp odd job man, he had in fact been teaching Alan the art of Taekwondo for about six months, Taekwondo being the Korean form of Judo. His name was Wan Ling Lee and he had never mentioned a daughter to Alan, but then why would he? Alan thought

It had started the Sunday after the previous Christmas when Alan had been in the gymnasium. Well you couldn't really call it a gymnasium, Alan thought, more a corrugated iron hut like all the others, which just happened to have half a dozen climbing frames around the walls, a couple of climbing ropes hanging from a girder in the roof, a punch bag and some padded floor mats to exercise on. Alan had been having a bit of a workout, as he had been doing since arriving in Korea, trying to keep in physical shape and all that. When Wan Ling just happened to wander in to the gym to do some maintenance work and after watching Alan working out on the punch bag for a while went over for a chat.

He mentioned Taekwondo to Alan, which was something he had never heard of, although he knew a little about judo, Wan Ling went on to explain some of the benefits, beginning with the relaxation part and then the martial arts part. He showed Alan some simple moves that would help him relax at the end of a stressful day which would also encourage a good nights rest, although Alan felt sleep wasn't really an issue, due to the long hard days he experienced. And then he went on to show Alan how to use his weight in both attack and defence and it just went from there. Alan felt it had been great and had taught him a whole new method of relaxation and self defence. Alan also found him to be a really nice guy too.

The week leading up to Sgt Brown leaving Korea was manic, Alan just hadn't realised what his total job had involved. Not only was he now responsible for the vehicle movements from 78 Coy, but for all the vehicle movements for the whole of the division. This included the Canadians who operated out of 78 Coy, plus he had to also coordinate everything with the Aussies and the Yanks, ensuring vehicle availability to get supplies, ammunition and troops to the front line of all the various divisions.

'Bloody hell,' Alan had thought at first, 'what a job.' But thanks to the expert guidance of Sgt Brown, or Harry as he now was, Alan soon got to grips with things and what had originally seemed a daunting task was to turn out to be really rewarding, even if it did consume nearly eighteen hours of each day.

Alan had thought that his previous role up and back to Tokchon was knackering, but the new role took far more out of him, it wasn't the physical side of things as before, now it was the mental tiredness and he was thankful to Wan Ling for the Taekwondo classes. Alan's second in command, Corporal George Bingham was an old Soldier by Alan's standards, having been in the mob for some six years, but never once showed any jealousy or animosity towards Alan because he had been overlooked for the job. He had in fact told Alan on the QT that he knew he wasn't up to doing the job and was glad when they made Alan up and appointed him. Luckily they got on great together and made a really good team. And Alan had to admit that Capt Mason was a brilliant boss, always available twenty four seven if there were problems and knew all the knobs to push to get Alan out of trouble if and when any arose.

Alan's introduction to the Sgt's Mess was quite a night and something that he certainly hadn't expected, but it was apparently tradition. Alan found that he would also have to contribute to the Mess Fund, which really was just a way of making sure there was always a good supply of alcoholic drink available. A special dinner was arranged for the Friday at the end of Alan's first week as a Sergeant, it was also doubling as a farewell dinner for Harry Brown.

In all there were twelve Sergeants in the Mess, Company Sgt Major Phillips was the king pin though. The others were made up of Staff Sgt John Howe who worked in the Admin Office for the Adjutant; along with

Sgt Gordon Jones, there were the two from A and C Platoons, James Smith and Bill Hawkins, two from the REME, another two from the Catering Corps and a further two from the Ordnance Corps.

The major difference between Alan and the rest was that he wasn't only the new kid on the block; he really was a kid by comparison to the rest of them. The majority of them were more than thirty years of age and some, especially the Sgt Major and Staff Sgt, were probably nearer to forty, all of them career soldiers with lots of service in, but they treated Alan like an equal, which Alan thought was brilliant. The dinner lasted several hours, with yarns being spun by each and every one of them, the stories getting more unbelievable as the drink flowed and the evening wore on. Alan decided to be a listener on this occasion, but all in all they were a nice bunch of chaps and he had a great time.

In the meantime Alan had been building up a very nice relationship with Kim Song Lee. Being the youngest Sergeant in the Mess they just hit it off. Alan had more or less got over Charlie, her replacement at the NAAFI was a girl called Jane and not at all Alan's sort he felt, even though she was an OK kind of girl. Not that Alan had any intention of making a play for her, especially with Sue still around at the time and her knowing how it was with him and Charlie.

But Kim Song, well she was just different. It had started when she happened to burst into Alan's room one morning while he was standing stark naked. He had just returned from having a shower and was about to get dressed when the door opened, she hadn't realised Alan was still in the room and was coming in to clean. Alan didn't have time to cover himself up in any way and she just stood there and gawked at him.

Then she smiled and said, "you are full of big surprises Sgt San," with the emphasis on the word big. Alan just smiled back, but felt that a connection had been made between them even though it was a couple of weeks before anything further developed.

It was a Sunday morning and George Bingham was on duty in the Transport Office, Alan wasn't reporting in until midday, having not had a break for the past two weeks. He was lying on his bed when there was a knock on the door, Alan grabbed a towel and put it around his waist then walked towards the door to open it, but before he got there it started to open and Kim Song put her head around the door. She jumped back saying, with a surprised voice, "Oh I sorry Sgt San, I didn't realise you still here. I have brought Dobby back." Dobby being the Korean word for laundry. "Please I call back later, I sorry," she ended and started backing away from the door.

"No you're alright, bring it in," Alan said, "I was just about to get up anyway."

She entered Alan's room and emptied the contents of the laundry bag onto the bed and started sorting through them and placing the various items, his shirts, underwear, socks etc into the various draws where she knew they went.

As she was putting Alan's underwear away she was making a real meal of it, folding and unfolding and then patting them, so he said in a cheeky sort of way, "Do you like playing with men's underwear?"

Kim Song smiled and said, "yes, but only special man."

"Am I a special man?" Alan asked.

"You special man," she replied, "very special man Sgt San."

"So why am I special?" Alan again asked.

She blushed and hung her head as if embarrassed and he said, "You don't have to be shy Kim Song, because I think you're a bit special too." This made her blush even more.

Alan walked across to where she was standing; she looked up at him and smiled. He leant his face towards her and gently kissed her cheek, she turned her face upwards and he placed his lips on hers. At first she didn't respond, possibly Alan thought because she was shy, but then she seemed to relax and it was as though any shyness had been banished and she pressed her lips against Alan's moving forward into his arms as she did. Alan could feel himself growing hard under the towel that he had around his waist and was now pressing against her stomach; Kim Song was aware of this and pushed herself against him, all the while letting small moans escape from her lips as they continued to kiss.

Alan slowly moved towards the bed and sat on the edge, bringing her down with him as he did, she didn't resist. They continued kissing for some time and Alan slid his hand inside the top of her blouse, again she didn't resist as he fondled her breast and then slowly lowered the two of them into a lying position on the bed.

Her hand then went beneath the towel and took hold of Alan, their lips parted for a moment and she said, "you have very big one Sgt San, I saw before and I wanted ever since. You very special man, I play?" she said stroking Alan up and down as she said it.

"Yes please," Alan said, "you play," was all he could muster as she gently stroked him.

The exploring continued and Alan slowly removed her blouse and bra, kissing her breasts as he did so; she had the most beautiful nipples he had ever seen, they must have stood out almost a full inch from her breasts. Kim Song was letting out little moaning noises as Alan played with her body; he was really taken with her nipples and kept sucking and tweaking them, much to her pleasure. Alan then removed her trousers, then her knickers and started fondling her between her legs; again she moaned and then said, "Oh Sgt San, I want you inside me. Please Sgt San, I need very much."

Alan moved his body over so he was kneeling between her legs; he slipped on a French letter which he had taken from the drawer in his bedside cabinet, and then gently pushed himself inside her as she lay on the bed with her legs akimbo; it was a sight to behold as her pink lips parted allowing him inside her body. She was small in comparison to Alan and he did wonder whether she could cope with his full length, but the female body is an amazing thing he thought.

Once Alan was fully inside they lay fairly still, both of them just enjoying the feeling of being together, then she started to move beneath him, slowly at first, then gaining pace until they were going at it hammer and tong. She then started to let out small screams saying at the same time, "faster, Sgt San, faster, oh please faster." And he did, until they both climaxed with an enormous gush, Alan could feel her juices running all over him as he came inside her, luckily he had the French letter on, so it was safe for him to stay inside her as they both came.

They lay in each others arms for ages afterwards and she quietly said, "I been wanting do that since first day I saw you Sgt San. You very special man Sgt San, very lovely man." When she said lovely it sounded more like lubberly and Alan thought it had a really nice sound to it.

"You are a very special girl Kim Song and I hope we do this many more times," Alan said.

"We do whenever you want Sgt San," she said. "You want do again now?"

How could he resist and they did, not just once, but twice. By the time Alan was ready to go on duty he was knackered before he had even started, but in a very nice relaxed way. And that was the start of Kim Song and Alan and what he liked most of all, was that she was always there for him whenever he wanted her, willing and more inventive every time, she was a dream come true he felt, especially in the semi hell hole that he was destined to stay for sometime yet.

Chapter 38

During September there was to be a huge turnaround of troops in the division. The Norfolk Regiment were returning home to the UK and being replaced by the First Battalion the Duke of Wellington's Regiment. There would be an advance party arriving in the middle of the month who would replace the Norfolk's at the front line, allowing them to return to base and then along with the remainder of the regiment ready themselves for leaving Korea. The remainder of the Dukes as they were known, would then be arriving towards the end of the month and a huge operation would be needed getting them to the HQ base and the Norfolk's out and aboard the boats taking them back to Kure on the first leg of their journey home.

September was therefore a real buzz month, everyone worked practically twenty four seven to get the troops in and out and there was going to be no let up after the Dukes were in place either, it was business as usual with just a different name tag. Alan also knew that it wouldn't be long before the weather would be turning once again and winter would be upon them and he felt that he needed a break to set him up for the long hard slog that he knew lay ahead.

As another six months had passed by, Alan was due for a further entitlement to R&R which he decided he just might take. George Bingham would be leaving in a few weeks, because his tour of duty was almost up and Alan wanted to get the R&R in before his leaving and before the bad weather arriving. So after a chat with Capt Mason they agreed a date of October the sixth, which was a Monday Alan contacted both Les and Cocker, but only Les was going to be able to make it, so they set the date.

Alan knew it was going to be a very different experience to his previous visit to Tokyo, but had decided that he was going to enjoy it in spite of that. Before they left they had planned a whole schedule of must do things and places to visit. The same rules applied as previously, that they had to report back to the YMCA house each day, but as Alan at least had planned to stay there each night anyway, this wouldn't prove to be a problem.

They flew on the same type of plane at previously, a Douglas C47 Skytrain, but on this occasion Alan enjoyed the flight much more, really relishing the whole experience. Once at the YMCA in Tokyo they got together the maps they needed to put in place the final touches to their planned week of sightseeing. They checked out different restaurants to eat at each day and of course made sure that they would have ample time for lots of drinking and relaxation.

One of the highlights of the trip was to be a visit to Mount Fuji which was the highest and probably the most photographed mountain in Japan; it was only about sixty miles south west of Tokyo and apparently had a good rail service. After good night out on the Monday, when they had feasted on Chinese food and drank far too muck saki and beer they were off on the trip to Mount Fuji. They caught a train from Tokyo at just after nine o'clock on the Tuesday morning and arrived just over an hour later. During the train journey they were able to view the mountain from a distance, but up close Alan was in awe, it was just so majestic to say the least.

From what they had read, the best way to view the mountain was from a boat on one of the lakes and they had decided to head for Lake Ashi which was highly recommended in the leaflet they had read. This meant a short bus ride, where they then got on board a passenger boat for the guided tour. Unfortunately the whole commentary was conducted in Japanese, so they didn't learn too much, but the views were breathtaking which Alan thought certainly made up for that. There was also a small exhibition centre at the foot of the mountain which covered the history dating back to the year dot almost, including some detail of the last volcanic eruption which occurred over two hundred year previously. By mid afternoon they were just about Fuji'd out and made there way back to the train station for the journey back to Tokyo.

Tuesday evening was a repeat of Monday, they ate Chinese food and drank the local beer and more of the rice wine called saki. Alan came to the conclusion on the following morning that it was the saki that provided them with the thumping headaches which they had both woken up with, and said to Les that perhaps they ought to steer clear for a couple of nights, well of the saki anyway.

Over the days that followed, they visited the Ginza Mart several times and spent loads of dosh. Alan bought a couple of presents for Kim Song; one was a silk nightie, the other a bottle of perfume. He also bought several Tee shirts, a couple of pairs of casual slacks and a pair of white leather moccasin shoes, which looked really cool with his new strides he thought. Les did something likewise and they even dressed in them on a couple of their days out, different from wearing uniform that's for sure, Alan had thought at the time.

During the week they absolutely gorged themselves on Chinese food, they both felt it was fab and also hoped that it would help tide them over until they were on their way home from Korea to start enjoying proper food once again. Alan, with some hard persuasion had managed to keep Les away from the local talent; even though some of them were bloody gorgeous he'd thought and had to admit it was very, very tempting. He didn't want to be a spoil sport, but also didn't want Les going back with another dose of clap, or himself for that matter, not with Kim Song waiting for him. But they did take in several strip shows, which made for a bit of fun; it just made the beer that much more expensive, what with the silly prices they charged in the clubs, but a bit of fun as well, and they both thought it was worth the extra.

Like all good things however, Alan's week came to an abrupt end and with Les they were on the plane heading back to Kimpo and the drudge that was Korea.

In a way Alan thought that he was pretty lucky, because he did have Kim Song to look forward too, 'lucky me,' he thought.

The plane landed at Kimpo at three in the afternoon, and once back at 78 Coy, Alan said cheerio to Les and made his way to the Transport Office to check in with Capt Mason. Everything was fairly OK; George had managed well in Alan's absence, but said how glad he was to see him back to take over the flak once again. Alan spent a couple of hours getting up to speed, before going to the Mess to freshen up before dinner and guess who was waiting to greet him when he entered his room, none other than Kim Song.

When he had entered she was sitting on the bed with not much more on than the smile on her face. "This is a nice surprise," Alan said, walking towards her.

"I like making nice surprise for Sgt San. You like what you see?" she said.

"I like very much Kim Song," Alan said bending to kiss her, fondling her breast as he did.

She reached up towards Alan and they kissed passionately, within minutes he was undressed and laying with her on the bed. And it wasn't long before they were making love.

"I glad you home Sgt San," she said as they lay on the bed exhausted after their love making, "Kim Song miss you very much."

Kim Song was pleased with the presents that Alan had bought for her and said that she would thank him properly at the weekend, because she knew he would have a full half day off. With that she left and Alan finished unpacking his small suitcase and putting his clothes away and once again dressing in his combat suit ready for his evening meal.

As the month ticked away the weather was getting colder, it was the end of October and Alan knew the snow would be falling any day soon; he was just thankful that he had Kim Song to keep his bed warm from time to time, which was great.

Alan was now starting to encounter the same problems that he had endured the previous winter, but from a different perspective, he didn't just have his own platoon to worry about like the previous year, it was now almost every bloody lorry in the whole of Korea. They were experiencing huge difficulties in getting supplies to the front line; and Alan's job was becoming more demanding. Trucks were freezing up and there had been a bad run of trucks sliding off the roads in to the Paddy Fields, the REME had their work cut out just keeping the Company up to quota.

Then in late November there was another problem, almost everyday the supply runs were coming under more attacks from the Chinks in and around Gloster Valley, it appeared that the Chinese had set up camp east of the Valley and were making one hell of a nuisance of themselves. Brigade HQ had to once again send in a Troop of Para's and SAS to get the little buggers sorted, it took in all about two weeks to see em off, but luckily, Alan had heard, there had been no serious casualties, just a couple of badly shot up trucks, just more work for the poor REME lads, he had thought at the time.

As Christmas approached it was announced that there would be a two day cease fire, something which hadn't happened the previous year or any time before that and everyone was looking forward to a two day break, although Alan knew that the run up to it would be pandemonium. More trucks and more runs were needed to get enough supplies to the front line to tide them over; they were doing three runs each day for a week to make it happen.

When Christmas did finally arrive Alan looked forward to the break, although he knew that he would have certain things to sort out, especially where Les was concerned with the staff cars, his Boss had a busy schedule, a visit to the front line, a first for Les and there were several visiting dignitaries that had to be shuttled around.

Christmas day was on the Thursday and on the Christmas Eve there had been a real good drink up after Dinner in the Mess and it was past midnight before Alan was in bed. Kim Song had said that she would try to visit him sometime during Christmas Day morning and it was almost nine o'clock before Alan woke. He needed the loo badly and decided that he would have his shower at the same time, the Sergeants and Officers were serving the other ranks at lunchtime in the Cookhouse and the Sgts were not eating Dinner until five in the evening. When Alan returned to his room, he got the shock of his life; Kim Song was sitting in the middle of his bed, naked with just a red ribbon tied around her. Alan just looked in amazement at the sight in front of him.

"This you're Christmas present Sgt San," she said, sounding the word Christmas as Clissmas and the word present as pleasant, and it was pleasant Alan had to admit, very pleasant.

Alan walked towards the bed and felt himself growing beneath the towel around his waist as he approached her, "god you look lovely, what a super present," he said.

When Alan reached the side of the bed she lifted her arm and pulled the towel away and he was standing directly in front of her in all his manful glory, she reached out and taking hold of him gently pulled him closer, at the same time kissing him. She then opened her mouth and started to suck him, gradually taking him into her mouth as she did, although she only managed about three to four inches, about a third of his full length, he was in pure ecstasy, 'this feels so bloody good,' he thought, he had never had this done before and found it sexy and so bloody erotic. Try as he may, he just couldn't control himself and was soon gushing into her mouth; she parted her lips slightly letting some of the juices flow down her chin and swallowing at the same time. What Alan found amazing, was that he had remained rock hard, even after cumming the way he had.

She moved herself backwards onto the bed and lay down spreading her legs wide, saying, "you want kiss me Sgt San?"

Alan didn't need asking twice. He knelt on the floor putting his head between her legs and leant into towards her kissing her soft puffy lips, she let out a little moan, "you suck me Sgt San," and he did as she suggested, he felt that she tasted sweet and salty at the same time, a taste that he had never experienced before.

Then Kim Song pushed Alan's head away gently and lay back on the bed with her legs still apart saying, "come on my Sgt San, I need you, you cum inside me now."

Alan slipped on a French letter just before he entered her and she cried out in ecstasy as he pushed himself fully inside her, still wondering how on earth she managed to take every inch of him as he did so They started slowly at first, but gradually increasing their thrusting until they both exploded together, with Kim Song softly screaming as she did. She said, "you very lovely man Sgt San, you make Kim Song very happy." Alan didn't know about making her happy, but blimey she certainly made him happy that was for sure.

They lay in each other arms with Alan still deep inside her, they kissed and he played with her nipples which were fully erect, she pushed his head down so that he could kiss them, while at the same time stroking her hands up and down Alan's body. This was starting to excite him once again and he could feel himself becoming hard inside her. "You fuck me again Sgt San?" she said and he did, not just once, but in fact several times before she departed just before lunch.

At one o'clock Alan dressed in his combat suit and made his way across to the Cookhouse, it was the Officers and Sergeants job now to make a fuss of the junior NCOs and the other ranks. Each one of them had been given two bottles of beer each, large bottles of Asahi beer, which was the local brew. The Cooks had rustled up some chickens from somewhere and had cut these into quarters, together with mash, cabbage, peas and a Yorkshire pudding; they had gone to great lengths to make it look like a proper Christmas dinner and it certainly did. They had also managed to get some ingredients to make a large Christmas Pudding and the Adjutant had supplied some Brandy to set it on fire, this being done to large cheers from the lads. It was just after three o'clock by the time it was all over and Alan made his way, together with the other Sergeants back to the Mess for a couple of beers, before getting ready for their own dinner later in the evening.

Chapter 39

Christmas and New Year went by very quickly and it was back to business as normal once again, getting supplies to the front line at Tokchon. The snow had gradually built up to a couple of feet deep during January and being hard packed on the roads made driving conditions difficult, if they weren't already difficult enough with the condition of the roads generally, Alan thought. Again the trucks were experiencing a lot of breakdowns, the REME lads worked their butts off to keep things fully mobile, or as near as dammit anyway. The trucks also had to have the snow chains on the tyres once again and this slowed progress making their journeys even longer than normal, everyone was getting knackered and irritable and just longing, either for their time to go home, or at least the warmer weather to arrive.

It should in fact have been Alan's time to go home, or at least have a posting away from Korea at some time during January, because the normal length of a tour of duty should be between twelve and fifteen months. However Alan had been asked by Capt Mason if he minded staying on a few more months, which he had agreed too. He didn't mind too much because he had the added bonus of more of Kim Song, which of course the Capt didn't know about; well Alan didn't think he did anyway, but who cared, he thought.

Capt Mason was himself leaving Korea at the end of March, his tour being well and truly over, having been there almost two years and again he had asked if Alan minded extending his stay to at least see his replacement bedded in, so to speak. Alan wasn't sure who the new boss would be or what he would be like, just have to wait and see. He would have to be a real good un to follow the Capt; he had thought at the time, he was certainly a hard act to follow.

Les and Cocker were both leaving at the end of February, Les was going to Hong Kong, it appears that his Boss was being posted there and wanted Les to go as his driver. Cocker was off to Malaya, apparently still working with the MASH team that he had been with since his arrival at Inchon and luckily for him his nursey' girl friend was going too. So in a couple of months it would be all change and Alan would be on his lonesome, well he still had Kim Song he thought to himself, so not too bad in the short term.

During the months following Christmas Alan visited Kim Song's home on several occasions, she wanted him to meet her mother, or Mama San as she called her and so did her father Wan Ling. Their house was about half a mile from the Camp, it was really no more than a mud hut, but they were very proud people. They all slept together on the floor, on one large mattress type thing, not a mattress as you would expect, but like two sheets joined together and stuffed with something that felt and smelt like goats' hair or possibly sheep's wool. There was a small table at one side of the room, where everyone had to sit cross legged to eat and there was a fire in the middle of the room that burned wood. They were real nice people and they really appeared to like Alan even though Mama San couldn't speak very much English, she always made him welcome.

When the time came for Les and Cocker to leave Alan had to admit he was quite choked, after all they had been together and been through a hell of a lot together for the previous two and a half years. They had had a few drink s at the PX the evening before and Alan managed to go to Kimpo to see them off, they were flying to Kure where they would be stationed for about a week, then they were sailing to their different destinations, they all promised to keep in touch, Alan just hoped we would find the time too.

There had been several changes in drop off zones at the front line; as well as dropping off supplies at Tokchon, supplies had also got to be taken to what was known as The Hook. This was a new front about twenty miles east of the Gloster Valley which had been opened up by the Dukes in early March, when a whole load of Chinks had invaded from the north. This was adding extra pressure on the lads that's for sure. Alan went on one of the first runs to suss out any problems they might encounter and gave the Platoon NCOs a full run down of what to look out for. He also explained that because of the heightened risks involved due to enemy fire, there may be some occasions when an NCO or additional driver would have to go with the convoy riding shotgun with the first vehicle.

All these issues were things that Alan could have well done without, with troop replacements arriving few and far between, 78 Company were very much under strength. Plus he also knew that his new boss would be arriving soon and he would have that problem to contend with as well. Alan just hoped that he was going to fit in straight away and not need too much mollycoddling. It had only been Alan's juggling with vehicles and drivers that had kept things moving with any sense of cohesion since Christmas and he could well do without any other side issues if he was to continue to be able to do so.

Capt Morrissey arrived in the middle of March to take over from Capt Mason and Alan's first thoughts were, 'I'm not impressed.'

He had such a different demeanour about him, very starchy, very distant and he very much wanted to be seen as the boss. Capt Mason spent two weeks with him going over the operation, but Alan could see that they were in for some changes, he just hoped that he liked them; otherwise he would be putting in for an early transfer that was for sure.

Luckily the weather was starting to change, the snow had disappeared and they were now once again moving into the rainy season and the different problems that they presented. Capt Morrissey insisted on a morning parade each day, which was new, in the past Capt Mason had just relied on Alan to do roll call. Harry Green, George Bingham's replacement, and the rest of the lads were miffed to say the least, there was enough stuff going on each day, without the need for all this were Alan's thoughts at the time. Anyway they just got on with it and hoped that after a while, when he saw the workload that everyone had, he would drop it, especially with the new Hook scenario.

The other thing that was very noticeable to Alan and the others was that Capt Morrissey wanted to be saluted at every touch and turn. They had all got used to the one salute in the morning and then one at the end of the day when they left the office, or if Capt Mason had left first. Not now though, whenever anyone approached the new Capt he expected to be saluted, before any word was even spoken. It really pissed Alan off and all of the others.

Capt Mason had a leaving do the night before his departure and Alan was invited to the Officers Mess for a final drink with him before he left. Alan did manage to have a chat about his feelings and those of the lad's regarding the parades and the saluting bit and he said that he would have a word, not only with Capt Morrissey, but also with the Adjutant, "leave it with me, I'll see what I can do," he had said.

During the second week in April, Capt Morrissey wanted to make the trip to the front line at Tokchon and to The Hook, to see what the situation was like there and to try to understand a little more of what the Drivers had to cope with. Alan had left Harry Green in charge of the Transport Office and drove the Capt up to Tokchon in the Ford Willys Jeep, accompanying the normal daily convoy headed by George Hall. George was the Cpl who had taken over B Platoon from Harry when he had been acquisitioned by Alan to the Transport Office.

Being at the beginning of the rainy season, the weather was dreadful, the rain was sheeting down and although there was a special fitted tarpaulin type cover around the sides of the Jeep, it didn't really keep the weather out and both Alan and the Capt got soaked. Capt Morrissey was not a happy bunny.

At the first stop he said, "Sgt Gray, do you think it would be drier for me in one of the Lorries?"

"I'm sure it would be sir," Alan said, "I'll arrange for you to travel with the lead truck. Driver Hall is a good Driver and well experienced in these conditions."

Alan wandered up to the font vehicle and called, "Driver Hall, you're going to have company."

"Who's that Sarge?" he asked.

"Capt Morrissey, he's getting a bit too wet in the Ford Willys, just be a good boy now and no scares," Alan said with a smile.

"What about the twenty five pounders when we get there Sarge, do I tell him, or just let him enjoy the experience?" he replied laughing.

"Just let him enjoy the experience," Alan answered as he walked away.

Capt Morrissey pulled on his poncho and Alan walked with him to the first lorry, once he was aboard he went back to the Jeep and drove to the front of the convoy and led the way towards Gloster Valley and beyond. It was a fairly uneventful trip, there was some small arms fire as the convoy went through the Valley and Alan sent out a couple of short bursts from his Sten gun just to let them know that they were armed and fortunately there was no further reply. As the convoy approached Tokchon it enjoyed the normal arrival barrage, only on that day they seemed to put on an even better show than they normally did, Alan grinned as he heard it. John Hall told Alan later that Capt Morrissey had almost shit himself when he heard the noise of the guns.

The rain had stopped by the time the lads had unloaded and were ready to make the trip to The Hook and then back to Inchon and Capt Morrissey chose to ride in the Jeep once again. He didn't say too much about the gun barrage, other than asking Alan was it a normal thing. Alan did wonder whether the Capt had thought that it was a special welcome for him on his maiden run.

Alan decided that we would bring up the rear on the journey back to base, just to let the Captain know what it was like for the Drivers further back in the convoy, all the shit getting on the windscreen the almost impossible visibility that they experienced. Well he did say he wanted to find out what the conditions were like for the Drivers, well today he had it at first hand and Alan had made sure that he did in no uncertain terms.

After thirty minutes they drove off of the main drag towards The Hook for the last drop off of supplies and they hadn't gone very far when they were engulfed in a heavy barrage of gunfire and a mortar bomb exploded just to one side of the Jeep. This time Alan was sure the Capt shit himself. He sat in the Jeep bolt upright, his face ashen and clinging on to his seat for dear life.

"What's happening Sgt Gray," he said in a somewhat shaky voice.

"It's just the chinks giving us a bit of a going over Sir," replied Alan.

"But what do we do, is it safe to continue," he asked.

"Not really Sir, but we have no choice; we've got to get the supplies through. We'll just sit it out for a while, the lads from the Dukes will be on to them in a jiffy and get them sorted, and then we should have no more problems."

With that Alan got out of the jeep taking cover behind it as he did and he let go a magazine from his Sten gun. Again he could see the Capt almost shaking in his seat. Alan signalled for the other drivers to get down from their trucks and take temporary cover until he was sure it was Ok to proceed. Alan gave it a further fifteen minutes and as there had been no more enemy fire, he signalled for the drivers to re-mount their vehicles and they pulled out for the remainder of the trip to The Hook to drop off the supplies. In all, including the skirmish when they had been making their approach, the round trip to The Hook and back to the main road took just over an hour and a half.

Luckily the convoy didn't come under any more small arms fire on the trip back, through the valley but then, just as they approached the outskirts of Seoul, one of the trucks had a blow out and the wheel had to be changed. Alan gave the Driver a hand, together with two of the other Drivers, while the others stood watch with Sten guns at the ready, just in case there was any form of ambush, which had happened on several occasions on this particular stretch of road.

Where they were parked up changing the wheel, was close enough to the main town for the enemy to have hidey holes and yet still go unnoticed by the local gook soldiers, but far enough away to give them their easy escape with any loot they were able to get their hands on. Again the Capt just sat in the Jeep looking very sheepish and not venturing out after Alan had told him that there could be an ambush.

In all it took almost forty minutes to change the wheel, mainly because the wheel nuts were almost welded on due to the battering the trucks took on a daily basis. It was almost eight o'clock when the convoy finally arrived back at Camp and Capt Morrissey soon took his leave, 'back to the comfort of the Officers Mess no doubt,' Alan thought as he went to the Transport office to check with Harry that everything was A OK. Thankfully he was a good second in command and had everything pretty well stitched up for the day and ready for all systems go the following morning.

Alan was in the Transport Office at just after seven the next morning, having told Harry to take an extra couple of hours off. When Capt Morrissey arrived at half past eight Alan got the lads on parade and he asked, "Where is Cpl Green?"

"I've given him an extra two hours before reporting for duty this morning Sir," Alan replied.

"See me in my Office after Parade is over Sgt Gray," he said in an offhand manner.

"Yes Sir," was all Alan said in response.

He had spent almost fifteen minutes inspecting the lads, pulling several of them up over scuffed boots and un-Blanco'd belts and gaiters and when he was through told Alan to dismiss them and get them back to work, which Alan did.

As soon as everyone was inside and at their desks, Alan checked the detail for the day ahead, when he was happy that things were in hand, he made his way to the bosses' office. "You wanted to see me Sir?" he said.

"Yes Sgt Gray. I am not happy with the turnout of this Platoon; we have to set an example. And I would also like to be informed as and when you decide to give any member of this Platoon special time off. Is that understood?" he finished.

Alan was raging, even after seeing the situation for himself with regard to the hazards that everyone works under and knowing the conditions these lads are living under, he has the bloody nerve to raise such bloody petty matters. Alan knew he had to be careful, but he also knew that he had to make a stand, 'Christ he's only been here two bloody weeks; he hasn't got a fucking clue.' Alan was thinking as he stood there, then he responded to the Capt.

"If I may say so Sir, for the past nine months I have been running this Office under Capt Mason and my staff have been commended by both the Adjutant and the Commanding Officer for the way we have kept transport running through the whole of the commonwealth division during that time. We have a very functional unit here Sir and I cannot stand by and watch, as I see the morale going down as it has during the last two weeks."

The captain glared at Alan saying, "What are you saying Sergeant, that my arrival has spoilt your cushy little set up and that I am the cause of this drop in morale?"

"Not exactly Sir, but what you have to realize is that this is a war zone as you saw for yourself yesterday and there is no time for bullshit, we are not in Aldershot or Blandford now Sir, this is Korea and there is a war going on."

"I don't care whether it's Korea or Timbuktu Sergeant Gray, war or no war, I will have my troops properly turned out each day, there is no excuse for slovenliness."

Alan new he was beginning to lose it, "You saw first hand yesterday the driving conditions that they face each day, but have you taken the trouble to see first hand the conditions that these soldiers actually live in and their toilet facilities Sir? Because if not then I suggest that you do, you might feel differently about this matter then Sir."

Alan paused to let what he was saying sink home before continuing in as controlled a manner as he could, "My main concern Sir is that the men take care of their personal hygiene and are clean and tidy, which they are, in spite of their very limited facilities. Yes they may have scuffed boots and un-Blanco'd belts and gaiters and even unpolished brass buttons, but they all have a very serious and demanding job to do and bullshit doesn't get the job done Sir, as you saw for yourself yesterday!" Alan could feel his voice rising as he spoke, but just couldn't stop himself.

"Sergeant I believe that you are overstepping the mark, this is bordering on insubordination and if you are not careful you could find yourself on a charge, I will not be spoken too like this!"

"Sir you can place me on a charge if you wish, but I will not stand by and watch my team being demoralised in the way they are. Right now I am requesting a hearing with the Adjutant and the CO if necessary, this matter has to be sorted and now." Alan finished, then after saluting walked towards the door of the Captains office.

"Come back here Sgt Gray," the Capt called. But Alan kept walking.

"Sgt Gray I order you to return to my office right now!" again Alan ignored what was said and kept going straight out of the door; there was no turning back now. He new he had to see the Adjutant and quick.

As Alan stormed through the main office all eyes turned towards him, they had obviously overheard some if not all of the conversation. He crossed straight to the main office block and after entering asked to see the Adjutant. Alan had to wait ten minutes before he was called in.

The Adjutant looked up at Alan as he entered and after saluting he told Alan to take a seat. "So you've been having a run in with your new boss Sgt Gray, he's just been on the blower to me, says if he doesn't get an apology he will be placing you on a charge. So what has brought this on, a bit out of character if I might say so?"

Alan spent the next ten minutes explaining the situation to Capt Jones who listened intently before saying, "Unfortunately this is Capt Morrissey's first time in an active service theatre, I did have a word with him as you had requested and I know that Capt Mason also did before he left us, but he said he wanted to try things his way, so I let matters alone. However after this I believe I will have to have a word, can't afford to have problems down there, your office's role is vital to the functioning of the whole division. Leave it with me Sgt, go to your Mess and cool off a little; I'll get a call to you when I've had a chat."

"Thank you Sir," Alan said, stood and after saluting left the Adjutant's office, making his way to the Sgt's Mess.

It was an hour before Capt Morrissey sent for Alan; he had sent L/Cpl Harrison over to the Mess, where he had been informed by the Adjutant that Alan would be. Alan took his time in making his way back to the Transport Office and arrived some fifteen minutes after Harrison had left.

After knocking on the Captains door, Alan entered and saluted before saying, "you wished to see me Sir."

"Yes Sgt Gray, take a seat. I believe that we have got off on the wrong foot and I want to put matters right.

The Adjutant has explained what an excellent and vital job you and your team do and have done for many months, and the last thing I want to do is to put a spanner in the works, so to speak. I have just come from a regime where 'bullshit,' as you call it was a number one priority; I obviously got it wrong with regards to matters here. I want you to inform the men that as from tomorrow we will be reverting to the system you had in place prior to my arrival; that is not to say that I will accept any slovenliness on their part. I will turn a blind eye to Blanco and boots, but personal hygiene is key. Is that understood?"

"Yes Sir. I will inform them and rest assured we have never had and I would never allow a situation where personal hygiene or slovenliness ever became a problem, even with their limited facilities. By the way Sir, have you been to see what they have to contend with?"

"Not yet Sgt, but I will. Perhaps we could go now; you can give me a tour, so to speak."

And Alan did. The Captain was appalled at the conditions that the lads had to contend with, especially the toilets and washroom and couldn't believe that Alan had in fact been living under those same conditions for his first nine months of his time in Korea. He made a big thing about saying that he would try to get conditions improved, although Alan knew he was banging his head against a brick wall on that front. It had been tried before. But thankfully it was back to normal and Alan was just pleased that he had averted what could have been a bloody awful situation.

Chapter **40**

In the weeks that followed the Capt threw himself into his job, obviously trying to show Alan and the rest of the lads that he was really an OK sort of guy. He made several runs to the front line, not just with the supply convoys, but also with the troop carrying vehicles of A Platoon moving squaddies from the main garrison to the trenches, where he could see first hand just what the poor bastards at the front line had to cope with. Alan had always felt that the conditions at 78 Company were bad, but those poor blighters were sleeping under canvas.

Alan was managing to see Kim Song about every two weeks or so and that was a wonderful light relief for him, he felt lucky especially compared to those poor buggers at the front.

It was towards the end of May at the height of the rainy season, that the Dukes at The Hook had an awful time of it, they encountered a huge artillery barrage from the enemy and then waves of Chinks swarmed over them, initially knocking them back from their positions. But being the bold lot that they were, they fought back furiously until they had once again regained their front line trenches.

This action though was causing major supply problems, especially at their real time of need. Trucks had to be escorted in and out of the drop zone it was a bloody nightmare for the Dukes, but also for the lads of 78 Company. Alan in fact had to muck in and take control of several convoys, leaving Harry to man the shop.

As May ended and June came and went, the weather started to hot up and it was a case of putting the ponchos away and getting back into Olive Greens. July was a real heat wave and the vehicle problems were coming thick and fast, but now it was back to the over-heating rather than the rain and slush they had endured for the previous six weeks or so. Luckily the problem at The Hook had gone away, the chinks deciding they were not up for the fight with the Dukes any longer. Alan was also pleased that the REME boys, both at Inchon and also at Tokchon, where they had a small field workshop, managed to keep the company fairly mobile.

As it got hotter, Alan noticed that the bloody mosquito's were starting to bite once again and most of the lads were trying to keep the little buggers at bay by smearing on an awful smelling lotion that the medics had supplied, it stank so bad Alan had thought, that it should have kept almost anything away. Alan only used it very sparingly and then used to splash on loads of aftershave and give himself a real dousing of his body spray when he knew Kim Song coming to see him, just to cover up the awful smell, although she didn't seem to mind one way or the other.

During early July Alan had noticed a huge increase in demand for staff cars; he was having one hell of a job getting enough to meet the needs. High rankers were flying in and out of Kimpo on a daily basis and requiring to be taken to Seoul, the front line and just about everywhere, together with an armed escort each time. Alan was starting to wonder what all the activity was, but try as he did, he couldn't get answers from anyone as to what the activity was all about.

Then, right out of the blue on Monday the twenty seventh of July a message was relayed to everyone from the Commanding Officer that an armistice had been signed and that fighting had now ceased, just like that. A Demilitarised Zone or DMZ as it was to be known, was to be set up, this would be two and a half miles wide and stretch the one hundred and fifty miles from coast to coast at a point level with the geographical line of the thirty eight parallel. The next task was the withdrawal of troops from the front line to behind the new DMZ.

It was quite weird really, Alan thought, one day they were at war and the next it was over. He also felt it was going to take quite a while for everyone to adjust that was for sure, even though there was a hell of lot to be done. The whole system went into overdrive for the next month; the whole of August was taken up with troop and munitions transportation, Alan was working around the clock to get things organised and the Drivers were putting in eighteen hours each day. Some troops were flying out from Kimpo and others were being ferried across by sea from Inchon, all headed for Kure to await troop ships to either take them back to the UK or on to other postings. For Alan and his staff it was manic.

It was during the last week in August that Alan was sent for by the New Adjutant, a Capt Bligh. He had taken over from Capt Jones during May when his tour had come to an end. Alan knocked and waited for his call before he entered his office and saluted.

"Sgt Gray, good of you to come, please take a seat," he said. "We have been checking up on your records and it appears that you have served well over your scheduled time here and as the hostilities are now over, we have decided that you will be shipped out in the next couple of weeks. What I would like to know from you, is who would you suggest as your replacement, after all you know your chaps pretty well and what the job entails, even though it will take on a very different look from now on."

Even though Alan knew his time was up and shipment home was due, it still came as a bit of a shock to him when Capt Bligh said it.

"Yes Sir, I realised that my time would be up fairly soon, but I haven't given much thought to a successor, may I have a day to think this through. I think I would also like to chat this through with the person I think would be best suited before actually stating this. Is that alright?"

"Yes of course Sgt Gray, just pop in when you have had time to give it some thought. I have also asked Capt Morrissey for his thoughts, but I know you have a much better knowledge of your team than he does, if you know what I mean," he said, tapping the side of his nose as he did

"Yes Sir, I do. I will be back to you in twenty four hours." With that Alan saluted and left his office.

As he left the Adjutants office Alan couldn't help but think, 'blimey it feels like I'm redundant.' After all the action and all the problems that he had encountered during the past twenty months, it was suddenly over; this was going to take some getting used too that's for sure, he thought. And he strolled back to the Transport Office to think things through.

Alan already had the person in mind, it was just a matter of would he want the job. After George Bingham's time was up and he had left to go to Malaya, Alan had chosen Harry Green as his replacement in the Transport Office and he had proved to be an excellent choice. Harry was a regular with over two years service in, he had been at 78 Coy for just over eight months, spending his time with B Platoon after Brian May had been sent home for demob. He was in fact not too dissimilar to himself, Alan had always thought, a good grafter and he got lots of respect from the rest of the team. Alan decided to arrange to have a drink with him in the NAAFI to chat things over that evening.

After getting a couple of coffees, they sat at a table away from most of the other guys there. "I won't beat around the bush Harry," Alan started, "but I'm going to be made redundant, they're sending me home to blighty in a couple of weeks and the Adjutant has asked me to suggest who I think would be the best guy to take over the top job. I would like to recommend you, but not of course without chatting it through with you first. So what do you say?"

"Bloody hell Sarge, that's gonna be a blow, we'll miss you that's for sure. Do any of the others know?"

"No, not yet Harry, but they obviously will pretty soon. So how do you feel, do you think you could handle the job?"

"I've never given it much thought really, you've always been there, so I've always had someone to guide me. Bloody hell, me the boss? Christ it's a big step."

"You'll be made up to Sergeant of course and all the perks that go with that. There's the extra dosh for starters and the Sergeants quarters and the Mess are a bloody site better than your current digs I can assure you." Alan replied, smiling as he said the last few words.

"Well, if you really think I'm up to it Sarge, then yes it would be an honour to take over from you. I just bloody hope I can do the job as well as you've done it all this time."

"No sweat Harry, you'll be just fine," Alan assured him, "otherwise I wouldn't be recommending you. After all if you don't turn out to be the right guy, they'll have me to blame won't they?"

"Yeah, but by the time they find out, you'll be bloody miles away," he said and they both laughed. "But what about Morrissey, does he know about this?"

"Yes he knows I'm going, but that's it so far. But he doesn't know who I will be suggesting not yet anyway, but the Adjutant will take my call on this one I know, we have already had a chat. He will be talking to Morrissey, but I know whose recommendation he will take."

They both stood and shook hands and Harry said, "Thanks Sarge for your trust, I'm grateful."

"You might not be saying that in two or three month's time when the weather starts to turn and winter sets in," and again they both laughed. "But not a word to the others until it's official, OK?" Alan finished.

"Yeah, goes without saying," Harry replied.

"We have a deal then." Alan said, "I'll go and see the Adjutant first thing in the morning and we can start to get you ready for the take over." And with that they parted company, Harry back to his billet and Alan to the Sgt's Mess for a night cap.

Alan suddenly thought, 'how is Kim Song going to take this.' He was soon to find out and not very well is all he could say.

Chapter 41

When Alan told Kim Song that he would be going home in two weeks, she burst into tears, "No Sgt San, you no leave me, please you no leave me," was all she would say.

"I can't help it Kim Song, my times up and I have to go. I'm as sad as you, it's been so good, but there's nothing I can do about it, I leave on Tuesday week." Alan didn't know what else to say or do, there wasn't anything he could do about it, and he had already overrun his normal tour time by well over six months.

Alan was in fact due to leave Korea on Monday the twenty forth of August. He would be flying from Kimpo to Kure and was scheduled to join the Empire Fowey for the homeward trip sometime during early September. There had been a rumour that the ship had broken down on its outward journey and therefore there could be a delay. If there was, it would mean that he wouldn't be home in time for his proper demob date, but he wasn't too worried about that little fact, after all, he thought, what was he going to do when he did get home anyway?

On the Saturday before Alan was leaving there was a farewell party in the Sgt's Mess, it was fun, but also tinged with a lot of sadness. Korea had been a real bitch, Alan had thought inwardly, but an experience that he would never forget. But he had been very lucky really he thought, firstly having Charlie for several months before her sad demise and then there had been Kim Song, wow. How on earth was he going to be able to go back to life before the army and certainly life before Korea, he just didn't know?

When Kim Song went to Alan's room to see him on the Sunday morning before he was due to leave she was very upset, knowing that this would be the last time they would meet this way. They kissed as they slowly undressed each other, savouring each moment knowing that this would be their last time. Alan wanted it to be special and felt he would like it to last forever, if there was such a thing.

They had both reached the point of no return and as Alan was about to enter her young body, he reached for a French letter but she stopped him, saying, "I want Sgt San to leave me special present, you no use today," and she took the French letter out of Alan's hand and tossed it on the floor.

"Kim Song I can't do that to you, it wouldn't be fair and what would your Papa San and Mama San say?"

"Papa San and Mama San they both like you very much Sgt San and they want you leave present for me," she replied.

"Only if you are sure Kim Song," Alan said.

"Me sure, me very, very sure Sgt San, let's make baby Sgt San."

And with that they did just that, although whether they actually did Alan would never know. All he did know; was without using the French letter their love making had been extra special, so special that they made love three times during that morning before they said their last goodbyes.

When Kim Song finally left his room she was distraught and Alan was extremely sad and very upset, this had been a wonderful relationship. Never did Kim Song ever ask or expect anything of Alan, she was always there when he wanted or needed her, never questioning him, never doubting him and never demanding anything from him. It seemed that she just wanted Alan for being Alan and no more. 'If only I were to be able to find someone like her back in blighty,' he thought, 'then life could be bliss.'

On the Monday morning Alan called in to the Transport Office to say his final goodbyes, He had handed everything over to Harry the previous Friday.

Even Capt. Morrissey appeared to have a tear in his eye as he shook Alan by the hand. "Thank you for everything Sgt Gray," he said, "and good luck with whatever you do in the future. You know you have a fine career ahead of you if you ever decided to re-sign, think about it?" And with that Alan left to get onboard the Jeep that was taking him to Kimpo and the first leg of his journey home to the UK.

Chapter 42

The flight to Kure took three hours; Alan was on board a small sixteen seater twin prop plane and once it had landed he was taken by jeep to the main HQ Base in Kure, where he would be staying until the ship arrived. Quite what duties Alan would have while he was in Kure he wasn't sure, but probably not a lot, well he hoped not anyway, just have to wait and see, he thought.

He reported to the Admin office and after signing in, was shown to his quarters; a meeting had been arranged the following morning with the Commanding Officer, who would give Alan his instructions for the time before he boarded the ship to head home.

As expected, Alan wasn't going to be doing very much; the Empire Fowey was due to dock on September the eighth and had a turnaround time of five days, which meant it should leave on Monday the fourteenth, this gave Alan around three weeks of leisure, which he felt he could certainly use after the hectic last few months in Korea.

Apart from reporting each day to the Duty Sgt, Alan was virtually on leave so to speak. He spent the time browsing the shops; he wanted to send some gifts home to his Mum and eldest Brother and Sister, who were both married. He had in fact seen some china dinner and tea services when he was in Tokyo on R&R and got the idea then. He felt that they were very different from what one sees back home and hoped that they would like them, so after some extremely hard bargaining with the Japanese shopkeeper Alan managed to get an excellent deal, including shipping back home and a full written guarantee and insurance of safe arrival. He did wonder how watertight the guarantee was, but what the heck.

Alan also took the time to pick up some gifts for his other Brothers and Sisters, mainly small items that he could take with him packed in his luggage, he got a couple of cameras and three cigarette lighters which were shaped like small cameras on a tripod. Alan didn't smoke himself, but as he knew his Brothers did, he just thought that they might like the idea of the gimmicky little things.

Alan bought himself a new watch, but his main treat was a new camera, it was the latest top of the range Nikon, or so the chappie in the shop had told him. The one Alan had bought back at Aden on his outward journey had served him well and he had taken some really great photos during his time in Korea and also when he was in Tokyo. 'Also be good to get them into an album when I get home,' he thought and that thought inspired him to purchase a beautiful black wooden photo album which had a hand painted picture of Mount Fuji and the ornate Otorri Gate on the front, god knows how he was going to get it all home, but he felt sure that somehow he would.

During the second week that Alan was in Kure, he arranged with the CO that he be granted a special pass to allow him to take a three day trip to the sacred island of MiyaJima. Alan had purchased a small weekend type holdall case which he packed with his toilet requirements and several changes of civilian clothing. He caught the train to Hiroshima which was about eighty miles away; this was where one of the Atom Bombs had been dropped during the Second World War. Again Alan took loads of photos of the buildings that had been left as a reminder to all of that awful day towards the end of the war, plus more of the town that had arisen from the ashes so to speak. He could only but admire their sheer resilience in these matters and how quickly they seemed to put their lives back together.

Then in the late afternoon, after a very full day of sightseeing, Alan boarded the boat to take him to the island. Accommodation had been arranged on the island in a small hotel come guest house, it was the structure of the building that struck Alan as very unusual. All the walls consisted of wooden frames, which were then covered in a special parchment type paper which was stretched very tightly over the frames. This apparently was the normal building practice it appeared, all very strange but it looked attractive, not too sure how practical it was though, Alan had thought, especially in bad weather.

Alan spent the next two days almost aghast, just enjoying the most wonderful sight seeing experience of a lifetime. He visited the beautiful Otorri Gate; which was made from the wood of camphor trees and was in fact over fifty feet tall, with a roof span of over seventy feet. The two main pillars of the gate were each made from a single tree which had a thirty foot circumference, so pretty large and very impressive. The ornate carvings he felt were something to behold, that was for sure. The Gate actually stands in the sea leading to one of the islands most important shrines. Alan didn't understand too much of the history, some of it dated back to about five hundred years BC, but he found it fascinating all the same.

He sailed on a small junk type boat, again with what appeared to be parchment sails and the boat did a circular tour, taking him through the centre of the Otorri Gate, again for Alan loads of photo opportunities.

The whole island of MiyaJima was surrounded by beautiful forests and a low mountain range, but in fact was only about twelve square miles in size. Alan found that it housed some of the most wonderful Temples, Pagodas and Shrines in the whole of Japan; all with there own history. He thought that it was probably the most beautiful place on earth that he had ever seen and over the past two years he had seen plenty that was for sure. Alan spent hours just walking through the woodland paths where thousands of domesticated deer lived and roamed, he found it hard to believe the tranquillity of the place, especially after his experiences of the past eighteen months or so.

After returning to Kure it was back to some form of normality once again. Alan spent more time shopping but also spent a good deal of time either in the gym, in the swimming pool, sunbathing, or playing football, he wanted to be one hundred percent fit for when he eventually got home. Not that he was out of shape, after all, he thought, how could he be with what he had endured over the past twenty months.

Alan's football was still as sharp as ever he was pleased to say; he even played in a couple of matches, scoring a goal in the first and a hat trick in the second. Was it still possible to resurrect that long ago burning ambition he had of making a career out of the game, Alan pondered?

The Empire Fowey arrived a day late, but was still ready for leaving Kure on the fourteenth of the month. Apart from Alan's two kitbags, he also had a large metal suitcase that was packed full of the gifts he had purchased and the various mementos that he had acquired during his stay in Korea and his trips to Japan. Together with all the other troops, Alan boarded the ship and made his way to his allotted troop deck, which was B Deck, only one deck below the main decks.

Alan was to be in charge of half of B Deck with another Sgt, a chap called John Travis who was in the Royal Engineers in charge of the other half. Alan thought he seemed to be a good sort of guy, also just finishing his time, he had been stationed in Seoul, but had only been there one full year. Back home he lived in Hampshire, just outside of Portsmouth, so not too far for him to go home when the ship finally docked at Southampton. Alan hit it off with him from the word go, so he felt that hopefully it would be a good trip all round.

When the ship left port the quayside was full of cheering Japanese, whether they were saying goodbye or saying good riddance Alan wasn't really sure, but he felt it was yet another great experience, just as it had been when they had left Southampton almost two years before. John and Alan stood together just enjoying the whole experience before wandering to the bar for a beer.

As a Sgt, Alan found that he had far more privileges than when he had gone out to Korea on the Empire Orwell, they ate in a separate dining room and their Bar was separate, so no long queues for a beer or meals as before.

After getting their drinks they walked to a table, "so what are you going to be doing when you get out?" John asked.

"I wish I knew," Alan said, "I always wanted to be a professional footballer, but what with the last wasted three years in the mob, I don't think I'll make it now."

"Depends on how good you were, or rather how good you still are," he said, "I used to play a bit before I joined up, I played for a team called Fareham and was also on Portsmouth's books, but again whether I've still got it or they've got a vacancy for a Goal Keeper, who knows. Otherwise it's back to the building site. Who did you play for?" he asked.

"I played for a club called Brentwood in Essex; I was on Southend United's books, but again who knows? I'll probably give it a shot when I get back. You never know, may even find ourselves on opposing teams one of these days." And they both laughed.

"So what work did you do before you joined up?" John asked.

"I worked for Sainsbury's, the grocers. I was a counter hand. I did most things, from cutting cheese with a wire, boning and slicing bacon, to plucking and trussing turkeys. Really exciting stuff as you can imagine. But god knows what I will do when I get home, certainly not that, especially after what I've been through over this past three years," Alan finished.

"How about you," he asked John after a short pause.

"Again I don't know for sure." John replied, "I used to work for a builder before I joined up, but I'm not sure whether I want to be wheeling wheelbarrows again. May train as a brickie or a plasterer, there are possibilities, just have to see what's available. I also think there's some form of free training available for ex squaddies, so may be worth looking in to"

They continued to chat for a further half an hour before making their way to the Sgt's dining room for dinner.

Chapter 43

The journey home to the UK took six and a half weeks; the ship stopped at the same ports as those it had on the outward trip, but this time in reverse. First there was Hong Kong and after re-boarding Alan palled up with another RASC Sgt, Reg Harris; he had been stationed in Hong Kong and had known Les for the short while he had been there. He in fact told Alan that Les had gone home for demob during early July.

Then it was on to Singapore, where together with John and Reg, Alan visited Raffles Bar once again. This was followed by Colombo, and then on to Aden. It was just before arriving in Aden that the ships problems had started and it limped the last two days into port. It appeared that the engine problems that the ship had experienced on the way out had not been properly sorted and that meant there was going to be a long delay in Aden while the repairs were completed. It was a case of waiting for spare parts to be flown out from the UK.

Aden, as Alan had experienced on the outward trip was a real shit hole, it was filthy, the people were dirty and rude, they spat in the roads as though it was the normal thing to do and everywhere it just stank. After the first three days half of the troops were down with dysentery, which in other words was sickness and the shits, so this meant that hygiene on the troop decks and everywhere on board was now a top priority. Luckily Alan managed to keep himself more or less free of a serious bout, but he did feel sorry for the poor bastards who had caught a real bad dose, spending all day with their heads down the toilets.

Alan still managed to do some shopping in spite of the place; the prices were just too good to be true, almost half what they had been in Japan for what appeared to be the same goods. Alan did wonder whether the items he purchased were as good, only time would tell he thought. The ship stayed a full week in Aden before it was ready for the off and then it was up through the Red Sea and the amazing Suez Canal, before turning into the Mediterranean Sea and heading for Gibraltar and finally the Atlantic Ocean for the last push towards home.

Although all the places that Alan visited on the voyage were exciting, the magic he felt wasn't quite the same the second time around. He spent a lot of time taking photos with his new camera, even though he had taken loads on the way out, there were just so many different things that he was seeing on his second visit that he hadn't really noticed the first time. He felt this was probably because he was in such awe of the whole experience on the outward journey.

On board ship Alan carried out his deck responsibilities, which were quite simple really and he managed to spend a good deal of time building up his sun tan, he wanted to look good when he finally hit home shores. He had many a good night with John and Reg in the Sgts Mess Bar, they played cards a lot and swapped yarns from back home and also since being in the mob. This certainly helped to pass the time and take any boredom out of the trip.

Alan often wondered how Les and Cocker had got on at their new postings, he had written a couple of times to both Les and Cocker, but had received only one reply from each. Writing was always a problem and he knew that it was a time thing, which none of them ever seemed to have enough of; something that always seemed to get put off until tomorrow and then tomorrow never came. But in spite of that Alan had made his mind up that he would definitely contact them both once he got home.

The Empire Fowey docked in Southampton on Thursday the twenty ninth of October in the early afternoon, even though it was raining there was a still a large crowd on the quayside to cheer the ship home. Together with all the troops on board Alan was standing on the deck leaning against the railings waving; he felt ten feet tall, like a real homecoming hero. In a way he thought, 'suppose I am,' hadn't thought too much about it before, so he just enjoyed the moment.

The next task for Alan was to get all the chaps on his troop deck on parade ready to claim their kit, also to claim his own at the same time, but what with everyone being so excited it wasn't the easiest of tasks, but they all got there in then end. Alan then marched them down the gangplank and on to the quay, where placards were being held up to guide each different Regiment and

Corps to their transport for their onwards journey's to the various holding camps.

It didn't take Alan long to spot the RASC placard and after saying goodbye to John Travis, he walked with Reg Harris carrying their kit to the awaiting lorries, there were two. They were once again heading for Borden Camp, which is where the adventure had started some two years earlier. Being the only two Sergeants, they each climbed into the cab of the trucks alongside the Driver for the hour long journey.

The trucks arrived back at Borden at four thirty in the afternoon where Alan would be spending the next few days prior to demob, they were met by a Sergeant and two Corporals, The Corporals marched the other ranks to a Barrack room where they would be staying, while the Sergeant took Alan and Reg to another block, where they had a single room each, They had both been invited to eat and relax at the Sgts Mess once they had got themselves sorted out, which didn't take either of them too long. The Sergeant that had met them also explained what would be happening during the next couple of days.

Reg in fact still had a year to serve and was to be advised of his posting the following morning, at which time he would then be off on leave for fourteen days. As far as Alan was concerned, he had a meeting with the Adjutant at ten thirty in the morning and matters would be arranged for him after that meeting.

They had a great time in the Sgts Mess, all the other Sergeants being dead interested in both Alan's and Reg's stories of their sorties across the other side of the world and what's more the beer flowed freely, in more senses of the word than one. Unfortunately for Alan he awoke the following morning with one hell of a thick head, not what he really wanted for his up coming meeting with the Adjutant, 'but my own silly fault, no one else to blame, ' he thought as he got himself up, showered and dressed.

In all Alan was with the Adjutant for just over an hour, during which time he did his utmost to persuade Alan to sign for another term. Offering him a really cushy posting to Paris, where he would head up the transport section of CRASC, which was the Command centre for the RASC throughout the whole of Europe. Alan would in fact be back working with his old Boss Capt Mason, who in fact now was Major Mason, having been promoted for his new job. He would also be promoted to Staff Sgt if he accepted, again with the additional dosh that went with it.

Alan couldn't help thinking that it was very tempting, after all what had he got to go home too, not a lot really he thought. The Adjutant would not accept an on the spot decision from Alan, he was to go away and think things through during the next forty eight hours and another meeting was set for the Monday morning of the following week.

And my goodness, Alan did some soul searching over that weekend. He tried hard to weigh up all the advantages of staying in the mob, the promotion and the extra dosh that went with it. There was the cushy posting to Paris back with his old Boss. Then there was the camaraderie, which he had always thought was really great, the feeling of being someone, being looked up to by the other ranks and of course the benefits of all mod cons once again.

Then Alan considered being a civvy once again, his home wasn't much to go back too, almost like Korea all over again with no mod cons, but just not as cold. But at least he would be his own man. He felt that being a soldier was OK, but then when he thought it through had to admit it was a bit restrictive and he had been at it for three years. 'I could always re-join I suppose, if civvy street didn't appeal after all, must ask the Adjutant about that possibility tomorrow,' Alan decided.

The next thought was, 'what would I do for work as a civilian once more,' he knew he had got to earn a living and he certainly didn't fancy Sainsbury's again, not exciting enough after what he had been through during the past three years. Then he thought that perhaps some sort of driving job maybe, or working for a transport company as transport manager, after all he had the experience, well army experience anyway, whether they felt that would be enough, he didn't know. His brain ached with trying to think this thing through and when he went to bed at the end of each day, he was no nearer to a decision, but he knew that he had to make one.

This was now decision time. Alan arrived at the Adjutants office at ten thirty as previously arranged and after a few preliminary words he asked Alan if he had reached a decision.

"Yes Sir," Alan replied, "but I have one question first,"

"Of course Sgt Gray, what is it? I'll be only too pleased to help."

Alan then asked him about the possibility of re-joining, if Civvy Street didn't work out.

"With your record Sgt Gray," he started, "re-joining would not be a problem. But whether you would be accepted back at your full rank may be in question, this would be dependant on the length of time you were out of the service. But a straight answer to the question is yes, you would be very welcome back. So have you reached your decision?"

"Yes Sir I have," He replied, "I am taking my Demob."

"Very well Sgt Gray. I am disappointed and I know that Major Mason will be also. But it is your decision and we will stand by it. If you would like to see the Quarter Master Sgt, he will fix you up with all you need and also offload your kit from you. Then, after lunch you will need to go to the Pay Office to collect your final payment, they will have it sorted out by then."

The Adjutant stood from his desk, extending his hand, saying as Alan took his hand to shake it, "You will be sorely missed Sgt Gray from what I have learned about you, you have been a good soldier. I wish you every success in whatever you do in your knew life and you know where we are if ever you change your mind. Good luck."

Alan stepped back coming to attention and saluted the Adjutant saying, "Thank you Sir, and if things don't work out for me, I will be in touch. I've enjoyed my time with the Corps." And with that he turned and left the Adjutants office. Alan just hoped he had made the right decision, he knew that only time would tell.

After calling at the QMS's office to make the necessary arrangements, Alan went to his room in the Billet and collected his kit for handing back. In all it took three hours to get things sorted. Alan was measured for his Demob suit, which would be ready the following morning and after selecting a shirt and tie, a pair of socks and shoes, an overcoat and even a hat. Alan chose a trilby, not that he had ever worn one before and wasn't likely to wear this one, he thought, but it was on offer so he had it. Alan was just left with his battledress uniform and the remainder of the clothes that he was wearing to see him through the day, until changing in to his Demob clothes the following morning. It did feel strange, he thought, very strange.

Alan's visit to the Pay Office was a nice bonus though, because not only did he get his pay for the past week, but also for the next four weeks, which was payment in lieu of army leave that he was owed. The Pay Master also gave Alan his Savings Account Book which is where his weekly savings over the past two years had been paid into, when he opened it he was gob smacked. It showed a total of five hundred and seventy three pounds, four shillings and sixpence.

That evening Alan had a few beers in the Sgts Mess, 'my last as a soldier,' he thought as he drank. He purposely didn't overdo matters as he had a couple of nights previously, knowing that he had to make the journey back to Essex the following day, but it was a pleasant enough evening and at just after eleven he bedded down for the night. Alan was awakened by the normal reveille call at six thirty on the Tuesday morning and got himself shaved and showered and ready for the day ahead, and a whole new beginning.

After breakfasting in the Sgts Mess Alan wandered across to the QMS stores to collect his demob suit, it fitted a treat he thought, but it also felt quite funny after wearing army clothing for so long. Alan walked back to the Sgts Mess in his new outfit to collect his bags, which he then loaded into a Jeep that was taking him to the Railway Station in Aldershot. Alan took one final look back as he left the camp and then just like that, almost in a winking of an eye, it was all over.

Chapter 44

The train shuddered to a stop at Waterloo Station, which fortunately woke Alan from his slumbers and brought him back to the real world. After stretching to get himself fully awake, he stood and pulled his bags from the overhead luggage rack, there was his metal suitcase, purchased in Japan on his homeward journey and the large sports holdall; both were stuffed with his memorabilia and the clothes that he had received from Borden Camp, plus those of course that he had purchased in Japan when he had been on R&R.

Alan struggled off of the train and started to make his way towards the Exit gate. Walking just a few steps in front of him was a dark haired young girl; probably no more than sixteen years of age, she had a very trim little figure, but her face looked full of woe. Alan just couldn't help noticing as she had walked past him, and wondered why someone so young would look like she did. The next thing, she dropped her purse, which got kicked away by a big chap who was walking across Alan's path. Alan walked forward a few steps and bent to pick it up calling after her as he did, but when he looked up to see where the young girl was she was gone, Alan couldn't see her anywhere. It was as if she had disappeared into thin air.

Oh shit, Alan thought, 'what do I do now?' No one took any notice of his actions and there he was standing in the middle of the bloody station with a girl's purse in his hand and he had completely lost sight of her. Alan picked up his bags and made his way to a small café and sat at a table, a young female waitress soon turned up, and he ordered a cup of coffee while he decided what to do. After the girl in the café had brought the coffee to Alan and he had paid, he opened the purse to see if there was any information inside so that he could perhaps contact her. There were several one pound notes and coins in the purse, and then in a pocket in the side of the purse he spotted a card with an address and telephone number on, it was an address in Kensington.

After drinking his coffee Alan made his way to where the telephones were situated and after putting a shilling in the slot, he dialled the number on the piece of card. A rather posh sounding male voice answered and Alan explained what had happened and was somewhat surprised and taken aback at his response.

"Thank you for being so honest." He said, before continuing. "Can I ask a big favour of you? That is of course if you are able to and have nothing planned at this moment in time."

"Well that of course depends on what you had in mind," replied Alan

"Could I perhaps ask you to get a taxi to bring you to the address on the card with my daughter's purse, I will of course pay the taxi bill when you arrive and then put you back in a cab to take you to your destination, wherever that may be?"

Alan thought for a moment before answering and then said, "Yes I'll do that for you, I'm not sure how long it will take, but I will be with you as soon as possible." Before putting the telephone down Alan gave him his name and he in turn said that his surname was Wilcox.

After gathering his bags up, Alan went out of the Station and got in the short queue of people waiting for cabs and luckily didn't have too long to wait. He gave the driver the address and they set off.

Alan's knowledge of London was very good, mainly based on his previous experience when he had served at 20 Company in Regents Park, even if it probably was a bit rusty from his two years away, so he knew it wouldn't take too long to get there. It in fact took twenty five minutes, mainly due to heavy traffic at that time of day. Alan asked the cabbie to wait while he went to the door of the address that he had been given, it was very swanky and the driver didn't hesitate.

Alan rang the doorbell on the very imposing front door, which was opened by a very attractive girl of about twenty. "Can I help you?" she asked in a very broad Irish accent.

"Yes I'm here to see Mr Wilcox, my name is Alan Gray."

"I'll just go and get him," the girl answered and she was gone, leaving Alan standing on the doorstep. He couldn't help but ogle a little at the swaying hips as they disappeared down the long hallway.

A very tall gentleman approached the door, extending his hand to Alan as he did. "Thank you very much for doing this. I'll just go and pay the cabbie."

Alan walked with him to the taxi, ready to make his onwards journey and the tall gent said, "could I ask you to pop inside for a few moments for a chat, I will call another cab for you when we have finished?"

Alan thought for a second before agreeing, this meant off loading his bags from the cab, which he did and then carried them up the flight of steps to the house where the tall gent ushered him inside.

Once inside he led Alan down the long hall and they entered what Alan assumed was a study. He then asked, "Would you like some refreshment, a cup of tea or coffee maybe?"

Not wishing to be rude Alan accepted. "Coffee would be fine," he said and the tall gent picked up a telephone and spoke in the handset and he then offered for Alan to take a seat, which he did.

After Alan had down, sat he asked, "I really appreciate what you have done for me young man, but what sort of employment are you in that allowed you to come to me so quickly?"

"Well at the moment I'm not employed," replied Alan. "I have in fact just been demobbed from the Army and I am on my way home that was when I spotted the young lady drop her purse."

"Ah I see," he replied, "that accounts for it, and what regiment were you in and where were you serving before you were demobbed."

"I was in the Royal Army Service Corps," Alan replied, "I have just returned from Korea."

"Very interesting," he replied, "and what are you going to do now that you are a civilian once again," he asked.

"I haven't decided yet," said Alan, "got a few weeks to think about that. Just depends what's available, I've been away from civvy street for over three years and don't really know what there is on offer," he finished.

They sat in silence for a few moments and just at that point the young Irish girl who had opened the door arrived in the room carrying a tray with two mugs and a pot of coffee on. After he had thanked her and she had left the tall gent poured coffee for them both and handed Alan a mug.

"So what rank were you in the service," he asked,

"I was a Sergeant," Alan answered.

"Will you excuse me for a moment, I just have a telephone call to make, you said your name was Gray didn't you, what is your Christian name?" He asked.

After Alan told him, the tall gent left the room. 'Bloody lot of questions,' Alan thought, 'after all I have done him a real big favour and all I get is bloody twenty questions. Drink my coffee and go when he comes back,' Alan decided.

The tall gent must have been out of the room for over fifteen minutes, and when he returned he offered Alan more coffee, but he declined saying that he had better be on his way.

"Before you go young man," he started, "I have a proposition for you. I'm a retired Lt. Colonel; I in fact retired at the end of the war, but still have many friends and contacts in the service. I hope you don't mind, but I have been checking up on you."

Alan had to admit to himself right then that he was a bit miffed to say the least, 'you do someone a bloody favour and this is the thanks you get.' Alan was just about to blurt out that he didn't think that was a very gentlemanly thing to do, when the tall gent must have realised and held his hand up in apology saying. "I should have asked first before I did so, so please accept my sincere apologies and let me explain. Are you sure you won't have some more coffee?"

Alan decided that perhaps he should and accepted, thinking that it might settle him down a bit, but also decided that if what he was going to say wasn't pretty damn good, then he was going to be off like a shot, he was starting to get a bit pissed off to say the least.

"OK," he started, "I am very grateful to you for returning my Daughters purse and when we have finished our chat I will put you in a cab to take you wherever you wish to go, as I promised earlier. But as I said, I have a proposition for you. You don't have to give me an answer right now, you can think about it over the next day or so, but I can't wait too long. Perhaps you will understand why when I tell you what it is I am proposing."

Alan had to admit he was intrigued and he felt that the gent or rather the Colonel could see this, so after a short pause he continued.

"First of all, do you mind if I call you Alan?" he asked.

"That's fine by me," Alan replied and the Colonel continued.

"Well Alan, first of all let me tell you something about my Daughter. She has just turned eighteen years of age and unfortunately she has got herself mixed up with a rather odd crowd known as Beatniks. It appears they are waging some sort Cultural Revolution generally rebelling against society; she seems to hate everything that I and her Mother stand for. She has had a very good education, but has been dropping out of college lately due to this new group she is involved with. My main concern is that I know she has been smoking marijuana and that could be the start of a long slippery road. Two days ago we had a massive fall out and she has left home. She stormed out wearing just what she stood in at the time and obviously carrying her purse, which she has subsequently lost, hence your involvement finding it at Waterloo Station." He paused, letting Alan take in what he was saying.

"Now Alan," he continued, "this is where you fit in. But only of course if you are prepared to do so. I don't want to get the police involved at this early stage; I want to see if I can find her without going down that route. I would like to hire you to firstly find her and then persuade her to come home."

Alan was gob smacked; he just sat not knowing quite what to say. The Colonel could see that Alan was confused and unsure and said, "That is why I said that you could think about it for a day or so. But as you probably know from your army training, trails go cold very quickly, so expediency is of the utmost importance. If you say no, then I will have to hire someone else, and damn quick."

"What makes you think that I could find your Daughter, rather than employing a professional private investigator," Alan asked.

"Well firstly, as I said earlier I did a little checking up on you and you have excellent references from your ex-service bosses and secondly I like your honesty. There are not many chaps who would have returned that purse in the way you did, they would have opened it, taken out the money and said 'thank you very much.' But not you, that tells me an awful lot about your integrity and I need someone with bucket loads of that if I am ever going to see my Daughter again." Again he paused, giving Alan time to think before going on.

"Let me tell you what I have in mind," he said. "You need a job, I need you, or rather I want you. I am prepared to pay you one hundred pounds a month and all expenses paid. I will provide you with a car and an up front float of say, two hundred pounds. If you are successful and bring my Daughter back home, there will be a bonus of one thousand pounds for you. Now I know that is far more than you could earn in most forms of employment that you are trained to do, so I will let you go now and will await you answer, but it must be by Friday at the very latest. Here is my business card," he said holding forward a smart looking card he had taken from his wallet.

Alan took the card and said he would be in touch, one way or another and with that the Colonel picked up the telephone and rang for a taxi. After shaking hands Alan left in a somewhat state of bewilderment and asked the cabbie to take him to Liverpool Street Station. Once there he got a train to Brentwood and made his way to his Mother's home, the time was five thirty in the afternoon.

Chapter 45

Alan's Mum was really pleased to see him and cried after giving him a big hug, saying how silly she was crying but couldn't help it because she was so happy. Funny really Alan thought, he could never understand why people cried when they were supposed to be happy. His younger sister Vicky was also there to greet him and she gave Alan a huge hug. She was still living at home and had grown into a real cracker, which made Alan think, 'I bet she's broken a few hearts from time to time, or if she hasn't so far she certainly would in the future.'

In fact Vicky wasn't Alan's real sister; she had been adopted by his Mum & Dad when she was two years old, both of her parents had been killed in an air raid during the war and there apparently were no other relatives. All of the family from his parents to his brothers and sisters had always treated Vicky as one of theirs, as a real sister, but Alan was all of a sudden viewing her slightly differently, especially after the way she had hugged him. When he had left home to join the army she was just another skinny thirteen year old, but wow!, the transformation was amazing, he could hardly believe his eyes.

Kate, Alan's middle sister was at the house and gave him a hug after Vicky had let him go, although she no longer lived at home. Kate was engaged to be married but a date hadn't been set, 'just some time later next year,' apparently had been suggested. Her boyfriend was an ex-soldier who worked at the Ford Motor Company where Alan's Dad had worked, although they apparently never knew each other, or so Kate had said.

Eddie, who had also been in the RASC, was still living at home, although Alan's Mum had said that he was also planning to get married early the following year. Eddie was out with his girlfriend right then, they have been looking at somewhere to live, but Alan's Mum had said, 'he should be home anytime now.'

Alan's brother Charlie wasn't married, but lived at his girlfriend's home in a town called Ongar about seven miles away and he would be popping round later to see Alan. He had to admit he was really looking forward to seeing his brothers again; it had been a long time. Both his eldest Sister and Brother had married while Alan had been away in Korea and had told his Mum that they would call round sometime later in the week. Mum had made plans to do a special welcome home dinner for Alan on the Friday evening when she knew they could all be there. Alan thought it sounded great and Mum had certainly been busy trying to make his homecoming a bit special, which he thought was nice.

After the hugs and the tears had settled, they were all full of questions; Alan found it a bit difficult really to answer all of them, because they were aiming questions at him so fast and furious. What had it been like in Korea, was it really as cold as Alan had said and what was Japan like, did he enjoy being at sea and was the Suez Canal amazing, it just went on and on, or so it seemed to Alan at the time. He probably spent three quarters of an hour giving them a bit of the background to what he had been through but it was endless, so Alan then tried to change the subject back to them and more local matters, finding out what they had been up to and he was pleased that it worked, or seemed to for a while anyway.

They all chatted generally about each of them and what they had been up too while he had been away; then out of politeness Alan asked about Uncle Les and Aunt Jean. Not that he thought they would ever have asked after him while he had been away, especially bearing in mind the way things had turned out back then.

Alan's Mum did drop something of a bombshell though by saying, "I don't think I told you, your cousin Jenny got divorced."

Alan was taken aback; divorced; he didn't even know that she had been married. He hadn't heard from Jen since about two weeks after they had been caught by her Dad and then out of the blue his Mum says that.

"When did that happen?" Alan asked as casually as he could.

"Oh, about six months ago I think," she replied.

"Had she been married long?" Alan asked.

His My Mum thought for a moment, "A couple of years or so maybe a little bit longer. I think it was just before you finished your basic training, so when would that be, sometime in February fifty one, or thereabouts. Perhaps you girls can remember?" she said speaking to Alan's sisters.

They concurred that it was in fact February nineteen fifty one, which was just a month or so after Alan and her had been caught by her Dad. Alan just couldn't believe what he was hearing.

"Were there any children?" He asked, again trying not to show too much interest.

Alan's sister Kate answered. "There was only the one boy I believe; he was born in the September of the same year, so I think it may have been that sort of situation where they had to get married to save face. The wedding was only a very small affair from what I can remember. Uncle Les and Aunt Jean were very quiet about the whole thing. We weren't even invited," she finished.

"Who did she marry," Alan asked, again trying desperately to not show too much interest about it.

"Some chap called Brian Jones, I never really knew him," said Vicky.

Brian Jones Alan thought, 'I can't believe that.' He knew that he had dated Jen just before Alan and Jen had started their affair, but he just couldn't imagine her marrying him. Alan just sat and tried to take in the situation. She had had a son. He couldn't believe that she would have had another relationship straight after he had gone away, specially the way they felt about each other at the time. 'So was he my son?' Alan thought his brain racing.

He couldn't help thinking what a bloody mess he must have left behind, he also felt it was no wonder Jen didn't write, or perhaps felt she couldn't write, what with Alan being away and the way her Dad was about their relationship. Perhaps Alan's Sister had been right and it had been an arranged wedding and poor old boring Brian just happened to be set up. Blimey, Alan thought, this whole thing is surreal.

Alan tried to put it out of his mind and concentrate on other matters. It was strange being home, being a civilian once more. He had no mates that he could phone and meet to go out with, they had all moved on, some had got married, or so his Mum had told him in her letters during the years that had passed, although funnily enough she had said nothing about Jen. Some of his ex mates had moved away and some were even in one or other branch of the armed forces, so apart from the offer from retired Lt. Col. Wilcox, what had he got? he thought, not a lot really.

His Mum's house was still as outdated as when Alan had left over three years ago, with the exception of electricity. There was still no mains water, sewage or gas, so it was back to real basics once again, might as well have stayed in Korea as far as facilities were concerned, Alan thought with a smile. That really did just about sum it all up, although he wouldn't ever say anything to his Mum, because he wouldn't want to hurt her feelings. 'So where do I go from here?' was all he could keep thinking right then.

Alan's Mum had cooked a nice dinner, which he ate together with his Sisters. Eddie still hadn't arrived home but Alan knew that Charlie was popping around later to see him; he had told Mum that he and Eddie would take Alan out to the Pub for a few beers to celebrate his homecoming. Some homecoming, what with the Jen scenario and his new potential employer, Alan was in a state of real flux that was for sure.

Charlie and Eddie arrived almost together, more by coincidence than planning, but Alan felt it was really good to see them after so long. Eddie had got himself a car, it was a Wolsley 10 and in pretty good nick, or so he said, while Charlie had a BSA 350 Motorbike. After a short chat, it was decided that they would go off in Eddie's motor to the Pub and Vicky insisted on going along too, she said she wanted to show off her big hero brother, back from Korea, and everyone laughed.

Alan enjoyed the drinks with the family, but tried not to have too much on that Tuesday evening, his Brothers had taken him on a bit of pub crawl; visiting all the old haunts from previous years and they had bumped into several old faces as they did. Luckily the Pubs closed at ten o'clock on weekdays, so it was only just after ten thirty when they all got back to his Mum's place and although Alan had had quite a lot to drink in a fairly short time, was still OK and slept very well.

The time was eight o'clock when he awoke the next morning, and he was pleased to say he didn't have a hangover. He got out of the bed and after putting his dressing gown on went to the kitchen to make a cup of coffee, his Mum was already there making breakfast and Vicky was sitting on a kitchen stool in a very short nightie, looking very adorable, Alan thought. His Mum gave him some toast to be getting on with and said that she was cooking him eggs and bacon, which she did and passed the plate to him when she had finished cooking it.

Alan had a lot of things he had to see to before the end of the week when his decision was needed for Lt Col Wilcox. It was Eddie's day off and his car was on the driveway and Alan needed a favour from him, he wanted to borrow the car to go into town. Eddie entered the kitchen about ten minutes later and after saying hi to all present sat at the table and took a slice of toast that his Mum had placed on a plate.

Alan took the opportunity then by asking Eddie, "Is there any chance I can borrow your car for a couple of hours to pop into Brentwood? I've got a few things I need to do."

"Yeah, that's no problem bruv," he replied, "as long as you're back by mid afternoon at the latest."

"Thanks Eddie, I'll be back long before that, you're a gem'"

During the conversation the previous evening, Kate had mentioned that Jen still worked at the hair dressing Salon in Brentwood where she had before; so Alan's plan was to try to meet her in her lunch break. Why he was doing this he wasn't sure, but he just felt that he had to know. He also needed to buy some new clothes; his wardrobe consisted of what the army had given him when he left earlier in the week and the items he had purchased in Japan, which was no where near enough for everyday use and some weren't even suitable for the time of year anyway.

Chapter 46

At just after ten thirty Alan left his Mums home and drove Eddie's car into Brentwood, after parking in the free car park at the rear of the Sainsbury's store where he used to work, he made his way along the High Street to a new Men's wear shop. Alan looked in the window and could see that it was very fashionable, not that he knew what the latest fashions were, but he knew he was about to find out. A quick chat with a young shop assistant who was about twenty years of age soon put Alan right and within an hour he was walking out of the store with a new wardrobe of clothes and a large hole in his savings.

The next stop was the local departmental store, where he purchased a sensibly sized suitcase, Alan was now thinking ahead, he needed something to transport his new wardrobe there and then and if he accepted the job with Lt Col Wilcox, as he probably would the way he was thinking right then, he knew he would be doing some travelling and needed the wherewithal to do so.

The time was almost twelve thirty when Alan piled all his purchases into the boot of his Brothers car and quickly made his way to the coffee bar opposite where Jen worked; this Alan remembered from before, was where she normally went for lunch. After ordering a coffee he sat in a window seat where he could keep watch for Jen to arrive and she did, at just before ten minutes to one. She looked just as beautiful as Alan last remembered her, slim, long flowing blonde hair and very smartly dressed.

She didn't notice Alan as she entered and he let her order her lunch, which consisted of a sandwich and a cup of tea, she took these to a table across the other side of the café from where he was sitting. Once she was seated Alan stood and taking his coffee with him he walked to where she was sitting. Just as Alan reached the side of her table she looked up, her face was a cross between shock and surprise.

"Alan?" she said in a hesitant voice, "Alan, is it really you?"

"Hi Jen, yes it's really me. Can I sit down?"

"Yes, yes of course." she replied, again the hesitancy when she spoke "When did you get home?"

"Just yesterday, although I've been back in the UK for about a week. I'm out of the army now. So how are things with you?"

"There're just fine," she answered, "still working at the Salon, assistant manageress now, for what that's worth. But yes, I'm just fine."

"My Sister Kate told me you got married some time ago."

"Yes, but it's over now," she said looking down at the table as she spoke. "It just didn't work out, but never mind I've moved on now."

"I'm sorry we lost touch Jen," Alan said, "I did write several times, but when I got no answers I guessed that you had found someone else."

"It wasn't quite like that, but it's a long time ago and best left that way," she replied.

Just as she said the last words they were joined by a chap of about the same age as Alan, slim build and dark hair, he leaned down towards Jen and kissed her on the cheek, "Hi Hon, sorry I'm a little late, got held up. Is everything alright?" he said looking at Alan as he did.

"Hello darling, yes fine," she said to him smiling as she did. "Oh by the way this is my cousin Alan Gray, we go back a long way as you can imagine, he's just returned home, he's been in the army. Alan this is my fiancé William, William Shore."

Alan was taken aback, but tried not to show it, "Oh Hi, pleased to meet you," he said standing and shaking his hand, "As Jen said, as cousins we go back a long, long way, just got home and guess who's the first person I bump into, small world isn't it. Anyway, I must be going I might see you around sometime Jen, who knows." And with that Alan left.

'One problem solved, well partly anyway,' he thought, 'no point in sticking my oar in where it obviously wasn't wanted, or needed for that matter.' He felt that by introducing him as her cousin she had drawn a line under them and made it quite clear that that was it, 'just have to let sleeping dogs lie, as they say, after all her Son may not be mine anyway and I'm certainly not going to find out by the looks of things, so time for me to move on as well,' Alan thought as he wandered from the café.

After the short stroll back to the car park, Alan drove his Brothers car back to his Mum's place and off loaded his purchases, taking them into the house and sorting out a space to hang them in the bedroom. Like old times he was sharing a room with Eddie, but thankfully, he thought, not a bed.

Eddie worked for a company that collected milk from farms and delivered it to a local dairy where it would be processed into milk that was ready for the shops. Because of the nature of the work he was up early in the mornings at just after five thirty, the bonus for him was that he finished by just after one o'clock lunch time. Alan spent a fairly quiet Wednesday evening at home, relaying a few more stories to his Mum and Vicky, who seemed to hang on every word that he said. The whole evening she just sat in her chair with her eyes never leaving his face, he felt it was a little embarrassing really; 'but that's young sisters for you,' he thought, 'well not so young anymore and not really my sister.'

At ten thirty Alan decided to call it a night and said goodnight to his Mum and Vicky before doing so. Eddie was already in bed and fast asleep, he had been out with his girlfriend Jean during the evening and had literally said goodnight to everyone as soon as he had arrived home, Alan felt that he obviously needed the shuteye due to his early mornings. Alan's Mum said that she was off out fairly early on the Thursday morning because she still had to buy a few more bits for Friday evening's dinner and would see him later in the day. Alan thought it was just great to be back in a fairly comfortable bed again, even if he didn't have the mod cons but he had to admit he slept pretty well, obviously all the things going on around him were catching up.

Alan spent Thursday just mooching about, he spent some time getting his clothes sorted into matching outfits and made a list of a few more items that he felt he needed. At just after midday he caught the bus to Brentwood and called in at the men's fashion store he had visited the previous day to purchase the items he had listed down. The young man was very pleased with his additional sales, once again giving Alan advice based on his knowledge of the fashions of the day. The evening was spent at home chatting with his Mum and Sisters and once again they pestered him with questions, but he had to admit, he was enjoying it really.

Chapter 47

On Friday at just before midday Alan walked the half mile up the lane to the main road and made his way to the public phone box, he had made his decision. Taking Lt Col Wilcox's card from his wallet he dialled the number, a few moments later Alan heard the familiar voice on the other end of the line.

"Hello Mr Wilcox, it's Alan Gray," he said, "I'm calling as agreed and I have an answer for you."

"Hello Alan, thank you for calling, and what is your answer?" he asked.

"I've given things a lot of thought and I would like to accept your offer. What do I do now?" Alan said waiting for his instructions.

"Alan, I'm so pleased, I can't thank you enough. What I would suggest is that you get yourself over to my home on Monday morning at around ten o'clock and we can get things sorted out from there. Just buy a single ticket, because I will have a car sorted out for you by the time you arrive. I have started working on some ideas and managed to get loads of information that should be useful; the rest will be down to you. I look forward to Monday." And with that he put down the phone.

Alan just stood for a couple of minutes gathering his thoughts and just hoping that he was doing the right thing, but he knew that only time would tell. After leaving the phone box Alan wandered slowly back to his Mum's place in deep thought.

The Friday evening was really good; Alan's Mum had gone to loads of trouble to make it nice for him. He felt it was good to have all his Brothers and Sisters there altogether, along with their respective wives, husbands and girlfriends and of course Alan was the centre of attention, especially where Vicky was concerned, she seemed to be at his side the whole time. His Brothers had had a whip round and had bought stacks of beer and wine and they all celebrated handsomely until very late into the evening.

The time was about ten thirty when Alan dropped his little bombshell; everyone was well and truly merry and all in all had had a great evening. Alan picked up a spoon from the table and rapped it against the side of an empty wine bottle to get everyone's attention.

Once they were all looking he started, "the first thing I would like to say is how good it is to be home again and to see you all. Also a big thank you to Mum for this lovely spread and to you lads for the booze, it's been great. I would also like to let you into a little secret that I have said nothing about over these past few days, mainly because I hadn't made a decision. But today I did."

They were now all sitting or standing, listening to every word Alan was saying, even more so now, so he continued. "I won't go into all the detail, but just to say that I have been offered a job by a retired Lt Col who lives in London and I start on Monday. He is supplying me with a car and I will probably be travelling quite a lot in this country and maybe also in Europe. At this stage I will just say that the job he is offering me is to find his daughter, who has run away from home." And there Alan left it, while they all started chatting amongst themselves and looking in his direction as they did.

Vicky was the first to approach Alan, saying, "Does that mean that you will be leaving home again?"

"Well on and off, yes I suppose I will," he replied.

She just looked somewhat downcast and looked up at him, "I'm so sorry; I was looking forward so much to having you back and before you've even got here you're off again." She was almost in tears as she said the last words and this really puzzled Alan.

Eddie and Charlie were the next at his side full of questions, and Alan took a little time going over what had happened and how the offer had come about and what it was likely to entail, although as he said, he still wasn't sure about so many things himself, one of them running through his mind right then being, 'am I doing the right thing.'

The End

Find out the answer to Alan's question and how he progressed in his new role as: ***The Hunter*** to be out soon.

Other Titles by Adrian Gere:

The Advisor ISBN 1-4241-3897-3

Synopsis

After almost two years of record breaking success with
investment company Global Portfolio, Alan Harper is
shocked to learn they are closing their UK operation.
Sitting in his office, Alan reflects on those two years;
how he first got involved in the world of finance and the
twists and turns his life took along the way. Also, he
reflects on his meeting with Tara, a stunning lady who
filled six months of his life until a tragic accident brought
matters to a sad end, and then his opportune meeting
with Shelly in Thailand, that was to prove a breath of
fresh air back in the UK.

This story unlocks some of the mystery surrounding this
area of financial services, the huge potential earnings,
the benefits for high level performers, and of some of
the tricks used by rogue advisors to line their own
pockets. The book concludes by touching on the
inducements offered to lure top advisors to rival
companies, which will be revealed in the sequel *The
Partner*.

Return from the Dead ISBN 978-1-4489-1974-1

Synopsis

James Grant was a top Financial Advisor with an International Wealth Management company. In May 2000 he faked his death in a boating accident on the Isle of Wight and his wife claimed over £2 million from the Insurance Company, which was also his employer. Unbeknown to his Wife and anyone else, James Grant had lived a double life in Portugal until he found out that his wife was going to receive further money from his ex employers and make a new life for herself in Peru with a new man friend.

James wasn't bothered about the new man friend, but he was bothered about her collecting more cash from his ex employer, because he had planned to collect these monies himself in due course by way of pensions and other payments, although not certain at that point in time how. So in January 2005, five years after his faked death, James gave himself up to the police claiming to be suffering from amnesia and in doing so incriminated his wife Jane, who was brought back from Peru and together they faced charges of fraud.